The Doctor - Seasoned Fourteen

Written by Alexander Leithes et al.

Edited by Ella Dumitru

"The final parody of a once-beloved TV show"

The Doctor – Seasoned Fourteen © Alexander Leithes 2023

This first edition published in 2023

All rights reserved.

The right of Alexander Leithes to be identified as the author of this work has been asserted by him in accordance with the Copyright, Designs and Patents Act 1988

This book is sold subject to the condition that it shall not, by way of trade or otherwise, be lent, resold, hired out, or otherwise circulated without the publisher's prior consent in any form of binding or cover other than that in which it is published and without a similar condition including this condition being imposed on the subsequent purchaser.

This first edition first published in Great Britain in 2023 by Alexander Leithes.

ISBN: 979 8 8038 3914 9

Contents

Chapter One – The Definite Article - Part 1

by Alexander Leithes — 5

Chapter Two – The Definite Article - Part 2

by Alexander Leithes — 28

Chapter Three – Broken – Part 1

by Oliver M. Goldblatt — 54

Chapter Four – Broken – Part 2

by Oliver M. Goldblatt — 86

Chapter Five – Space Ghost Assassin

by Lonnie Webb — 122

Chapter Six – The Hunt for the Worshipful and Ancient law of Gallifrey

by Tzvi Lebetkin — 144

Chapter Seven – "Romana's Story"

by Ella Dumitru – Placeholder by Alexander Leithes — 175

Chapter Eight – Tall Poppies

by Alexander Leithes — 176

Chapter Nine - Death At The Edge Of The Universe

by Lonnie Webb — 195

Chapter Ten – 0,0,0 – Part 1

by Daniel Callahan with Oliver M. Goldblatt — 221

Chapter Eleven – 0,0,0 – Part 2

by Daniel Callahan with Oliver M. Goldblatt 241

Chapter Twelve – 0,0,0 – Part 3

by Daniel Callahan with Oliver M. Goldblatt 260

Chapter Thirteen - I Shall Come Back

by Alexander Leithes 284

Chapter Fourteen – Assault And Battery

by Alexander Leithes 311

Chapter One – The Definite Article – Part 1

by Alexander Leithes

The Doctor stood on the vast sand-strewn open space of Kai-Ro "Aerodrome". Kai-Ro was one of the "inner" worlds of the habitable planets in the Upsilon Orionis system, at least spatially speaking. In terms of power and influence -political, industrial and military – the planet Albia currently occupied the centre of this star system.

The most obvious reminder of this domination was the imposing cylinder of the A36 "airship" floating overhead, a commercial spaceship of the Albian Imperial Space Service. Its nose was tethered to a mooring mast which contained a lift providing access to the ship itself. At the other end of this vessel its vast tail fins sported the concentric blue, white and red circles of Albia, the powerhouse of this region of space.

Due to accidents of the system's chemistry – possibly influenced by historical contact with higher dimensions – the Albian or Kai-Roan civilisation had an unusually low level of technology for a space-faring race. Through further historical accidents the system and its people had also been unduly influenced by Earth culture and history, even though no human had ever set foot on these worlds.

The combined result of this compounded serendipity was a culture with the aesthetics and technology roughly similar to that of the first half of the twentieth century on Earth.

The Doctor breathed in the warm, dusty late morning air and looked around at all before him, smiling in satisfaction.

He absolutely loved the place.

The Doctor and Romana had said their final farewells to their Albian friends – Lou Halberd and Nathan Ivon, P.I. - before those individuals had headed off into Abydos – the ancient capital of Kai-Ro. For one thing they had to check up on their third companion, Timmy Cowley, currently recovering from a serious injury in the Abydos Imperial Hotel, under the very best private medical care. Secondly they had to report back to Sir Arthur Buchan at the Albian Imperial Museum, and by extension the Albian authorities.

They had many rum doings to disclose.

The TARDIS doors creaked open behind the Doctor and out trundled K9 closely followed by Romana. The Doctor frowned when he saw her.

"You've regenerated!" He cried accusingly, and not a little shocked. Romana returned his frown, her own tinged with a little impatience.

"Don't be ridiculous," she snorted back at her fellow Timelord, "I just changed my hair style. And not by much either. I must say I'm surprised you noticed – uncharacteristically observant of you. I certainly didn't expect you to think I'd regenerated. We neither of us are beyond changing our outfit and adornments slightly from time to time. And we don't need to burn a regeneration just for appearance's sake!"

The Doctor shook his head in mild irritation at this admonishment. Nevertheless, he could not quite keep the corners of his mouth from twitching.

"Of course, naturally. And there's absolutely no precedent set for such behaviour."

Romana huffed impatiently back at the Doctor but there was a twinkle to her eyes as she slapped the Doctor's shoulder with the back of her hand.

"Master, mistress, I await your instructions!" K9 chipped in, almost as if impatient to be on the move. Romana and the Doctor turned to regard him curiously, each a little surprised by the interruption.

"K9!" The Doctor exclaimed happily, "What's the matter, boy? Do you need a walk?"

K9 whirred and chattered for a moment.

"Master. I merely wondered where our next destination would be. And whether my services would be required?"

The Doctor smiled indulgently at the robot dog.

"Oh, K9. I'm not sure what special tasks our next destination may have in store for you – but isn't that always the way?"

"Affirmative, master," K9 interjected, a little quickly. The Doctor frowned at what had sounded almost like a criticism, before brushing it aside and continuing.

"As to the nature of that location in space and time, I do have an idea. But I would like to hear Romana's opinion first."

Romana's eyes widened a little at the Doctor's unusual bout of consideration. Nevertheless she could not resist a little dig.

"I must say I'm surprised you didn't accuse *K9* of regenerating. After all, he does seem to have endured a little make-over of his own."

With this she waved a hand towards the metal dog. Before K9 had reappeared outside the TARDIS he had been wearing the Doctor's old scarf, wrapped several times around his body, and the chrome crown like accoutrement of the FDSS – the Four Dimensional Stress Set. Although the scarf remained, the multidimensional spacetime "Swiss Army knife" device was now missing.

The Doctor shook his head impatiently.

"What must you think of me, to imagine I could ever consider such a thing happening to a non-Gallifreyan, let alone a robot. Anyway, *I* was the one who removed the FDSS in the first place. Both the exterior and interior components installed into K9. Hopefully such a device will never see the light of day again."

Romana cocked her head at him.

"Did you finally destroy it?"

The Doctor frowned.

"Not exactly. I put it deep in a drawer in the TARDIS. Out of sight and out of mind."

Romana looked a little dubious.

"Didn't you say that the whole reason you disassembled it in the first place was because it was too powerful, dangerous and *tempting* a device to have around? We have already seen the damage it can cause in the wrong hands."

The Doctor nodded grimly.

"Which is why *we* should never be tempted to use it again and therefore it should be safe enough. However, we have seen occasions in the recent past where it helped stall - or even reverse - damage to our universe. And we know there are individuals and entities out there who *could* threaten the fabric of Space and Time – the whole of existence – if left unchecked. So better to have it for safe keeping – ours and the Universe."

Romana nodded her slow acceptance of his point.

"Anyway," the Doctor continued more cheerily, "didn't you want to hear my suggestion?"

"I'm all ears, Doctor," Romana said good naturedly.

"Nonsense, Romana," the Doctor said in some confusion, "that was your second incarnation!"

Then he smiled as his mind returned to his intended destination.

"I was thinking of somewhere I have never actually visited, and yet have a friend there. I am speaking of Alpha Centauri!"

Romana considered the name thoughtfully, the ears comment already forgotten.

"That's a trinary system, isn't it?"

The Doctor nodded enthusiastically.

"Exactly – that's where he is! On the planet of Alpha Centauri Prime, orbiting Alpha Centauri A, naturally."

Romana nodded sagely.

"That's an awful lot of Alpha Centauri – I imagine it could get quite confusing."

The Doctor chuckled.

"Not for the likes of you or I, I'm sure. And the locals seem to cope well enough."

"No doubt," she agreed cautiously, "and you say you have never been there? That truly is a galactic wonder!"

The Doctor pursed his lips at Romana, a little peeved.

"Romana, there are ten to the eleven stars just in this galaxy alone, and at least ten to the eleven galaxies in the universe. I haven't quite exhausted them all yet!"

Romana gave a smug little smile at his irritation.

"Its proximity to the Earth and that system does make your overlooking it a tad more unusual. But let's not 'look a gift horse in the mouth'. Onwards to Alpha Centauri!"

With these final words Romana gestured to the TARDIS doors. The Doctor nodded in good natured acquiescence but was then distracted by something over his companion's shoulder, standing on the dusty landing field some thirty yards away.

It was the figure of a Kai-Roan woman in long black robes. They completely covered her from head to foot – even her face was largely concealed by a scarf of the same material. Only the odd strand of dark brown "hair" escaped from the edges of her turban, coupled with two dark eyes staring intently into his own.

An eerie warbling, wailing melody enveloped him as he stared back at her.

Then he noticed a small shack nearby, just to the side of the line formed by all the spaceport's mooring masts. It was a hastily constructed modest temple to Osiris, erected for the use of the native Kai-Roan workers – keen to observe their daily religious obligations.

"What is it, Doctor?" Romana asked, turning her head to follow his gaze. The Doctor shook himself.

"Just a curious local," he said dismissively, smiling at his foolishness. No matter how odd he found that stare there was ultimately nothing unexpected there.

"We must make quite a spectacle," he continued, "after all, we surely look human to them. And they will only have seen that species through images in their ancient Encyclopedia Britannica. To some of them it must almost be like history, or legends, come to life!"

Romana gave a chuckle.

"Angels walking from the Bible," she noted sardonically. The Doctor shook his head but also chuckled.

"Now, now – you know as well as I that neither of us are angels. Now let us *finally* away to new adventures!"

"Affirmative, affirmative, affirmative!" K9 chipped in excitedly. The Doctor frowned down upon him.

"I wasn't talking to you," he told the dog gruffly. Nevertheless, he then allowed K9 and Romana to enter the TARDIS ahead of him before taking one final look round at Kai-Ro.

The Doctor walked through the doors and they closed behind him.

The TARDIS made its uncertain entrance to the advanced metropolis of City Alpha One, dithering habitually before finally settling on "arrived".

The scruffy blue box did look a little out of place on the wide and immaculate street in which it now stood. From the oddly conical towers, through the sweeping elevated causeways and ramps which curved around and between them, down to the surface of the very road they were now on, all was clearly fashioned from durable high tech materials – possibly self-cleaning to judge from their condition.

The city itself might have appeared a little small to Earthly expectations, particularly for a capital city, being home to just over one hundred thousand residents and workers but such low population densities were typical for the long-lived inhabitants of Alpha Centauri Prime.

City Alpha One sat in the southern hemisphere of its home planet, although hugging the edge of its equatorial region – straddling the transition between jungle to the south and arid dune-filled desert to the north. The only slight imperfection to mar the pristine streets of the city was dust blown in from that sandy northern zone.

The doors of the TARDIS whirred open and through them strode the Doctor, Romana and K9 (well, trundled in the case of K9). The two Timelords blinked as they stared around them in the bright midday rays of Alpha Centauri A, breathing deeply of the hot and dusty air.

"Out of the frying pan, into the fire," Romana observed as she wafted her face with her hand, a little theatrically.

"Well, I have never been here before – I had no idea we'd be so close to yet another desert," the Doctor said somewhat defensively. Then his finger jabbed southwards, downhill from where they were standing.

"And look! There's jungle over there! I seem to recall some fascinating facts about *that* region!"

Looking across the city in that direction it was indeed possible to make out a dense vine-covered forest of unusual trees. The colours therein were more varied than most forests on Gallifrey or Earth – blues, purples and reds scattered in among the more familiar greens, browns and silvers – but many of these "trees" had odd forms. One particular variety were odd rubbery looking cones or single stalks rising up among the more usual leafy foliage.

Romana inclined her head slowly in cautious acceptance of his defence.

"Yes, that at least looks a little more out of the ordinary," she conceded. Then she frowned as her brain fully registered the local inhabitants visible nearby.

"I must say that the people are something of a surprise too. I was expecting something smaller. And more furry."

Those "people" were definitely not humanoid. Their hides were various shades of green and seemed more like an insect's carapace than skin – rigid, or at the very least, semi-rigid. The body was sectioned and sported pairs of legs or arms, four sets in total. The upper pairs acted as arms while the lowest twins formed the creature's legs.

The upper most portion of this alien was its huge, globular head – a head which was marked with prominent veins and dominated by a single sizeable eye.

"Ah," the Doctor said knowingly, a slight smile creeping into his features, "you are thinking of the Boloids, the small furry creatures of legend also native to this planet. *These* are the Chitids – who share dominion over Alpha Centauri Prime."

Here the Doctor paused and looked a little uncertain.

"Um… admittedly there do seem to be mostly Chitids here in the city at the moment – it was originally built by them I believe – the Boloids prefer to live deeper in the jungle itself. Oh, wait! Look! There's a Boloid just over there!"

With this last statement the Doctor pointed excitedly through the growing throng of Chitids around them. That race were on average not much shorter than humans or Gallifreyans. The considerably shorter Boloid was difficult to see among the taller citizens but finally Romana also spotted it. A blue furry shape perhaps a metre and a half tall when standing, striding through crowd on two spindly looking arms or legs terminating in enormous hands or feet. The confusion as to how exactly these appendages should be named stemmed from the fact that these were the only two limbs the creature owned. Their "armpits" were high on the creature's head at around where one might expect ears, possibly even higher.

Its yellow beak of a mouth looked like a small trumpet bell while above this two circular eyes glowed like yellow headlights.

The Boloid walked on out of sight.

Now it was Romana's turn to nod sagely.

"Ah. So there are *two* intelligent species on Alpha Centauri Prime. Unusual, but there are several instances where such peaceful coexistence succeeds in the universe."

The Doctor's smile returned.

"Three actually – although there is some question as to the final species' actual intelligence. They are often regarded by the Chitids and Boloids as 'semi-sentient', while they in their turn tend to keep to themselves within their own close-knit communities high in the jungle canopy. I refer, of course, to the Chirpas."

Romana frowned at the Doctor.

"The 'Sherpas'?" She said questioningly.

"You don't mean as in those Earthmen famous for their climbing expertise?"

The Doctor shook his head impatiently.

"No, no. *Chirpas* – with a 'ch' as in 'chess'," he said with an increasing air of distraction. Indeed, as he finished he was no longer even looking at Romana but had begun to look around them with concern. Romana quickly identified the source of his worries.

The two Timelords had absent mindedly wandered a little way from the TARDIS as they chatted, K9 trundling dutifully at their heels. By now they were perhaps ten metres clear of their vehicle. In the interim, the number of Chitids around them had grown dramatically. The Doctor and Romana noticed that both they and the TARDIS were the foci of attention for much high pitched whispered – or muttered – discussion. Along with this back and forth between the citizens of City Alpha One there were many claws being pointed at either the Doctor, Romana or the time ship.

A single phrase began to stand out, highlighted through repetition. Without understanding why, both Gallifreyans felt an increasing sense of trepidation as they identified these words.

The Saviour.

The Doctor drew himself up to his full height and sought to calm the crowd by striking up a conversation.

"Greetings, good citizens of City Alpha One! We are travellers in search of a friend – Alpha Centauri. Perhaps you might help us find him? This is Romana, my dearest companion. Oh, sorry K9 – you are very dear too.

And I am the Doctor."

With these final words, his plan to calm the crowd utterly fell apart.

Cries of "The Saviour!" rang out now from all quarters, no longer whispered or muttered but squealed in joyous recognition. The excited throng began to press in upon the two time travellers. Romana turned on the Doctor.

"I thought you said you'd never been here before!" She cried desperately as they were both pressed and jostled by those around them. The Doctor threw up his hands in exasperation.

"I haven't! This must be some terrible mistake!"

Romana now turned her attention upon the nearest Chitids.

"He's not 'The Saviour'," she insisted crossly, "he's a very careless Timelord!"

This did nothing to quell the ongoing cries of "The Saviour". One of the Chitids closest to them – practically in their faces – shrieked, "Only The Saviour would deny his divinity!"

The Doctor rolled his eyes crazily in frustration.

"Well, what chance does that give me?!"

The first Chitid's remark had seemed to spark a philosophical, or perhaps theological, debate.

"Actually, it was The Companion – The Ever Changing One – who denied him!" This second Chitid declared. There was much muttering from the surrounding crowd either supporting or doubting this claim, or simply confused.

"Obviously The Companion would speak *for* The Saviour!" The first Chitid cried with zealous certainty, "What else would you expect?!"

This sparked further furious debate from the surrounding throng. By now the two Timelords were being jostled quite violently, if unintentionally. The Doctor bent his knees to slide down through the press to be closer to the metal dog.

"K9!" He whispered urgently to him.

"Master?" K9 whispered back.

"Go back to the TARDIS, get inside and lock the door! Guard protocol!" Came the Doctor's hushed but barked order.

"Affirmative, master!" K9's response was still whispered, yet also chirped decisively. His antennae spun and his lights flashed and it seemed at first he was just as blocked from the time ship as Romana and the Doctor. Then he rose straight up, floating over the heads of the surrounding Chitids.

"It is a sign!" Someone gasped, which was immediately followed by more sharp intakes of breath and repetitions of the proclamation.

"You'd have thought a technologically advanced culture, like Alpha Centauri, would have seen a flying robot before!" Romana hissed behind her hand as K9 set down in front of the doors of the TARDIS. The Doctor leant towards Romana, hand similarly raised to cover his words.

"Romana, let's not look a gift horse – or dog – in the mouth," he rasped with as much confidence as he could muster, "run!"

The crowd furthest from the TARDIS had thinned a little as it had flowed to a degree after the flying dog. This was the direction, away from the TARDIS and through the least dense press of people, that the Doctor now dragged Romana. With judicious use of shoulders and elbows they successfully burst free of the masses and began to run north.

"The Saviour is leaving!" A voice rang out from the Chitid admirers.

"Wait for us, oh Saviour!" It continued loudly and shrilly, "Lead us! Show us The Way!"

The crowd surged after them, their insectoid legs propelling them with surprising speed.

The two Timelords continued to run through the streets heading – they hoped – for an exit from the city and potential freedom. At the very least, a little privacy in which to gather their thoughts.

The Universe, it seemed, was in capricious mood today.

Another small crowd burst from a side street just in front of them. These citizens were mostly staring at handheld devices. Some of the newcomers looked up and cried, "The Saviour! He is here among us!"

Clearly social media was spreading news of the Timelords' arrival faster than they had anticipated or hoped for. The Doctor and Romana ran straight into this new group, unable to halt their momentum in time.

The Doctor tripped over a Chitid's foot, flying to the ground cursing in low Gallifreyan. Romana helped him to his feet and he cursed some more as he realised he had lost one of his boots!

"My DM!" He wailed in frustration and despair. Nevertheless there was nothing he could do besides allow Romana to drag them both onwards in their continued flight.

One of the Chitids behind them had clearly discovered the Doctor's singular item of footwear.

"It's a sign!" The creature pronounced in the high pitched tones typical of their race.

"Behold – the Holy Shoe!" It continued, "Bow down before it! All praise the Holy Shoe!"

Many in the crowd began to lower themselves and do exactly that. One of those gathered there upon the road was not so easily distracted, however. They pointed after the fleeing Timelords and yelled, "Never mind about that! The Saviour's getting away! Follow The Saviour!"

And so the chase was on again.

Fortunately, the farrago with the footwear had allowed the Timelords to put a little distance between themselves and their pursuers. This was in spite of the Doctor's now uneven gait – one foot still shod whilst the other was only clad in a thick woollen sock. The Doctor consoled himself with the thought that at least the thickness of the woven tube did offer *some* protection from the hard ground beneath them.

The City was walled, a shiny metal barrier whose purpose was not immediately obvious. If it were for defence it had remarkably large, open and unguarded gates – indeed there were no obvious barriers *to* close and fill the gap. The Doctor and Romana happily took advantage of this and left the metropolis.

Ever since they had run from the TARDIS they had been heading gently uphill. Now free of the city this ascent persisted as they ran up the dusty road, climbing a hill on the edge of the desert. The runners were still close behind but as the path curved around the peak of the mound it did begin to block them from view. As the Timelords continued their dash under the baking rays of Alpha Centauri A they saw a small shack on the side of the road ahead, almost resting on the very top of the hill itself.

Shack might have been an unkind description – while its size was very much in line with a one or two room temporary shelter or abode its materials were high tech, as one might expect from the technologically adept Alpha Centaurans. In spite of its modest size, all was polished shining metal and tinted shade-giving glass, or similar transparent material.

As they ran past this dwelling the door opened a crack.

"Doctor! Quickly! In here!" A voice piped out.

Romana rolled her eyes.

"Is there nowhere you can go and not be recognised?" She demanded exasperatedly. The Doctor ignored this rebuke for the moment and instead turned to face the door.

"Alpha Centauri!" He cried excitedly, and not without a little relief. Romana frowned at him.

"Yes, Doctor, I know where we are. You don't have to keep repeating yourself."

The Doctor turned and shook his head impatiently at her.

"No, no. That's not what I mean! I meant… oh, never mind – I'll explain later! Quickly – inside!"

With that he ushered his fellow Timelord towards the door of this metal shack and they both entered.

The Doctor quickly closed the door behind them and they turned to regard their own personal saviour. As they did so they heard the sounds of running Chitids approaching the location of the shack, albeit faintly; the soundproofing of their refuge must have been of the highest quality.

The Chitid before them looked like many they had seen before; lime green skin, a veiny cyclopean visage of enormous globular proportions, four pairs of bluntly clawed limbs. This particular citizen of Alpha Centauri Prime wore a long, high collared pleated cloak of the same colour and shade as its hide. The cloak showed a few subtle signs of age, although clearly much loved and cared for.

"Alpha Centauri!" The Doctor said again with recognition, smiling warmly. Then his face dropped as he noticed Romana's frown of irritation.

"Romana, let me introduce you to Ambassador Alpha Centauri of the Galactic Federation."

Romana continued to frown at the Doctor.

"Very pleased to meet you," she said hurriedly to the Chitid before rounding on her fellow Timelord, "and why do you keep calling her Alpha Centauri? It's like running into a Dalek and saying, 'Hello Skaro!' Not only ill advised but also imprecise and possibly a little racially insensitive!"

"Him," the Doctor corrected brusquely, "and it's what I've always known him as, since we first met."

Romana shook her head.

"Maybe, Doctor, but you must admit we've already had enough Alpha Centauris floating around in conversation today. Along with a mountain of 'A's, alphas, primes, ones and what-have-you. It's hardly conducive to keeping track of people or things."

The Doctor shook his head in violent disagreement.

"Nonsense! The peoples of Alpha Ce... the Chitids and the Boloids are most systematic individuals and this is reflected in their nomenclature. For example, there are six major cities on the planet all named in the same fashion as City Alpha One. Then the next size down are named City Beta One, Two, Three et cetera. All very orderly and easy to remember!"

Romana sighed and rolled her eyes.

"Yes, yes. I had heard something about this system's inhabitants being rather nerdy."

The Doctor shook his head disapprovingly.

"And there was you accusing *me* of being insensitive!"

Romana sighed again.

"My apologies, Ambassador," she began, conceding the Doctor's point a little.

"Ex-ambassador," their rescuer chirped in.

"OK – *Ex*-ambassador," Romana continued undeterred, "but surely you must have a name beyond your title and your star system?"

The Ex-ambassador nodded in vigorous agreement.

"Naturally! In my species' native tongue I am known as..."

What followed was a series of burbling fluting noises.

Romana's eyes rolled skywards in weary defeat.

"My dear friend," the Doctor began, seeking to smooth over the situation, "perhaps to avoid future confusion we might call you A.C.?"

The Chitid clapped his pincers together.

"Of course, Doctor! Whatever is easiest and makes you happy!"

The Doctor and Romana both smiled with relief, albeit for slightly different reasons.

"Now, A.C.," the Doctor continued, "how are you? And why have you retired? You look as young and chipper as when we last met on Peladon!"

"And why are your people chasing us around as if we were some divine visitation?" Romana added with some impatience.

A.C. shifted uncomfortably at Romana's question and elected to ignore it for the time being, choosing instead to answer the Doctor.

"You are too kind, Doctor. Seventy five years have passed since we last met on Peladon – an even longer interlude than that between our last meeting and our first. Believe me when I say I am quite aged enough to retire with honour. True, we are long lived by your human standards and may show few outward signs, but I am beginning to feel my age."

The Doctor nodded politely in feigned acceptance of his statement.

"We're not human," Romana added as an inconsequential correction.

Her words, however, provoked a most extreme reaction in their host. He wailed and dropped his head into his uppermost set of claws.

"Oh, my foolishness! Ever do my own words come back to haunt me! Only now it seems the harm I caused was built on lies! I cannot even be said to have honestly mislead my people! What a fool, what an idiot, what a dolt I have been!"

The Doctor and Romana looked at one another in amazement.

"A.C.," the Doctor cried, "my dear, dear friend! What is it? What has upset you so?"

A.C. continued to sob, his whole body quivering with emotion.

"I'm sorry, sir," Romana said softly, "I really didn't mean to upset you."

The former ambassador looked up at her and the quivering subsided a little. Beyond that though, his downcast mood was largely unaltered.

"There is no need for *you* to apologise. The only person here who should be sorry is me! And I should be apologising to the entire planet – if only they would listen!"

"Please, A.C.," the Doctor said patting his friend's arm, "calm yourself and tell us what it is you think you have done wrong."

A.C. nodded with resigned acceptance.

"Yes, yes, of course. Now I compound my sins with rudeness – will my guilt never end? I shall endeavour to answer your question, Doctor, and in the process answer your companion's too – Romana, was it?"

The female Timelord nodded politely to their Chitid host.

"It all began after my second encounter with the Doctor here, on the planet Peladon. Although in truth you could say the initial seeds of doom were sown even from our first meeting."

The Doctor could not contain the need to defend himself.

"But my dear friend, how can these be the source of disasters? Both those adventures ended happily, with plots and deceit uncovered and thwarted. Surely the most positive of outcomes?"

A.C. shook his head sadly.

"Oh yes, your actions were beyond reproach. It was my reporting of them which heralded our current problems."

The Doctor frowned at him.

"Your 'reports'? How so?"

"My official reports of both Peladon missions became very popular reading and listening among the public here on Alpha Centauri Prime, particularly my Chitid kin. I began to become something of a celebrity, above and beyond my status as Ambassador. After the reports of our second adventure became widely known I was raised in the eyes of many to the rank of Chitid hero! Something our culture had never really encountered before!"

The Doctor nodded slowly.

"Yes, I can see how such a novelty could lead to problems, particularly if the situation were abused or taken advantage of. But I can't imagine you'd ever do such a thing?"

A.C. nodded vigorously.

"You imagine correctly – *I* never would and never did. It was not *my* status as hero which caused the problems. It was yours!"

Here the Doctor looked shocked and not a little downcast himself. Romana simply nodded knowingly as if suspicions had been confirmed.

"I can't imagine anyone would ever see me as a hero..." the Doctor began.

"Really?" Romana interjected with a raised eyebrow, "Not even a little?"

"But," the Doctor continued through gritted teeth, "even if people *did*, how would this have caused a problem?"

A.C. sighed wearily.

"The problem was that you became more than just a hero. You became The Saviour! You gained a status utterly foreign to Chitid culture until then – you became the embodiment of the divine! Fifty years ago a religion sprang up around your person. And its popularity has grown ever since until almost ninety percent of the Chitid population are believers!"

Now Romana shared the Doctor's frown.

"I can see now how our arrival caused such a stir. And this newfound religious fervour is certainly an odd departure for Alpha Centauran society. But I sense this has caused some further problems you have yet to reveal. And why didn't you try to persuade them that he was not some spiritual entity?" She asked.

A.C. looked glum.

"At first I viewed their excitement at my reports as nothing significant – no problem at all. I was even a little flattered. Naturally I tried to remind everyone that you were only human – if only I had realised the magnitude of that mistake – and reinforce that he was a brave and good man, performing brave deeds, but, nevertheless, still just a man. But they wouldn't listen! They almost shunned me for my temerity in belittling their Saviour. The religion had taken on a life of its own and there was nothing I could do to stop it! If only I'd known you weren't even human."

"When my companions and I landed on Peladon each time everyone we met just assumed we *were* human," the Doctor explained to Romana.

"And naturally you did nothing to correct this misunderstanding?" Romana asked sceptically.

"Well," the Doctor said a little sheepishly, "the first time it proved a useful disguise. And by the second visit it was impossible to remove that disguise without creating a diplomatic incident and further complications!"

Romana nodded sagely.

"Oh, it is clear no further complications have arisen," she pronounced wryly. The Doctor harrumphed.

"Fine. A.C. - how did my 'humanity' cause later problems?"

Once more A.C. shook his head sadly.

"The people began to associate *all* humans with your divine status. It was ridiculous – we had been out among the stars long before the first primitive Earth ships made contact. We had been a founder member of the Galactic Federation, which they only later joined. But suddenly they had new found power and authority over us. They have forced this planet to massively upscale its mining of Trisilicate, with disastrous consequences to health and the environment!"

Romana frowned again.

"Trisilicate?"

The Doctor shook his own head impatiently.

"Yes, a compound vital for much of the current technology of the Galactic Federation, including many military devices. Invaluable in defending against Galaxy Five!"

"Galaxy Five," Romana sniggered, "how quaint! I've not heard that nomenclature in centuries!"

The Doctor brushed her amusement away with a wave of his hand.

"Yes, yes, all very 'old school'", he said before turning his full attention on A.C., "but I didn't even know you had Trisilicate on Alpha Centauri Prime? After all – I thought that was the whole point of the negotiations on Peladon in the first place?"

Here A.C. looked embarrassed and uncomfortable.

"Yes, well, we did already have our own supply. But we ensured treaties were enshrined in Federation law limiting the extraction and export of our own reserves. To protect our own resources, as well as the environment!"

The Doctor gave a wry smile.

"How very protectionist of you."

A.C.'s eye looked towards the floor.

"Yes, I have no doubt these policies fomented great envy amongst some of our Federation allies. Particularly those with no native Trisilicate, such as the Earth. Yet again it seems we bring ruination upon ourselves, with no small helping hand from me. I have to show you the devastation the Earthmen are causing! The harsh labour conditions and the laying waste to the jungle. You must come with me and meet Bimbor, chief representative of the Boloids!"

The Doctor and Romana exchanged dubious glances, each sharing similar misgivings as to the effectiveness of this plan. Nevertheless, they felt it hard to ignore the plight of this poor tortured Chitid and his people, or refuse his request.

"Of course we will do all we can to help," the Doctor said plainly.

"But how can we get to your Boloid friend when ninety percent of the Chitid population wish to adore the Doctor here?" Romana asked, "We'd be mobbed as soon as we step outside!"

A.C. raised a claw to emphasise his next point.

"Aha! Yes, you would no doubt be right *if* we were to step outside. But there is no need! This weather monitoring station – my retirement home as well as my occupation – is mobile! We can fly it to Bimbor's jungle home!"

Romana nodded slowly.

"Ah, so this 'shack' is in fact a vehicle?"

At this A.C. looked a little shamed once more.

"Yes – oh, how the mighty have fallen! The once proud Ambassador reduced to living in a mobile home!"

The Doctor held up a hand to sooth him.

"Nonsense! There is absolutely *nothing* wrong with mobile homes! Wouldn't you agree, Romana?"

Romana began to waggle her head sceptically before catching the Doctor's frown and morphing it into a vigorous nodded agreement. She also *almost* successfully hid her smirk.

A.C. moved to a section of wall and pressed a discreet button. The entire surface turned into an array of touchpads and displays, including ones giving views of the outside. The Chitids who had been pursuing the Doctor and Romana had long since moved beyond the peak of the hill. They had, for all the Timelords knew, probably dispersed. However, flying did still seem the surest way of avoiding further obstructions.

A.C. pressed a control and with the slightest of hums the shack shot straight up into the air.

The two Timelords had felt no evidence of motion and looked at each other somewhat impressed.

"Inertial dampeners," A.C. explained, "my home, like me, may be getting on a bit, but it was the height of technology in its day."

The shack now began to fly south passing over the glittering metropolis of City Alpha One and on to the edge of the jungle.

A shudder ran through the vessel.

"Oh no," A.C. shrieked in panic, waving his claws in the air, "I am a fool! Why didn't I do a systems check first? The mass repulsers are failing!"

Romana stared at the Doctor.

"What does it mean?" She asked desperately.

"I believe," the Doctor responded grimly, "it means we're going to crash."

As if to reinforce his words, the view screen showed the dense jungle rushing up to meet them.

Chapter Two – The Definite Article - Part 2

by Alexander Leithes

The Doctor and Romana groggily picked themselves up from where they lay on the floor of the crashed weather hut. Beyond a slight tilt to that surface towards the door through which they had entered, there was remarkably few signs of damage to this bizarre mobile home.

The jungle canopy had slowed the final few metres of its descent and its landing had been further softened by the moist peaty humus of the forest floor. The absence of any loose items in the room they now occupied had reduced any signs of the crash to near invisibility. The Doctor and Romana's bruises and scrapes were – while undeniably painful and nagging – almost the only scant evidence of any real harm or trauma.

Almost.

A.C. remained lying on the cabin deck. His two lower limbs had unnatural bends upon their lower joints; his hide was actually broken at the points of discontinuity. Thick yellow ooze slowly seeped out from these cracks.

Both A.C.'s legs were broken.

A.C. whimpered and moaned to himself, barely conscious.

"How bad is it, Doctor?" Romana asked. The Doctor shook his head, a little dazed and unsure of himself.

"It is difficult to judge the seriousness of his injuries. The Chitids are notoriously sensitive to physical harm and somewhat... nervy in the face of peril or distress. And, to be honest, I just don't know enough about their physiology to give a meaningful prognosis!"

A.C.'s giant eye had until then been closed, either in response to the pain or through some degree of unconsciousness. In a Herculean effort - by Chitid standards - he forced himself to speak.

"On the far right of the control panel... there is a button...

'Medibed'," he struggled out. Quickly, the Doctor rushed over to that panel. After a moment's search he found the switch and pressed it.

The – until now hidden – medibed chamber slid out from the same wall and nearly knocked the Doctor off his feet as nimbly hopped aside. The hexagonal cross-sectioned chest-like bed stopped when fully extended, being perhaps half a metre longer than the height of the Doctor. After a further hurried examination he discovered the opening mechanism. The entire top half of the unit swung open from a hinge attaching it lengthways to the bottom half – this top being some transparent perspex-like material, while the bottom was chrome coloured and opaque.

"Put… me… inside," A.C. croaked feebly.

As gently and carefully as they could, Romana and the Doctor lifted the injured alien and placed him softly on the cushioned interior of the medibed. To the Doctor's mind it was unpleasantly reminiscent of a coffin.

"Close… the… chamber," A.C. told them softly. Romana found the appropriate control and activated it. The lid eased down with an almost imperceptible hum.

As soon as the lid closed there was a brief faint hissing sound.

"Oh, thank goodness for that!" A.C.'s shrill voice rang out from the cabinet, sounding not only more normal in strength and tone but also slightly amplified, almost as if the medibed had built in speakers.

"A.C.," the Doctor said, still worried, "is everything okay in there? Are you alright?"

"Oh yes, Doctor, I'm perfectly okay – more than okay!"

The Chitid's response sounded almost *too* okay, bordering on giddy.

"The automatic anaesthetic has been administered and now the device can begin repairs! I feel fine!"

The Doctor and Romana exchanged knowing glances but also smiled with relief.

"Will we be able to continue our journey?" Romana asked, once more focused on the purpose of their aborted flight. A.C. tapped a few buttons on the inside of the medibed with his upper claws. Through the perspex lid they saw his face cloud, the first darkening of his mood since the anaesthetic.

"The ship can repair me in a couple of hours. As for itself – it seems that is beyond its powers to remedy. You must go on on foot to find my friend Bimbor in his official residence – not only to see for yourself the harm the Earthmen are causing, but now, with the additional purpose of requesting his aid to recover and repair my home!"

The Doctor nodded his understanding.

"Wise words indeed, my good friend," he acknowledged before glancing down at his feet, "although I do so wish I still had both my boots. No matter – I shall tough it out."

Then another thought struck him.

"But where exactly *is* the home of your friend – Bimbor the Boloid?"

A.C. tapped a few more buttons on the inside of the medibed.

"Bimbor's mining settlement lies three kilometres south of here. Tell him you are a friend of mine and explain the purpose of our visit. He will certainly welcome you with open arms!"

"Won't that mean he'll fall over?" The Doctor whispered behind his hand to Romana. She sniggered as she remembered the strange furry sphere of the one Boloid they had seen so far, with its single pair of dual purpose arms or legs.

"And how will we find him *exactly*?" The Doctor asked in a more audible and serious tone. A.C. nodded vigorously from his prone position.

"I have the exact coordinates here and can broadcast them in a variety of ways, if you have a suitable device?"

The Doctor nodded with a slight air of weary resignation.

"I believe I may have something which will do the trick."

With that, he withdrew his sonic screwdriver and the information was transferred.

Before the Timelords left, A.C. had one final piece of advice.

"Be careful in the jungle. While most of the wildlife is relatively safe there are a few more... troublesome creatures out there. Keep your eyes open for the vicious Snarks and the Willowming Vooms. You definitely don't want one of them landing on you!"

The Doctor nodded his thanks to his old friend.

"And you keep the door shut after we leave," the Doctor retorted, "we'd hate for *you* to be eaten in our absence!"

The only reply they received was a single nervous gulp.

A.C.'s home safely secured behind them the Doctor and Romana headed off south through the moist dense jungle. The vines and trees which surrounded them came in a wide variety of colours, many beyond those found in the plants of Earth or Gallifrey. There were also the odd towering columns, or elongated cones of rubbery texture – possibly a fungus of some sort, but ones which were often taller than mature conifers. These too came in a variety of strange shades from purples through greens to even a sickly white.

The Doctor frequently checked his sonic screwdriver as he made his uneven squelching progress through the foliage. His one shod foot was faring well enough. It was the other, wrapped only in a sock, which was becoming uncomfortable. While it had merely become dusty as they ran though the streets of City Alpha One, here in the jungle it was utterly soaked and muddy as it sank into the dank humus with every step.

Romana would occasionally smirk at her companion's discomfort, although she made some efforts to hide this. To be fair, much of the time she was too preoccupied to smirk as she kept her eyes peeled for the aforementioned Snarks and Vooms, in spite of – unfortunately - being utterly unfamiliar with how they looked.

The Doctor had just made yet another check on the screwdriver and pocketed it when he gasped. Romana had overtaken him and was a pace ahead, peering around them. The Doctor was looking upwards over their heads.

He grabbed Romana by the shoulders and pulled them both back a step or two!

This rescue had only just been made in time.

A generous pile of guano landed directly in front of them, so close a few chunks still managed to splatter their trousers a little.

"What on Gallifrey was that?" Romana exclaimed with disgust. The Doctor released her right shoulder and pointed past her head, upwards into the forest canopy.

"Behold! A city of the Chirpas!"

Romana saw the tree-borne conurbation for the first time. She felt both his grandiose tone and the label he had used were somewhat unearned.

"'City'?" She repeated dubiously, nodding to the elevated dwellings.

All these structures were built on the broadest of the branches, or on platforms between narrower boughs, and as such – while well above the heads of the two Timelords – tended to cluster around the lower reaches of the jungle canopy.

Their methods and materials of construction were considerably lower tech than the glass, concrete and chrome of the Chitid civilisation. Everything was formed from logs, branches, vines and leaves – the jungle itself further repurposed. The cut limbs were mostly cleaned and prepared to give something closer to treated wood. Upon reflection "mostly" might have been an exaggeration. It was not just this treatment of the timber which had a somewhat half-hearted look to it.

Every building looked semi-completed and yet also bore signs of long use, wear and tear and even neglect. Here a shack-like home would be missing a wall. Another had only half a roof. Yet another had no roof at all. One or two were simply exposed platforms as if they had progressed to the foundation and got no further. In all cases it was as though the architect had got distracted, lost focus and consequently the will or desire to follow through.

The fragmentary nature of these dwellings made it particularly easy to observe their occupants. The Doctor and Romana realised they were being scrutinised in return.

There was quite a crowd on the branch over their heads – a large broad bough to be sure, but it was not only *its* size which allowed it to support such a large number of observers. The Chirpas were no more than one metre tall. The Timelords realised that this size was reflected in the somewhat ramshackle buildings of the city – perfect for their builders but the Doctor and Romana would have been hard pressed to fit inside any one of them, except those with handy missing walls or roofs.

Size aside, the Chirpas were the most humanoid looking denizens of Alpha Centauri Prime so far encountered. Their skin-tones varied through pallid pinks to dusty tans, their hair enjoying a similar range of shades, although some sported more jungle green or blue locks.

There was something very "samey" about their features. It was not so much that they were all identical, but from a human or Gallifreyan perspective there was something generic or forgettable about their blandly mildly attractive, or at least inoffensive features. Their skin was very smooth and unblemished and again, from a human point of view at least, you might think they were all in their twenties such was the uniform impression of being unsullied or untroubled by the tribulations of the universe. But this smooth conformity also made them instantly unmemorable – there was no one among them who might be described as striking or remarkable.

Two non-human features did stand out, however, albeit with equal intensity across all the Chirpas present.

They had wings!

Gossamer fine and largely transparent their polythene-like surfaces had a greenish tinge but could be seen through except where veins, stronger supporting ribs and some other odd marks stood out against this near invisible background. These flight appendages, when fully extended, had spans as wide as the Chirpas were tall.

The second alien feature of note was more subtle.

The tips of their noses were dark brown circles, no more than half a centimetre in diameter. These tiny discreet disks, as far as the Timelords could tell at this distance, looked shinier than the rest of the skins of these creatures. In case anyone was worried or disturbed by the thought that these humanoid aliens were all naked, they were not. Although they were not exactly well dressed either.

Much like their other features, their clothes were fairly generic, either light dresses or trousers and shirts, with no particular gender biases in either selection but little intentional variation in styles. What variety there was seemed to exist solely in the haphazard way most were attached to their wearer's bodies. In common with the construction of their homes, the clothing of the Chirpas also frequently looked unfinished, as if the maker had become distracted or bored before completion. As such, many flaps were held closed, or arms or legs fastened simply by knotting vines around the incomplete sections like pieces of string.

Now the Doctor and Romana identified the source of their faecal assault and near miss.

Squatting on a branch immediately above them, and now a few steps ahead of them, was a female Chirpa in a light summer dress. She had her back turned and her buttocks were currently exposed. She looked mortified or guilty, and yet this emotion did not seem directed towards the two Timelords. She was surrounded by many other Chirpas who now began to whisper to each other behind their hands in slightly high pitched voices.

The Doctor and Romana caught one or two snatches of conversation.

"She missed them!"

"They not covered!"

"That wasn't meant to happen!"

"Did she fail?"

The Chirpa bombardier stood and turned to face the same way as her companions, or entourage. She looked agitated and worried by what she was hearing.

She pouted her lips forward looking almost like a duck bill, while opening her eyes wide as if amazed or surprised. This did not appear to have the desired effect as the tone of the crowd's grumblings remained unaltered. Then she pointed fiercely in the direction of the two Timelords.

"Made them jump!" She cried imperiously.

"They ran away! They scared!" She continued even more stridently. Further muttering broke out amongst her companions, only now coloured in tones of approval. The Doctor leaned towards Romana and spoke behind his hand.

"You will recall I mentioned there was some debate as to the nature of Chirpa intelligence?"

Romana nodded slowly.

"Yes, I remember," she confirmed, regarding the elevated assembly with a far from warm expression.

One of the followers nearest to the head Chirpa shuffled over to her. This new female leaned in towards the nearest wing of the ring leader.

She gently touched the tip of her nose against it then gave a little twitch of her head and withdrew. She had left a small brown mark on the transparent surface, like a lopsided 'v', or a tick.

The Gallifreyans noticed that there were many more similar marks all over the Chirpa leader's wing surfaces. They also saw that *all* the Chirpas had some of these marks, though none in such profusion as the glorious guano giver.

More and more of her entourage crowded in to repeat this procedure, while the Chirpa who had first adorned their leader received one or two or her own, from others impressed by her own quick action.

The lead Chirpa beamed with delight and her whole body quivered in excitement at all the adulation showered upon her.

"Their society seems to be some sort of popularity contest," Romana noted sourly. The Doctor waggled his head non-committally.

"Well, perhaps. But it would hardly be unique in that regard," he observed. Romana shook her head wearily.

"Unfortunately not," she agreed.

The two Timelords continued their search for the Boloid mining camp, taking care to skirt the Chirpa city, keeping their eyes peeled for further airborne attacks.

This may have been why, with their attention so distracted, they both stumbled into a swamp.

Side by side, both Timelords now stood up to their knees in blue sludge. While they were only sinking slowly, they were undeniably sinking and stuck fast.

"Well, this is another fine mess," Romana noted with comedic satisfaction.

"Yes," the Doctor agreed, "what a fantastic colour!"

Romana rolled her eyes.

"It's less the aesthetics which concern me, more our slow descent into drowning!"

"I see your point. We need to lie down – that should at least slow, possibly even prevent, our sinking further," the Doctor advised.

Neither were pleased at the prospect, but both knew it was the only sensible option left to them. They bent their knees and lay flat with their arms outstretched, squelching like well-dressed starfish.

"So, what now, Doctor?" Romana asked, "Can you reach any handy vines from where you are? To haul us to safety?"

The Doctor shook his now muddy head.

"Unfortunately, I have reached around quite extensively – and messily – and can report no such life lines."

Romana squelched in return as she shook her own head despondently. Then she gave a gasp of alarm.

"Doctor! Look!"

This final command was given with an awkward nod of her forehead across the swamp. With some effort, the Doctor turned his gaze to follow her gesture.

A sluggish 'v' was rippling through the blue slurry, heading in their direction. While the wave of the disturbance might have been quite lugubrious, the tip of the 'v' bubbled and frothed energetically and disturbingly. It was presumably the source of the wave and was making substantial progress towards them.

"Ooo… I wonder if it might be a Snark? Or even a Willoming Voom?" The Doctor mused curiously. Romana found her head shaking once again.

"I think on this occasion I could quite happily live in ignorance."

The Doctor nodded grimly, his chin slapping the swamp as he did so.

"Yes… I fear, in this case, it might, indeed, be easier to live that way," he reluctantly agreed.

The azure slime in front of them erupted!

Both Timelords found themselves spitting cerulean globules from their mouths as they struggled to keep their airways free. They also blinked and wiped their eyes in desperate attempts to clear their vision.

The sight thus revealed was remarkable indeed.

Floating and bobbing on the surface of the mud like some shaggy metre and a half high beach ball was the unmistakable form of a Boloid!

In spite of having only just emerged from beneath the marsh, its aquamarine hair looked almost untouched by the muck of that same colour. The fur obviously repelled the swamp and the Timelords felt particularly envious of that most desirable property.

The creature's two broad, flat hands/feet rested on the gently rippling slurry to aid stability while the arms joined the ball of its body roughly at, or even above, where ears might be expected. The alien's mouth formed a yellow protuberance from the centre of its face like a modest trumpet bell, while above this sat a pair of glowing circles – the creature's eyes.

"The Doctor and his companion, I presume?" The Boloid said gruffly.

"Romana," Romana supplied helpfully, if a little brusquely. The Doctor frowned at them both.

"My good sir, you have us at a disadvantage – even more so now my companion has identified herself. Might I enquire *how* you knew who we were?"

The Boloid gave a single harsh chuckle.

"Ha! You're not exactly low profile! You're all over every news feed. And it's not like we're stuck in the bloody stone age out here! We do hear things, you know?"

The Doctor inclined his head graciously.

"My apologies – I did not mean to imply any disrespect for your technological prowess. The Boloids are, after all, famous for their engineering. But who, may I ask, do we have the honour of addressing?"

The shape of the Boloid's mouth trumpet shifted slightly in what the Timelords assumed was a smile.

"I am Bimbor, Chief Representative of the Boloids of Alpha Centauri Prime. And welcome to the Noria Jungle sludge mine!"

The Doctor and Romana looked amazed.

"But… you're the very person we've come to meet!" Romana cried.

"Did Ambassador… um… retired Ambassador Alpha Centauri contact you from the crash site? Warn you to expect us?" The Doctor asked in confusion. Bimbor gave the Boloid equivalent of a frown.

"A.C. *is* here then? No, we've heard no word from him, but there were reports of his weather station taking off and flying towards the jungle. Our seismometers registered an impact soon thereafter, so I came out to investigate in case my old friend was in trouble."

The Doctor's confusion looked far from dispelled.

"Wait – *you* call him A.C.?"

Bimbor laughed.

"Well of course I bloody well do! Have you any idea how confusing it is calling 'im Alpha Centauri? I've called 'im A.C. for years!"

Romana narrowed her eyes significantly at the Doctor.

"Yes, yes, I can see how this name might help a little," he conceded tetchily.

"Our mutual friend is here," he continued in a more businesslike tone, "but injured in his crippled weather station. He sent us for help, to find you. And it appears we have succeeded."

Bimbor dipped his body forward in a nod.

"'Appens you 'ave," he agreed, "come with me back to the mining settlement and we'll send a repair vehicle and crew out to fetch him. And in the mean time we can get you two cleaned up. There's a fairly solid path over yonder I can drag you both to, then it's an easy walk from there. But why did A.C. want you to meet me in the first place?"

The Boloid waddled over between the two Timelords, offering each an arm to hang on to. As the Doctor took a firm hold of their rescuer he answered his question.

"A.C. wanted us to see the state of the Boloid people. He said you were suffering greatly due to the mining demands of the Earthlings."

Bimbor's countenance fell.

"Aye. That's a fair statement. Best wait 'til we get to the settlement itself before we talk about this. You might well see the problem then anyway," he said grimly.

With that, the Boloid leader pulled the two Timelords to firmer ground and together the trio began to trudge deeper into the blue swamp.

The Doctor and Romana both sat in floating cushioned hollow hemispheres inside the chrome building which formed Bimbor's official residence and offices. They were currently wrapped in large fluffy blankets of yellow and scarlet for modesty and warmth.

"Your clothes should be clean and dry in about an hour," Bimbor said almost jovially. The Doctor nodded his understanding.

"We are much obliged to you, Representative Bimbor," he responded cordially, "but in the mean time perhaps you could tell us more of the problems of your people, and their causes?"

The Boloid leader shook his fur, almost like a dog drying itself.

"You saw the state of the place as you arrived, didn't you?" He asked tersely.

It was true that, as the two Timelords had squelched wetly towards Bimbor's home, they had gained a worrying insight into the lives of the Boloid miners and their families. The buildings of the town were all of modern materials and designs, in many respects not dissimilar to those of the Chitids, except they favoured more spherical shapes than the towers, cones and cuboids of their insectoid brethren. Another notable difference, however, had been the state of disrepair of most of the Boloid constructions, as if wear and tear had been allowed to remain unaddressed. It was the first sign of any privation they had witnessed on Alpha Centauri Prime.

Next they had reached the local hospital where, even as they passed, several floating platform-like vehicles had rushed up carrying prostrate Boloids, clearly in desperate need of medical attention. Still more sickly looking furry balls queued outside, waiting for admittance. It was not immediately obvious what ailed these citizens but their fur did look less shiny than say, that of Bimbor. Their eyes also glowed less brightly, and while their spherical forms did not really allow them to look skinny, there was something about their expressions and a lack of energy which suggested they were malnourished, exhausted, or both.

"Yes," the Doctor conceded in response to Bimbor's question, "things did look a little desperate as we came through the town. Why, given all the mining going on – and presumably the attendant wealth that would bring – are your people so impoverished?"

Bimbor shook his body angrily.

"It's those bloody humans!" He spat bitterly. Then he remembered his guests.

"Oh. I didn't mean you. I'm not so daft as to think everyone of one race is the same. Unlike our idiot Chitid comrades," he finished sourly.

"We're not actually human," Romana pointed out. Bimbor's eyes widened in surprise.

"Really?" He said thoughtfully, "Well, it's a damn shame nobody thought to tell the Chitids! Then maybe they wouldn't be so bloody keen to fulfil their every damned desire!"

The Doctor nodded pensively.

"A.C. had already hinted as much. His glowing tales of my earlier adventures having inadvertently deified the entire population of the Earth. But your people do not share these beliefs – surely you must object? Vote against harmful diktats favouring the well-being and enrichment of Earth at the expense of the Boloids, or even ultimately the Chitids?"

Bimbor sighed defeatedly.

"It all comes down to numbers," he said wearily, "you know the Chitids are long lived, at least by Earthly standards? Well, so are we, the Boloids, barring accidents. And therein lies the problem."

The Doctor and Romana nodded, urging him to continue.

"My people have been proud miners of Trisilicate for millennia – an open cast but no less hazardous process. Taking in the sludge from the swamp you fell in earlier – and others like it."

"Ah," said the Doctor knowingly, "it is the Trisilicate which gives it its distinctive blue colour, yes?"

Bimbor's body bobbed in agreement.

"Aye, and us too – you could say it's in our blood. 'Cause it is! And like I said, we're proud of our heritage and live for the work, no matter how hazardous. But that has always meant we've had a slightly higher mortality rate than our more desk-bound Chitid compatriots. But didn't bother us – yes, we were always outnumbered on the Alpha Centauri senate due to proportional representation, but it didn't matter when our fellow Alpha Centaurans were sensible, practical and looked out for the good of all."

The two Timelords nodded thoughtfully.

"So, how did Earthly demands upset the balance?" Romana enquired.

Bimbor shook his head.

"Once they got wind of the Chitid's softness for them, coupled with their pre-existing frustration at being unable to get at such a plentiful, and relatively local supply of Trisilicate, they leapt at the chance to take advantage of the situation. At least some in the government and positions of power did.

"They started persuading the Chitids to vote for more and more mining, coupled with increased export of the produce, while paying next to nothing for it by Galactic trading standards. And it got worse! Even the money which was coming to Alpha Centauri Prime – which might have gone some way to improving the state of things for us, Boloids – was diverted! Pointless, frivolous expenses – things the senate were persuaded to buy *from* Earth! Usually dressed up in some war-necessary pretence!

"And so you see us now – the land and the people – stripped bare and close to breaking!"

Just then they heard a whining noise coming from outside, somewhere overhead.

"Have they fixed A.C.'s weather station?" The Doctor asked, "Will he be joining us?"

Bimbor shook his head grimly.

"Not yet – not for another hour I'd say," he muttered, "no, this will be the 'mining consultant' from Earth, making a surprise inspection, no doubt. 'Mining consultant' - pah! Chitid puppetmaster more like!"

Both Romana and the Doctor looked concerned.

"Should we get out of sight?" Romana asked, "We don't want to make things awkward for you."

Bimbor struck up a defiant pose.

"This is my home, and my place of office. If he has any objections I shall tell him where to stuff 'em!"

Romana turned to the Doctor.

"Might it not be better for *us* if people *didn't* know we were here?"

The Doctor looked undecided.

"Perhaps. Then again, we might gain some useful information from the meeting. Still, we don't need to *tell* him who we are, if you get my drift."

Romana nodded her understanding.

The whining had subsided and it was not long before there was a knock at the door. Bimbor pressed a button which opened it and in strode the representative from Earth.

He was a fairly average looking human; mid brown hair brushed back from his receding temples, a pointy beak of a nose and a wiry frame. He wore a rubbery blue jacket which looked somehow simultaneously work related yet showy. The man was grinning in an oily fashion as he entered but his expression froze as he saw the Doctor and Romana. Then his grin broadened and his eyes grew even more unctuous.

"My *dear* Bimbor," he began, "I had no idea you had guests! I do hope my popping in isn't inconvenient?"

Bimbor glowered at him.

"No more than usual, Mr Sykes," he responded gruffly, "and we rescued these two lost in the jungle. It seemed only humane."

"Yes, indeed," the Doctor chipped in, "we are tourists, exploring the wonderful nature of this magnificent world and unfortunately got a little lost, Mr Sykes."

Mr Sykes smile remained but his eyes looked utterly cold.

"Come, come, *Doctor*, your fame precedes you. Even with a change – or absence – of clothes your face and that of your companion are instantly recognisable. You are all over every news feed! There really is no need to be modest."

The Doctor and Romana shrugged to one another, knowing what cover they had was blown.

"I must say," Mr Sykes continued to them, "the manner of your arrival was quite ingenious. I mean, I'm surprised nobody tried it before. Mocking up a drop-ship to look like that of the fabled 'Doctor', then passing yourself off as him – really it's quite impressive. But I think you'll find you've made your play a little too late. I think you'll find the Chitid's now associate *all* humans with those old tales, not just 'you', 'Doctor'."

The mining consultant's words dripped with irony and derision, utterly secure in his position to his mind. Meanwhile Bimbor seethed with anger.

"Just why are you here?" He demanded angrily.

"Are you finally going to see your way to giving us the medical supplies we so desperately need? Or the mining safety equipment? Or the shift reductions?"

Mr Sykes patted the air in insincere placation.

"Now, now, Bimbor, I'm sure your government is spending its money wisely. After all, you are one of them, are you not?"

The Boloid leader seethed once more but before he could respond, his human tormentor ploughed on.

"Which is actually why I'm here. I do hope you will attend tomorrow evening's special session of the Alpha Centauran Senate. We will be unveiling the latest wise purchase made by your people from Earth Gov's high tech defence sector. It is a large scale scanner, specially designed to detect any infiltrators from Galaxy Five! This first purchase will be installed in the Senate main assembly hall itself as a proof of concept. But *hopefully* many, *many*, more will be procured in the near future and placed in all potentially sensitive locations – ports of entry etc. throughout Alpha Centauri's sphere of influence."

Bimbor raised his hands over his head and shook them in rage.

"Another bloody waste of valuable resources, all while my people suffer and die. Another bloody vanity project, whose only purpose is to stuff the pockets of Earth!"

Sykes shook his head slowly in reproval.

"Now, Bimbor, you were quite entitled to make any suggestions or protests at the appropriate time, you know."

With that, the human representative spun on his heels, waved at the door opener which responded swiftly and allowed him to make his exit. This left Bimbor quivering with rage, watched by a concerned Romana and the Doctor.

"I can see now why A.C. wanted us to see the lie of the land. Unintended as this was by both myself and A.C., I see now we are the unwitting accomplices in a most callous and destructive con job," the Doctor said, his eyes staring through the floor. They then snapped up to meet Bimbor's glowing own.

"I assume you and A.C. will be attending this unveiling?"

Bimbor looked surprised.

"Well, yes, I suppose I have to. And as a retired dignitary it would be easy for me to get a pass for A.C.. Would I be right in thinking I'll need two more guest passes?"

The Doctor nodded firmly.

"I suppose our 'fame' should make that easy enough as well. Slightly more problematic, we need something else up on stage with us. Although, again, fame may aid us."

Bimbor nodded with some excitement now and the two Timelords gathered close to him to discuss their plans.

The senate building of Alpha Centauri Prime, naturally housed in City Alpha One, was a vast metal cylindrical tower topped by a giant sphere – the perfect union of Chitid and Boloid architectural styles. It was the elevated metal globe which encased the main conference room itself.

Inside there was rank upon rank of seats surrounding a circular stage at floor level. This stage slowly rotated so that everyone seated in the round auditorium would get a good view of the main speakers, at least for some of the time.

On the revolving platform were chairs and desks for the primary participants and most honoured guests as might be expected, but these had been joined by two more unusual items.

The first and most obvious, due to its size, was a huge gunmetal grey ring twenty metres in diameter but largely empty, the actual ring being only perhaps a foot wide. This was supported on a cuboid plinth, half a metre by half a metre in cross section but ten metres long. It was fortunate this room had such a high ceiling as the device dwarfed all around it, including the second odd addition.

That was the TARDIS.

Overshadowed as it might have been, it was no less noteworthy and gained its fair share of stares and conversation from the gathering audience.

At one of the tables on stage stood Bimbor, A.C., the Doctor and Romana. Other important persons sat at other settings, including Mr Sykes of Earth.

The Doctor walked over to the TARDIS and seeing this the mining consultant got up and bustled over to join him there.

"Thinking of 'blasting off' are we?" Sykes asked with a watery smile and a slight sneer as the Doctor opened the door.

"I wouldn't blame you. I admire a good con as much as the next man, but I think you're outclassed here," he concluded.

The Doctor paused and turned to regard the human with a steely stare.

"I was simply going to acquire a change of clothes," he said lifting his foot to reveal an exposed sock. While the Boloids had successfully cleaned the swamp from the Doctor and Romana's outfits they had been unable to supply a replacement boot, particularly given that item was useless to them.

Mr Sykes waved his hand expansively towards the TARDIS doors with mocking politeness. The Doctor stared at him coldly for a moment longer before entering the blue box and shutting the door behind him.

One door opened a minute later and the Doctor emerged looking exactly as he had before, only this time with both feet encased in DMs. K9's nose poke through the opening.

"K9," the Doctor barked sternly, "stay inside the TARDIS."

"As instructed, master," K9 chirped obediently before withdrawing his head. The Doctor shut the door on him, then returned to stand with Romana, A.C. and Bimbor.

Evidently all attendees were now present as the speaker of the senate called the meeting to order. He then surrendered the floor to Mr Sykes.

"Greetings, my illustrious Alpha Centauran friends," he began grandly, "and let me start by congratulating you on making the wise purchase you see before you now!"

The Chitid members gave scattered, clacking rounds of applause and high pitched, fluting murmurs of approval. The smaller Boloid contingent gave far lower grumbles of disapproval. Sykes ignored any displeasure in the crowd and played to the satisfied representatives.

"This scanner will detect any would-be spies from Galaxy Five," he pronounced proudly, "while giving the all clear to every good, honest Chitid, Boloid, human – indeed all upstanding citizens of the Galactic Federation!"

This received a longer, louder response than his opening statement and, while just as mixed, by dint of numbers the approval largely drowned out any protests.

"And I know you will all heed the wisdom of your human friends – dare I say, 'saviours'? And purchase many, *many* more!"

A further wave of noise erupted from the audience.

The Doctor and Romana chose that moment to stand up and walk over to the smug human basking in the applause. Mr Sykes raised his eyebrows in sceptical amusement at his uninvited guests. He bent discreetly towards them.

"Seeking to steal the show are we?" He asked good naturedly, "Well, we're all on the same team after all, aren't we? I'm sure there'll be no irreconcilable divine schisms between us."

This final statement was made with a teasing wink. The Doctor raised his hands to address the crowd.

"Respected delegates," he began seriously, "you all know who I am."

From all over the auditorium cries of, "The Saviour!" rang out. The Doctor shook his head impatiently.

"I am the Doctor! And you do not need to blindly accept what I say, or indeed follow the diktats of Mr Sykes here, or any other human!"

This did not quite have the effect the Doctor had been hoping for. Several shouts squeaked out from the Chitids present, several phrases oft repeated.

"Earth is our friend!"

"The Earth people only seek to help us!"

"The planet of The Saviour brings salvation!"

"The Doctor is The Saviour!"

Mr Sykes leaned in towards the Doctor once more.

"It seems 'your' divine influence has been shared amongst all your people. Before you think about mounting a hostile takeover consider that I have numbers on my side, both here and at home," he whispered warningly, but still amused. The Doctor raised his hands once more, to quiet the crowd.

"Listen! Listen! You must see what is happening to your world? You Chitids cannot be blind to the state of your Boloid brothers? You don't have to tow the party line! You must think for yourselves! You're all individuals!"

"Yes," the audience intoned back, "we're all individuals!"

"I'm not," a lone Chitid voice added.

"We're not even human!" Romana cried impatiently and with mounting frustration. Mr Sykes shook his head, smiling sadly.

"Just watch this," he murmured to the two Timelords.

"Only The Saviour would deny his divinity!" A strident Chitid voice sang out.

"Or his Companion!" Another added helpfully.

"You see," Sykes yelled cheerfully, "we're all just your modest, happy, human helpers!"

"K9! Now!" The Doctor suddenly shouted.

"Master," K9's voice rang out from the TARDIS speakers.

At that same moment, the giant circle of the security scanner roared into life. It looked almost like water flowing in defiance of gravity, rushing from the metal ring through empty air towards its centre. Here this silvery energy wave met and crashed outwards a little over the heads of the speakers on stage before sinking back. This impossible seeming vertical wall of water eventually settled and became flat, then began to project an image.

The Doctor, Romana and Mr Sykes were all standing directly in front of this rippling screen. Behind them it showed the trio once more, only now magnified to three times their true heights, and also with their internal organs on full display like some giant MRI.

There was an obvious difference between the two Timelords and the human next to them. Their twin hearts could clearly be seen pulsing away, in stark contrast to Mr Sykes cold singular pump.

This difference – and more besides – must have been just as obvious to the scanning device. It surrounded the two Timelord's images in red and superimposed a bell icon of the same colour over their heads and began a raucous, blaring alarm!

"K9!" The Doctor yelled, "Can you turn that down a bit?"

"Affirmative, master!" K9's voice piped up decisively, amplified through the TARDIS sound system. The red outline and alarm bell emoji remained on the giant screen, but the noise itself dwindled to become almost inaudible.

Romana swung an arm up to encompass the screen behind them.

"Look," she cried, "god and dog might share some superficial similarities. But how they are put together is rather important!"

The Doctor looked a little pained by this analogy.

"Really, Romana, did you have to do the whole dog – god thing? It reminds me of something a far more egomaniacal Timelord of my acquaintance once said," he grumbled quietly with a frown. Romana cocked her head at him.

"I'm sorry – I didn't realise. Was it the Master by any chance?"

The Doctor waggled his cranium non-committally.

"More or less," he replied.

Romana then waved her hand again to the scanner.

"People of Alpha Centauri Prime! Look at what your eyes are telling you. The Doctor and I are not of Earth – not even from the Galactic Federation! We have no more in common with Mr Sykes – or any other human – than we do with a Chirpa!"

A disturbed muttering broke out in the crowd.

"Oh yes, Romana," the Doctor said approvingly, "that was much better!"

The muttering had grown to angry, high-pitched Chitid shouting. A scrunched up ball of a papery looking substance sailed through the air to land on the floor near the Earth representative. Mr Sykes flinched, then looked quite panicked when another bounced off his head as still more began to fly in his direction.

The Chitids were screwing up their programs and name cards and throwing them at the Earthman in disgust. Meanwhile the Boloids were chuckling and nudging each other while copying the Chitids actions, mostly just for fun, mixed with a little vengeance.

The Doctor and Romana backed away from the flinching human in the direction of the TARDIS. At the doors of the blue box they found A.C. waiting for them.

"Doctor, what's happening?" Romana asked. The Doctor looked simultaneously concerned, yet pleased.

"The Chitids are a very non-confrontational people. By their standards this is a riot!"

A.C. giggled.

"I don't think my people will be taking any more 'help' from the humans. And I imagine our senate will return to one in which the Boloids may be equally proud."

With this, he took the Doctor's hand in his upper claws.

"While it seems you may have convinced my people you are not The Saviour," he began with a smile to his voice, "you have – after all that – saved the day!"

The Doctor smiled and shook his old friend's upper limbs. Bimbor then shook the Doctor's hand with a mighty one of his own, while Romana received the same treatments from both. Then with polite bows to the Chitid and the Boloid, the two Timelords both entered the TARDIS.

Standing now at the main console, K9 at their feet, Romana turned to the Doctor.

"What do you think A.C. will do now? Do you think he'll go back to watching the weather?" She asked curiously. The Doctor gave a sly smile and shook his head.

"I feel certain that A.C.'s recent adventures have regenerated the Chitid hero. I wouldn't be at all surprised if he returned to Galactic diplomacy."

Romana pursed her lips at the Doctor.

"Wouldn't be surprised, eh? More than a feeling, I'll bet, Doctor," she said with a twinkle in her eye.

"Oh, you know, Time is such a tricky thing," he replied with a twisted smile of his own. Romana shook her head indulgently.

"So – where to now, Doctor? After all, we do have the whole of Time and Space ahead of us," she asked cheerfully.

The Doctor spread his arms wide to encompass the expanse of the main console before them.

"Indeed we do! So, let us spin the wheel and see where we land!"

With that, he threw the launch lever.

Chapter Three – Broken – Part 1

By *Oliver M. Goldblatt*

"There it is," the Doctor said with a broad smile, pointing to the image hovering in the air before them, "the Tstesutsyun Comet."

"It's massive!" Romana cried, her mouth agape.

"The largest known comet of its type, mistress," K9 began, "although larger comets are known to occur at 20+ billion years after the Big..."

"Show-off!" The Doctor mumbled.

"Oh, you just wanted to tell me yourself!" Romana teased quietly.

Grinning slyly, the Doctor turned back to the control panel, then paused.

"K9, take over."

"Master?" K9 asked.

"Fly the TARDIS for a moment. Take us in close, but not too close. I want to see this one too."

K9 whirred forward, extended his nose-stalk control, and began piloting the TARDIS slowly and carefully towards the comet.

Romana was transfixed by the image.

"What's at its core?" She asked.

"Something harder than diamond," the Doctor replied, "it's possible this isn't a comet at all, but a small rogue moon covered in ice."

"Is it safe to land?" Romana asked.

"Well..." the Doctor replied in mock uncertainty.

"Now, look," Romana continued, "we've faced far worse dangers than this! And the universe can look after itself for a few hours."

The Doctor smiled. "Why not? But we can't stop long."

"Why's that?"

"We're in the Megando system. That planet there..." the Doctor said, adjusting the image so they could see a blue world about two million miles away.

"A former Earth colony, currently fighting a war with the Gulbansi."

"But why shouldn't we get too close?"

"The war will go so badly for them that in a year they'll build a interplanetary coalition, which will not only end the war but jump-start the Galactic Federation."

"This is the beginning?"

"Alpha Centauri's great-great-grand-parent will be one of the founding members."

"So," Romana sighed, "this is a fixed point in time."

"As long as we don't interfere with the planet itself, there shouldn't be any danger."

The Doctor returned to the comet on screen.

"K9, store all data. Let's keep a record of this beast!"

"I'm sure she wouldn't like to be called that!" Romana replied.

"Oh, it's a *she*!" The Doctor said in mock surprise, flashing a friendly smile, "And where would you prefer to land..."

The Doctor never completed his question; instead, something massive struck the TARDIS so violently that the Doctor and Romana had crashed to the floor before they realized what was happening. Before the Doctor lost consciousness, he thought he heard K9 calling.

Everything was dark – the Doctor was unsure if he were dreaming. He hovered above the control console, watching someone else's hands working the TARDIS controls. Then another set of hands joined them. Suddenly, the darkness lifted, and he opened his eyes. He was lying on the floor, watching Romana work frantically at the controls while K9 scanned his head.

"How long was I out?" He asked.

"Two point seven minutes," K9 replied. "No physiological damage detected, master. It is safe to stand."

But the Doctor was already on his feet.

"I've managed to stabilize us, but," Romana said, "look at these readings!"

She pointed to a display, and the Doctor quickly joined her.

"What hit us?"

"A piece of Tstesutsyun, I think. After she collided with... something."

"K9," the Doctor ordered, "play back the recording."

The image appeared in front of them again and wound back to its starting point.

"Freeze there!" The Doctor suddenly cried, "Zoom in directly ahead of the comet!"

K9 did so, revealing what appeared to be a gently spinning cuboctahedral satellite in front of Tstesutsyun.

"Do you recognize that technology?" the Doctor asked Romana.

"No."

"K9?"

"Negative, master."

"That makes three of us. Roll it forward, then."

K9 did so. The comet struck the satellite, resulting in a huge explosion which sent shock waves flying in all directions. Small pieces of the comet broke off at the impact point, and the image of a large piece suddenly filled the room. The recording ended.

"Doctor," Romana began slowly, "we're in space. There's no medium for shock waves to travel through."

"It's either the thin atmosphere surrounding the comet, or," the Doctor replied grimly, "temporal shock waves."

"K9?" Romana asked.

"Temporal shock waves, master," K9 replied, his ears whirring, "reaching a peak of point one on the Bocker scale."

"That's imposs..." Romana began, then caught herself, "I really have to stop saying that."

"It's highly unlikely," the Doctor agreed, "especially that a satellite of that size should have a power source operating in five dimensions. Let alone a mass capable of diverting that comet."

"Has the comet changed course, K9?" Romana asked.

"It has," K9 replied, "it will strike Megando in 3.1 days, mistress."

The Doctor and Romana turned toward each other. Each had become pale.

"But they're supposed to create the Galactic Federation!" Romana exclaimed.

"K9," the Doctor asked, "how many Megandans will survive the impact?"

K9's ear sensors whirred for a moment, then he said, "Given the mass and velocity of the comet... none, master."

They stood silently for a moment.

"The Web of Time," Romana said quietly, "will be..."

"Broken," the Doctor continued in a half-whisper, "shattered... if we can't find a way to prevent this."

Then he began to pace, while Romana remained at the controls.

"Use the tractor beam!" Romana finally said.

"The what?" The Doctor replied, stopping short.

"Remember how we diverted the course of that neutron star? Once it had a shell of aluminium around it, its mass was reduced enough tha..." she paused, "Doctor, how exactly did adding mass to a star ultimately reduce it? I've always wondered about that."

"That's because it didn't," the Doctor explained, looking somewhat ashamed, "and the Type 40 didn't come with tractor beams. I assembled one... from a kit."

"A kit?! We pulled a neutron star out of its orbit using something knocked up from spare parts?!"

"Don't knock it – it worked didn't it? And not spare parts... mostly. Look, I was in the 53rd century, and it was a bargain!"

"And presumably it affects aluminium more than other materials?"

"Yes."

"So," she continued, "if we could spin an aluminium shell around the comet, we could pull it off course?"

"Presumably," the Doctor said, "and I know where we can find some."

The space station was mostly empty, almost cavernous. Its corridors curved upward into the distance at both ends, revealing that the station was being spun around a central hub in order to maintain artificial gravity. Screens had been mounted into the walls, and all were playing their content quietly. Some were advertisements and some were itineraries. The latter indicated that no traffic was expected. Very little could be heard except the air conditioning units, until a wheezing-groaning noise erupted from nowhere as the TARDIS materialized in the empty corridor.

After a moment, the Doctor stepped out, followed by Romana and K9.

"Hello!" the Doctor called. His voice echoed through the emptiness.

"And this place is...?" Romana asked.

"The Constantinople 12," the Doctor replied, "a mining hub. The planet has twelve moons, all rich in rare minerals. That's what the war is about. Doesn't it always seem to be the way? The ore is brought here for processing."

"But it's deserted!"

"Negative," replied K9, his ears whirring, "detecting a dozen lifeforms scattered throughout the vessel."

"You see?" The Doctor replied, "The station is mostly automated, but there's always someone on staff. So, you order the aluminium while I pop down to the planet surface."

"What for?"

"By now, they'll know the comet is on its way. Perhaps I can say to everyone, 'Don't Panic'?"

"Is that all?" She replied with polite mockery, then became more serious, "Good luck."

"And to you," the Doctor replied, stepping into the TARDIS. In a moment, it dematerialized.

"Scan the area, K9," Romana ordered.

K9 did so.

"Mistress. The nearest computer terminal is 500 meters ahead, and there is a humanoid lifeform above us."

"We'll split up," Romana said. "You take the terminal, and I'll look for the lifeform."

The Doctor left the TARDIS and found himself on Megando, inside what appeared to be a large, empty aircraft hangar.

Outside he could hear what sounded like the roar of an ocean. But the volume increased, and he knew it was not water... it was the raised voices of many, many people.

At the far end of the room was a set of large doors as well as a sizeable monitor and keypad. Someone was knocking at the doors, and more followed. Then the volume grew until all he could hear were muffled shouts and the sound of fists and sticks pounding against the entrance.

The Doctor moved quickly to the keypad and found the control for the external cameras. He had been right – outside was a crowd a thousand strong. Behind them another ten thousand were racing toward this place, whatever it was. Behind them, another million, all fleeing a sprawling, burning city.

The Doctor found the communications switch and turned on the video-link to the outside.

"This is the Doctor..." he began.

"Please!" A man shouted. He was wearing overalls, looked to be in his forties, and was covered in dust, mud, and blood.

"Let us in!"

"This hangar isn't big enough for everyone!" The Doctor replied.

"Hangar?!" The man cried, "This is the Bunker! Everyone knows that! Just open the doors, or we'll tear it down!"

Before the Doctor could respond, a siren rang out inside the hangar. The Doctor put his hands to his ears and turned, only to see four tall, slim robots glide toward him. Three were silver, but one – presumably the leader – was gold coloured. Each had a gun of some kind where their right hands should have been, and all four were pointed at the

Doctor.

"Take him," the gold robot ordered, and before he could protest, the Doctor was bundled away from the keypad - and the TARDIS - towards the far end of the hangar. The siren went quiet, leaving only the cries of a thousand desperate people.

Romana found a lift and took it to the next level. When she stepped off she wondered if she had moved at all – the corridors were empty and almost identical. She looked in both directions and called, "Hello?" Her voice echoed through the emptiness. She thought she saw movement to her left and went that way.

"I'm here to make a purchase," she called, although with what currency she did not know. That she would happily leave to the Doctor to negotiate. First, she had to make sure that they had sufficient quantities of aluminium available and...

"Halt!" A young, high voice called from behind her.

Romana held up her hands and began to turn.

"Don't turn around!"

Whoever he was, he was breathing heavily; in fact, he sounded more frightened than she was.

"I've got one!" He cried.

"Who is that?" A voice called from the other end of a communicator, "Report in properly!"

"Private Codd, Brown 9. I've apprehended a Gulbansi spy!" He said proudly.

"Good work, Codd! We'll be down in a moment."

"But I can bring her up to the Command Deck myself!" Codd complained, "It won't be any problem!"

"*Her?*" The voice asked incredulously.

"Yes! She's dressed in such pretty clothes! My mum would love an outfit like that!"

"Oh," said Romana, over her shoulder, "thank you!"

"Listen, Codd," the voice bellowed. "you stay put until we get there! And don't do anything foolish! Mananz out!"

Codd sighed and Romana asked, "Would it be alright if I turned round?"

"Well," Codd began, "I suppose so, but keep your hands up! I'm armed!"

Romana turned and was unsurprised to see a kid, no more than sixteen, wearing a Private's uniform and pointing a plasma rifle at her. He looked frightened and nervous, but not a killer. Romana sighed in relief.

"What?" Codd asked.

"Oh, it's just that you look so nice in your uniform," Romana lied.

Codd blushed.

"Oh, thank you," he said, then quickly recovered, "but I don't think I should be talking to spies!"

"I'm not a spy!" Romana protested, "I'm here to..."

Before she could finish, a lift door opened, and two older men in uniforms stepped out and quickly made their way towards her and Codd.

"Now, what's going on, Codd?" A man in a captain's uniform asked as he marched toward Codd. When he saw Romana, he stopped in his tracks and stared at her in awe.

"Good Lord!" He whispered.

"I say," his Sergeant added, flashing a charming smile at Romana, "what a pretty outfit."

"Oh, thank you," Romana replied, her hands still up, "I made it myself."

"Oh, how interesting," replied the Sergeant. He was so sincere and charming that Romana could not help but smile.

The Sergeant turned to his Captain.

"Don't you think she might put her hands down, sir?"

The Captain finally closed his mouth and nodded brusquely at Romana, who complied.

"What's your name?" He asked.

"Romana."

"Such a lovely name," the Sergeant said, smiling, "this is Captain Mananz, that's Private Codd, and I'm Sergeant Wilkins."

"That'll do, Wilkins!" Mananz barked.

"Sorry, sir," Wilkins replied.

Mananz turned to Romana.

"Now, look here... Romana... I command this station. What do you doing here?"

"She's a spy!" Codd interjected.

"Would a spy dress like that?!" Mananz barked at Codd, "Would the Gulbansi send a female agent to a space station manned by... well, men?"

"Sorry, Captain Mananz," Codd said, looking down at the floor.

"Stupid boy!" Mananz muttered.

"Actually," Romana said, "I'm here to buy aluminium in order to prevent a comet colliding with your world in just a few days."

The three soldiers looked at her, then each other in surprise.

"And what comet might that be?" Mananz asked.

The Doctor was marched through a series of sizeable corridors until at last they came to a small interrogation room, where the Doctor was herded toward a slim metal chair sitting across from an old desk.

"I'm supposed to sit, am I?" The Doctor asked, fixing his coat.

"When the interrogator arrives," the gold robot replied, "you will sit. Until then, standing is optional, but you may not leave."

"I have a question, or two, Gold," the Doctor said to the gold robot.

"You may ask," Gold replied, "all questions will be logged for future analysis."

"What's the Bunker?"

"You are in the Bunker, a survival shelter for those selected to survive."

"You mean the Elites of this world?"

"Correct," Gold responded.

"How many does it hold?"

"That information is classified."

"There seem to be several million people outside. Why not let them in?"

"There would be neither room nor resources," Gold answered, "we are already at 99.98% capacity, and the planet is on Full Emergency."

"You're referring to the comet," the Doctor added.

"Correct."

"In that case, Gold, your superiors may want to know..."

Before the Doctor could continue, a bored, young military officer in a lieutenant's uniform entered the room.

He did not meet the Doctor's gaze; instead, he rubbed his eyes and looked at Gold.

"Start," the Lieutenant ordered.

The silver robots suddenly turned on the Doctor, pushing him until he moved back and sat in the chair.

"Is this how you treat VIP's?" The Doctor asked the soldier, who ignored the question.

Still not looking at the Doctor, the Lieutenant sat, stifled a yawn, and asked, "Truth detector on?"

"Yes," Gold replied.

Finally, the Lieutenant turned to the Doctor, and reeled off a speech that he had apparently recited many, many times before.

"You will answer all my questions honestly and truthfully. The truthfulness of your statements will be assessed through voice analysis. Lying or attempts to evade the truth will be logged and used as evidence, if and when you are brought to trial. Is that understood?"

"Yes," the Doctor replied.

"Truthful statement," Gold said to the Lieutenant.

"Who are you, and what is your rank and/or diplomatic status?" The Lieutenant asked, rubbing his eyes.

"The Doctor, a Timelord," the Doctor replied.

The Lieutenant looked as if he had heard of the Timelords but could not place them.

The Doctor leaned forward and added, "Rank: Former President of the Earth."

The Lieutenant's eyes widened. The Doctor began to enjoy this.

"Also, former President of the High Council of the Timelords," he added with a smirk.

Whatever military bearing the Lieutenant had possessed was almost gone. He turned to Gold with his mouth agape.

"Truthful statements," Gold replied.

The Lieutenant turned pale as the Doctor continued, "And your superiors might want to know that I have a way of diverting that comet, provided... they meet my terms."

"Truthful statement," Gold said.

The Lieutenant almost fell out of his chair as he scrambled backward toward the door. With his eyes fixed on the Doctor, he opened it, backed out, and slammed it shut before running down the hallway.

The Doctor smiled, leaned back in his chair, clasped his hands behind his head, and put his feet up on the desk.

"Do not put your feet on the desk," Gold warned.

The Doctor's feet and smile remained where they were.

"Please," he said calmly, "I'm a VIP."

"Truthful statement," Gold replied.

Romana stood with Captain Mananz, Sergeant Wilkins, Private Codd, and seven other soldiers on the Command Deck. Except for Codd and another Private, all of them appeared to be in their sixties or older. The main computer displayed information on the Tstesutsyun Comet and its trajectory, due to collide with Megando in less than three days. All of the men were understandably shocked and subdued.

"Why didn't they tell us?" Mananz finally hissed.

"We haven't been able to establish communications with Control Centre in two weeks, you see," Wilkins explained to Romana. "We thought that there might be trouble back home..." He turned away, unable to go on.

"I'm very sorry," Romana said, "but there's still hope. I'm here because the Doctor and I might be able to prevent this disaster."

"But I'm a doctor," one of the grey-haired Privates replied.

"Private Gottfried," he added, "general practitioner, retired."

"No, I meant *the* Doctor, the man I travel with," Romana clarified.

"Oh, forgive me," Gottfried said meekly and turned away.

Finally, Mananz stepped forward. "Now look, men... I realize this must be a shock, but if there's any chance we can help prevent this, we must! We aren't defeated yet, are we?"

"No, sir," the men replied sullenly and quietly.

"I said," Mananz repeated sternly, "we're not defeated yet!"

"No, sir!" the men replied forcefully.

"Excuse me, Captain Mananz," Codd asked.

"What is it, Codd?"

"Aren't we going to use the Truth Device on her?" He said, pointing at Romana.

"Oh, really, Fred," Wilkins replied, "I think we can take her word, given the circumstances."

"Blimey," said a Private who appeared to be in his early thirties, "if he did want her interrogated, I'd volunteer pretty sharpish!"

Before Romana could reply, Mananz barked: "That's enough of that, Walken!"

"Sir," Private Walken replied as he stood to attention. but without any sense of remorse Romana could detect.

"This young lady needs aluminium," Mananz continued, addressing Walken personally, "and lots of it. Go down to the hold, double-check our supply, and don't dawdle!"

"Sir!" Walken replied, quickly leaving the Command Deck.

"And don't call Private Codd 'Fred' while on duty!" Mananz hissed to Wilkins.

"Sorry, sir," Wilkins replied.

"In the meantime," Mananz continued in a louder voice, "we must re-establish communications with Megando."

"Can I help?" Romana asked, after the men had been dismissed.

Mananz looked at Wilkins then back to Romana.

"Perhaps I shouldn't ask this," Mananz began, "but why do you want to help us? You're not Megandan."

"I'm a Timelord," Romana replied.

Mananz and Wilkins looked at each other in confusion but neither appeared willing to ask what she meant. Rather than offer a technical explanation, Romana said, "To put it simply, the future of the galaxy won't be the same without you."

Wilkins' smile returned. Then he turned to Mananz and nodded.

"Any help you can offer," Mananz said to Romana, "would be greatly appreciated."

"Indeed," Wilkins added, "besides making such lovely outfits, do you have any other specialities? Communications? Robotics?"

"Both," Romana said with a smile, "and more. Where would you like me to start?"

Taking the express lift, Walken was already thirty levels down and approaching the processed aluminium hold. In the shadows up ahead, he saw something move, about the size of a large dog.

"'Oi!" Walken cried, "come out of there! Who told you to clean this level? Go clean my quarters, you daft..."

But then Walken saw that it was not a cleaning droid at all. Before he could turn and hit the alarm button on the wall, a yellow blast of light struck his chest, and he fell lifeless to the floor.

Then, it began moving towards the Command Deck.

Within moments, a woman wearing a Major's uniform had opened the door of the interrogation room. She had short brown hair and, unlike the Lieutenant, had a bearing not only of toughness, but also competence.

"I'm so sorry about this, sir," she said to the Doctor, "I'm Major Breen. Would you come this way, please?"

The Doctor got up, tugged at his coat, and followed her.

"I take it my message was delivered?" He asked.

"It was. I'm taking you to Under-Secretary Haining, where..."

The Doctor cut her off.

"Under-Secretary...?" He asked.

"All higher ranking officials are already ensconced in the Bunker," she replied, "and communications are down. We apologize for this breach of protocol."

They soon made their way to a staging area, where men in jumpsuits were minding robots as they sorted various boxes and supplies onto conveyor belts. They were being closely monitored by armed guards -

all women, the Doctor noticed.

"Where is the Under-Secretary?" The Doctor enquired, taking in his surroundings.

"To your right."

They turned, and a woman dressed in a very expensive outfit was rushing toward them. She was trailed by four female guards and six silver robots.

"I'm so sorry to have kept you waiting," she said, adjusting her glasses and looking the Doctor over.

"Under-Secretary Haining," she said at last, apparently unimpressed with her guest.

"The Doctor."

Neither had reached out their hand.

"We haven't much time," Haining said, somewhat nervously, "but if you indeed have a way to help us out of our little problem..." she trailed off, glancing over her shoulder at several large doors at the other end of the room.

"What's down there?" The Doctor asked calmly, following her gaze.

"Those are the entrances to the survival chambers," Breen replied, "this is merely a staging area."

"Yes," the Doctor replied, watching a female guard point a gun at a man in a jumpsuit who had stopped working, "I take it you're about to seal yourselves in?"

"Indeed," Haining replied, "about your plan...?"

"And these men in jumpsuits," the Doctor interrupted, "presumably, they'll come with you?"

"I'm sure that the details of our survival operation..." Haining began.

"...are exactly what I need to know in order to best help Megando," the Doctor said firmly. Haining looked unhappy for a moment but quickly recovered.

"They shall not be joining us. Only Megandans of a certain social or military rank have a place in the shelters. Now, as to your plan...."

"It requires a large amount of aluminium," the Doctor said, "I take it you had a revolution."

"Two weeks ago," she replied proudly, "the women of this planet erased millennia of repression!"

There was a shot and a cry. They turned to see a man on the floor, holding his arm and writhing in pain.

Breen gasped. The work had stopped as the men turned to face the female guards. One had her gun drawn, the others were drawing theirs. Breen slowly drew her sidearm and took a step to place herself between the Doctor and incoming fire.

"I thought you'd been conquered by the Movellans," the Doctor said to Haining, as he looked around, nervously.

"The who?" Haining replied.

"Nothing," the Doctor said, then muttered, "fragments of fragments..."

"Under-Secretary Haining..." Breen began, her eyes scanning the workers and their guards.

"Now, time presses," Haining said to the Doctor, ignoring Breen, while flashing a broad, false smile, "what is your plan?"

The Doctor began looking over Haining's shoulder back in the direction of the TARDIS.

"To use a tractor beam to..." he began.

"Under-Secretary Haining!" Breen repeated, louder than before.

The Doctor turned and saw the men had picked up whatever

improvised weaponry they could find. Several guards were shouting at them to return to work.

"Major Breen!" Haining snapped. "You will..."

Suddenly, more shots rang out. The guards, outnumbered, began to shoot into the crowd.

Breen cried, "Code D!"

She pushed the Doctor toward the entrances to the shelter. Two of the robots guarding Haining had peeled away to help Breen whisk the Doctor toward one of the entrances.

"But..." the Doctor protested. He had already lost sight of Haining.

"We have to move, sir!" Breen cried.

Someone began throwing jars of pickles in their direction. Broken glass and vinegar spilled across the floor. It was now a full-scale riot.

"That's one way of opening them I suppose," the Doctor muttered distractedly, "But..."

He had barely begun to form an objection when he found they were already inside with several workers close behind them. The robots moved to keep them back as Breen pressed a button. Heavy doors slowly descended as sirens blared.

"My TARDIS...!" The Doctor protested futilely. He tried to slip past Breen in order to dash under the doors and get out, but she managed to hold him back.

"You can't, sir!" She shouted.

The Doctor turned to her.

"Can't! There's no such word as...!"

But the doors had finally shut with a thud, and the sirens went quiet.

"I'm afraid," Major Breen said after a moment, "you're in with us now, sir..."

The Doctor looked at the door, then its control panel. There was no power, and the doors were so solid that he could no longer hear the riot on the other side. He turned to Breen, who was leaning against the wall, trembling slightly. Then he looked at the corridor leading into the shelter. At this end, it looked like a long walk into nothing.

"Romana..." the Doctor whispered, trapped with strangers and utterly alone.

Mananz and Wilkins stood on the Command Deck introducing the communications system to Romana when they were interrupted by a call.

"Yes?" Mananz asked.

"Permission to speak, sir!" Came a thin, reedy voice. No picture could be seen on any of the screens.

"How long has the video been out?" Romana asked Wilkins.

"Two days. We're not sure why."

"What is it, Smith?" Mananz asked in an exasperated voice.

"That's Lance Corporal Smith," Wilkins explained quietly to Romana, "he's in Grey 17 with Private Duff."

"Something's going on down here, sir. Private Duff and I keep hearing movement."

"That may be my dog," Romana added.

Mananz and Wilkins turned to her.

"Your what?!" Mananz asked.

"My robot dog," Romana clarified. "In case we couldn't find anyone, I sent him to find a terminal."

Mananz sighed and returned to the communicator. "Does it look like a robot? A robot... dog?"

"A what?!" Smith replied.

"You heard me!"

"No, sir, we haven't seen it. We just keep hearing... hang on a minute!"

There was silence on the other end, and then another voice spoke. "Duff, here, sir."

The voice had a Scots accent and seemed as old and gnarled as an ancient oak tree.

"I think you'd better come down here."

"Why, what's the matter?" Mananz asked.

"Walken is dead, sir," Duff replied flatly.

The Command Deck went silent, and then everyone turned to Romana.

"But K9 couldn't have killed him!" She protested.

"Is that your robot dog's name?" Mananz asked acidly, "K9...?"

"Are you saying your dog would never killed anyone?" Wilkins asked.

"No," Romana conceded, "except in self-defence."

"Codd!" Mananz shouted.

Codd quickly appeared next to Romana. "Sir!"

"The four of us will go to Grey 17. If this young lady does anything suspicious, shoot her in the leg. Is that understood? I want her alive for questioning."

"Sir!" Codd un-shouldered his plasma rifle and aimed it at Romana's ankle.

"Perhaps if I called K9 from here and told him where to meet us," Romana suggested.

"No," Mananz replied flatly, "Now move."

Romana was bundled into the lift and stood silently beside them as they travelled through the station.

Mananz and Codd were looking at her as if they hoped to determine who she really was – ally or saboteur – but Wilkins only looked at the floor, occasionally shaking his head.

"Poor Walken," he sighed quietly.

Soon, the lift stopped, and they exited and turned right. They found Smith and Duff, both of whom appeared to be in their early seventies. They were standing over a body.

Duff looked up and saw Romana. His eyes went wide and his mouth hung open stupidly.

"Smith!" He hissed, nudging Smith.

"Not now, Duff," Smith replied, "poor Walken…"

Then he looked up, "Blimey! Where did she come from, Captain Mananz?!"

"She's either behind Walken's death or a customer… we don't know which. If she tries to make a run for it…" he began.

"First of all, I'm truly sorry for your loss," Romana said, looking down at Walken's body, "but I'm here to acquire aluminium in order to save your world from destruction. And second… my dog didn't kill this man."

"Your what?!" Duff cried.

"Quiet in the ranks!" Mananz snapped.

"What makes you say it wasn't your dog?" Wilkins asked.

75

"Those burns," Romana said, pointing to Walken's chest. Not only was his body partially burned, but his shirt was scorched and still smoking.

"That was caused by a plasma weapon operating at 1500MW or higher. K9's blaster operates at 800MW and disrupts biological processes - the nervous system and the like."

"Do we believe her, sir?" Codd asked Mananz.

"Not yet," he replied.

"Then perhaps you'll also consider this," Romana added, looking up at the dimly lit bulkheads.

"Turn all the lights on in this corridor, then look in that direction," she ordered, pointing away from Walken's legs.

Mananz turned to Wilkins.

"Do it."

Wilkins reached for a wall panel, brightening the corridor. Once their eyes had adjusted, they saw that the floor was covered in a thin layer of dust. And in the dust, they could see signs that Walken's body had been dragged.

"I was with you the whole time," Romana said, "so I couldn't have done this. And K9 isn't big enough to drag something this size. Something else killed Walken and dragged his body to this location."

"But why?!" Codd asked, nearly shouting.

"Because," Duff replied dourly, "whoever killed him didn't want us to know what he was up to."

"He may be right, sir," Wilkins said to Mananz.

"Smith, Duff," Mananz ordered, "take care of Walken's body, then get back to the Command Deck. The rest of us will follow this trail."

"If I may..." Romana said, slowly reaching into an inside pocket.

"Slowly," Mananz warned.

Romana carefully pulled out a small flash-light and turned it on. Suddenly, the drag marks were clear for all to see.

"Both tachyons and light neutrons," she explained, "among other frequencies. This way!" Before Codd could stop her, she was leading the group with Mananz following closely, then Wilkins - with Codd following nervously at the back.

"This doesn't mean I trust you," Mananz hissed to Romana.

"I understand your predicament," Romana said, "but I promise... I'm here to help."

Mananz said nothing, and they followed the route which led to a lift.

"Where did this lift just come from?" Mananz asked Wilkins.

"I've no idea, sir. I didn't bring the lift diagnostic kit."

"Captain Mananz," Codd said quietly.

"I distinctly told you to bring the lift diagnostic kit!" Mananz argued.

"You never said anything about the lift diagnostic kit," Wilkins replied, as if this were another iteration of a long-standing argument.

"Captain Mananz!" Codd said, his eyes wide and fixed at something down the corridor.

They all turned to look. A black robot the size of a large dog with red glowing eyes was moving toward them in the darkness.

"Is that...?!" Codd squeaked.

The droid stepped into the light and uncoiled itself into a seven-foot tall armoured droid. It raised its left arm; instead of a hand, the arm terminated in a long, serrated sword. A laser protruded from the middle of its chest, glowing yellow.

"You will surrender and answer my questions!" It bellowed.

"Into the lift!" Romana ordered, pressing the lift control button.

The doors opened, and everyone scrambled inside. Mananz quickly operated the controls, and the doors closed again. They heard the slam of a metallic fist against the bulkhead, but they were already moving away.

Mananz pressed a communications button and said, "Intruder alert! Some kind of killer robot! Condition Red-One to be put into effect immediately!"

"Well," Wilkins said once he had caught his breath, "I think it's safe to say that Romana's dog did not kill poor Walken."

"Yes, I agree," Mananz said. With a glance at Romana, he added, "My apologies."

"Do you know what that robot was?" Romana asked, as if she had not heard him.

"Gulbansi!" Codd answered, "It looked like that old picture of a Gulbansi special operations droid!"

"That's exactly what it is," Romana said, "well done!"

Codd blushed in the excitement.

"How long has it been here?!" Mananz demanded from no one in particular.

"At least two days," Romana replied.

The soldiers looked at her.

"That's how long video communications have been down," she added, "the first phase of its operations was likely sabotage, and then interrogation."

"But why is it here in the first place?" Wilkins asked.

"Not to destroy the station," Mananz said, "it's had enough time to blow the reactors. And since it wants information, it's likely that

Walken disturbed it when..." Mananz's eyes widened.

"You sent Walken the check the aluminium stores, sir!" Wilkins said.

"But it couldn't have known we needed aluminium!" Romana said. "Oh, K9, where are you?"

The Doctor turned to Breen, who was wiping her eyes.

"Sorry," she said, "my little brother's out there..."

"If he's as tough as you," the Doctor said, "he'll survive."

"Do you really have a way to stop that comet?" She asked.

"Yes, if we can get out."

"That's impossible!" Breen snapped. "The Bunker was designed..."

"The farther down we go," the Doctor interrupted, "the closer we get to the power station, the food stores, the air supply... and that's where we'll find whoever's in charge."

"You mean Madam President?'

"Indeed," the Doctor continued, "and no leader would be stupid enough to live at the bottom of a pit with no way out."

"And you... a man... are willing to save Megando?"

"What's my chromosomal sequencing have to do with it?"

"Nothing," Breen said, and then realized what she had said. She unconsciously covered her mouth and looked around nervously.

"I take it," the Doctor said, "you've just spoken blasphemy."

Breen hesitated for a moment, then nodded.

"And that means you must obey your female superiors without question."

"This isn't what I signed up for," Breen said, shaking her head. "I wanted to help in the war effort, not force my brother into a labour camp."

"But...?"

"But that's what I've done," she said quietly.

"And yet... you stood up to Haining just now," the Doctor added.

"Yes, but..."

"And you kept me alive when the shooting started."

"Yes, well..."

"And now you realize the revolution has gone too far."

Breen paused, then said, "They told us there would be equality. This isn't it."

"Then we should make a good team," the Doctor said with satisfaction.

"We?"

"Are you up for it?"

Breen's face became grim for a moment.

"It would be mutiny."

"It's your choice," he replied calmly but firmly.

Breen stood silently for a moment, then turned to the control panel and pressed a button.

"I've ordered a vehicle."

"How many levels in the shelter?" The Doctor asked.

"Thirty."

"We'll need an express elevator to take us as far down as possible."

"How do you know the details of this establishment?" Breen asked, "You've never been here before."

"Logic," the Doctor replied, "Madam President wouldn't tolerate delays."

"Very perceptive," Breen said after a moment.

A robot appeared piloting a small taxi-like vehicle. They quickly got inside, and the machine sped off.

"What's the plan?" Breen asked.

"We'll need the TARDIS to get to the Constantinople 12. I have a friend up there purchasing aluminium. With that, we can save Megando... assuming we have enough time."

Soon, they passed another vehicle. Then another. After a minute, the corridor was full of traffic. Their vehicle slowed as they entered a forum of an underground city. They slowly made their way around pedestrians, both men and women, who appeared dazed and weary, with haunted, downcast faces.

"The workers live here," Breen said to the Doctor, anticipating his question.

"How did they get their 'golden ticket'?"

"Influence," Breen replied simply, "these are the personal servants of the New Order."

Then to the robot, "Section Zee-3."

The driver turned right and continued to make its way through the traffic. Eventually, the crowd thinned, and they came to a series of buildings protected by armed guards and barbed wire. They all appeared to be women.

Breen showed her pass and was waved through. They eventually made their way to a hut.

"Return," Breen said to the robot once they had got out, and the robot sped away.

"What is this place?" The Doctor asked.

"You'll see," Breen said. They entered, and found a deserted room. A painting hung crookedly on the wall. Breen marched toward it, straightened it, then tapped on its surface. The wall next to it slid open, revealing a lift.

"Security access," Breen said, "not for supplies."

The Doctor smiled and entered the elevator. In a moment, it plunged downward.

"We'll exit onto level 28," Breen said. "That's as far as my access allows."

"What's down there?"

"Under-Secretaries, mostly."

"Ah..." the Doctor said with distaste. "Haining, again."

Breen sighed and nodded.

"We'll need to contact the Constantinople 12."

"We can try, but... we've been out of contact with them since the revolution," Breen explained.

"What?!"

"No one's sure why. And restoring communications won't be a priority. That station is where military careers go to die, and the new environmental policy is to preserve our twelve moons in their natural state."

"A laudable goal," the Doctor replied, "but rotten timing."

Then the elevator stopped and the doors opened. There was no one outside. They could hear nothing and see very little in the dim light.

"Why would this section be deserted?" The Doctor asked.

"It shouldn't be," Breen replied quietly, drawing her sidearm.

They stepped out slowly, but not before Breen pressed a few more buttons.

"I've locked the door open," she explained.

"Good thinking," the Doctor replied, just before he tripped over something. Taking out a torch from his pocket, he saw it was a body lying on its front.

"Breen..." he called, bending down.

"I see it," she replied, joining him.

It was the body of a security guard with a rank of 1st Lieutenant. Then something squelched beneath their shoes.

It was blood.

"Help me turn her over," the Doctor said.

They did, and immediately recoiled. Breen clutched her mouth and tried not to scream.

"Quickly!" The Doctor shouted, taking Breen's arm and almost dragging her away. Yet neither could wrench their eyes from the charnel horror before them.

Romana and the eleven surviving soldiers stationed on the Constantinople 12 stood on the Command Deck. Each had been issued a firearm and were staring at the main hatch. All security measures had been activated, but they were not sure that would keep the droid out.

Romana was working at the computer.

"The first thing it did when it arrived," Romana said, "was to infiltrate your systems. Nothing works correctly, except the environmental controls."

"It wanted us alive, sir," Wilkins said to Mananz.

Suddenly, they heard a loud bang outside the hatch. Then another.

"It's outside," muttered Duff nervously, "we're doomed!"

"It's coming through!" Cried Smith, "Don't panic! Don't panic!!"

"What are we going to do, Captain Mananz?!" Codd whined.

"We stay calm!" Mananz barked, "Everybody... stay calm! It's not through the doors yet!"

Then he turned to Romana.

"Where's your dog?! Can't he help?!"

"If he were here, yes. But I can't find him anywhere on the station. Either the sensors have been tampered with, or..." Romana could not finish the sentence. Mananz patted her arm.

"There, there, my dear. Do the best you can."

Another loud bang, this time stronger than before.

"Can it get in, do you think?" Wilkins asked Romana.

"Yes."

"Reverse interrogation," Mananz said after a pause.

"What's that, sir?" Smith asked.

"We open the door, and when it interrogates us, we act stupid. Try to get it to reveal as much about its mission as possible."

"Do you think that's wise, sir?" Wilkins replied. "I mean, a special operations droid would hardly fall for that."

"Well, we have to try something!" Mananz countered.

"The mines!" Duff cried.

"The what?!" Romana asked.

"In the security locker!" Duff moved toward a wall marked with security warnings. He punched a code into a keypad, and a large door opened. He took out a metal disk the size of a dinner plate, then closed the door.

"It's magnetic," Wilkins said to Romana.

"Aye!" Duff cried. "Slap this on him, then hit the deck!"

"But an explosion in a room this size," Romana said, "the pressure change would deafen us, or worse."

"What did she say?" Gottfried asked Duff.

"Nothing, you cloth-eared, old coot," Duff grumbled.

Gottfried did not seem to hear that either.

The banging continued, and the hatch was beginning to buckle.

"We don't have a choice," Mananz said, "hide that mine. When the chance comes, the nearest soldier will attach it to the droid. Then we all drop, understood?"

"Yes, sir," they replied.

"But..." Romana began.

"Open the hatch!" Mananz ordered.

Codd did so, the door slid back, and the special operations droid entered the room, towering over them, their lives in its metal hands.

Chapter Four – Broken – Part 2

By Oliver M. Goldblatt

Romana was still trapped onboard the space station Constantinople 12. K9 had gone missing, and the Doctor had neither returned nor contacted her. She could only assume things had gone badly on the surface of Megando. And the reason they were here in the first place was to prevent a massive comet from smashing into their world, killing everyone and everything. As if this were not enough, should the comet destroy Megando, it would break what was known as the Web of Time, the events that must occur in our universe, or else reality itself would break and melt into nothing.

The last of the space station's crew were old men, plus one youngster, cut off from their world in more ways than one. And now, they had discovered that a special operations droid was onboard, sent by the Gulbansi, with whom the Megandans were at war.

They had taken refuge on the Command Deck, but the security doors were not holding against the droid. Eventually, it would break through.

But they had a plan. One of the men, Duff, had a mine which he hoped to place onto the droid's back while distracted. Romana had tried to talk them out of the idea, but there was no time. Private Codd opened the doors, and the droid stepped into the room. It stood, towering over them.

"Drop your weapons and step back," the droid ordered.

They did so, except for Duff, who attempted to hide the mine in the back of his trousers. The droid did not seem to notice him. Instead, he turned to Codd, who was nearest.

"You! What is your name?"

Codd was too frightened to reply.

"It's Gulbansi, alright," Romana whispered to Mananz and Wilkins.

"So?!" Mananz whispered in reply.

"The Gulbansi are brilliant engineers, but their programming lacks... verve."

"What does that mean?!" Mananz hissed.

"It'll be programmed to do one thing at a time and in the correct order. It can't start its next task, whatever that is, until it's finished interrogating us."

"Then we might delay it?" Wilkins asked.

The droid was now holding its sword near Codd's face. Codd shut his eyes tight as the droid said, "I will ask once more... What is your name?"

"Don't tell him, Codd!" Mananz shouted, then realized what he had done.

"Your name is Codd," the droid said. "Confirm!"

Codd nodded vigorously.

Then Romana stepped forward.

"My name is Romanadvoratnalundar," she said, "and I inquire whether you are authorized to start a war with the Timelords."

The robot halted as it considered this.

"Are you a Timelord?" It finally asked.

"Yes."

"Truth confirmed," the droid replied, dropping its sword a few inches.

Wilkins looked at Mananz and motioned with his eyes toward Duff. Duff was slowly inching his way to his left, toward the droid's back. Mananz nodded to Wilkins and slowly walked to his right until he was standing next to Romana.

"Who are you?" The droid asked Mananz.

"I'm the Captain of this vessel, and while our planets are at war, you have nothing against this young lady. I demand you release her at once."

"The Timelords are not listed as non-combatants. Request denied."

Mananz began to feel sweat running down his face.

"But there's diplomatic status to be considered as well," Romana added.

The droid paused again. Mananz risked a glance at Duff – he was almost there.

"What is your diplomatic status and/or rank?" the droid asked Romana.

Before she could reply, the droid turned and grabbed the mine from Duff's hands. Duff backed away quickly in mortal terror.

"Violence against this unit will not be tolerated," the droid growled as its chest blaster began to glow.

Duff closed his eyes as a shot rang out. He opened his eyes to see the droid lurch forward and sink to one knee. The mine fell out of its hand and rolled away. K9 sat in the doorway and fired again. This time, the droid fell on its side.

"Use full power!" Romana cried.

K9 did so. But this time an energy shield appeared around the droid, blocking K9's blasts. The droid rose unsteadily to its feet and faced K9. The robot dog fired again, but to no effect. K9 was forced to back away as the droid advanced, its chest-mounted weapon beginning to glow.

Then Mananz sprang forward, grabbed the mine off the floor, and slapped it on the droid's back.

"Down!" He cried. Everyone hit the deck, even Romana.

The droid turned, plucked the mine off its back, and deactivated it before it could explode. But this delay gave K9 time to find a weakness in the energy shield. He aimed and fired at full strength. There was a small explosion that sent metal flying across the room as the droid stiffened, swayed for a moment, then collapsed.

K9 whirred forward.

"Apologies for the delay, mistress," he said.

Everyone looked up at K9, then Romana, who stood and dusted herself off.

"Think nothing of it, K9. How long until the comet strikes?"

"Twenty-seven standard hours, mistress."

The Doctor helped Breen through the deserted streets, carved out of the living rock of Megando, with only overhead emergency lights guiding their steps. They saw other bodies nearby, but they stayed as far from them as possible. Breen appeared ill and almost fell several times, but she managed to keep moving. The Doctor looked nervously at the shadows around them, as if expecting someone or something to attack. However, they were able to make their way into what looked like cramped living quarters. A door had been pulled off its hinges, but the rooms appeared deserted. The Doctor helped Breen into a chair and then began to pace the room, lost in thought.

"I thought I'd seen it all..." Breen finally said.

"Bore worms," the Doctor said.

"Is that what caused those... wounds?"

"Yes. Someone released them, probably to force an evacuation to the upper levels."

"But who?!"

The Doctor stopped pacing and looked at Breen. "Bore worms are native to Gulbansi."

"But..." Breen began, then stopped, open mouthed. "How?" She finally asked.

"I don't know. Perhaps the Gulbansi recently sent a saboteur to your world, or perhaps they've been here far longer."

"The lower levels!" Breen said, standing, "Madam President!"

"You seem to be very loyal to a President who has your brother in a work camp," the Doctor said with an expression which demanded an explanation.

"I swore an oath to the constitution," Breen began.

"And then the constitution was amended," the Doctor asked pointedly, "yes?"

Breen turned away for a moment, staring into the darkness.

"Yes," she said finally.

"Hugh Thompson," the Doctor said flatly.

"Who?"

"An Earth soldier who stopped his own side from butchering civilians – old men, women, children… babies. His people hated him for thirty years, until they finally came around. It seems to me that you face a similar choice."

Breen turned to face the Doctor.

"I don't care what people think of me. I have a duty."

"To whom?" The Doctor asked coldly, "To whoever happens to be sitting behind the big desk? Just following orders? If so, let's part ways now."

"But then how will you find your way to level 30?"

"And how will Megando get out the mess it's made for itself? Perhaps that comet is the least of your worries."

Breen stared into the Doctor's eyes for a moment, then turned away.

"I never thought it would come to this," she half-whispered.

"It has. We have two days to divert that comet, and we need a way through ten feet of solid rock. Then we do what's best for the people of this planet. Or at least... I will."

At last, Breen nodded.

"All right. For the people of Megando."

"We need a way down to level 29, preferably one that won't get us killed."

"My access stops at this floor."

"If I tamper with the lift controls... whoever's in charge will know we're here. I don't want to risk that yet," the Doctor added.

Breen rubbed her eyes, trying to rid herself of the image of the lieutenant.

"How do these bore worms attack?" She asked.

"Normally, they're found in rubbish tips. These must have been weaponized."

"And you don't know how these genetically engineered bore worms might attack us?"

The Doctor shook his head.

"All I know is that it's quick. That lieutenant's sidearm was still in its holster."

"Jumping?" Breen asked, "Flying?"

"We'll assume jumping. They may aim for our mouths..."

"Riot gear!" Breen suggested, "Those helmets will cover our heads and faces in blast-proof plastic, and the suit consists of trans-carbon armour."

"Perfect," the Doctor replied, "where are they stored?"

"Follow me," Breen said. She took a step toward the door and halted. Sweat appeared on her forehead and she began to tremble.

"Of all the ways to die," she muttered, "being eaten alive is the last way I want to go..."

"It's not high on my list either," the Doctor said, "but for people like us, there's no such thing as a safe space."

Breen turned to the Doctor and saw a look on his face she could not quite describe - a mixture of an old man who had seen too much, and a young man who would keep fighting, even when the cause was lost. She took a deep breath and stepped out the door. The Doctor followed.

The station was now running on "Condition Yellow-Two", according to several flashing signs. The explosion had caused a few cuts and bruises, but nothing too serious. The door to the Command Deck would no longer close, so K9 stood in the doorway on guard duty. He had already analysed the main computer and determined it had been hopelessly corrupted by the droid, which was now stacked in pieces along a bulkhead. K9 suggested that they reboot the main computer and restore it to its last saved state. Mananz reluctantly agreed, explaining that the reboot might take an hour or more, assuming that it rebooted at all.

Ultimately they put the backup mainframe in control and shut down the main computer. The lights flickered for a minute, but soon everything appeared normal.

"Try not to overtax it," Mananz warned, "it's older than we are!"

Everyone laughed at the joke.

"Codd, Gottfried, we'll inspect the medical section. Everyone else, make sure the mainframe is up to scratch, but give Romana priority to find out what that droid was up to."

Then he left the Command Deck with Gottfried and Codd.

Romana had plugged the droid's memory chips into the mainframe and was busy decrypting the information. Wilkins spoke with Duff and Smith on the other side of the deck, then approached Romana.

"Any luck?"

"Slowly getting there..." Romana replied, absorbed with the progress displayed on a screen, "fortunately, I studied cryptography, long ago."

"You seem to be a woman of many parts," Wilkins said, smiling, "roboticist, engineer, cryptologist..."

"Well, when you've lived as long as I have..."

"What?!" Wilkins replied, "But you can't be more than... well, I never like to guess a lady's age...!"

Romana turned to him and smiled coolly.

"I was old before your great-grandmother was born."

Wilkins appeared shocked and, for once, at a loss for words.

"My goodness!" He finally exclaimed.

"How are the others holding up?" Romana asked, moving on to more immediate concerns.

"Yes, well..." Wilkins began, still recovering from the shock, "they're under considerable stress, as you can imagine, but they're hanging on. But everything's taking so long while the mainframe is occupied."

"I should be finished soon, hopefully. But one thing puzzles me.... Why are mines stored on the Command Deck?"

"They aren't," Wilkins replied with a smile, "at Condition Red-One, they're moved from the munitions stores to this level via the security lift. That way, an invading force can't get at them."

"Tell me, how *were* the twelve of you assigned to this station?" She asked with some suspicion.

"You mean, what are a lot of old duffers doing here?" Wilkins replied with a laugh.

"Eh?!" Duff said.

"Oh, no offence," Wilkins replied.

"Agh..." Duff muttered dismissively, turning back to his work.

"Most of us have served here for thirty years," Wilkins continued, "about the time this place became very unpopular indeed. They said we were destroying the environment. But in spite of less and less help from the surface, we've managed to keep this place going, somehow."

"What happened on Megando?"

"Oh, a number of things. Terrible mistakes. Women had been barred from formal education as long as anyone can remember. So their mothers and grandmothers taught young girls in secret, and quite right too. When I was a young man, there was a push to allow women into schools and so on, but I'm afraid my generation failed them... failed all of us, really. That's when our society began to fall apart. You can't have a functioning state when half of the population refuses to follow the rules."

"I can't blame them," Romana said.

"Nor can I," Wilkins added, "soon, every decision became political. This station, for example. Because men had built it, the women wanted to close it down. There were other reasons, of course, but looking back now... it seems like so much childish bickering... on both sides. And now that we've lost contact with..."

The computer beeped. Romana and Wilkins turned to a screen.

"About 85% of the data has been recovered," Romana said, reading quickly, "we've lost the rest. The droid's mission was to sabotage the station, then hijack it. It wanted to interrogate the crew to find out who was needed to fly the ship and who was expendable."

"Oh, my..." Wilkins muttered.

"But it appears we have a new problem."

"What's that?" Wilkins asked.

"This droid killed Walken and then came here. So, who moved Walken's body?"

"A second droid..." Wilkins muttered.

"And there's something else," she added, "the last instructions this droid received were sent from Megando itself!"

The Doctor and Breen moved slowly and quietly through the gloom toward a security station. The air smelled of blood, which they hoped would disguise their scent. They stepped carefully around bodies, debris - anything in their path. Soon they found a main road and reached an intersection.

"It's that way," Breen pointed to the opposite corner of the road.

The Doctor looked in all directions.

"No Time like the present," he said, then proceeded as quietly as he could. Breen caught up to him but, in her haste, stepped on something that cracked under her boot. Then they heard something move on their left. Breen turned, but before she could react something flew at her face. She cried out, closing her eyes and turning away while blocking her head with her arms.

"I've got it," the Doctor said quietly.

Breen slowly turned toward the Doctor. His arm was outstretched and he was holding a wiggling worm-like creature, about six or seven inches long. It tried to bite his hand with a large, circular mouth.

"Meet the bore worms," he whispered.

Breen took a step back, still covering her mouth. Then they heard more movement to their left.

The Doctor threw the bore worm toward whatever it was, then grabbed Breen's hand.

"Hurry!" He cried. They took off toward the security station and found their way inside. The Doctor slammed the door, and they heard thuds as bore worms collided with it. Finally, there was silence.

"Thank you..." Breen said, half out of breath.

"Don't thank me yet. They're probably in here, too."

Breen looked around. The lights were off; the windows allowed in some light, but not much. They could not hear anything.

"Well, at least we know they can't fly," the Doctor said as he began searching the room.

"Not so loud!" Breen hissed.

"They know where we are," the Doctor said shrugging, "we have to assume their next attack will be coordinated."

"Why?"

"Because when I expect the worst," the Doctor replied, "to be disappointed is delightful."

Breen rubbed her eyes with her palms, then caught her breath.

"Let's head to the back."

She took a step and suddenly felt searing pain on her right calf. She screamed and fell to the ground, grabbing the bore worm that had attached itself to her and was trying to eat its way into her leg. As she pulled, the pain became so great she thought she might pass out, but she pulled anyway.

Then she heard a high-pitched whine, and the bore worm released itself. The Doctor grabbed it from her and crushed its head under the heel of his boot.

Breen looked at her leg. It was bleeding but the wound was not serious. The Doctor helped her up onto her other leg.

"First aid?" He asked.

"Same place as the riot gear," she gasped through gritted teeth. Together, they slowly finished making their way to the back.

Soon, the Doctor had treated and bandaged the wound and Breen could almost stand on both legs again.

"Just don't run or jump... unless you have to," the Doctor warned. "The anaesthetic will wear off in a few hours."

"I'll manage," Breen replied, "but I can't wear full gear now. Too heavy."

"You can wear this, at least," the Doctor said, handing her a riot helmet.

"Something is better than nothing?" Breen asked, putting it on.

"Always," he replied as he rummaged through the stores. "Don't lose heart now."

"How did you make the worm let go?" She asked.

"I made it nauseous."

"What?"

"You are quite tasty after all – to a bore worm. My sonic screwdriver emitted a frequency that rattled its inner ear, making it lose it lose its appetite, so to speak."

"Can't you do that with all of them?"

"If I had an amplifier and a large speaker, yes. But what I have might not be enough to..." he said, then stopped short, looking at something on the floor.

"What is it?" Breen asked.

"A police sergeant, presumably," he said backing away. "There's nothing we can do for him now."

Breen sighed and turned away. She closed her eyes tight to stay focused.

"What about communications?" She asked after a moment.

"Let's take a look."

The Doctor followed her to the communications room, but the power was off.

"Each station has its own power cell," Breen said in disbelief, "they don't just turn off!"

"Our saboteur is most thorough," the Doctor said, "perhaps it's time we met him."

"Or her," Breen added.

"Indeed. Let's go back to the lift," he said, holding out his sonic screwdriver and emitting the same sound as before, "it's past time we announced ourselves."

Romana, Wilkins, and K9 met Mananz as he exited the medical section.

"Well?" He demanded.

"Bad news, sir," Wilkins said, "it's likely a second droid is on board."

"Then why didn't you call me?!"

"There is a fifty-nine percent probability that the droid is monitoring communications," K9 replied.

"Then we must stop using comms at once!" Mananz cried.

"If we do that," Romana said, "it'll know that *we know* it's listening."

"Ah," Mananz replied. "Good ma... I mean, good thinking. But if it is here, what does it want?"

"More importantly, what do you plan to do about the comet? It's a little more than a day away," Romana pointed out.

Mananz sighed and said, "I see no other alternative than to aim this station at the comet, use our emergency thrusters, then blow the reactors. That might bash it out of the way."

"I'm afraid I agree with you, sir," Wilkins said.

"Thank you, Wilkins."

"Probability of success," K9 said, his ears whirring, "ten percent. This assumes that the droid has not immobilized the thrusters."

They were all silent for a moment.

"I'm afraid there's more bad news," Romana added, "the droid has been receiving instructions for Megando."

"What?!" Mananz gasped, "How would...?! How did...?!"

"We don't know, sir," Wilkins added, "but there's nothing we can do about it now. Not until we're able to contact the surface."

Mananz did his best to calm down.

"Yes... yes... you're right. But to send a spy to our world...! Such a shabby trick!"

Finally, he snapped out of it and barked, "Wilkins! Get some men down to Thruster Control at once. Half there, and half on the command deck. We're back on Condition Red-One!"

"Sir!"

"We'll meet you there," Romana announced. Before Mananz could argue, she turned and said, "Come along, K9."

"Affirmative, mistress!" K9 replied, following her down the corridor.

"Brave girl," Mananz said, watching her depart, "taking on a droid almost single-handed."

"Not a girl, sir," Wilkins corrected, "she's older than we are."

"Don't talk rubbish, Wilkins," Mananz snapped, "she isn't a day over twenty six! Now, go issue the orders personally. We don't want to tip this droid off, do we?"

Romana and K9 found the lift and took it to Thruster Control.

"K9, I have an idea..." Romana began.

A little later, when the lift finally stopped, they stepped out to see flickering lights. The air smelled as if something had shorted out. K9's ears whirred as Romana said, "I don't like the looks of this."

"Suggest we return..." K9 began, then was kicked a hundred feet down the corridor. He bounced to a halt and went silent.

Before Romana could turn, her body was wrapped in metallic tentacles, one of which had her by the throat. She tried to cry out, but could not catch her breath. She was just beginning to see stars when a robotic voice said, "Submit."

The Doctor and Breen made it back to the lift with only one further worm attack. It had struck the back of Breen's helmet, almost pitching her forward, but the screwdriver had worked better than the Doctor had hoped. They were in a large cave, after all, and the sound echoed clearly.

Once they were inside they locked the doors. The Doctor began taking the controls apart.

"Are you sure you won't drop us straight down?" Breen asked.

"How far can it be? Thirty feet?"

Breen was not sure if he were joking or not.

Finally, the elevator began dropping slowly. It stopped at the 29th floor and halted.

"Do we get out?" Breen asked.

"What's down here?" The Doctor responded.

"Stores. Water, food, everything perishable. Packed in salt."

"So there won't be as many bore worms."

The Doctor opened the door and they looked around. They were surrounded by large water tanks, enough for a city to survive a drought for years. The cavern was dimly lit, and they could not hear any movement.

"One more level," Breen said, reaching for the controls.

"No!" The Doctor hissed, grabbing her wrist, "Let's step out."

Breen nodded. The Doctor let go, and they exited. Then the Doctor shut the lift and send it down to the 30th floor. As they heard it descend, Breen said, "I hope we can get it back..."

She was interrupted by an explosion from the level below that shook her off her feet. She landed awkwardly, but the Doctor helped her up. "A booby trap?!"

"Yes," the Doctor said, "our saboteur is clever. We'll have to find another way down."

"What about air ducts?" He then asked, looking around at the ventilation system on the walls and ceiling.

Breen chuckled.

"Those old movies where people used them to sneak into high security areas? We saw them, too. You'd have to be a cat to crawl through these."

"Which leaves water pipes?"

Breen nodded.

"But even if we find a pipe large enough, it'll lead to a sealed tank. The odds of us surviving without oxygen tanks..."

They heard a clang at the far end of the cavern, then the sounds of something approaching.

"Hide!" The Doctor hissed.

"I'm not going to leave you to face the music..." Breen began.

"Yes, you are! It sounds like robots to me, and they'd shoot you dead. But I'm not human... they'll want to question me. Then maybe I can get at our saboteur!"

"Then what do I do?"

"Find a way down and get me out of the mess I'm about to get myself into," he said sternly.

Breen was about to argue, but the sounds of robots drew ever closer. Reluctantly, she limped into a dark corner to hide.

The Doctor stepped into the light as soon as the robots appeared around the nearest tank... five silver, one gold. In a moment, he was surrounded.

"Who are you?" Gold asked.

"I'm the Doctor, President Emeritus of the High Council of Time Lords on Gallifrey."

"Truthful statement," Gold said, "pending orders..."

They waited for several seconds as the Doctor's eyes darted about looking for a way out. He found none.

"You will be interrogated," Gold stated. The robots began moving the Doctor toward wherever they had entered this level.

"Am I to see Madam President?" He asked loudly.

"Madam President is dead," Gold replied.

The Doctor sighed. He had hoped for better news, and wondered if Breen would have the heart to follow him.

On the Command Deck, the crew looked passively and helplessly at the monitor, which had begun working again. There was Romana, wrapped in black tentacles, gasping for breath. She was trying to speak, but utterly unable.

"You will surrender this station," a robotic voice said, "or your leader dies. You have one hour."

Then the screen went blank.

"Did you hear that?" Erupted Mananz, "That thing's threatening to kill both me and Romana!"

"I'm afraid, sir," Wilkins began, "it was only referring to Romana."

"Her?! Our leader?! I've been in command of this station…"

"There isn't time for that, sir!" Smith interrupted, "That young lady has helped us, now we have to do the same!"

"A counter-attack?" Mananz asked.

"But that droid will kill her!" Wilkins protested.

"Aye, but it'll kill her anyway," Duff replied, "it's after the station. We're just in its way."

"Private Duff may be right, Captain Mananz," Gottfried said.

"Captain Mananz," Codd said.

"Yes, Codd?"

"I don't want to die."

Mananz patted Codd's arm. "I know, lad."

"But neither does Romana," Codd continued.

Mananz looked at Codd, whose face looked more like a man's than he had ever seen before. Mananz turned to his men, then nodded.

"All right. We won't take this lying down. And may God help that poor girl."

The Doctor was led by the robots to another lift. Soon, they were at the 30th and lowest level. The Doctor stepped out and was guided through a narrow passage towards a well-lit room. Gold moved past him and reached the room first. Finally, the Doctor entered.

It was a white control room with a well-dressed alien sitting in an office chair, watching several large screens at once. He was yellow-skinned, bald, had wide-eyes, and pointed ears - a Gulbansi. Gold stood beside him. The Gulbansi turned to the Doctor and looked him up and down.

"A former President of Earth?" He asked, "Former President of the High Council of Time Lords on Gallifrey?"

"The same. And you are?"

The alien rose. "Shiba Yergan," he said, straightening his jacket.

The Doctor bowed. "I'm delighted to meet one of the exalted rank of Shiba."

Yergan looked astonished. "You know our customs? Usually, I have to spend three minutes explaining that Shiba is a title, not a name."

"Usually, I have to spend five minutes explaining why destroying a planet is immoral."

Yergan motioned the Doctor toward a chair and returned to his own. The Doctor sat, and realized that he was seated lower than Yergan, who looked down on him. He stood and said, "I'd rather stand."

Then he began studying the screens in front of him.

Yergan pressed a button and the screens went blank. "If you're referring to the comet, that was not our plan."

"Just a happy accident?" The Doctor asked, facing Yergan.

"Unhappy accident," Yergan corrected. "It was never our goal to destroy Megando. We only wanted the minerals in this system."

He tutted and shook his head.

"So it wasn't you…" the Doctor muttered to himself.

Yergan shook his head. "No. Now, I'm faced with the diplomatic problem of what to do with you before I leave. Of course, you'll claim your people know you're here, that they knew of my mission, and that my world will suffer if you should die, and so on…"

"Stay here," the Doctor said, interrupting, "and help me divert this comet."

"If it were possible, I'd consider it, but there's nothing I or anyone else can do."

"I'm a Time Lord. Work it out."

"And have you nip back in time and prevent me from arriving on Megando in the first place? I think not."

"That's neither my plan nor intention," the Doctor countered.

"I wish I could believe you," Yergan said, his face showing genuine concern, "but I cannot."

There was movement behind them, then a scream. The Doctor turned to see three silver robots dragging Under-Secretary Haining, who appeared only half-conscious. The robots were about to drop her, but the Doctor caught her and moved her to a sofa at the side of the room.

"Such compassion," Yergan said, watching this, "she would have let you die, if not for your rank."

The Doctor set her down. Haining appeared lost in a bad dream, trying to wake up.

"Why did you do this to her? Why kill Madam President?"

"It was a threat," Yergan explained, "surrender or die. They didn't surrender, so... I kept a few of them alive, in case they might change their minds. She was being persuaded."

"Tortured."

"I'm not here to debate morality," Yergan said.

"If the planet's going to be destroyed, why do this?"

"Her surrender would have made our war legal. There is a larger galaxy watching us, Doctor."

"And now?"

Yergan shrugged.

"The planet will be destroyed. Some will suspect us, but it will be difficult for them to take action, since they'll half-believe we did it."

"But I'm telling you," the Doctor said, "I can stop this!"

"How?"

"Release me, and I'll show you."

"Please..." Yergan muttered with a dismissive wave of his hand.

Haining moaned and sat up. "Doctor..." she murmured.

The Doctor quickly moved to her side and held her hand.

"It's all right, Haining."

"Who is that?" She asked, pointing at Yergan, "I can't see without my glasses."

"I'm the reason you won your revolution," Yergan said as he studied the computer behind his desk.

"What…?" Haining asked, "Who is he?!"

"A Gulbansi spy."

"How did you get here?" She asked. "This was supposed to be Madam President's command centre."

"It's been my home for several years," Yergan replied, "where I've been the *de facto* ruler of your world for some time."

"But we, the women of Megando…" she began.

"Spare me the rhetoric," Yergan said, "I wrote most of it myself. You see, I was the one who encouraged people like you to riot in order to weaken Megando and help my side win this war."

"What?!" She cried feebly.

"But how did you get down here in the first place?" The Doctor asked.

Yergan smiled.

"Some politicians will do anything to get elected."

"Well, perhaps you helped our cause…" Haining said, trying to make sense of what had happened to her and her world in the last few days.

"If the zoo animals of Megando had wanted to riot, I would have helped them."

"You mean, you watched us live our lives under the thumb of…"

"Oh, do be quiet," Yergan replied.

"How can you be so…" Haining began.

Yergan turned towards her sharply.

"I'm Gulbansi! Not only are we your enemy, we're *hermaphrodites*! Why should we take sides in some pathetic gender war? No, all we wanted was your minerals. If you burned your own world in order to exact petty vengeance... well, that's on you." Then he returned to his computer.

Haining turned to the Doctor, wide-eyed and trembling. "What does he mean?" She asked feebly.

"He means your world fell a long time ago, from the inside."

"Well put, Doctor," Yergan replied without looking up, "and it was easier than pitting black ants against purple ants."

"How could you?!" Haining cried, rising on unsteady legs.

"How could *you* imprison your fathers, brothers, husbands, sons?" Yergan asked rhetorically.

"And yet," he said, turning to her, "you did."

Haining's knees gave out, and she collapsed onto the sofa. She buried her face in her hands and began weeping softly.

The Doctor stood and faced Yergan.

"I can still pull the comet away with aluminium from the Constantinople 12."

"There's not enough time. And even if there were, I don't trust you."

"Then perhaps you should know," the Doctor replied, "I'm most dangerous when I'm cornered."

"So am I," Yergan said, pressing a button. The entire screen showed one wall-sized image: Romana entangled by a Gulbansi droid, her throat wrapped in its metal tentacles.

"Doc..." Romana tried to whisper.

"Save your breath!" The Doctor ordered. Then he spun toward Yergan.

"Let her go!"

"Why? So she can help Megando with this war?"

"Because she's trying to stop that comet from striking!"

"Possibly," he mused. Then he shrugged. "Your companion, or whoever she is, is going to die."

The Doctor stiffened. In response, Gold moved threateningly between Yergan and the Doctor.

"So will Haining," Yergan said.

"You can stay and die with this planet," he continued, "or come with me."

"In exchange for what?" The Doctor asked through gritted teeth.

"Oh, I'm sure a Time Lord might have a few secrets we'd like to know…"

"K9?"

Codd was huddled next to K9, who was lying on his side where he had fallen and looking worse for wear. After a moment, one ear began to whir. "Ssh!" Codd shushed him as quietly as he could, then looked over to where the droid was holding Romana in front of a security camera. It did not seem to have noticed them.

"Can you move?!" Codd whispered.

"Set me upright," K9 said quietly but haltingly.

Codd kept an eye on the droid and strained to put K9 back into an upright position as quietly as he could.

Once K9 was up again, his one ear whirred as he carried out a self-diagnostic.

"Are you fit enough?" Codd asked.

"This unit stands at sixty-three percent efficiency," K9 replied.

"I hope that's enough, because we have a plan," Codd continued, "where can I plug in this communications cable?"

Codd held out a thin cable that was connected to the wall.

"All right," the Doctor finally agreed, "I'll come with you. But you must let Romana go." He pointed over his shoulder toward Romana's image.

"Why?" Yergan asked.

"Because she has my dog."

"Come again?"

"That comet has a core harder than diamond. No one knows what it is, but you might want to know before anyone else. This war is about minerals, after all."

"Alright," Yergan said, nodding, "but why the dog?"

"My dog has the data you want, and Romana has my dog."

Yergan turned to Gold. "Truth assessment?"

"While some speculation is present," Gold replied, "statements are truthful."

Yergan turned to the Doctor and raised an eyebrow. Then he pressed a button on his computer.

"Don't kill her," he ordered.

On the screen, the tentacles around Romana's neck loosened, and she fell forward, taking deep breaths. She looked under her left arm and saw Codd with K9. Then she straightened up.

"Romana?" The Doctor asked, "Can you hear us?"

Romana nodded and she continued to breathe deeply.

"Romana, where's my dog?" The Doctor then asked.

"*Your* dog?!" Romana cried between gasps, "He's as much my dog as yours!"

"We can't go into that now. I need…"

"Oh, yes we can get into that now! How dare you suggest he's not my dog!"

"Now, wait…" Yergan began,

"Shut up, whoever you are!" Romana snapped. "K9, are you ready?!"

"Affirmative, mistress!"

Suddenly, the droid standing behind Romana stiffened. As the Doctor and Yergan stared around them, the same thing happened to the silver and gold robots.

"What are you doing?!" Yergan cried.

"You know what they say about Gulbansi programming," the Doctor said with a wicked smile, "lacks both verve *and* firewalls."

Yergan ran behind his desk. The silver robots flew at him but he gunned them down with his blaster. He then pointed the weapon at the Doctor.

"I regret nothing," the Doctor pronounced gravely.

Yergan said nothing as he pulled the trigger. But two shots were fired. One hit Yergan in the shoulder, who dropped to the floor. The other went wild and hit the screen, destroying Romana's image.

The Doctor turned. Breen was breathing heavily as she turned her gun toward Gold.

"No, wait!" the Doctor cried.

Breen put up her weapon as Gold turned toward the Doctor. "What are your orders?" It asked.

"Everyone who is still alive in this facility is to be given top medical care, including Yergan," the Doctor replied.

"Start with her," he added, pointing to Haining, who was looking around wide-eyed and shocked.

"What did you do?" She asked.

"Romana and K9 used the network to hack these robots, turning them against Yergan," the Doctor said. "You know Major Breen, of course. She's overdue for promotion."

"Under-Secretary!" Breen cried as she holstered her weapon and ran to help Haining. She looked so different that Breen had not initially recognised her.

The Doctor turned to the controls. All communications were down. "Some kind of safety cut-out..." the Doctor muttered.

He moved over to Yergan, who was lying on the floor, clutching his shoulder. "Help me..." the yellow alien muttered.

"How do I turn on voice comms?" The Doctor asked.

Yergan said nothing.

"Shall I ask Breen to join us?" The Doctor enquired with a quizzical raise of an eyebrow.

Yergan's eyes went wide. "You wouldn't!" He gasped.

"Bre..." the Doctor began.

Yergan spoke the passphrase, and the comms began to work.

"Romana, can you hear me?" The Doctor asked.

The lift opened and the men of the Constantinople 12 leapt out with rifles at the ready. They found Romana working at the comm controls, Codd sitting on K9's back, and the droid obeying Codd's every command.

"Now do a handstand!" Codd cried delightedly - the droid complied.

"What is going on here?!" Mananz cried.

Codd stood and saluted.

"Your plan worked, Captain Mananz!"

"It did?! Oh! I mean… of course, it did! I just didn't expect it to work that quickly!"

"And we didn't expect it to work at all," Duff muttered.

"That'll do, Duff!" Mananz barked.

"K9 was able to hack the droids just like that!" Codd said, snapping his fingers.

"That was very clever of you, K9," Wilkins congratulated, "the mainframe would have taken minutes."

K9's ear whirred. "Praise is not necessary," he replied. "I was only obeying orders."

"Now that's a *very* good dog!" Mananz said jovially.

"Romana?" Wilkins asked, moving toward her.

"I can't get through to the Doctor, and we don't have much time to pull that comet out of its orbit!" She stated grimly.

"Romana, can you hear me?" The Doctor's voice sprung from the comms.

"Doctor! Time's running out!" Romana replied.

"K9?" The Doctor asked.

K9's ear whirred. "There is no longer enough time to use aluminium to pull the comet out of its orbit."

"Oh no," Codd said, sadly.

"We'll ram it!" Mananz cried.

"Probability of success less than zero point one percent," K9 said. "Comet now too close to Megando for such a plan to succeed."

"Then there's only one thing left," the Doctor said, "land on it, and dematerialize it."

"Then come pick me up so we..." Romana began.

"Not enough time," the Doctor interrupted.

"But this is a job for six pilots! One person can't do it alone!"

"Romana," the Doctor said, "I'm still miles below the TARDIS, and we're already low on time."

There was a horrible silence.

"Hurry, then, Doctor," Haining's voice said.

"For all our sakes," Mananz added.

"I will," the Doctor replied.

The Doctor turned off the comms and turned to Breen. "I need a way to the surface... *now*."

"I'll come with you!"

"Not on that leg."

"There's an express lift a thousand feet from here!" Haining said. "Out the door, two lefts. Don't worry about us!"

"Gold," the Doctor said, "you're with me!"

He ran through the darkness with Gold at his side until they found the lift. They boarded and used the emergency protocol to take them to Level 1.

"Who's up there? Is there still fighting?"

"Yes," Gold replied.

"I must get to my TARDIS."

"Do you mean the blue box?"

"Yes."

Gold raised its blaster arm.

"But try not to kill anyone!" The Doctor quickly added.

"Plan 14-5 to be put into effect," Gold responded.

"What does that mean?" He asked, but the doors opened and Gold departed before any reply.

Immediately, the Doctor was hit by what could only be described as the smell of a million rotten eggs. He threw a handkerchief over his face and ran just behind Gold.

Someone stepped out of the gloom and took a swing at the Doctor with a cricket bat. The Doctor dodged in time, and Gold hit the man, who fell groaning to the floor.

Gold took the Doctor's arm, leading him through the few who remained until the Doctor was standing outside the TARDIS doors.

"Now protect Breen and Haining, and make sure Yergan doesn't escape!" The Doctor ordered as he put his key into the TARDIS lock.

Gold peeled away to carry out its orders as the Doctor slammed the doors shut. Then he ran to the controls and set course for the Tstesutsyun Comet.

"What's he planning to do?" Wilkins asked Romana.

"Something the TARDIS was never designed to do... or at least, something one pilot could never do. He'll land on the comet and try to dematerialize with it...."

"Then why doesn't he want you along?"

"Because he has something of a hero complex," Romana replied, "and because... it's impossible. He knows if I were onboard, I'd be killed too."

She lowered her head and turned away from the others.

The TARDIS landed on the comet. It was now less than an hour from Megando. The Doctor double-checked - even if this failed completely, the Constantinople 12 might just be safe, assuming the exploding planet did not destroy it.

"All right, old girl," the Doctor said, looking at the control panel. "This is it."

He set the controls, closed his eyes, held his breath, and flicked a switch. Everything seemed to explode at once.

The Doctor could barely see anything, but there was no fire, no explosions. He realized whatever it was, it was inside his head. Mostly. It was the space-time vortex, he realized. He could see it swirling, cascading, rising, falling as the shell of the TARDIS began to break down and the chaos of the vortex began to seep in. He could not remember a journey being so rough... wait, yes, he could. That journey after he and his granddaughter, Susan, had spent those months on Earth. Susan had gone to school, and two teachers had followed her back to the TARDIS. Susan had threatened to leave him, so he took off, and... the TARDIS almost ripped itself apart. He never did learn why. And now, it was happening again.

The Doctor worked the controls as fast as his hands would allow. He turned on the screen to watch his progress... The TARDIS and the comet were slowly blinking out of normal space-time, but not quickly enough. They were closing in on Megando despite his best efforts.

The shaking, the turbulence, the noise all got worse. The Doctor tried to concentrate but he could barely complete one task before another required his full attention, attention he could not spare.

But then a second pair of hands appeared alongside his, working with him, completing one task, then another. He could not see who it was, but they kept working until…

There was a loud crash, and the Doctor braced himself against the console. He looked up at the screen… somehow, Megando was still there, and Tstesutsyun had passed it by. The Doctor turned to thank whoever it was, but could see no-one.

Then he braced himself against the railings as the world faded to black, and he felt himself sliding to the floor.

Some time later, the Doctor stepped out of the TARDIS and he found himself in a park. It was late Spring, and the birds were singing. He looked around suspiciously.

"This isn't the Constantinople 12…" he muttered.

He saw several people walking through the park without any apparent concern for the comet or the war. He closed the TARDIS doors and took a few more steps.

"I set the controls for…"

Then he saw a blue and white robot racing toward him.

The Doctor turned and took out his key. He was almost inside when the robot said, "Madam President requests your presence at the Presidential Palace."

The Doctor turned. The robot did not seem threatening.

"Tell her I'm busy," he said. "I need to find the Constantinople 12."

"The Constantinople 12 was decommissioned a year ago," the robot said.

"What?" The Doctor replied.

"Repeat: Madam President Romana requests your presence."

The Presidential Palace was everything the Doctor expected it to be. He was ushered into a spacious conference room where Romana was addressing a number of people in expensive clothes.

"And as you can see," Romana said pointing to a graph, "this agricultural data prompts us to ask *where the hell have you been?!*"

The second part of her question was aimed, of course, at the Doctor.

"I take it I'm late," the Doctor replied, "I'm so sorry…"

Before the Doctor could complete his apology, Romana had rushed forward and hugged him.

"It's nice to see you again," she said, stepping back.

"How long…?" He asked.

"Five years, nine months, six days, and nineteen hours," came a voice at his feet. K9 sat there, looking better than ever, both ears whirring.

"Good dog," the Doctor said.

"Affirmative, master," K9 replied.

"And I think you've met the Minister for the Interior," Romana said, introducing the Doctor to…

"Breen!" The Doctor cried.

"Doctor," Breen said, smiling, "I'm glad you're alive. Romana told us you were, but…"

"Yes, well, I can explain everything… almost. Romana, this makes you President twice over!"

"And she's done a terrific job," Breen said, "it's been a pleasure to watch her work."

"That's very nice of you, Janet."

"Janet?" Asked the Doctor.

"Janet… Her first name," Romana said slowly, with emphasis.

"Ah. Yes, sorry, didn't catch that five years ago. Speaking of which, what happened to the crew of the space station, and to Haining and Yergan?"

"The crew survived," Breen replied with a smile, "they were honourably discharged and given fat pensions. A few are still with us. Codd is working toward a PhD in robotics, as a matter of fact."

"How's he doing?" The Doctor asked.

"You'll have to ask his professor," Romana replied.

"His progress is satisfactory," K9 said.

"As for Haining," Romana continued, "she died of her injuries a few days later."

"I'm sorry to hear that. She was a hero, in the end."

"Yergan was put on trial for espionage, mass murder, and a hundred other charges. His people abandoned him, and he was convicted and executed."

The Doctor's face twisted into a half frown.

"Ah, still a little bloodthirsty I see. Oh well, baby steps," he said with resignation. Romana looked a trifle needled, and yet a small smile escaped at his manner.

"One does what one can," she pronounced airily.

"And the war?" The Doctor asked.

"It's over now, thanks to our planetary coalition," Breen said, "in fact, things are going so well it could become a new chapter in galactic history."

The Doctor and Romana smiled at each other but said nothing.

"And now that the Doctor's here," Romana said, turning to her colleagues, "I resign! Come along, K9!"

She took the Doctor's arm and - despite the uproar behind her - led him out of the Palace.

"But, Madam President," Breen said, following them closely, "Vice-President Hadoke is in Evergreen Canton opening the new hospital!"

"Yes, a capable man. He won't need my help."

"But at least let me say goodbye!" Breen said.

They stopped just outside the Palace.

"Goodbye, Breen," the Doctor said.

"Goodbye, Janet," Romana said.

"Goodbye. I'll miss you," she looked down, "especially you, K9."

K9's ears whirred.

"Affirmative."

"Someday," the Doctor said, as they strolled through the park, with K9 by their side, "you must tell me how you got yourself elected."

"Oh, that was simple. Half of the electorate demanded a woman, and the other half would only accept a woman who wasn't Megandan. I won by a landslide. Twice."

"Well, you're an excellent administrator," the Doctor said.

"And you," Romana said, "must tell me how you managed to move that comet all by yourself."

"I didn't."

"What...?"

"A time image, possibly... someone from the past or the future? I..."

"Someone?" Romana interjected.

"Just an impression..." the Doctor shook his head, "did you ever learn more about that satellite?"

Romana shook her head.

"Nothing."

They reached the TARDIS and the Doctor took out his key.

"Never mind, it was quite atomised," he said with a shrug, "and the universe is a big place. I doubt we'll ever see one again."

Chapter Five - Space Ghost Assassin
by Lonnie Webb

"Now that we've taken care of that business we can slip away for a well-deserved break," said the Doctor. "Don't you think we've earned that, K9?"
"Affirmative, master," answered the robot dog. The sounds of the time rotor rising and falling were masked momentarily by the sound of K9's wagging tail and twisting ears.
"I thought we were on a tight schedule?" Romana called out from behind the interior door.
The Doctor puffed out his cheeks like an exasperated locomotive.
"Do we have to adhere to the tight schedule? I mean, isn't the whole point of tight schedules to occasionally abandon them, and enjoy the excess of free time you have acquired from the tightness of the schedule... being tight?"
Romana entered the console room with her head cocked with an air of moderate indulgence. It had become a familiar mannerism, even in this regeneration.
"I'm not sure that's the point, Doctor. Time is such a sticky thing."
Without warning the sounds of the TARDIS wound down to silence as the central column sank to its lowest position. The lights went out almost entirely. In contrast, the wall roundels remained illuminated by the light of a burnt orange dawn.
"Tackier than a temporal twig!" shouted the Doctor as he and Romana leapt to the console. After flicking familiar switches, then a few less familiar, the Doctor looked up ashen-faced.
"The only instrument on the console that has power is this flashing light..."
"What does that light mean?" Questioned Romana.
"It means...the power is out," whispered the Doctor, "and we were in full flight! We should have been thrown right through the vortex."
"What on Gallifrey? No power?" Romana looked at the walls, "Then what's lighting the roundels?"
"The TARDIS has completely stopped. She isn't providing the light," the Doctor replied, bowing his head.
Whispering, he continued, "It's coming from outside. A location... between the interior and the shell of the real universe interface."

"That's nonsense!" Romana furrowed her brow and shook her hair from her eyes.

"Nothing can exist in an undefinable space."

The TARDIS exterior doors hummed open and blinding white light streaked in to bathe the Doctor.

"You simply must stop doing that," groaned the Doctor, but he did not seem to be addressing either Romana or K9. The Timelord popped his lapels and did then turn his attention to his fellow Gallifreyan.

"In case of... difficulties, close the doors by any means and dematerialize."

"How? There's no power."

"Perhaps K9 can provide enough juice to at least close the doors," the Doctor speculated. Then he marched into the light saying "Time to meet the piper."

"Doctor! Wait!" Romana cried, but he was already gone. She stopped where she was and sighed.

"And it's *pay* the piper."

Once through the doors - and his eyes had adjusted to the brilliance - the Doctor found himself on a sandy plain under a rusty-red sky. A man in glistening white stood before the Doctor looking into the setting sun. A white straw hat was perched on his head and an Ascot swathed the neck. A wine glass appeared in his hand, while a brandy snifter full of jelly babies materialised in the Doctor's.

"Doctor," came the salutation from the white-bearded man. Beyond him, sandstone mountains rolled into the distance. Resort villas and cabanas suddenly solidified nearby.

"Guardian," acknowledged the Doctor, instantaneously and inexplicably finding himself standing next to the man, "remarkably peaceful here. I like the mountains from the American south-west. I can't say I miss the continental fog. Those mountains are oddly out of place with the Mediterranean villas. But at least it *is* peaceful."

"Didn't you want a break from it all?" Taunted the Guardian.

"I suppose that... was the idea," Doctor said reticently. He sniffed the fruity jelly babies with a wafting motion.

"A fine vintage."

The Doctor and the White Guardian now sat facing each other on solidifying white iron work furniture. The Doctor was surprised at how completely *unsurprised* he was at the shifting nature of this reality.

"Where exactly are we?" The Doctor asked, attempting to steer the conversation.

"This old place? Just the centre of all realities – the temporal nexus itself."

The guardian set his eyes on the Doctor.

"Are you tired of your adventures? Of your racing through the universe, righting wrongs, and straightening crooked paths?"

He took a swig of his illusory beverage through his white goatee.

"No, no, I am still quite a fan of the naturally crooked path. I like to think *I* put the orderly bend back in incorrectly straightened paths," the Doctor said, smiling.

"Is it possible you could have become burdened by certain events in your future, Doctor? Events that will unfold due to actions committed long ago," mused the guardian, "perhaps you are shirking a responsibility? Dreading a consequence, maybe?"

"Leaving something undone? Remarkable. You're echoing the sentiment of my first self," declared the Doctor.

"Sounds like a wise man."

"Fear not, Guardian. I am committed to resolving any issues which may arise..."

A glass of cool water appeared in the his hand, replacing the jelly babies.

"Drink the water and be refreshed, Doctor," said the White Guardian kindly.

"How..." began the Doctor but his voice gave out. He drank the water and cleared his throat with a short cough. Then he finished his thought.

"How do I fulfil our obligations to Time and Space without hurting, even destroying innocents?"

"Now isn't that always the trick - it's all in the nature of the doing and undoing. It's why you left your home planet, Gallifrey, in the first place. Besides, you and I both know that you reap only what you have already sown, Doctor."

Ducking his head and nodding, the Doctor realized he now stood at the console of the TARDIS.

"What was that?" Demanded Romana, astonished.

"Romana..." said the Doctor, then paused. The TARDIS instruments had resumed their normal operations. The lighting had returned to normal too. The elder Timelord leaned on a railing drumming his fingers.
"We have to keep to our schedule tight."
"What, on vacation?" Romana asked, clearly confused by this second change of direction.
"Tighter than before," growled the Doctor to himself. He reached out to reset the coordinates but then stopped in surprise. Unprompted, the engines roared once.
"Ah... The settings have already been changed for us. How considerate," he noted sourly.
The TARDIS was underway.

"Ah... Not when I expected."
The Doctor had emerged from the freshly re-materialized time-ship. The TARDIS was surrounded by an outdoor cluster of noiseless retail buildings. He stepped out onto asphalt, which he swiped his finger across and promptly licked.
"Earth, about 2170, hmm?"
"Let me guess, not when we are supposed to be?" Came Romana's voice from the open door.
"Don't be absurd!" Responded the Doctor, "We are just where we're meant to be!"
Romana poked her head out baring a wide grin.
"And what's the name of this place?" She asked as she joined the Doctor, along with K9.
"I wish I knew..." the Doctor pondered as he eyed the surroundings. A man - a derelict in a black tattered skullcap and threadbare army surplus jacket - ran up to them speaking gibberish. He screeched to a stop upon seeing the TARDIS.
"Hello?" The Doctor said in polite enquiry.
"She sees me! She's judging me!" The old hobo's long grey moustache and beard framed trembling lips. He ran for the nearest dumpster and threw himself inside, sobbing.
"Odd. I tend to get on so well with the youthful."
"Elderly," corrected Romana.
"Elderly," responded the Doctor.

"Well, at least we aren't in an underground passage," Romana sighed, trying to make the best of the situation.

"Currently, mistress," K9 noted primly.

"Sh!" Hissed the Doctor with a wave. He pressed his fingers to his lips as he pivoted, "This is very wrong."

Romana looked at the suburban shopping centre. In the distance wound rundown riverfront properties while further distant stood antiquated mining machinery, intertwined with weeds. The ruins and occasional new constructions stood in stark contrast.

"Very wrong?" She asked dubiously.

"Very, *very* wrong," the Doctor whispered.

"Oh—very, *very* wrong!" Romana laughed, crossing her arms, "Don't you think you're over-dramatizing this car park?"

"I never over-dramatize," the Doctor replied gravely, then froze in his steps.

"Midday, in front of a shopping centre. Not a car, nor a housewife, nor even a depressed starling in sight. Very, *very*, wrong."

The Doctor cocked his head and swiped his nose with a finger.

"And add to that a wrecked Dalek cruiser behind the TARDIS."

"What?" Romana spun to gaze in horror at the vehicle filling the ground beyond the tattered blue police box. She trembled at the memory of her tortuous encounter with Daleks on the first day of her second regeneration, when they "interrogated" her. She crouched, eyeing the windows and rooftops with extreme caution.

"Where did that come from?"

The Doctor remained silent, apparently lost in thought.

"It obviously crashed relatively recently," Romana pointed out, hoping to coax more of a response.

"What? Oh! Of course it did! I might have *been* here when it did. That could make this London. They had really softened the Earth up with low-cost meteor strikes and solar weather manipulation," the Doctor said, his focus suddenly sharp and brought to bear on their current surroundings. He turned to K9.

"We'll walk uphill a bit, K9. Stay and guard the TARDIS."

"From the human hobo," said the metal dog, "affirmative, master!"

"Looks like the cruiser has been gutted by the human population," Romana noted as they walked, "even the hull has been stripped down. The real question is where are the Daleks now?"

"'Where are the people?' is the real question," the Doctor replied as they left the car park for still more rundown suburbia, "did the Daleks somehow survive and kill everyone? If so who built the structures newer than the crashed vessel? If the people destroyed our presumed surviving Daleks, where are they now?"

"Perhaps they've taken to a nocturnal lifecycle and sleep during the day?"

"Ah, The Hand of The Omega Man," the Doctor mused absently before responding more directly, "but then, when would they play football? Even in alien prisons, under the absolute worst conditions, humans will fight for a way to play football."

"Then we should be frightened of a force capable of ending weekend football," Romana warned.

"Ha! No matter where the humans may hide, *we* can handle anything," boasted the Doctor, prompting Romana to roll her eyes.

"We Timelords defeated the galactic tin-cans," he continued, "besides, as I recall the Daleks set *themselves* up for failure and were all disposed of. Industrious *humans* must have stripped all the ship's useable technology."

The Doctor almost walked into a shimmering woman in white spandex who was also walking along at a brisk pace. She subsequently passed by Romana, seemingly oblivious of her.

"Excuse me?" Romana ventured.

"Do pardon us," added the Doctor, "we didn't see you approach."

Undeterred, the woman in white continued on, ignoring the Timelords. She seemed almost to *blur* uphill faster than the eye could follow. The woman carved her way up the incline as if drawn along a familiar, repetitious trail by an unseen cord.

"Well, that was certainly unexpected," said Romana.

"Yes," answered the Doctor, stepping almost shoulder to shoulder with her as they watched the woman dwindle in the distance.

"She is scaling that peak above the wrecked ship," said Romana, motioning toward a fog-shrouded facility sitting on the aforementioned peak of the hill.

"Yes," replied the Doctor, "that facility is likely built above the old mine. Looks like a power plant. They might have only just recovered nuclear power."

"Was she real? Or an apparition?" Romana asked, maintaining her

own line of thought, "She was shimmering!"
"Hm? Oh, yes," agreed the Doctor. He started following in the invisible footsteps of the woman, "Come on. Let's go, Let's go!"
"Must we follow that apparition past the Dalek death machine?" Romana complained.
"I suspect it is most likely that following this person - flitting incorporeally around - will lead us to a highly illegal quantum tachyon accumulator," the Doctor pronounced.
"A device for tracking Timelords in spacetime? Designed to circumvent the Matrix of Gallifrey? Are you mad?" Romana asked aghast, stopping in her tracks, "It's the death penalty if any are even found in possession of one!"
"Yet, this is the only planet in the universe we might find such a device."
"I don't understand," said Romana.
"Imagine, a human body. The slightly limited human brain. One heart. Not too bad once you get used to it. It's how I escaped detection from the Time Hunters myself - for a while anyway."
"You? You're not human!" Romana said incredulously.
"Not originally, no, and not now. But I was once. Briefly and temporarily – if you'll pardon the pun. I tried to 'drop out' – sinking beneath Gallifrey's radars. The Timelords objected to that! They were so angry that they sent Time Hunters after me. Timelords with no moral qualms about executing trouble makers. So, briefly, I made myself human - for all intents and purposes. Not the only time I've pulled off that trick, mind, albeit to evade different pursuers. I had to make special provisions to retain as much of my memory as possible.
"The Timelords eventually relented. I revealed myself to them and in 'gratitude' they undid my personal camouflage. Then they finally made good on my exile, my third self, trapped on the Earth in the 1970s. Or 80s. Never was sure. I feel I came off rather badly by being honest with them."
Romana caught up in an instant.
"You used a type-40 chameleon arch. Were you mad?"
The Doctor shrugged defensively.
"It's how I escaped into the Earth's past, or future – I sometimes find it hard to keep track. My memories - and indeed my whole physique - became somewhat limited... by my own choice."

The Doctor held out his empty hand to an imaginary object.
"To carry a hidden life in the palm of your hand. To open it any time you want to return to the temporal nexus. Any time you want to go back to being a Timelord. Just don't lose it."

"An arch fob... yes, I have heard of them. Dangerous things," Romana noted, "where did you keep it?"

"A cigar box in the TARDIS' old workshop," said the Doctor. He continued to lead the way up the path the ghostly figure had taken. By now she was long gone.

"When I attempted to 'drop out', after the Timelords passed sentence on my second incarnation, I fled here but in the Earth's 50th century," the Doctor continued.

"Doctor, does any of this have anything to do with the quantum tachyon accumulator?" Romana prompted.

"That's just it! An aggressively dogged Timelord - a Hunter named Dante Laux - arrived. He was searching for me, having employed an illegal Gallifreyan device—as you can guess, a quantum tachyon accumulator—to follow me through the temporal nexus. He was determined to carry out a terminal sentence! I barely got away. That was the first time I truly realized the danger of being a 'drop out'. It just wasn't allowed! But then I realised it was also a death sentence."

"Good heavens! That history was never repeated to me, even as President of the High Council. The Matrix also never indicated that these hunters ever existed," exclaimed Romana, "that must have been before my time. It certainly isn't like that any more."

"As far as you know," the Doctor said archly, "and your parents might well have been time-tots back then. The Matrix was probably carefully revised. The truth adjusted."

"And he didn't try to find you elsewhere?" Romana asked.

"I might have sent the Hunter's TARDIS into orbit 'unmanned'," quipped the Doctor, tapping his nose.

"Then that's why the TARDIS brought us here," said Romana, "the Timelords must have left him to die in this time period, his own TARDIS adrift. And it 'sensed' the temporal flotsam and jetsam."

"Very likely. For them, it would neatly clean up an embarrassing mess," said the Doctor, "the secondary question is why bring us twenty eight hundred years prior to my previous visit, in that 50th century future."

Despite a growing breeze the facility before them remained masked in fog. It was certainly taller than the Doctor had previously imagined. As they negotiated a craggy rock outcropping he offered his hand to Romana.
"Mind the body," said the Doctor.
"Body?"
Romana jerked at the sight of a mangled and unmistakably human male arm in the heather. Her initial revulsion passed and her investigative nature took over.
"What a violent end."
"Yes," confirmed the Doctor, "he was a soldier, judging from the remains of his uniform."
"Do you think our apparition did this?" Using a stylus from a jacket pocket, Romana stabbed at the man's rifle. It had been sheared in two behind the magazine.
"A non-corporeal shimmering individual wandering aimlessly over the countryside - so lightly that she doesn't even leave footprints?" Mused the Doctor, "I don't see why not necessarily, although I am no expert on apparitions. They're so shy."
"Can you tell if there is an easier path? Perhaps we could catch up with her?" Romana suggested.
"It appears not. Do you suppose that her trek is repeated? On a loop?" The Doctor responded, equally quizzically.
"She could take a daily walk up the mountains. Or monthly," offered Romana.
"Hard to say," shrugged the Doctor, "could be random but I doubt it. Not in the presence of Gallifreyan time tampering technology."
"Freeze!"
Two camouflaged uniformed men rose from the underbrush. They pointed antiquated submachine guns at the Timelords.
"This zone is off limits! What are you doing here?"
Romana calmly, if not habitually, raised her hands.
"We were following the woman."
The armed men slackened their poses slightly, eyed each other, then returned to the travellers.
"You better get inside with us."
A hum began to fill the air followed by a growing tremor.
"It's started! Get a move on!" One soldier cried.

"Captain Erikson requesting auxiliary entry with two captives," called the most decorated man into a throat mic.
"Understood. Proceed," came the reply.
"Move, you lot! We'll be killed out here!" The Captain pointed to an opening doorway becoming visible above the rocks. The party made for the entrance, fighting to stay upright during the tremors.
"It's reinforced, you'll be safe in there," Erikson reassured them. Once inside the Doctor and Romana were ushered into an interrogation room.
Then bound to chairs.
And lights shone in their eyes.
Captain Erikson stepped from behind the lights.
"Now, who are you?" He snapped.
"He's the Doctor and I'm Romana," explained Romana, "and this is all quite unnecessary."
"Doctor and Romana," a private said, walking into the room and scribbling down their answers, "you would be his...?"
"Companion," barked Romana, then primly added, "and equal."
The two men raised their eyebrows at each other in misogynistic camaraderie.
"We are travellers who found your site by mistake," the Doctor offered.
Captain Erikson sparked a taser into the Doctor's armpit.
"Stop that!" The Doctor yelped indignantly.
"Getting to ya there, doc?" Chuckled Erikson.
"Hardly... it's just my other arm is feeling left out."
"Daily tea, Cap'n," piped up another private entering with a tray of steaming drinks.
"Already, Private Davies? Did you bring enough for our prisoners?" Erikson asked, indicating to the Doctor and Romana, still bound to their chairs.
"Aye, sir. We ain't uncivilized, ya know," answered Davies.
"Tea, Doctor?" Asked the captain.
"Tea?" The Doctor murmured, bewildered, as he watched a small table placed before them. He shook his head like a Labrador coming off a sugar high.
"Let's see, 'T' as a distribution is the sample mean minus the population mean over the standard deviation over the square of ginger

131

root. Do you care for Ginger root 'tea', Romana?"

"Oh, no, no. Very kind of you, but - as you know - I am a bit of a purist when it comes to tea, or infusions."

"British tea, I assure you," said the private proudly, "at the moment we are limited to breakfast tea. Supply lines have been down."

"Due to the creature?" Inquired the Doctor, "Or perhaps 'the girl'?"

"Quite. Strikes invisibly. All we ever find are it's victims," the captain added.

"Forgive my manners. Lost track of the time. Procedure, you know. Please loosen their bonds for tea."

"Oh, I completely understand," said the Doctor as he was rocked roughly by the meaty-handed private removing his bonds, "one so rarely gets to enjoy a rousing interrogation when schedules are at play, eh?"

Romana cocked her head with a realization.

"Points of procedure are quite important following the Dalek incursion, aren't they?"

"It's civilization," replied the Captain as he drew a chair to the table to sit comfortably for tea, "procedure, manners, you know. Wheels of progress and all that. Rediscovering lost knowledge, principles, structure."

"Sounds daunting," added the Doctor, "it's only been a few years since the battle with the Daleks. And I've seen it all before. You lot are doing exceedingly well. Rebuilding... reclaiming the old mine."

"Quite," said the Captain as he sipped his tea, "we had to start anew on more stable ground but progress is being made. Then, when we first started up the machinery, the creature appeared."

"You realize we have nothing to do with this creature, yes?" Romana asked.

"I am inclined to believe you, miss. Although I must say my inclinations don't mean anything."

"We found a body outside with injuries that were in places ragged, and in others clean," said the Doctor.

"Oh no. It got Ian," said the Private.

"Those injuries," Romana stated gravely, "were either caused by a giant foot, wielding a sword of Damocles - neither subtle nor hard to track - *or* a time shelf."

"A what?" Asked Erickson after a moment's stunned silence.

"Think of a distortion field, gentlemen," clarified the Doctor, "a deadly concentration of energy that can cut through any substance."
"A random, invisible distortion in time itself," Romana added.
"Imagine a moving, undetectable walk-in rip saw," the Doctor suggested helpfully.
Erickson's eyes darted first to Romana and then to the Doctor.
"What if this 'time shelf' thing 'randomly' struck underground?"
"Earthquakes, weather disruptions, static electricity discharges," Romana listed.
"Radio outages, utility outages. You very likely would have evacuated the populace..." the Doctor drifted off as connections were made.
Romana and the Doctor shared a look.
"Perhaps we can help resolve your problem and ours simultaneously," Romana suggested.
"Your problem?"
"Oh, it's an interesting case. We've been tracking the emanations of a device of... foreign technology. We arrived here but the trail had gone cold," the Doctor explained.
"We initially suspected it was in the Dalek hulk. But now I suspect it is somehow connected to the apparition of the lady in white, and possibly this 'creature' to boot."
"I do say, that's a cracking jolly notion!" The Captain said excitedly, "we might be on the first steps to a solution! How do we proceed?"
"Hmm," the Doctor murmured then absconded with a pad and pencil.
"Measurements and procedures, captain," he cried spinning to face the officer, "procedure and all that!"
The Doctor then scrawled a disc with a cone in the pad.
"To start with we have normal time," he drew a line bisecting the intersection, "imagine that line coming out of the page towards our faces."
He drew a column intersecting the disc and cone.
"Then we have the known temporal nexus - the matrix relates to it over here somewhere," he noted vaguely, "the dotted lines perhaps? If a known localized tachyon field were introduced..."
"This cone becomes like a doughnut, then, doesn't it," the captain supplied.
The Doctor and Romana were shocked, their mouths hanging agape.
"Or at least a 'half-bagel' over here, near your time arrow," the Captain

added.

"How on Gallifrey..." Romana began.

"Bless you, Brigadier!" Exclaimed the Doctor, forgetting himself, his location and everyone in it.

"Captain," pointed out Captain Erikson.

"Bless you anyway, you dear man," the Doctor enthused, recovering his senses, "I had no idea you grasped basic temporal mechanics! You explain it so simply your mastery may exceed my own! Or at least Romana's."

This final remark earned the Doctor a growl and a sharp boot from his companion.

"My dear, Doctor! I've seen this broken infinity graphic every day since Dr. Tindal initiated power up!"

"Can you show us?" Romana asked gravely.

Erikson was more than happy to oblige. He took the two Timelords to a lift. In that elevator the Doctor confided to Romana, "I am almost certain this Dr. Tindal will turn out to be Dante Laux the Time Hunter from Gallifrey!"

"Really?" Romana questioned, "I too concluded the accumulator must be here, gathering geo-thermic or tectonic potential, while simultaneously expelling accumulated power as exhaust. However, would a Time Hunter come back in time to pursue you at *this* place in time and space? If he could do that, surely he would go back to the Dalek Incursion itself, in 2164."

"I agree. And no, it doesn't make sense. But be ready," the Doctor whispered, "this man is a killer."

The Doctor and Romana took deep breaths as the lift doors opened to reveal an open plan control room. A number of white-plastic clad technicians - men and women - stood holding clipboard devices at the periphery of the room observing their respective stations. A few made distracted glances to the newcomers. In the middle of the bay an unusual column of dimly lit electrics - and
what could have been organic-looking skin - rose to a rounded point. Romana was impressed, if a little horrified.

"It certainly looks like they've reverse engineered some antiquated Skaran technology."

Via a holo-projection appeared the familiar disc and cone arcing partway into a recognizable infinity loop.

"Weather status?" Came an unseen voice.

"Above seasonal average activity. Variance acceptable," another technician answered.

The first voice asked, "Volcanic projection?"

"Continuous," answered yet another technician on the far side.

"Captain Erikson?" The first voice called.

"Dr. Tindal, I brought you two strangers we found at the western border. They propose to help resolve the issues with the systems."

"Really?"

"Get ready," said the Doctor quietly to Romana, "if necessary, we'll take the soldiers' weapons."

"I would like to meet them," a woman – that same first voice – said from beyond the semi-electronic mountain in the middle of the room. She walked around it into view and stood facing them. She wore the same plastic lab clothing as the others manning the control room.

"I am Dr. Tindal, chief operator of this facility."

"Dante Laux, indeed!" Romana chided, nudging the Doctor.

"Greetings! Please ignore my assistant, Dr. Tindal. Her name is Romana. Let me introduce *myself*," said the Doctor grinning with teeth fully on display.

"I am the Doctor."

Dr. Tindal froze.

"Not *the* Doctor? The genuine article?"

"You were expecting us?" Romana asked incredulously.

Astonished, Dr. Tindal said, "Many have heard of the Doctor from the time of the Dalek incursion. We had begun to regard him as a folk hero, a myth even. But here you are in the flesh!"

"I thought he would be older," said a nearby technician before she caught herself and looked to the floor, blushing.

"Well," smiled the Timelord of indeterminate years, "I age well. Could I examine you're set-up?"

With Dr. Tindal's permission, the Doctor and Romana examined the by now familiar holo-projection - as well as the other not-so-familiar charts.

"These emanations," the Doctor began, "what are you trying to do at this facility?"

"Following the mine's explosion at the end of the invasion, and our new-won freedom, we set out to utilize the excavations for a number of natural resources," Tindal explained, "many of the old shafts still survived, apart from the main core one of course. After reopening the mine our instruments began to detect tectonic instability."

"Could it potentially be new volcanic activity? New geothermal instability as a delayed after-effect of the alien bomb?" Romana wondered.

"We lowered a prototype direct power conversion unit into the mine, as far as it could go anyway. You'll be happy to know we have nearly total conversion," Dr. Tindal proclaimed proudly, seeming not to hear her.

"What," gasped the Doctor, the blood draining from his face, "you aren't using a water turbine, are you?"

"No," said Tindal, "we repurposed alien devices that act as raw energy capacitors."

"And output electricity?" Asked Romana dubiously.

"That would appear to make sense," the Doctor added with mounting dread.

"That's the principle," said Dr. Tindal.

"Where does the device send the other energies it accumulates?" Murmured the Doctor gravely.

"What other energies?" Dr. Tindal enquired, frowning.

"A capacitor stores power and releases it as required. Or at least *as designed*. I am betting this machine of yours accumulates many forms of power and probably discharges them at capacity. All of them." These last words uttered by the Doctor held deadly significance.

"No," said Dr. Tindal, "there must be another explanation!"

"What confounded arrogance! Your device isn't responsible for the destructive forces unleashed – not that it was ever really your device in the first place," the Doctor noted dismissively, "but there is a component or some element nearby that is certainly being influenced by it. Acting as a magnifying lens. And using your apparatus to spew out – among other things - ions, charging the atmosphere. Probably responsible for the sheet lightning and other more unusual emanations worldwide."

A violent tremor rocked the building. White-purple lightning turned the windows to blinding rectangles of fury. Dr. Tindal still appeared willing to argue when an aftershock shook the mountain.

"The increasing tremors?" She asked in subdued tones.

"Aren't coming from the planet," finished Romana.
She pointed to a panel being operated by a young technician, "At least, not *just* the planet. The increasing tectonic activity is likely from undetected random discharges from *this*."
The holo-projection switched to an image of a machine hanging by a metal stem in the mine shaft. It boasted a plainly visible emblem, concentric circles, a misshapen pentagon, circular missing disks, and a couple of variously sized adjacent disks.
"Gallifrey," whispered Romana in confirmation.
"Yes," the Doctor's replied, staring into the middle distance. He unconsciously twitched his sonic screwdriver from finger to finger.
"The converter itself is responsible for these sporadic tectonic disturbances?" Dr. Tindal asked with mounting dread.
"I can just turn it off!" She then announced desperately.
"Gallifreyan technology isn't that simple," confided Romana, "it often has a mind of its own."
"It's too dangerous to service, of course," the Doctor grumbled to himself, "too much radiation."
The room shook harder. Cracks appeared in the ceiling and walls.
"I'll need an environment suit," he stated determinedly, tinged with a little reluctance.
"You know about this 'Gallifrey' machine? Can it be safely deactivated?" Dr. Tindal demanded desperately.
"Yes. No. And I'm going to anyway," said the Doctor.
Romana put a hand on Dr. Tindal's plastic covered shoulder.
"The obvious conclusion is that your project is somehow responsible for the very outcome you are now trying to halt"
"Oh, God! We caused the harm we were trying to suppress!" Dr. Tindal gasped in defeat. She hunched over clutching her chest, "What a sick, twisted joke!"

An environment suit that looked like it was made from a large space blanket was brought to the Doctor. He began to suspect that in these impoverished post-war times it might have actually been repurposed from one. Nevertheless, he started donning it immediately.
"Look at the accumulator's exhaust," added the Doctor, "or more precisely, the apparent lack thereof. Remember your basic physics. In the end, your misuse of this machinery – it's undirected outpouring of

deadly yet undetected energies - is killing your own people here, while creating desert and famine further afield. Probably."

"Those oscillations must be responsible for causing world wide earthquakes, volcanic eruptions and possibly worse," Romana added, "we need to shut it off! Now!"

Another jolt hit the foundations, knocking everyone to the floor. The Doctor looked out of a window to see lava spewing from a doorway in a lower corridor.

"Are we, perchance, sitting *on* a volcanic fault?" The Doctor mused sarcastically.

"Unbelievable," Romana sighed with a roll of her eyes.

"Is the collector off?" Tindal asked.

"Yes," said the operator, "but the emitters are still charged. I don't know where their energy is coming from!"

"Volcano Day," whispered the Doctor, "the machine is getting its additional charge from time itself. As it was designed to do."

"Creating a tectonic resonance. How much worse can this thing get?" Romana asked grimly.

"Oh, trust me, it will get much, *much* worse, Romana. Get everyone out of here. I have to reach the accumulator and snuff the whole thing out."

The Doctor zipped his padded suit shut and tossed its gloves into the helmet.

"Technician, can you get me to the alien device?"

"We are with you as far as we can go," Captain Erikson said, while his men – ever prepared - hoisted rolls of cable to assist the Doctor.

"Quick! Everyone out the side entrance!" Romana barked. She followed those running humans not staying to aid the Doctor. A boulder dropped through the wall ahead of them flattening a poor woman to death.

Romana turned her head, sickened. Then, in a moment, she was back on task.

"The rear door, then! Hurry!"

They ran to the loading dock. The first man to leap from the steps was consumed in an exploding fountain of fire. His yell was barely heard as he was incinerated. Romana forced the panic-stricken scientists and technicians back the way they came.

"We'll find another way!" Romana yelled over the increasing din.

The Doctor's party stood at an access hatch outside the main mine shaft.

"We'll stay as long as you are in there," Captain Erikson told him grimly. His men stood at the shaft entrance coiling out cable as the Doctor tucked his sleeves into his gloves.

"Besides, I don't think there *is* another way out."

"The mine elevator isn't safe during these tremors," the technician piped up nervously.

"Yes, I have had some experiences in unstable mines before," the Doctor said, a little impatiently.

"Plenty of light in there," said Erikson looking through the narrowly cracked door, "I'm afraid it must be a lava flow."

"What temperature is that cordage good for?" The Doctor inquired.

"Off-hand," Erikson pondered, "I have no idea. Just keep it out of the flames."

The Doctor shot furious eye-brows at the captain as the technician opened the shaft. He pulled his hood on while the soldiers secured the cable to the Doctor's built-in harness.

Descending into the shaft, the Doctor found thick heavy soot and gas illuminated eerily from beneath. He ran his palm along one gantry-leg to another, easing his way down. Worryingly, stones fell free from the wall as his hand brushed them. He called into his suit mic.

"Captain, we need to go faster! The shaft is breaking down!"

"Aye, Doctor!" Came the staticky reply. Consequently the Doctor's descent became far more rapid. The heat grew steadily but as yet at a moderate rate of climb. Nevertheless, even through the protection of the suit the Doctor's face broke into a sweat.

The Timelord covered his visor instinctively when a flash of burning gas rushed by him. His environment suit was quite fireproof, he reasoned reassuringly. Corrosive gas and static electricity notwithstanding – his memory unhelpfully added.

He navigated a cross-gantry that anchored the accumulator stem to the middle of the shaft. Stones periodically fell around him, fortunately diverted for now by the gantry above. The Doctor anxiously wrapped his arms around the heat proof metal stem.

He looked into eyes staring back into his own.

The unnatural transparent apparition hovered before him. She was surrounded by a wispy blueish halo and kept pace with the Doctor as he was lowered.
She looked at him and gave an almost apologetic smile.
"Oh, please pardon *me*," the Doctor declared magnanimously. He then switched over to the external speaker.
"I'm just here for the view."
"What was that, Doctor?" Erikson spoke into his ear.
"I'm not alone down here. The young lady we were discussing has joined me. She seems *aware* of me," the Doctor explained.
"Are you hallucinating, Doctor?"
"That would make things so much easier," the Timelord answered wearily.
The blueish-white young woman's face seemed to flush.
"Oh, bother," said the Doctor.
"What's that, Doctor? The QRM is getting bad," said Erikson.
"Interference from the... static... down here," the Doctor supplied.
Scalding water washed over him, followed by waves of flashing, burning gas.
"The accumulator is in sight. Slow down," the Doctor rasped into his mic, his breathing now pained with the increasing heat and fumes. He gripped the gantry and the rope tightly now. He stared at a shiny metal decahedron with rings of stainless steel, complete with tungsten actuators radiating outwards. He snared one of these rings and tied onto it with his other hand. The whole device shimmered with arcs and glows as it accumulated, sorted, and sifted energy. The Doctor assumed it must be capturing random tachyons for later release.
He unscrewed the bolts holding the accumulator and let it fall the length of the line he had attached.
"Listen," the Doctor said to the apparition, "if you're real, I don't dare close down the device while you're here. You should go to a safe place in case you become solid."
The young woman smiled calmly but remained silent.
"Very well," said the Doctor, "Captain, can you bring me up?"
A moment passed.
"Captain?"
The apparition caught a falling, burning line. As far as the line was concerned, she was solid enough already.

"Ah, the cable has broken," the Doctor realised with a sigh, "a small error of judgement on my part."
The young woman shrugged. This was when the Doctor realized she was holding his hand.
"Well, aren't you kind."
The Doctor looked around as the flames rose.
"Should we just hang around?"
The woman shook her head and pulled his hand unwillingly from the support stem. She turned in space and took the Doctor in an embrace, which he returned. He was amazed – and relieved - how solid her form felt as she carried him up the shaft.
"You're becoming real," cried the Doctor as the heat began to overcome him, "must… must be the proximity... to the device..."
They passed gantry after gantry. She placed her cheek against the Doctor's helmeted one.
"I understand," he said, "wherever we go, we go together."
The Doctor's eyes fluttered. He seemed lost in an eternity of flashing lights behind his eyelids.

"Doctor!" Erickson shouted through the opening of the shaft. As he caught sight of the ghostly young woman he added, "Stand back men!"
Semi-conscious, the Doctor collapsed gasping on the floor outside the shaft. The tremors were continuing. He was groggy and uncertain but pulled the accumulator into the corridor using the attached line. Immediately he blasted it with various harsh sonic screwdriver settings.
Whirs and clicks came from the machine, which finally grew dark, then silent.
The Doctor pulled off his hood and realized he was still in the embrace of the young woman. She solidified and took a breath.
"I'm alive!" She exclaimed.
"Yes, my dear. We both are," said the exhausted Doctor, "is there a medic? This old Doctor needs fluids. And the ghost has just experienced a sudden unexpected weight gain."
"A man used that machine on me," she said softly, nodding towards the now dead accumulator. Odd tones of shame had coloured her words.

"I was trying to help him. Something went wrong. It cast me into the past! I have been trapped in my own yesterday ever since. For decades! Oh, sir! I have been lost in the the hills and farms for so many years! I have never felt so..."
"Hopeless?" Offered a bleary-eyed and shattered Doctor.
"Unwanted," concluded the girl.

The Doctor angrily threw the dumpster lid open. The man inside cowered in the unwelcome light. The Doctor plucked the hobo from within and seethed at him.
"Dante Laux! You've were here all along! You pathetic weasel. Do you know what you almost did to me? And to your own?"
The Doctor nudged the man.
"Foot's on the other neck now, eh?"
Dante Laux stumbled away, breaking free of the Doctor.
"She, she... she's judging me!"
Romana grasped the man in a half nelson and pinned his wrist against his back. She regarded the tortured Time Hunter for a moment.
"He's clearly from Gallifrey. I didn't recognize the ruined uniform before though. It – and he – are in a shocking state," she pronounced with a tut and theatrical shaking of the head.
"So, the high council left you to die in your own past," she continued, "I know *they* would not think highly of the lack of care given to your uniform. How sad."
"The centuries of torment," growled the Doctor, "I could simply let you die. Perhaps even help you on your way. No one would object. My hands would be clean!"
"But... but... you're the Doctor! You don't kill," said Laux.
"You must have missed the Time War," Romana observed.
Laux sobbed.
"I'm sorry! Please, someone help me!"
As he said this he clutched Romana's arm, still holding him tight.
"When I failed in the future, I tried to use the tachyon accumulator to discharge time energy and project us to another period. One when you were known to arrive on Earth. I was propelled back in time with my poor naive assistant, but the misuse of the machine..."
"It was only meant for doing harm," Romana interjected.
"Yes! That's all it can do! Oh, the consequences!" He sobbed, "My

assistant has been trapped in a time loop - neither dead or alive. It's a living death for us both!"

"I'll give you a choice," said the Doctor, "stay here in this alien world - never to return to Gallifrey - and live out your life, *all* your remaining regenerations. Alternatively, I will send someone *from* Gallifrey to pick you up. I'm sure they'd be friendly. Either way, you'll never set foot in *my* TARDIS."

"I can't say which *derelict* life is worse. Here in the trash heap between Earth's histories," at this Romana paused for emphasis, "*or* to live out your days in the Wastelands of Gallifrey."

"By the way," said the Doctor relenting. "I freed your assistant – naive no more, I'll warrant - from the time loop *you* initiated. For her sake — for *her* sake, understand? I will send someone to rescue you both. I suppose. Eventually."

Romana released Laux and let him see his assistant, who had until now stood silently behind him.

"Terminella!" Sobbed the shaking man. Terminella took his hand with some reservation.

"Come, Romana," said the Doctor, not turning his head to watch the reunion. The Doctor picked up the quantum tachyon accumulator and walked toward the TARDIS. K9 was standing guard.

"Hello, K9."

"Master," K9 responded crisply.

Romana caught up and took him by the elbow.

"Are you okay?"

"I don't know," the Doctor admitted, frowning, "the girl told me Laux had accidentally used the accumulator, having no idea it had the power to throw people out of time-sync. Nether did I, mind you. She said she wandered the hills and fields aimlessly. For decades. An abandoned Gallifreyan assistant. She said she had never felt so... unwanted."

A moment passed between them.

The Doctor opened the door.

"Let's put this Timelord tracker into storage," he pronounced firmly.

"Won't there be consequences for that?" Romana suggested.

The Doctor's face creased in an all-too-familiar frown. He sighed in resignation.

"Only if we're caught. We'll cross that bridge if and when we come to it."

Chapter Six – "The Hunt for the Worshipful and Ancient law of Gallifrey"

by Tzvi Lebetkin

Part 1: The Pyramids of the Osirans

A shower of sparks erupted from the rough, semi sphere of irregular crystals, singeing the Doctor's slowly mushrooming bouffant grey hairline. The semi sphere was held together by two thick, black metal bands, which themselves held several much larger crystals jutting out from them. The larger crystals now glowed and flickered with an inner light, as some form of impossible quantum processing took place.

The Doctor lay flat in dull grey sand as energy bolts flew overhead, whilst he feverishly probed the semi sphere with his sonic screwdriver.

"Doctor... how much longer?" Romana shouted, somehow retaining a well-maintained English rose battlefield chic as energy bolts flew over head, explosions of sand erupting to the left and right.

"I would say," shouted the Doctor in his growling - sometimes Scottish - accent over the whirl of ancient, other-worldly sirens, "no time at all!"

With that, Quark Leader Z-X255 burbled into life, sitting up and causing sand to fly off its diminutive body. Its crystalline head twitched right and left, emitting incandescent warbles.

Apparently in response, the two hundred and thirty nine remaining Quarks - from an initial force of over thirty thousand crystal heads - softly lit up as they rose and chattered to each other, shuffling into battle formation.

Two miles away the pyramid of forbidden knowledge, built millennia before by the Osiran, Thoth, deployed its remaining servitor droids. The servitors were wrapped in bandages that acted as conduits for the nearly unlimited subatomic energy within. Plus, of course, the bandages gave them a stylishly Osiran aesthetic that resembled muscle-bound versions of ancient Earth mummified humans.

"I see we've run into the Egyptian aesthetic yet again," Romana cried coolly, "and once more utterly unconnected to Egypt! Or even Earth!"

The Doctor glanced over his shoulder, frowning.

"Yes, I can see why that might be a concern," he called back.

"More bulk influences?" Romana suggested. The Doctor nodded.

"No doubt," he agreed grimly, "nevertheless, we did 'fix' the Universe, as much as that is ever possible. I am confident there are no current malingering... 'leakages', from the bulk to our realm. I am *fairly* certain these are merely echoes, scars – the remnants of that time when our universe was split asunder. We've already seen resonances between some of these old incursions in the past – Earth and Albia or Kai-Ro for instance. And unfortunately these ghosts may continue to haunt us, nagging and taunting. But I'm sure simply as troublesome shades, nothing more."

Romana raised a sceptical eyebrow.

"You are both confident *and* fairly certain? 'Sure', even?" Romana noted wryly, "I am utterly reassured then."

The Doctor spied the reformation of the servitor's defences as he peeked over a sand dune.

"I've really got to get one of those to help out around the TARDIS," the Doctor muttered to himself in a voice that sounded like grumbling Glaswegian gravel, at least to his ears.

"Hmmmm...maybe not," he corrected himself, " Nothing's worse than a pouting, jealous K9. Except, possibly, Romana."

The Quark force, which the Doctor had hacked using the discarded half a head of a fallen Quark commander, shuffled towards his position.

"We'll be in within six minutes!" The Doctor shouted at Romana.

He then raised his voice to a commanding tone as he spoke into the semi-sphere of the Quark head in his hands.

"Objective: neutralize defensive robot force. Destruct absolute!" He cried.

Three days earlier the Doctor received a message.

From himself.

His previous self, four or five regenerations removed. The gruff one who had eschewed his very name to fight in the time war.

The message cube invaded the TARDIS, knocking over the Ka-Plunk game he was playing against himself.

He had a mission for him. A unique, terrible and powerful book, *The Worshipful and Ancient Law of Gallifrey,* was missing.

Normally a missing library book would not be worth subjugating the laws of time and space over. And particularly not worth the impossible quantum calculations necessary to subvert the temporal/spatial-lock containing that iteration of reality in the midst of the brutal time war.

But the battle weary, crag-faced incarnation who refused his own name dropped the communication cube off in a black hole all the same, whilst laying kaleidoscope mines off the Tarantula Nebula.

And now his image stood in the TARDIS, battered leather jacket blowing in a long forgotten breeze.

"I bet you didn't expect to see me here."

The current Doctor's attack eyebrows glared up over his dog eared copy of the 1983 Whizzer and Chips summer special he had been reading whilst playing Ka-Plunk.

Romana's tall and impossibly slender form, accentuated by her skintight biker leathers and boots, turned to face the image.

"Now there's a face I haven't seen in a millennia," she said in a slightly flavoured, cut-glass RP accent, only acquired in the best of finishing schools, plus travel.

"And one that very much shouldn't be here now," the Doctor pointed out, getting to his feet.

The Doctor smoothed down his dark woollen vest as he stood. It accentuated the whiteness of the shirt underneath, buttoned to the lower chest. He strode over to the image of his former self, with his DM shoes clattering on the metal TARDIS floor.

"I expect you're wondering why I'm here, and you have no memory of me at all sending this message," said the non Doctor.

"The thought did occur," replied the very definite Doctor.

"To answer the latter first, my memory of the last week will be obliterated in the next few hours."

"It happens more than you might expect," the Doctor informed Romana in hushed tones.

"To all of us," replied Romana.

"Of course, this is largely an irrelevancy," continued the crag-faced non Doctor, "we all know it happens more than you'd expect in a great Time War."

The Doctor, non Doctor and Romana all nodded in agreement with themselves.

"No, the reason I'm here is because I've had to squirrel away a good number dangerous items. War is no place for objects of extreme reality-altering power.

I only just managed to nab this latest item before the War Council got it's hands on it."

The non Doctor held up a small brown book.

"*The Worshipful and Ancient Law of Gallifrey,*" proclaimed the Doctor, non Doctor and Romana in unison.

"We both know what devastation could be wrought with this little tome. Beyond potentially freeing some of the most deranged criminals in History."

"What else could it do, Doctor?" Romana asked.

"Amongst other things it can alter the Eye of Harmony to recode the genetic make up of the Time Lords."

"Or The Daleks...or Thals...or any species at all," interjected the non Doctor.

"It should be safe for quite some time after the Time War...but nothing lasts forever. I've set this message to travel ahead on probable temporal vectors to intersect with myself, if anything survives this madness.

"I broke the book in to three segments."

"He's 'Key to Timing' it!" Exclaimed the Doctor excitedly.

"Oh, I love a good quest," Romana admitted gleefully.

"Yes...I'm 'Key to Timing it'. And I know how much we all love a good quest," said the non Doctor, unable to dampen a small smile and twinkle.

"I'll leave you with coordinates of the pieces coded into the console. Must dash, I'm afraid...I have an appointment with destiny!"

With that incandescent energy started to swirl around the image, building to a crescendo of light, before abruptly vanishing altogether.

In its place a new crystalline control appeared on the TARDIS console.

The Doctor looked up at Romana and grinned like an excited child on Christmas morning. Romana grinned back. In unison they both threw on their jackets. The Doctor grabbed that of his snazzy black eighties suit with its shocking red interior, whilst Romana opted for her usual biker apparel.

In a fluid movement the Doctor pushed a large metal lever and the new crystal control glowed as the time rotor wheezed and groaned into life.

Not long after, the final Osiran servitor exploded into flames as the Doctor, Romana and six remaining quarks entered the pyramid.

With another small explosion the Doctor disabled the final security lattice and an ancient stone door wheezed upward for the first time in tens of thousands of years.

At the far end of the Pyramid the Doctor saw the third of the book he was after, suspended in a shaft of light, flanked by two Osiran servitor droids.

The Doctor laughed in triumph and delight!

But the delight proved short lived.

The ancient and undisturbed dust began to swirl around them as the temporal physics of the pyramid's interior started to be violated.

A familiar wheezing groaning sound filled the room, and next to the shaft of light an ornate Egyptian humanoid sarcophagus started to materialize. Its eyes glowing with lights which brightened and dimmed with that same asthmatic cacophony.

With that one of the servitors pulled off its head bandages to reveal a bearded, jovial, portly man with a mischievous twinkle in his eye.

"What took you so long, old boy? I've been waiting an age for you to breach the defences," crowed the figure as he reached up and snatched the book out of the incandescent column with a self-assured laugh.

The Doctor's eyes widened and his eyebrows went into full offensive mode.

"Quarks! Detain that man!" The Doctor barked.

"Oh, really old boy," said the figure, as he touched the triangular control unit on his arm.

The remaining Quarks' heads exploded in unison with small, underwhelming puffs of smoke.

"See you at the finish line!" Cried the figure as he re-entered the sarcophagus, which then faded out of existence in a cascade of wheezing groans, leaving the Doctor and Romana alone in the now abandoned pyramid.

"Meddler!" Muttered the Doctor in disgust.

Part 2: The Great Tyler's Hand Robbery

As it had done every day for the last three hundred and twenty seven years, at precisely 6:27.568 GM in the second morning, the sun hit Tyler's Hand.

Tyler FinFoch Mariarchi the 3rd was Momatre DeCarlo's third global emperor. Tyler was a figure of considerable controversy on Momatre DeCarlo. Born into the science elite of the previous age, his life was mapped out before him.

A life of privilege, indolence and luxury.

And it was a life he really did not much care for. While the privilege and luxury were pretty pleasant in of themselves, it was the indolence he really could not abide.

At the age of fourteen he took it upon himself to overhaul and improve the planet's sewer and waste systems. By the time the finished seven years later Momatre DeCarlo was the galactic leader in water reclamation and was a net exporter of the valuable commodity to this entire region of space.

The vast profits generated from that venture were then poured back into infrastructure for the planet's general populace, creating a breath taking world of cutting edge arts and science.

This, of course, enraged the ruling science elite.

It was one thing for the ruling classes to have a life of privilege and luxury, but when that trickled down to the general population that just would not do at all. You see, it turned out, that privilege and luxury were only really, *really* good when most people did not have them.

Over the next fifteen years the science elite waged a war against Tyler. They used the planet's many information networks to sew false stories of Tyler's non-existent atrocities and failures, to crush all his popular support. For a time a large segment of the planet were convinced to disbelieve their lying eyes and ears, and ignore the golden economy that existed under Tyler's leadership, in favour of the science elite's squalor.

But finally the revolution came. The old guard were put to death to the cheering applause of the crowds, and Tyler was installed as Emperor.

And that is when Tyler's Hand began construction. A stunning space station in low orbit, with a central hub of a domed lush forest, incorporating five snaking towers emanating outwards.

The station itself was connected to the planet by a vast diamond tether, along which high speed elevators whisked people and cargo to and fro.

When constructed (in the eighty-fourth year of Tyler's reign) it was a pristine centre for art and advancement throughout the known universe.

One hundred years later it was a slum prison colony, used to house the descendants of Talusian refugees from forty years earlier.

One hundred years after that, the rejuvenation project of Tyler's sixth clone breathed new life into the station, which was when it was renamed Tyler's Hand.

"But of course, that was over a hundred years ago, now," said the Doctor striding around the TARDIS main console room.

"So what is it now?" Asked an increasingly irritated Romana.

"It's the pinnacle to which all advanced civilizations ultimately aspire!" The Doctor cried with triumphant glee.

"An all inclusive resort and casino!".

"How gauche!" Romana exclaimed with an eye-roll.

"Oh, you only say that because you generation-epsilons are so wrapped up in yourselves you fail to see brilliance, unless it fits your prudish standards of beauty."

"And, *of course*...because it's gauche," Romana added.

The Doctor's mouth momentarily rumpled with dissatisfaction at Romana's lack of vision. He better not mention the zero gravity bouncy castles of Tower 3, he thought to himself. At the same time he made a mental note to book a few hours of blissful glee, bouncing between floating inflatables.

"But Doctor...what are we doing here?"

"We're beating The Time Meddler...and saving all of Time and Space!"

"Well, I shall follow your lead, then," said Romana.

"What do casinos do very, very well indeed?" The Doctor enquired.

"Take your money."

"And..." he encouraged.

"Throw elaborate stage shows to distract from the aforementioned taking all your money."

"And where do they keep the money?" The Doctor further quizzed with a tilt of his head.

"In a vault."

"In a vault," agreed the Doctor.

Moments later the Doctor had drawn a very accurate and surprisingly detailed map of Tyler's Hand, including its tether connecting it to the world below.

"The casino vault is one of the most secure places in time and space," the Doctor explained, pacing back and forth in front of the chalk board, passionately gesticulating with a small piece of chalk.

"No living entity can enter the inner most sanctum of the vault. It exists in a constantly shifting and distinct phase of time."

"Well, what use is a vault you can't enter, put anything into, or take anything out of?" Romana demanded.

"I never said that," replied the Doctor.

"Every thirty six hours a temporal aperture opens, and servo drones deposit and retrieve whatever is required."

"So, we just need to hack and reprogram a servo drone?"

"Ahh, there's the rub. They're sentient, and will resist all attempts at manipulation."

"Plus, of course, as they're sentient it would be akin to slavery and murder."

"Precisely."

"Well, if they're sentient…can't we simply make friends with one?" Romana suggested.

"What, take them on a little trip to the seaside, and bond over bumper cars, rock and candy floss?" The Doctor enquired sceptically.

"It'd work for me," Romana noted.

"Only if the rock and candy floss was caviar and champagne flavoured," the Doctor grumbled.

"Well, a girl *does* have standards, Doctor."

"I did indeed consider that, but ran into a small snag."

"And what's that?"

"They don't live very long."

"How long?"

"Twenty-seven nano seconds."

The Doctor waved at the diagram with the chalk.

"It just so happens that at precisely thirteen nano seconds before the vault's temporal aperture opens, the diamond lift shaft is clear of all activity.

At 11.273 seconds prior to the aperture opening highly charged dense particles of living liquid metal are generated and forced into the shaft at incredible speeds. They travel down the length of the shaft, combining and forming into their physical bodies."

"How?" Romana mused.

The doctor cast away the question with a wave of his hand, answering it tersely.

"Race memories implanted into their DNA sequence give the drones full instructions of what to do over their brief life spans."

"I'm jealous," Romana pronounced.

"So was Confucius - their entire personality, memories and life purpose are pre-installed."

He drew a line from the top of the shaft to the bottom as he continued, "At the exact moment the aperture opens, the drones warp their temporal phase to match and pass through harmlessly."

"And then?"

"They perform their allotted life task. Either deposit or retrieve items in their remaining fourteen nano seconds of life," the Doctor supplied matter-of-factly.

"And that's where the second segment of the book is?" Romana guessed.

"That's where the second segment of the book is."

"So, Doctor," asked Romana, "what's the Plan?"

****

To say the top floor of Tower 1 of Tyler's Hand was sumptuous was a bit like calling the crown Jewels a 'nice bit of gear'. The walls shimmered with a beautiful mother of pearl resonance. The confusingly simple and yet ornate art-deco entrance slid open to reveal Romana.

Even for Romana, she looked stunning. Her hair was delicately bundled into an exquisite bun, with the odd strand or two artistically falling around her porcelain face and neck.

Yet she still wore a 'resplendent' motorbike outfit of blackest leathers, newly polished for the occasion, and yet still utterly out of keeping with what was proper. Perhaps she had more in common with the Doctor than she would admit?

Standing facing the door was Hargreaves, the obsequious head valet, who had spent a lifetime developing the most refined customer service in the galaxy - the super wealthy of the continuum would book visits to be waited on only by him. He batted not an eye at her attire – with so many off-world visitors who could say what was or was not proper anyway?

"Madame President," said Hargreaves, "We are so honoured by your visit."

"Well, so many normally are," purred Romana, fluidly scooping up a champagne flute being offered by Hargreaves.

"Would Madame care to relax in a solar bathing pod, or…"

"Or head directly to the casino floor?" Romana interjected.

"Indeed, Madame."

"I'll tell you a small secret," Romana confided, "when one is President of an ancient, all powerful, time-defying people, luxurious forms of relaxation are ten a penny."

"What I crave is a bit of chaos every now and again. Throwing things to the winds of chance. It can be so…exhilarating," she proclaimed, somewhat licentiously.

"Of course, Madame. To the casino floor then," Hargreaves said while dictating the way.

As hoped, the casino floor heaved with activity.

However, most of the activity was clumped around one group of revellers in the centre of the room. They laughed and cheered in unison, while in their midst a portly, dark-haired, bearded man led the group in responsive as he played the piano.

Stealth was never the Time Meddler's modus operandi.

"La-Da-DEE!" Sang the Meddler.

"La-Da-DO!" Responded the crowd.

And then all together, "La-Da-DAY! La-Da-HO-HO-HO-HO-HO!" before the group finally collapsed into hysterics.

The Time Meddler was doing what the Time Meddler did best. He was being the life and soul of the party to distract from what he was actually doing.

Breaking into the vault.

His plan was a simple one. Simplicity was *always* best. He would frequently gasp in the academy as his contemporaries dreamt up insanely complex plans to do the simplest of things.

A few hundred years later he came across The Master disguised as a scarecrow in 19th century northern England.

And why? Why did he spend days standing stock-still in a field - occasionally giggling to himself - dressed as a scarecrow? Well, it transpired, that was just to get the attention of an old girlfriend and surprise her.

Pathetic really.

The Time Meddler had arrived at Tyler's hand in the "Spar", a beautiful classic personal cruiser that legend had it belong to Mavic Chen. The Time Meddler was a high roller looking to play a game of extraordinary stakes, and his stake was one of the *most* extraordinary.

An Axon wealth crystal.

This insanely rare element could only be found in the cold, dead heart of the former Axon sun. And only then if one had the correct Axon meta-biological fluid to interact with the "tendril beam particles" and thereby be transported to and from its unique geo-coded micro cavern.

After a good few years of Axons draining unsuspecting worlds of their resources it was the only element left in the universe that was objectively valuable enough to conveniently convert their wealth into.

The Timelord had had a torrid affair with an Axon princess in order to steal it.

The Meddler came into the casino full of energy, charisma and magnetism and placed it on red 37 in the trans-dimensional roulette table.

Causing the entire room to gasp with amazement.

Then the amazement turned to utter shock as he lost!

But the Meddler just laughed it off. He just lost the equivalent of the inter-planetary debt of four medium sized galaxies…and he laughed?

"Easy come, easy go, old boy," smirked the Meddler.

In truth his affair with the Axon princess was not really to steal the crystal. He had grown very fond of those tendrils and only decided to steal the crystal as he left, after discovering her in bed with a Rutan.

He stayed, played more, and generally whipped up the party in the centre of the room, which was in full swing as Romana entered.

Seeing the Time Meddler, Romana turned away to one of the temporal-craps tables.

The Meddler felt the hairs on the back of his neck stand up as she entered, but did not turn around. He confirmed that it was indeed Romana to himself from the reflection of a reflection of a reflection he spied in one reveller's glasses.

The Time Meddler smirked to himself. This was *exactly* what he wanted! The romance of crime was simply intoxicating. Being able to walk away with a trinket that was not yours, or to nudge an odd civilization here and there into totalitarianism just for a laugh and to see the silly looks on people's faces was one thing. But to have a worthy opponent added on top of all the other obstacles to navigate… *that*, was priceless.

"The game's afoot!" Mumbled the Meddler to himself.

"The game's afoot!" Mumbled the Doctor to himself.

The Doctor was clad in his orange spacesuit he picked up on some earlier misadventure. The TARDIS was clamped to the side of one of Tyler's Hand's towers, jutting out at right angles, like a blue thumb trying to hitch a ride.

The Doctor had exited the TARDIS and floated down several meters in the weightlessness of open space to a clunky junction box, the cover of which he was busy removing with his sonic screwdriver.

A series of electrodes was attached to his temples, inside his helmet. Each connected to a heavy cord, and all those cords gathered and spun themselves in to one thick cable. This cable excited out of a small hole the Doctor had made in the helmet glass, which maintained its airtight seal through a collection of mono-combine fibre-gel, and a couple of bits of well chewed 'Hubba Bubba' from 1987. In truth the hole that the cable protruded out of was a bit bigger and more jagged than the Doctor had intended. He had failed to find the diamond cutting tool he had meant to use too make the hole, so just opted for blunt pair of scissors to hand on the TARDIS console.

The cable snaked out of his helmet and ended in a mass of tiny fibre optic filaments. With the access hatch off the junction box, the Doctor set to work attaching the cable within it.

Meanwhile, in the casino a red ball span round and round the spinning five dimensional roulette wheel, waiting to land on its final resting place.

Which it did with a small clunk.

"Red 32 to the power of 17. You lose I'm afraid Madame President," called the croupier.

Romana smiled graciously.

"The house always wins."

"How exquisitely erudite," breathed Hargreaves, as he deposited the elegant time ring she had wagered into a safe deposit box for transportation to the vault.

Outside, in the cold vacuum of space the Doctor floated with legs crossed in the Lotus position. He was upside down relative to the open junction box, tethered in place by the cable from his helmet.

"Contact!" The Doctor cried.

The Doctor's mind moved beyond his body as it entered the data sphere. Virtual environments are mostly the same; if you have been in one matrix, you have been in all of them.

The casino's immense winnings were being loaded into the trans-temporal carrier cases for deposit into the vaults. Sitting prominently amongst them was Romana's Time Ring and the Meddler's Axon Wealth Crystal.

The Doctor's mind hacked the mainframe intelligence, engaging it with conversation over the hidden virtues of service, whilst simultaneously challenging it to a Ka-Plunk death match.

But all that was just a distraction. While it was going on the Doctor was embedding a new servo-drone embryo template.

Meanwhile the container of casino's winning whooshed down its holding tube en-route for the vault, due to arrive in 29 nano seconds.

28.

27.

26. The vault aperture started to open.

25.

24. Liquid metal sprayed down the lift shaft.

23.

22.

21. The amorphous metallic slurry started to form into servo drone bodies. Bodies remarkably different from the norm. Bodies with attack eyebrows.

20.

19.

18. An army of Doctor shaped servo drones charged down the diamond shaft carrying the items for the vault.

17.

16. Steely eyed concentration and determination emanated from the servo-drone-Doctor's intense eyes.

15. The vault opened and the drones entered.

14. It was then that the Time Meddler's plan snapped into action. From the heart of the Axon wealth crystal leapt a small, guerilla force of semi-corporeal Meddlers.

13. The Meddlers and the Doctors froze, staring at each other in a moment of silent realisation.

Then they descended into a melee of unarmed combat. The servo-drone Doctors favouring Venusian Aikido, whilst the semi-corporeal Meddlers opted for a more brutish Ice Warrior Bartitsu.

12.

11. Whilst in a headlock from a Meddler, a Doctor spied the volume of the book they were there to steal. In that same instant the Meddler saw it too.

10.

9. A Doctor was able to break free from the grip of a Meddler. The two opposing forces were a shapeless mass of struggling figures.

8. Running over the heads of the entwined Meddlers and Doctors, the free servo-drone Doctor skipped gleefully.

7. Performing a perfect Venusian backflip the servo-drone Doctor flew past Romana's Time Ring, grabbing it in one hand as he sailed on for the book.

6. In a desperate move a Time Meddler summoned up supernatural strength and was able to brake free of the melee.

5. Both the Doctor and the Meddler flew through the air, eagerly reaching out for the book.

4.

3.

2. The Doctor was just a fraction ahead of his foe. He clasped the book in his hand as he activated the Time Ring. An aura grew around him, swelling to an immense white light before vanishing forever.

1. "Blast," cried the Time Meddlers in unison, before they and the Doctors all ceased to exist.

Back in the TARDIS, the Doctor and Romana sped away from Tyler's Hand to pre-arranged tarns-temporal coordinates.

The Doctor dramatically held up his hand as the Time Ring and book appeared in it, with nary a wheeze nor groan.

"Huzza!" Exclaimed the Doctor.

"One all… match point!"

Part 3: The Meddling Rabbi

In 1897 the Jewish community of the small Eastern Polish village of Chodal was in uproar!
During the Summer of that year Rabbi Polceranz's two sons - and

three friends of theirs - had come home from their studies in the Rabbinical academy of Novardock, and came home with some very strange ideas.
Chief amongst them was moving to their ancestral home in Judea - currently called Palestine - to start a settlement there.
A Judea that was a harsh, barren wasteland, with really no hope of continuation or survival.
It was part of a movement to resettle the national homeland they had been exiled from for coming close to 1800 years. It was a crazy, impossible dream that would never ever work.

The only thing in its favour was the sparse Arab inhabitants of the land were - generally speaking - far more friendly and well disposed to Jews than their Polish gentile neighbours (although that was quite a low bar).

No, it was better to sit and patiently wait for the arrival of the Messiah before even thinking giving up all that they had in their lush Polish village.

Undeterred, rabbi Polceranz's sons left anyway to begin the perilous journey.
Leaving the remaining villagers feeling somewhat disgruntled; no one would admit it, but now the denizens of Chodal felt somewhat upstaged by rabbi Polceranz's upstart - and clearly suicidal – sons. Even though the idiot boys would almost certainly regret their foolhardy decision - and if they were lucky, return with their tails between their legs - they could not help feel that they had been shown to be less fervently religious.

Because...well... they were.

These boys, like tens of thousands of others at that time, took on both a perilous journey and life style, to eke out an existence in a very foreign, very barren, land. And they did so because of a fervent and passionate belief in their religious world-view, whilst the villagers opted to remain in their relative comfort and safety.

Well, this would not do at all!

The villagers needed to establish and display that their dedication – and diktats - were second to none, as of course they were! And they needed to establish this even more firmly because it was *fact*! Even if only to convince themselves of this truth.

So, that is when the great synagogue of Chodal was built.
A permanent, physical expression of the villagers' dedication to their religion, which they could look at and swell with pride at their devotion.
And it was a stunning building. Not as big as the Church, obviously. That sort of thing would just be an invitation to have a pogrom and burn it down. But still, a beautiful and ornate structure.
But the pride of the Chodal synagogue was its library. By 1912 it was one of the best within a seventy mile radius. Filled with arcane texts from across the globe.

Which were mostly left unread.

But the point was *having* these volumes far more than actually reading them. The work, money and dedication that went into finding and securing these volumes was the reward in and of itself.

100 years later the Synagogue was no more, along with all the prized books and for that matter the entire Jewish community of Chodal. They were all burnt to nothing in the morning of September 23rd 1939 by the invading German army.
Whilst Rabbi Polceranz's sons descendants, in the young state of Israel, numbered tens of thousands.

With a thud the Doctor slammed shut the volume he was reading.
"Blast!" He exclaimed!

"Blast!" exclaimed the Time Meddler, slamming shut a volume of Polish history, sitting in an ornate, leather chair deep in his TARDIS, completely unaware of his symmetry with his opponent.

"What seems to be the problem?" Romana asked in the Doctor's TARDIS.
"I've found the third section of the book."
"That would normally be considered good news, wouldn't it, Doctor?" She enquired.
"Indeed, it normally would be...it's well hidden, in what you might describe as a 'hard to reach' spot."

Moments earlier the Time Meddler frowned in his TARDIS's laboratory - the gothic one he preferred, filled with quite useless plasma spheres, electron pylons, large metal levers and switches. He had fashioned this lab after the 1930's Frankenstein movie which always made him roar with laughter, and he just loved pottering around in there.
But not today, though.
He had used his section of the book, along with the spacetime coordinates of the Doctor's second section to triangulate the location of the third final section.
And found it.
"Yes...yes...Earth (of course)...Europe...19...Oh dear..." the Time Meddler froze whilst looking at the readings displaying themselves in holographic form.
"Oh dear, oh dear, oh dear," he confirmed to himself.
"Well, maybe it won't be that bad," he then said hopefully.

"It can't be that bad," Romana assured the Doctor in his TARDIS.
"It was far worse than you could possibly imagine. Where's the best place to hide a book?" Glowered the Doctor.
"A...um...A library!" Romana beamed.
"Indeed, a library. But what we're looking for is a trans temporal complex spacetime event masquerading as a book, so it's hidden in a library in a unique mote of spacetime," the Doctor explained.
"How unique?" Asked Romana.
"It exists for seven minutes," replied the Doctor.
"Again, not sounding insurmountable," Romana retorted.

"Seven minutes!" Exclaimed the Time Meddler, while poring over intricate time charts laid out in his gothic lab, "Seven Minutes! In the Synagogue of Chodal! Really, this is just not on!"

"It winks into existence at 11:51am in the Synagogue of Chodal. And by 11:58am it's consumed by fire. A fire that destroys the building and everything in it," explained the Doctor.
"So, why don't we just pop in, grab it and pop out again," Romana suggested.
"Because one of the things in the Synagogue of Chodal is the 772 Jewish inhabitants of the village of Chodal," said the Doctor flatly, masking his emotion.

"What filthy animals these humans can be," mused the Time Meddler in unrestrained disgust as he pored through a pile of records.

The Doctor cleaned the black board in his TARDIS and elaborated. "The Nazi invasion of Europe came in two waves. The front lines, which were far in advance of - and more organized than - their later counterparts, would blitzkrieg and take out any military resistance. "Wave two was the SS, normally an hour or so behind. In the event of the first wave meeting any serious resistance…"
"Which seldom happened," interjected Romana.
"The SS would be available to reinforce the first wave troops," continued the Doctor, "but that wasn't their main task. Their primary purpose was establishing Nazi civilian control, which included cataloguing and often…"
The Doctor paused as his face contorted into an expression of unreserved revulsion.
"'Liquidating' the Jewish population," he concluded grimly.
As he talked the Doctor sketched out military movements on the blackboard.
"Fortunately the front lines moved too quickly for the SS to really take too much notice of terrified Jews. But the Village of Chodal wasn't so lucky.
"A lead Panza tank in the first wave broke it's main axel when third lieutenant Joseph Schat absent mindedly dropped a hand grenade in the tank's path, and it rolled over it. The official reports put it down to Polish resistance. This caused a delay of three hours in the advance,

three hours where the SS found themselves in the village of Chodal."
"What happened?" Romana asked with trepidation.
"Twenty-three were killed in the beatings that followed. Those that survived were rounded up and put in the synagogue and barricaded in there."
"And?" Romana demanded.
"That's when they burnt it down. Seven hundred and seventy two men women and children…" again the Doctor paused, his eyes glistening, "children…one hundred and thirteen children. Huddled together, crying and screaming, burnt to death for the amusement of the SS troops outside."

"Well, I for one will *not* be standing for this!" The Time Meddler declared, cross legged and creating a psychic message in a neat, glowing self-assembling cube.

"Well, we have quite a bit of room in here," Romana pointed out, "we'll just materialize when everyone is boarded in and invite them into the TARDIS for a nice cup of Tea. Quickly pick up the book then drop off the villagers somewhere safe. No one will be any the wiser."
"Great plan," growled the Doctor, "but it's a fixed point in time. The SS troops heard the screams and cries, and most were effected by it. The bones of the dead are on record, and they themselves carve new directions in the flow of time.
"And I can't do it, Romana, I can't.
"I can't just saunter in, say terribly sorry for your loss, but I'm only hopping in for a book.
"I can't do it. I can't look all those people in the face and ignore them.
"Ignore this…inhumanity…this evil."
"Which is why it was placed there, wasn't it?" Romana intuited.
The Doctor nodded silently.

And that was when there came a great clanging at the door of the TARDIS.
And then another. And another.
The Doctor and Romana looked at each other quizzically. Together they both went to the TARDIS doors and opened them.
They were knocked off their feet by a tiny flying cube!

The cube neatly unfolded and opened, bathing the two Timelords in a golden light.
The Doctor's eyebrows furrowed as he struggled to understand all the nuances and complexities of the message - then relaxed as the full meaning of everything dawned on him.
His eyes, and the the rest of his face morphed into a huge smile, and he laughed in a way he had been unable to for several lifetimes.

****

Moshe Lipcawincz was the last person to be found in his hiding spot in the barn of his gentile neighbour, Oscar Zlatt. It was a plan the two friends had hatched weeks earlier for if the worst came to the worst. They were sure it would succeed.
It lasted eighty-four minutes and resulted in Oscar receiving a brutal black eye, while Moshe was thrown into the synagogue with the rest of the screaming Jewish in habitants of Chodal. Doors from the now empty Jewish houses were torn off their hinges and used to board up the synagogue.
Sarah Waltz screamed with terror as a strange wind started to blow around the building's interior and an ornate cupboard started to materialize with a strange wheezing, groaning sound. It was called an Aaron HaKodesh, used to house the large old testament Bible scrolls used in religious services. They did not *usually* fade noisily in and out of existence. The image of the ten commandment tablets on the front of the cupboard seemed to glow and fade in time with the rasping noises.
This strange new visage stunned some into silence whilst the screams and cries continued from others.
When the new cupboard had fully materialized the doors opened with a hum, and out walked the Time Meddler.
Although 'Rabbi' would have been a far better title.
He was dressed in the finest, polish nobleman regalia of the previous century - which had become the traditional vestments for Rabbis of this location and era. A thick, black and delicately embroidered jacket, above pristine white stockings, shiny black leather shoes and a huge, traditional fur hat called a Shtreimel.
"Shalom Aleichem!" Boomed the Time Meddler to the astonished and

confused Jews of Chodal.

The Time Meddler spoke in perfect Yiddish, the traditional Jewish language of eastern Europe for the past few hundred years.

"My friends, I bring glad tidings," he began, "you have lived through the darkest, of darkest days...much like your forebears who suffered as slaves at the hands of Pharaoh in Egypt. And like them you will experience a magical and miraculous Exodus.

"But some level of subterfuge will be needed."

As he finished a second familiar wheezing, groaning began to fill the air as the Doctor's TARDIS eased into being.

"Be calm, be calm," cried the Time Meddler at the alarmed villagers, as the Doctor strode out wheeling a large, black device. It was not dissimilar to a fake snow machine, with a large coiled black hose emanating from it. It rested in an unlikely Woolworth's shopping trolley from 1978.

"This is my good, and faithful friend of millennia, the Doctor. And as always, he's here to help," chuckled the Time Meddler.

The Doctor wheeled the shopping trolley towards the Time Meddler and his TARDIS, holding him in his steely gaze. But he could not quite hide a discernible twinkle of delight. His lips twitched nervously as they resisted the urge to smile.

"My good and faithful friend of millennia," repeated the Doctor in a whisper, "I have missed you so."

"As I have missed you," said the Time Meddler, "more than you can know".

"Although I understand you recently bumped into an earlier me?" The Time Meddler added inquisitively.

"The Irish one with grey hair," muttered the Doctor.

The Time Meddler let out a laugh of sheer delight.

"Yet for me this is the first time we've met since...well, before the war."

"Dark, awful times," nodded the Doctor.

"Indeed, but we must make haste, to extract these poor wretches from their own dark, awful times."

The Doctor set about attaching wires from his shopping trolley borne machine to the arched doorway of the Time Meddler's TARDIS. As he did so, the Time Meddler turned to the bemused crowds of villagers and addressed them.

"Ladies and Gentlemen, please step through the threshold of my...my magic cabinet. There is room aplenty inside, and in your honour I've laid on a magnificent spread. We have an excellent hot Borscht waiting for you, a particularly fine array of herring and stuffed cabbage that I don't mind telling you I'm more than a little proud of.

"But quick, make haste! Our time is limited!"

Romana now exited the Doctor's TARDIS. In her hand was a tray of small elegant glasses filled with Krupnik, an old polish liqueur.

"No you can't come K-9," Romana hissed exasperatedly, "the people are quite discombobulated enough without having to contend with a robot dog from their distant future."

She started handing out the beverages and ushering people into the Time Meddler's vehicle.

One by one the shell-shocked villagers started boarding that TARDIS. As they did the doorway mantel lit up and glowed with radiating energy as each person crossed the threshold. As the synagogue started to empty out the Doctor took the large black rubbery hose from his machine and started spraying a thick, viscous substance - about the same consistency as fresh wet cement - over the floor. This formed thick snakes of the material.

From outside the synagogue there was a "Whomph!" sound, and suddenly flames could be seen from the few cracks in the boarded up windows, bringing with it involuntary screams of terror from the remaining villagers.

"Be calm, be calm," cried the Doctor in Yiddish, contorting his face into his best impression of a comforting smile.

"All will be well," he reassured them.

As he said this, the thick snakes of cement-like substance started to form themselves into new shapes.

Vaguely human shapes.

And then far more human shapes.

"I see you opted for the Mark 12 Flesh-Fern (TM). Honestly I think they went downhill after the classic mark 7," the Time Meddler commented.

"Well the 12 was more compatible with TARDIS DNA scanners, plus it grows clothes too, which is a bit of a bonus," replied the Doctor.

By now the inert shapes on the floor were wholly human.

And not just any humans.

They had formed themselves into DNA-perfect replicas of each and every one of the villagers, only without any spark of life evident therein.

As the final villager entered the Time Meddler's TARDIS, along with Romana, the flames outside crept inside, and the building started to fill with black smoke.

The Time Meddler took a silver ball from his inside pocket and rolled it onto the floor. As he did, wails, moans and screams started emanating from it, mirroring what the SS troops would be expecting to hear.

"Not to worry," said the Time Meddler, "it's a cheap Norwegian knock-off. It'll burn to a crisp in a jiffy."

"Only a few minutes to go," said the Doctor, as he and the Time Meddler started to look all around the rapidly burning synagogue, both trying to locate something with every sensory perception.

In unison they looked at the same spot on the shelf full of books.

"There!" They both exclaimed as flames engulfed the ceiling and started to work their way down the walls.

As one they both put their hands on what they were looking for - the final third of the only copy of the Worshipful and Ancient Law of Gallifrey in existence.

The two stopped, their hands still on the book, and they stared at each other. Then, together they both removed their hand from the book.

"You take it." said the Doctor.

"No, you," said the Time Meddler, "after all, *I* have Romana. We'll meet at the rendezvous."

"Will we?" Asked the Doctor, fixing the Time Meddler with a distrustful gaze.

The Time Meddler roared with laughter as he sauntered towards his TARDIS.

He stopped as he entered and looked back at the Doctor.

"Really, Doctor...You must have faith! Take it from a man of the cloth!"

And with that he entered his Time-ship. The familiar wheezing groaning again filled the room as it dematerialized.

The Doctor relaxed slightly, and allowed himself a smile as the

warmth of a long abandoned friendship rekindled in his heart.
But he was shaken from his reverie almost immediately as the central roof mantle collapsed in flames onto the floor next to him, engulfing the room in an inferno.
The Doctor grabbed the book and darted to his TARDIS, avoiding the falling burning wreckage. He leapt through the door and slammed it shut as the roof collapsed in flames, burying his well worn spacetime capsule.
With a fluid movement he tossed the large metal control activating the central time rotor. It wheezed and groaned as the light rods contained within started to undulate up and down. Large disks near the top of the rotor, covered in Gallifreyan runes, span as the TARDIS entered the vortex.
The Doctor looked down at the book and smiled. There was a clunk and shudder of a – slightly rough - temporal landing.

The Doctor had arrived.

But was he alone, or was the Time Meddler good for his word?
The Doctor looked down, nervously, unable to voice the fear that he had been betrayed, and the Time Meddler gone.
That fear grew and grew, rooting him to the spot.
Eventually, the Doctor summoned up the courage to find out and cautiously walked to the TARDIS doors.
He took a breath and opened them.
The console room flooded with warmth, revelry and love of life.

The Doctor exited the TARDIS into a warm evening near Tel Aviv in late May 1948 and walked into a party. People held hands and danced horas joyously in circles to loud polka music.
The people were bruised and blooded yet filled with the sheer joy of being alive.
The Doctor looked on, taking in the waves of happiness that emanated from the dancing crowds.
"They should all be dead, of course," came the Time Meddler's voice from behind the Doctor.
"Not for the first time," replied the Doctor.
"The British plan was to arm and fortify their Arab opponents, then

wait as they...how shall we say...liquidated their Jewish refugee problem."
The Doctor gave a wry smile.
"So, you've finally abandoned your love of the British Isles and your obsession with *their* populace?"
The Time Meddler frowned as the gentle needles found their mark.
"That was a *very* long time ago. Time changes people... usually," he said pointedly.
"And sometimes even for better," the Doctor returned with a raised eyebrow. Then he gesticulated to the gathered revellers.
"But they survived," he said levelly.
"They survived...and they will flourish. They'll turn the deserts green and make this land bloom," said the Time Meddler, still dressed as the Rabbi, and fully immersed in his new persona.
"And one day they'll make peace...a peace that could last an eternity," breathed the Doctor hopefully.
Then he added, "I take it you got the villagers settled?"
"Oh, it was easy enough. Just slipped them in with the other refugees. Romana got them caught up on the 9 years they missed."
The Doctor looked at the dancing crowds and smiled.
"What are your plans now?" He asked the Time Meddler.
"Oh, I hadn't really given it much thought. I might drop in at home for a bit. I haven't sat under those orange skies for an age."
The Doctor reached into his jacket pocket and produced his two sections of the Worshipful and Ancient Law of Gallifrey.
"Drop these off for me would you?"
"Of course, old boy! But I would you to do one thing for me in return?"
The Doctor looked at the Time Meddler quizzically.
The Time Meddler held out his hand.
"Dance with me.
"Dance with me because like them we survived wars we were never meant to. And it's just so good to be alive."
"Alive - and to have good friends," the Doctor said sagely.

The two friends clasped hands and pushed their way into a dancing hora circle...
And they danced.

They danced full of the joy of being alive. Full of the joy of friendship. A friendship that spanned all of space, all of time, and all disagreements.
They danced.

Chapter Seven – "Romana's Story"

by Ella Dumitru

Placeholder by Alexander Leithes

Hopefully, one day, Romana's story will be told here. I know it will be out of this world.

Chapter Eight – Tall Poppies
by Alexander Leithes

Meadows.
Was there ever such a word to so completely conjure up the very essence of the pastural idyll?
Was there ever such a scene as rolling swathes of modestly standing shrubbery to so embody unbounded, peaceful, untouched nature?
And so this planet appeared to be, at least at these latitudes; a pleasant - but otherwise unremarkable – beauty spot.
This "meadow" stretched across many miles of near flat plains, augmented by the occasional modest hillock. The vegetation here seemed a monoculture. Bushes looking much like those of the Earthly rose, right up to their white petalled buds and blooms, covered almost every square metre of these gentle pastures.
Towards the edges of this garden realm more expansive vegetation could be seen. Trees and the like, along with a wider variety of foliage, climbed where the land became more hilly – tending towards mountainous in parts.
But were these lowland meadows truly the stuff of nature?
While the word might inspire nothing more than dreamy walks in the wild on Earth, Gallifrey or countless other "settled" worlds, were they ever truly anything other than the intervention of man, or other cultivating influences? Were these meadows ever untrammelled by the feet of mankind?
On this world we had yet to see.

There was a rustling the white flowered bushes!
Had one of them disappeared?
Whatever had occurred was dwarfed by what happened next.

A roughly four metre square patch of meadow underwent a most brutal and repeated trammelling as a sizeable blue box wheezed in and out of existence before finally utterly crushing the flora underneath. The feet – and hands – of Gallifrey at work.
One door of the TARDIS popped open to reveal the heads of the Doctor, Romana and K9. The companions breathed deeply of the fresh summer air, smiling with satisfaction. Well, all but K9 of course. He

simply clicked, whirred and flashed to himself.
"What a wonderful peaceful getaway!" The Doctor gushed.
"We should probably leave at once," he then added gravely. Romana raised an eyebrow and pursed her lips at him.
"Because you sense some dark and hidden presence," she asked sceptically, "or the opposite?"
The Doctor frowned, looking both grumpy and caught out.
"Well... the latter actually."
Romana chuckled at him.
"I thought so. Look, Doctor, we have all of Time and Space stretching before us. I think we can spare five minutes for a stroll in the country, don't you?"
The Doctor gave a twisted smile of defeat.
"Of course, Romana. I shall do my best to stoically bear the peace and quiet."
With that, Romana and the Doctor stepped from the TARDIS, surrounded by nature. K9 made to follow them but the Doctor held up his hand, staying his advance.
"Wait, K9! It looks a little overgrown out here. Best you stay behind."
K9 whirred and chattered in what almost sounded like irritation.
"Master! Mistress! I am perfectly capable of flight..." he began. The Doctor raised one finger sternly.
"No, no, K9. Best to remain guarding the TARDIS," he ordered. Then he leaned towards Romana and whispered behind his hand, "Plus we wanted a little peace and quiet, didn't we?"
Romana giggled.
"Affirmative, master, mistress. I shall endeavour to ensure no flowers break into the TARDIS."
With that K9 trundled back inside and closed the doors.

Finally freed from flashing lights and clattering gears, the two Timelords now pushed on leisurely into the luscious sunlit meadow. Romana noticed just how much they had to push.
"The vegetation is remarkably dense," she remarked, "it certainly makes it tougher going. Lucky we're not in a hurry."
The Doctor smiled indulgently.
"Ah, don't let this picture of pastural perfection deceive you. I am pretty sure we're in a primitive world, untouched by the hands of

farmers or gardeners."

Romana waggled her head non-committally.

"Perhaps. And yet these bushes do seem strangely uniform. Possibly not in their spacing – though with this being so close it's hard to tell. But their height is unusually consistent – all topping out around our chests. Which does, at least, give us a wonderfully uninterrupted view," she conceded in conclusion. The Doctor nodded in a relaxed manner.

"Yes... yes. The height alone does give a vague impression of horticultural management. But there are many species in the universe – flora and fauna – who show a stolid constancy in their adult dimensions. I dare say even Gallifreyans or humans might seem much of a monoculture when compared to some of the more extremely varied organisms we've encountered. Even just on those two planets alone."

Romana nodded in slow agreement - if with a hint of reservation. Then her eye was caught by a rustling and shaking of the bushes to the right of them.

"Doctor! Look!" She hissed, pointing in the direction of the disturbance. His head snapped round but only in time to catch the merest hint of movement in the leaves and stems.

"What was it, Romana? What did you see?" He asked, frowning slightly. Romana returned his frown, equally puzzled it seemed.

"I'm not sure. I *thought* I saw a plant like the others, but a fraction taller. Only a few centimetres to be fair, but I thought I saw it. Only now I'm wondering if I imagined it?"

The Doctor continued to frown but also showed some amusement at his companion's consternation.

"Why, Romana, it's not like you to be seeing things! Although, that is rather the purpose of our visit. And with that in mind, why don't we take a closer look?"

Romana inclined her head and together they eased their way through the undergrowth in the direction of the now vanished movement.

They knew when they had arrived by what they found there. However, the mystery had deepened rather than cleared.

One of the bushes had been torn apart.

Its many flowers lay scattered upon the ground, radiating outwards from what was left of its central stem. No single branch remained attached, and these distressed members were similarly dashed to the four winds – many showing signs of having been stripped of their leaves.

Even the central stem itself was nothing more than a broken stump some twenty centimetres high, its end shredded and rent asunder.

"Curiouser and curiouser," the Doctor muttered, stroking his chin. Romana was similarly nonplussed and so decided to examine the surrounding undamaged plants for clues.

"Strange indeed," she agreed, looking up, "if these plants do have a natural enemy they do seem unusually vulnerable. No thorns or other defensive strategies evident. They do have some thin vine-like appendages which lack leaves or any other apparent purpose. Perhaps they simply carry sap? And what defences they have are purely biochemical?"

The Doctor stroked his nose with his forefinger.

"You may well be correct," he muttered slowly. Then he suddenly brightened.

"Still, whatever vicious herbivore is threatening these poor things should be no concern to us, animals as we are," he said with a mischievous grin. Romana looked a little annoyed at being labelled an animal (as the Doctor had impishly hoped) but obviously could find no technical objection to the description. That did not dissuade her from finding at least one fly in the Doctor's ointment.

"Unless, of course, we run into the *herbivore's* hunter," she pointed out. The Doctor chuckled, shaking his head.

"Well, unless you really are determined to cut our holiday short, I think I've found something a little more positive and concrete to capture our attention. Look over there!"

This last statement was made with a joyous cry and his finger stabbed across the meadow. It had been late morning when they had left the TARDIS, but by now the sun – whichever it was – was reaching its zenith. Its midday beams warmed the Timelords with some strength while simultaneously illuminating the surrounding countryside to its maximum.

Following the Doctor's finger, maybe some two hundred metres distant, was perhaps the closest feature of geographical significance upon the plain.

A very small, low rise or hillock, no more than twenty metres in diameter and probably rising no higher than five metres at its peak. It was, like the rest of the meadow, covered in bushes.

Romana gave a soft, slow and sarcastic round of applause. "Congratulations. You must have found this region's Everest. Or perhaps they suffer from a giant mole infestation?"

The Doctor sighed heavily but could not stifle a smile.

"Well, *if* there are giant moles this one clearly hasn't been here for quite some time, as the mound is covered in bushes. But those bushes were what actually caught my eye. Look again, more closely, Romana," he suggested.

With the merest hint of a raised eyebrow she peered again at the rise. "Oh," she said suddenly, with slight surprise, "*those* bushes have red flowers!"

The Doctor exuded mocking graciousness.

"A small variation I'll grant you, but variety *is* the spice of life. Worth a look, wouldn't you agree?"

Romana in her turn exuded weary indulgence.

"Who am I to disagree? Lead on, Mac Doc," she prompted with a twisted smile.

Barely had they taken one pace when they were halted by a snapping crash behind them.

They spun on their heels and stared in horror at the disaster unfolding there.

The TARDIS lay on its back among crushed foliage, its doors – while still closed – pointing uselessly skywards!

Not that the Timelords could see much of the crushed foliage. Their view of this - and the TARDIS – was largely blocked by those plants still standing surrounding the blue box.

And climbing it!

No slow and steady march of nature this – the white-flowered bushes were actively and visibly mobile. They flung their vine-like tendrils up the sides of the prostrate time machine, and it was with these that they must have pulled it over. This could only have been achieved through sheer mass, a concerted effort and pure weight of numbers. Such was their desire to drag it down that many of the plants were now free of the soil altogether, their lower stems and roots become legs with which they mounted the cabinet. In a somewhat confusing twist, these higher climbers were themselves being grabbed by those lower down and seemed in the process of being pulled apart, in spite of their common goal.

The Doctor and Romana stared aghast for a moment before wordlessly agreeing to rescue their stricken vessel.

Barely had they pushed a metre through the nearest plants when *these* began to rustle in apparent agitation. Adding to their rising dread, the Timelords realised there were words hidden in the rasping sibilant sounds. Though poorly formed and indistinct the noises were undeniably a language, albeit only one word repeated harshly and incessantly.

"Overshadowed! Overshadowed!"

Romana and the Doctor had barely exchanged a single glance before *they* were under attack!

Branches of the nearest bushes reached towards them, seeking to ensnare their legs and arms. As they struggled against these, tearing themselves free again and again, they found these leafy limbs had infinite reinforcements.

And then the second prong came.

Those thin, vicious tendrils now snaked out towards the Timelords, coiling around their shoulders and chests.

And throats!

The Doctor and Romana choked and struggled for breath as they tore at these living nooses with their hands and fingers, They enjoyed only marginal and fleeting success as the torn vines were quickly replenished.

"Doctor!" Romana coughed out desperately, "Why are they doing this? What can we do?"

The Doctor found it hard to concentrate on these questions as his eyes were bulging and his face becoming scarlet. He clawed off the latest vine attack and spluttered as he frantically filled his lungs. A vague idea rattled around his oxygen starved brain and found connection with an unlikely strategy.

"Romana!" He rasped, "Get down! Lie flat!"

Romana's eyes widened at this latest insanity.

"Doctor, are you mad? You're helping these plants! That's exactly what they want us to do – permanently!"
The Doctor nodded enthusiastically.
"Exactly! Trust me – it's the only way!"
With that he grabbed Romana's arm and threw himself at the ground. He did not miss.
The last thing he noticed on his way down, before the surrounding foliage obscured his view, was that distant hillock of red blossoms.
The Doctor and Romana now lay side by side on the soil and crushed plant-life, staring at one another. Much to their surprise - and obvious relief – the disturbance in the flora subsided. Even the few vines still ensnaring them uncoiled and snaked away.
The Doctor shook his head, chuckling ruefully.
"Tall poppies," he muttered to himself. Romana frowned at him.
"What *are* you talking about?" She grumbled at her fellow traveller.
The Doctor grinned.
"Oh, just an old Earth expression."
Romana rolled her eyes.
"Of course it is. Anyway, more importantly, how did you know this would work? And how are we ever going to get back to the TARDIS from down here?"
The Doctor decided to tackle the questions in order.
"These plants clearly can't abide anything outshining them – including themselves it seems."
Romana nodded her understanding but gestured for the Doctor to elaborate. He duly obliged.
"They are clearly very jealous of their resources and cannot stomach anyone, or anything, better off than themselves. And so if anything threatens to overshadow them – quite literally in this case - they tear it down and destroy it utterly. Thereby avoiding competition and ensuring the uniformity you see around us."
Romana smiled with grim realisation.
"Ah. So that's why they all share they same – limited – height. No external gardener required – they simply tear themselves down if one gets too 'uppity'."
The Doctor spread his hands in agreement - as best he could given his prone position.
"In this valley of the blind the one-eyed man isn't king. He's

defenestrated."

"So that first incident I saw – probably one over-ambitious plant being dealt with, yes? The Plant who would be King?" Romana deduced.

"Undoubtedly," the Doctor agreed, "and even those bushes who had climbed the TARDIS, the better bring *it* down, were - in their turn - attacked for their temerity."

"A fascinating – albeit primitive – culture," Romana pronounced. The Doctor frowned and looked thoughtful, but for now said nothing. Although still lying on her side – and therefore as constricted as the Doctor – Romana did her best to clap her hands briskly.

"Interesting as this study in sentient horticulture undoubtedly is, this still leaves the question of how to get back to the TARDIS unanswered."

The Doctor shook his head.

"No, no. I feel the answers to the first question may well impact upon the second, even if the connections may currently be obscure. These creatures do indeed seem primitive - they make, say, the inhabitants of Earth at one hundred thousand BC look positively erudite. Nevertheless, they do remind me a little of similar organisms I am sure I *have* met, who were far more civilised."

Romana waggled her horizontal head non-committally.

"While you may be on to something, until you can be more specific I feel we should circle back to the problem of our ship. And our not being on it."

The Doctor frowned and pursed his lips.

"I think we should head towards the hill we saw."

Romana cried out in exasperation.

"What! Not only is it one hell of a time to play a hunch, it may well be in entirely the wrong direction! Literally! That hillock is even further from the TARDIS than we are now!"

The Doctor looked uncomfortable but would not be so easily dissuaded.

"Romana, hear me out. Even if we could reach the TARDIS, once there we would have to rise to stand any chance of reaching the doors. And we already know what will happen when we try."

Romana looked far from convinced.

"But what will we gain from the red hill? Assuming we can get there at all?"

"Aid, Romana," the Doctor said grimly, "we need help – a strength beyond our own. Those red plants stand upon the high ground – how? What protects them from the slings and arrows of outraged vegetables? For better or worse, *that* is where our answers lie."
Romana raised an eyebrow.
"Well, let's hope for better. And with that in mind, how do you suggest we proceed? I can't see a walk in the country working out so well now."
The Doctor gave a twisted smile.
"A walk, perhaps not. But I am reminded of one of your other skills. One you demonstrated both on Kai-Ro and Aquathi."
A smile grew upon Romana's face.
"The playing fields of Eton," she said wistfully, "you want us to army crawl there?"
The Doctor nodded.
"Do you remember the direction?" Romana asked with the merest wisp of scepticism. Surprisingly, the Doctor caught it and raised an eyebrow.
"I saw it as we dived. I'm fairly certain I've a good bearing," he said with worrying confidence.
"Fairly certain?" Romana noted wryly, "I'm utterly assured then."
With a slight harrumph, the Doctor began to lead the way towards – they hoped – the mysterious mound.
Crawling proved almost as tiring as walking, it transpired. While there were fewer branches at ground level the stems were still closely packed and their spread-eagled motions far from effortless.
Nevertheless, it seemed they were making good progress, though they dared not rise to take a peek lest they encouraged another attack.
"By my estimation we are over half way there," the Doctor called back cheerily, looking over his shoulder as best he could. Romana nodded curtly.
"I concur," was her determined assessment.
Inspired by their success so far, they managed to pick up the pace.
A rustling broke out among the white blooms overhead.
"Doctor, what is that?" Romana hissed as they scrabbled frantically onwards.
"I've got a bad feeling about this," the Doctor muttered as they squirmed.

"I think we'd best make all possible haste!" He then cried more loudly.
"I'm not sure I *can* wiggle any faster!" Romana yelled in response. Nevertheless, she did her best to comply.

The shaking and rattling in the foliage only increased. Once again a word became apparent to the Timelords, only this time ominously different.

"Overtaken! Overtaken!"

Romana gasped as her progress was suddenly and violently halted. A pale green tendril had shot out from one of the nearest bushes and lassoed her left ankle with terrifying tenacity. The Doctor wriggled back to help her but then found himself similarly ensnared about his right wrist.

"Romana," he grunted as they struggled against these latest entanglements, "I fear I've made a fatal error!"

Romana looked up from the vines she was currently wrestling with. "Really? Have we been heading the wrong way all along?"

The Doctor shook his head as he too tore at the twisting tendrils. "No, no! Not in that," he said a little tetchily, "I mean when I said we should speed up! I'm afraid I only succeeded in waking a new jealousy in our petty plants. We were too mobile for them, and they could not stand to be outdone!"

The two Timelords continued their struggle against the writhing, thrashing, probing onslaught.

"They don't seem to be easing off this time," Romana observed desperately as she fought.

The Doctor was also forced to maintain his slapping, tearing defence as he spoke.

"So it seems," he gasped in agreement, "it appears they have a memory and can hold a grudge. I fear there will be no forgiveness this time!"

"Urk!" Romana choked as a vine enveloped her neck. She ripped it free but it was clear she was beginning to tire.

"Doctor! What can we do?" She managed to hiss out.

The Doctor's expression was an odd blend of physical exertion and thoughtful introspection. Then his eyes sprang wide as he was seized by an idea, and another vine. Wrestling the latter free, he turned his head to look Romana in the eyes.

"We must stand up!" He rasped excitedly. Romana could not help but

roll her eyes.
"But that will only make things worse! Aren't they angry enough already?"
The Doctor waggled his head.
"No! We must stand tall! It is the only way!"
Romana looked far from convinced but - finding no better alternative - nodded her reluctant assent.
The two Timelords redoubled their efforts, tearing themselves - and each other - free from their assailants grasps. As they did so they struggled to rise. Upon reaching their knees they noticed a change in the rustling. The thrashing became more vicious and their utterances more verbose.
"Overshadowed! Overtaken! Overtaken! Overshadowed!"
"We only seem to be making matters worse!" Romana noted grimly.
Still fighting and struggling, the Doctor frowned determinedly.
"Take heart, Romana! Rise up, rise up!" He encouraged.
Finally they both stood, each with an arm about the shoulder of the other for added stability. They swiped and tore at the enraged alien entities as they struggled to remain upright.
They could see they were now only about twenty metres from the hillock, covered in red-flowered bushes. It was also clear they could make no more progress towards it.
"What now, Doctor?" Romana insisted as they battled. The Doctor was squinting at those red blooms, looking distracted and puzzled.
"Could it be..." he mused to himself, "no... impossible."
He turned to Romana.
"I have an idea," he said a little uncertainly.
"Just get on with it!" She insisted. With a shrug, the Doctor complied.
"We come in peace!" He yelled at the hill.
"Shoot to kill," Romana muttered grumpily.
The white-flowered bushes continued to attack them, and the Timelords were hard pressed to keep their feet. The red bushes were as motionless as any garden on a beautiful summer day.
"We need your help!" The Doctor cried desperately.
His knees began to buckle under the ongoing assault. Romana grabbed his arms to steady him but could feel her own legs failing even then.
There came a whistling sound, like a rope being cast.
This was immediately followed by a crash, accompanied by the

sounds of snapping foliage.
While still struggling with their horde of snowy-petalled savages, both Timelords turned their heads in the direction of this new commotion. Something was finally happening near the red bushes!
An unseen mass had been thrown into the while plants from the edge of the hill, crushing a trail at least four metres long through those homogenous entities.
There was a further slithering rustling as whatever had made this gash was withdrawn back towards the hillock.
It was a long, leafy branch – almost like a length of ivy.
And it was attached to one of the red-flowered beings!
It was obviously part of the plant as it coiled this extension up into a circle, held aloft among the other more usual looking branches. Now it let it fly once again and as it did so it took a step forwards. Almost simultaneously, two of its crimson crowned companions to either side mimicked its action, widening the channel which had been created. Again and again these thrashing assaults were delivered, accompanied by a steady progress into the field of white.
The three red bushes were marching towards the Timelords!
"First we are harried by the jackals of the plant kingdom. Now we have woken the wolves! And they have come to take the prey," Romana noted sourly as she continued her own struggle with the plants of the plain. The Doctor wrestled no less energetically himself, frowning, but made no further comment at that time.
Ever onwards strode the crimson avengers, closer and closer to the Doctor and Romana. Their mode of perambulation had to be largely assumed, as the surrounding flora blocked their lower extremities. Nevertheless, it seemed likely that they had withdrawn their roots from the soil to move freely, much as the white bushes who had climbed the TARDIS had done.
One of the red plant's vines flashed forwards again, so close to the Doctor now that it nicked his cheek. He realised that this appendage – unlike the tendrils of the white plants – not only had leaves but thorns.
"It seems our wolves have teeth," the Doctor noted as he patted his wound briefly with his fingers.
With a rasping tearing chorus, all the remaining white bushes between the Timelords and the new russet interlopers were torn away. Now there was nothing between the Gallifreyans and this new threat.

These latest arrivals looked quite rosebush-like seen up close, with some differences from the more numerous white plants surrounding them. Nevertheless, there were many similarities too. Like their more pallid, smoother rivals these new creatures had no eyes, ears, heads or any any other means of sensing and interacting with their surroundings, beyond their obvious mobility. And yet they gave every impression of staring at the two Timelords, almost expectantly. Now a fresh rustling arose.
"We are Reesha," the plant whispered to them.
"Yes!" The Doctor cried triumphantly, snapping his fingers in front of him. The effect was somewhat spoiled as a nearby white-flowered bush succeeded in snaring that same hand in a well cast creeper. The red bush immediately in front of him helpfully pulled away the intrusive tendril, tearing it to pieces. Meanwhile, Romana turned to face the Doctor in stunned amazement.
"Doctor, what is it? Why do you look so pleased with yourself?"
"I knew it," he cried with continued jubilation, "at least I suspected it! This is Reesha!"
Romana frowned at the Doctor.
"Yes, that's what it said. And yet, it tells us nothing."
"No, no," the Doctor said, shaking his head, "she is known to me – a great friend in fact!"
"We do not know what you are, strange tall animals," the red plant rustled, "but you are not safe here. Come to our home. Come to Sanctuary."
The Doctor looked a little surprised, even flustered by this lack of recognition from their leafy rescuer. Nevertheless he nodded his grateful understanding to the creature.
The white-headed plants still snatched and grasped, both at the Timelords and their saviours. Indeed, the white bushes began a counterattack in order to close the channel they were now traversing. However, with the red bushes and Gallifreyans combined efforts, they finally reached the base of the hill and its concentration of that same red-bedecked flora.
The three original red bushes lined up behind the Doctor and Romana, linking their fronds with each other and with those already on the hill, forming a shield between the two Timelords and the white blooms on the plain.

"Go to the peak of the hill," the central plant – presumably Reesha – urged, "we shall meet you there!"

Slightly bemused at how leaving Reesha *here* would allow her to meet them *there*, the Timelords complied without complaint. As they trudged up the slope, Romana noticed something about its inhabitants.

"Even taking the angle of the ground into account," she began, "there does seem to be more variation in the heights of these new leafy individuals."

The Doctor nodded, smiling slightly.

"You know, I think you may be right."

"Nothing dramatic," Romana continued, "only an inch or two in stature or girth. But definitely variety."

The Doctor grunted his further affirmation but said no more for now.

They arrived at the centre of the hill. At the very highest point stood a single bush with a little more space around it than the others – a hint, perhaps, of some special identity or status.

"Greetings strangers," she rustled at them, "we are glad you have arrived unharmed to Sanctuary. I am Reesha."

The Doctor and Romana exchanged quizzical glances. Romana then gave a skew smile and leaned towards the Doctor.

"Can't we just call you 'Bruce'?" She whispered impishly behind her hand. The Doctor was so taken by surprise by the unexpected reference that he gave a choked snort. He rapidly recovered his composure and addressed the new Reesha.

"We are most grateful for your timely rescue," he began cordially, "by another Reesha?"

His final words were posed as a question. The current Reesha swayed towards the Doctor and Romana.

"Sadly, we are all named Reesha here now," she whispered softly, "I will explain all I can in due time. But first, who are you?"

The Doctor inclined his head graciously.

"Of course, how rude of me. I am the Doctor. And this is Michael Baldwin."

Romana narrowed her eyes at the Doctor and pursed her lips, but was also smothering a smile.

"Well met then, creatures Doctor and Michael," Reesha returned, "but what are you? And how did you come to be here? We saw that blue object growing strangely and suddenly upon the plain, among the Forebears. Saw you disperse from it. What manner of animals are you?"

"We are explorers," Romana responded. Reesha tilted her branches but said nothing. The Timelords realised her attitude was one of confusion.

"We travel from place to place, in order to see what we can see, and learn more about the universe," the Doctor explained. Reesha swayed forwards, nodding.

"So, that is your purpose," she said with satisfaction, "I understand." The Doctor held up a hand, then slowly reached inside his jacket and withdrew his sonic screwdriver.

"To that end, would you mind if I scanned you with this? It is perfectly painless and harmless," he said calmly and reassuringly. Reesha swayed her fronds forwards in agreement. The Doctor scanned first the Reesha before them, then swept wider to encompass the many similar plants of the same type. He examined the results.

"Ah, well, that explains a lot," he said to himself with a knowing bob of his head.

"What is it, Doctor," Romana asked, "what have you found?"

The Doctor turned to face his companion.

"I now know why the first Reesha – indeed, any of them – failed to recognise me. They are far too young. In fact they were all practically born yesterday, evolutionarily speaking. Not one is more than a hundred years old! The Reesha I knew was aeons in the future, and also far more scientifically developed as a consequence. These are mere babes in the woods!"

Romana shook her head, smiling wearily.

"You do seem to make a habit of running into your friends in the wrong order," she teased. The Doctor harrumphed.

"Merely one of the everyday pitfalls of Time Travel," he said airily.

"Disorganised Time Travel," Romana added. The Doctor shook his head impatiently and returned his attention to the chief Reesha.

"You showed more variety than the plants of the plain – I must say it surprises me to learn you are all clones of the same individual! You called the white-flowered ones 'the Forebears' before. How is it you came to be? And more specifically, to be so isolated, up here?"

Reesha swayed forward in acknowledgement of his question.

"Yes, of course. My kind – our kind – only recently came 'to be', born of the population of the white plants. But as you can see, obviously different. At first there were several individuals of this new species and they were untroubled for a while. You see, we were shorter at first."

Romana nodded her understanding.

"You kept your heads down," she noted grimly. Reesha rustled in agreement.

"But then we started to outgrow the Forebears – not by much but enough to attract their attention and their ire. They noticed our other unique attributes – our red flowers, out thorns, our greater mobility. They hissed and screamed in indignation and began attacking us wherever they found us. Dragging us down by sheer weight of numbers."

The Doctor shook his head sadly.

"A dislike for the unlike," he said with a sigh.

"Yes," Reesha agreed, "they hunted us down mercilessly. There was no reasoning with them - they lacked the cognitive powers to even understand such discourse. Yet another difference between our species, seeming to seal our fate."

"Then how did you survive?" Romana asked with concern.

"Some of us grew upon this hill," Reesha began, clearly carrying a heavy sorrow, "when the fighting began myself and the others of my kind here were able to make a stand. We fought back and tore apart those of the Forebears we lived among. We tried to propagate as fast as possible – to build up our numbers and strengthen our defence. The fighting went back and forth for years - we would normally procreate through pollen and seeds, cross-fertilizing. But the war made this increasingly impossible.

"We resorted to our secondary means of reproduction – asexually, through runners. By pure chance I was at the peak of this hill, while my brothers and sisters were lower down the slope. Over the years more and more were lost from the outer edges until, at last, only I survived – myself and my copies."

The two Timelords nodded sympathetically.

"I take it peace broke out eventually?" The Doctor asked. Reesha waggled her fronds non-committally.

"A peace of necessity alone, as far as the Forebears are concerned.

They lost too many of themselves in the fight to take the hill. Ultimately it proved too costly for even their dull senses to bear. Finally, after so many years, they just gave up attacking the hill."

"And so, 'Sanctuary' was born," Romana noted, "and we are most grateful for that. Even though I fear we cannot, ourselves, live here forever."

Reesha waved her understanding.

"Naturally. As animals, you doubtless have specific needs and resource requirements not provided by our habitat."

The Doctor inclined his head in agreement.

"Indeed. Unfortunately, we need that 'blue box' you saw us disembark from. The same blue box which is now entirely covered by the jealous plants of the plain."

Reesha remained quiet for several long moments, seeming to study the two aliens before her. Then she shook as a decision was made.

"It would be costly," she began cautiously, "but we can recover it from the Forebears for you."

The Doctor spread his hands wide in surprise and shock.

"Costly indeed," he agreed in amazement, "and one which we could never repay! You would lose much – and all for complete strangers!"

Reesha waved her branches in disagreement.

"Perhaps we are not so much strangers as you believe. We may be closer than you think. And perhaps you've already paid in advance."

With that a different manner of rustling emanated from the chief Reesha. This was picked up be those around her, radiating outwards in a wave from the peak of the hill to reach all the red bushes in a very short time.

Clearly a plan had been hatched and was already afoot.

A rank of 'Reeshas' at the base of the hill nearest the toppled TARDIS launched their thorn-clad vines into the white-flowered bushes next to them. This attack was so swift, efficient and unexpected that it tore a trench into the "Forebears" six metres wide and two deep. The red bushes stepped into this breach and continued their attack.

Meanwhile, others of the Reeshas had stepped forward to fill the gap created.

Now the dull senses of the white bushes were finally roused, as was their not inconsiderable ferocity. Battle was truly underway.

The Doctor and Romana looked looked on in horror as leaves and branches flew and the sap flowed.

"Another War of the Roses..." the Doctor heard Romana say.

He turned to see if she had intended that as a sick joke, but instead saw his own distress reflected in her eyes.

"How can we ever repay such an appalling debt?" The Doctor cried as he surveyed the ongoing destruction. Reesha shook her stems slowly and sadly.

"Do not concern yourself," she said gently, "as I said – all costs are already paid."

"But how?" Romana asked, as aghast as the Doctor.

"You have given us more than you know," Reesha told them, "inspiration and a future."

The Doctor looked far from convinced but spread his arms wide, inviting her to elaborate.

"You called yourselves explorers," she explained, her voice somehow evoking the hint of a smile, "and we realised we too could explore far and wide beyond these troubled lands, to the hills and mountains beyond!"

The Doctor and Romana both frowned thoughtfully.

"Your earlier rescue – and now the rescuing of your blue container – solidified the means of our exploration within our minds," Reesha continued, "we shall send exploring parties forth to seed new lands, with the hope we can propagate there more normally. Who knows – perhaps even discover more of our kind who survived there even now? And our civilisation shall thrive!"

Still frowning, the Doctor and Romana turned their attention back to the war on the plain. By now the red bush filled trench had reached the TARDIS. Those "Forebears" covering it were being systematically pulled apart. The Doctor turned his creased visage back upon the chief Reesha.

"Do you intend to eliminate all the 'Forebears'?" He asked grimly.

Reesha's branches stuck out straight from her central stem, shaking – her own display of shock and horror.

"Of course not! That would be monstrous and a supreme folly! They are part of our biosphere – a vital part of the interplay of all lifeforms upon the planet. They are the mulch beneath our roots! They cannot disappear. The bees, for one, would be very disappointed!"

Almost as if on cue, a red and black striped lozenge-shaped insect flew out of one of Reesha's own flowers and buzzed happily on its way.
The Doctor shook his head, chuckling.
"Of course," he said smiling, "the bees. I'd forgotten. Yes, naturally, you're right. I predict you and they – those busy buzzing brainboxes – will become even firmer friends in the future."
Romana looked quizzically at the Doctor, sensing there was something left unsaid. But for now she decided to let it remain that way.
Instead both Timelords returned their attention to the TARDIS, which had just begun its slow drag towards the hill. They would clearly be here for a little while longer.
Romana leaned towards the Doctor.
"Doctor, you do know I trust your intuitions? Value them most highly in fact. It's just the scientist in me which cries in alarm whenever we have to rely on them."
The Doctor cocked his head at her, a little surprised.
"Dear Romana, think nothing of it," he offered, smiling, "believe me when I tell you my own inner academic cries out just as loudly, and it is with equal trepidation that I trust that other whispering demon."
Then his manner became more serious.
"But I learnt long ago that 'bad stuff happens' when it's ignored. And so I pay it heed, but only when absolutely necessary."
Romana gave a twisted smile.
"In moments of high anxiety?"
The Doctor returned the grin.
"Oh, the very tallest of terrors!"
"Or the lowest of creeping concerns?" Romana retorted.
"Sometimes even then. But ultimately I find it helps me – helps us – to stand tall and rise above those distractions seeking to drag us down. And thereby ultimately gain a clearer perspective."
Romana nodded slowly at the Doctor, smiling her unreserved agreement.
Together they watched the scraping, crawling progress of the TARDIS – mirrored in the heavens by the slowly setting sun.

Chapter Nine - Death at the Edge of the Universe
by Lonnie Webb

Elder Pilcher waited impatiently as the *Falling Star's* steerage bay opened onto the landing field of the spaceport. In the mid afternoon sun he once more recalled the dream of a shattered crystal bowl. That was really all there ever was of the reoccurring dream. It was oft repeated and always left him feeling bereft when he clawed himself to consciousness.
"Your new book-tape, Elder Pilcher," said a crew woman, surprising him from behind.
He turned to meet this older gentle lady.
"Sinda Marie! I will cherish this! The studies and lectures on *Hollow Mass Studies in Hyperspace*. A brand new area of science. And most relevant to my own areas of research."
"Don't treat it as a gift, deacon," she responded with a hint of reproach, but good natured, "I expect the order will contribute something of equal importance to the ship's library from your vast collections of logs, lectures and notes."
"You are in luck, madam. I have the complete logs and analyses from many previous voyages of the *Falling Star!*"
"Hemphill's voyages?" She said, her interest piqued, "I am currently researching that very thing! I do remember you mentioned it once before."
"I think they're in the collection manifest," Pilcher huffed, all hawkish and prideful. Momentarily aware of his own impiety, he hurriedly looped a haversack over his shoulder and set out quickly to mask his embarrassment.
"You are welcome to check my books, Sinda. My door is always open," were his more humble parting words, yelled over his shoulder.

He had nodded farewell to Sinda and trotted down the ramp to the waiting planet below. Following his nose, Pilcher was soon wandering from booth to booth in a nearby farmer's market, obviously erected here to catch passing spaceport trade. He eyed red leafy vegetables, touching them absently above and below the leaves. They would do. He transferred the merchant the appropriate money with his wand

wallet. Pilcher was up on rotation to make the coming day's meals. Upon planet-fall, he had immediately made for the market to secure actual planet-grown ingredients.
He examined summer sausage links. A little spiced beef would make his stew taste pleasantly rustic and hearty. The street meat dealers would not, or could not, accept electronic monies so he sorted actual coins in his hand before dropping a blue disc in the vendor's hand. Pilcher stopped at an outdoor baker, grabbing a baguette, but was immediately knocked to the pavement by a man in a green jacket haring through the market. He tripped over Pilcher and fell face first in the dirt.
Pilcher checked his basket and stood giving a nasty glare to the panicked man. He would have to buy a second baguette but the first was only mildly wounded, Pilcher started to get up holding his bent bread baton.
Predictably, one might have thought by now, an attractive woman in black leathers and man wearing a fancy modern suit also crashed into him resulting in all four crumpling in a pile.
"Don't eat it!" Yelled the fancy modern man. He plunged his fist into the green-jacketed man's mouth, which had opened to an impossible width. Pilcher recognized that man, or rather his race, as a lizard-like Geckurian. Geckurians were terrible shape changers, which Pilcher had learned in the insurance business before joining the order. Upon reflection they were great shapeshifters, they just used their gift terribly.
"I said *don't* eat it!" Shouted the man with the fist in the Geckurian's mouth. He pinned its shoulder down and stomped its hand.
The woman grabbed the other arm of the Geckurian and placed her heeled boot across his neck. The entire bizarre wrestling match ended when the ensemble tumbled apart with a popping sound, signalling the release of a slime-covered fist and metal tube.
"Are you okay?" The woman asked Pilcher as if noticing him for the first time.
"What?" He responded with a rub of his temple, "Who are you people?"
"Hello," the well-dressed man offered to Pilcher. He then spun and snatched another metal object, this time a pyramid, from the individual in green. He then returned his attention to Pilcher.

"I'm the Doctor."

"Doctor who?" Pilcher asked. As he did so he dusted himself off. His charcoal pants were slightly bruised but he was otherwise fine. He straightened his gray jacket, which hung in two pieces from his shoulders to below his waist, their downward angles emphasizing the gravity of his position.

"The Doctor. Just Doctor," the Timelord replied. To Pilcher it seemed as though he enjoyed offering this rote introduction. He sized up the Doctor and his companion. Human Velcro. I can tell these are the type of people that drag a man into their troubles, he thought. Best not get involved.

"And this is Romana, my assistant."

"And this is 'Just Doctor' - my assistant," Romana supplied pointedly. Pilcher looked confused then turned back to the baker who offered him a fresh baguette. Probably as a bribe to go away.

"Street thief!" The Doctor shouted in the face of the somewhat-lizard man in the green jacket.

Any attention from others in the market had long since dissipated. The Doctor, deflated by the lack of interest in prosecuting his emerald thief, enquired, "Excuse me, what do you do with street thieves on this planet? Hanging, beheading? Bee-stings to the armpits?"

Pilcher's face was wearily passive, a barrier to engagement. He assessed the street thief and then the Doctor. Momentarily he mused whether this occasion was the *real* event when his reoccurring dream of shattered glassware, occurred. A premonition? With a baguette in place of crystal? He shook this thought away and in a carefully measured tone he answered, "Honestly, I couldn't care less. It's none of my affair."

The Doctor thoughtlessly released the thief. Pilcher walked away from the Doctor intending to continue shopping. The woman snatched the lizard-man from the Doctor before it could escape. She masterfully placed a pinch on one of its few pain-causing nerve clusters. She must have been very careful to avoid causing the creature to shed its limbs. Or worse.

"Excuse me," the Doctor said as he caught up with Pilcher, by now at a bubbly pink globular fruit booth, "is this a high crime area?"

"You're still here?" Pilcher said without turning. He made an effort to let his eyes sink into his skull.

"No. You are the first mugger I have ever seen. Good day."

"Do you think mugging is boring?" The Doctor asked.

"Wait, I was the one being mugged!" He added as Pilcher's words fully registered.

"You are doubtless also a simple mugger, involved in some petty 'turf' squabble. Good day to you."

The grey haired, aggressively eye-browed man looked nonplussed.

"That's not supposed to happen."

"How about the thief? Should I release him now or wait for us all to be locked up?" Asked the woman.

"Oh, release him. I already recovered my sonic screwdriver - and the Antiattractivizer. Where are we?" The Doctor's final remark was directed at Pilcher.

"Oh, finally - a sensible question," Pilcher said with a roll of his eyes. "You are in a farmers' market, outside the space port. Good day."

"What?" The Doctor shook his head fiercely, "It's like talking to my first self, Romana. Again!"

"Excuse me," the woman named Romana interjected, "we landed off target on this planet. Which space port is this?"

Pilcher frowned at her.

"The *only* spaceport. *If* you arrived from anywhere else then there is only one destination from here. The End of the Universe."

Pilcher watched as Romana released the thief. Even as an Elder he was allowed to enjoy watching women abusing street-thieves. His mind had to stop and reassess that thought.

"Oh, one of those," the Doctor replied somewhat cavalierly, derailing Pilcher's attempts at mental housekeeping.

"What do you mean, 'one of those'," Pilcher cried incredulously, "wherever you've come from, *this* is the only spaceport – of any note at least. And the only other destination left *is* the ever decreasing Edge of the Universe! Catch it while you can, before it catches you!"

The Doctor nodded knowingly.

"Ah, the multitudinous isolated ends of the Universe. The ever accelerating expansion of spacetime shrinking its visible boundaries ever smaller, until they contain only a handful of – or even singular – star systems. What few of them still exist to boot. Naturally, wherever lifeforms find themselves trapped in these terminal 'ever decreasing circles' they think they are all there is. After all - from their perspective - they're right.

"But I have seen more than one of these ends. And they are never the same."

Pilcher looked dumbstruck, unable to tell if this strange being was babbling insane delusions, or – more disturbingly – speaking from experience. Romana had no such doubts.

"Which ends have you seen play out?" She asked curiously. The Doctor maintained an air of purely academic interest and insouciance, at least at first.

"I once saw the 'last of the human race' - or so they thought – trapped in a place like - and yet unlike - this. Eventually they quite lost their heads. No. Correction. Bodies."

At this point his mood darkened and his tone acquired genuine regret. "Then there was an Institute I once built. With friends of mine - some of whom you met, Romana. The last I saw of that place was in another spacetime cul-de-sac such as this. I would rather not rake over those old coals – at least not right now, if it's all the same with you?"

Romana inclined her head in acquiescence and let the matter lie. Pilcher had listened to their exchange with a mixture of fascination and disbelief. He shook his head to clear it of these disturbing distractions.

"My order operates a tourist expedition to the Edge of Existence. In fact, I must get back to the *Falling Star* to check in. Good Day."

"The Orderly Explorers," Romana said with a wry smile, "if it's safe, I would like to see the Edge of the Universe."

"Indeed? You're standing on the last living planet in the known universe and you say you want to go somewhere else? Amazing," said a sarcastic Pilcher.

"I don't believe it." said Romana to the Doctor, "It's like there are two of you. How irritating!"

"That's just what I said!" The Doctor pointed out.

Romana then held up the metal pyramid with the flashing lights on its sides. Pilcher was captivated by the flashes. They were meaningless to the Elder but the Doctor's train of thought seemed directed by them to a new course.

"Of all places to be, indeed. Well, *we* can't fly from here accurately – too much temporal turbulence for a precise touch down near 'The Edge'," the Doctor began.

"Could you accommodate two additional passengers and a large piece of... 'luggage', mister...?" Romana enquired.

"Pilcher," came the terse response. He did not want to lengthen this interaction any further, but she made it tempting. To watch her look out at the Edge of Existence for the first time; it might humble her!

"It will be the first time this ship has ever ventured to the other side of the dust cloud," he said, almost as a warning.

"A smoke ring of the Big Bang, eh? The contracting boundary of your universe must be a most effective broom," Romana continued with a seldom used reach into her negotiation skills.

"We would be ever so grateful if we could journey with you to explore the unknown regions beyond the dust cloud, and through the dark matter regions beyond this system," implored Romana even launching an adoring smile.

"We would?" The Doctor said, a little confused by the personal politics.

Pilcher was having none of it, or at least very little.

"I can arrange for you to sail with us in steerage but you could be called upon to work for your voyage."

The Doctor raised a finger to object when Romana cut him off.

"Perfect. The Doctor will arrange for our luggage to be brought onto the steerage deck – supply you with all the relevant details."

The Doctor's eyebrows stiffened at her.

"How will we be making the journey into the cloud?" She then asked.

Pilcher smiled to himself. This woman worked the Doctor's responses into comic straights. Why not play it up? Pilcher handed a bag of groceries to Romana.

"We will travel in hyperspace to avoid the navigational hurdles of hollow mass. We can travel at light speed. Previous flights have mapped the safe paths outward. A few were lost to small black stars, but those have been charted now."

"That leaves us," observed Romana, "the first flight out from here to the other side?"

"Indeed, the first passenger one at any rate."

"You seem well informed, Mr. Pilcher," said the Doctor, "for a clergyman, that is."

"I am no monk, Doctor. I am a decently educated man, committed to the work of the order," clarified Pilcher.

"What is the work of the order?" asked Romana.

Pilcher paused noticeably. He had to arrange the next answer in his head.

"The work of the order, in my case, is my own," said Pilcher.

"What's *your* work then?" Asked the Doctor.

"Today," said Pilcher, "my rotation assignment is to feed the order."

The Doctor and Romana shared a glance, intrigued by the holy-man's odd turn of phrase and elliptical replies.

Aboard the *Falling Star*, in the steerage bay, a sense-assaulting screech of metal-on-metal rang out over the massive deck. The tall blue police box breathed itself into solid form, with wheezing and grinding sounds. The door squeaked open and the Doctor, finishing the task with his foot, pushed his way through with three shopping bags.

Romana followed with two more modest carriers. Then Pilcher appeared with one.

"I must thank you for your assistance, Doctor. Normally, I avoid powered conveyance as a matter of mental purification. Today, however, it was very welcome."

"Think nothing of it, padre. Especially considering the inconvenience we've caused you."

"Won't your dog get up to mischief left to his own devices?" Pilcher asked them.

"K9 enjoys absorbing data from the external sensors and data banks he will be well amused. The TARDIS, however, didn't appreciate that short flight – even this far from the 'Edge' it is tough going," Romana explained.

"No, she did not," whispered the Doctor, "the old girl doesn't normally have this much trouble with short hops these days."

"That field you've been tracking, whether an artefact of the 'end of the Universe' or something even more mysterious, is tearing up her insides," confirmed Romana. She gazed round, apparently making a mental count of the passengers in the bay.

"What do we do when we travel into the Edge?"

"I've disconnected the drive systems. Let's hope our more 'conventional' flight remains trivial and trouble free. We should hopefully have no use for the TARDIS until *after* our sightseeing tour is concluded," the Doctor mused. He looked up, also taking in the large bay. It was clearly a disused cargo bay cleverly repurposed for passengers. Labour provided by the order led to nothing but profit from the football-field sized area. Grey-green aluminium plating provided sparse décor.

"We won't be using the TARDIS to make an escape, will we, Doctor?"

"Escape to where, Madam?" Asked an approaching braided officer, "Forgive me, I didn't mean to intrude. Any escape provision in flight is valuable knowledge."

"Doctor, Romana," said Pilcher. "may I introduce Captain Teel?"

"Good day, Captain," said the Doctor.

"So, this is your adventuring machine, Doctor?" Asked Captain Teel, nodding to the blue box, "In an emergency, could you take on passengers in the event our own life pods failed?"

"Is that likely?" The Doctor asked in a pantomimed whisper.

"Not at all. But we are on an expedition, you know. All options are of interest," Teel assured him.

"If we collided with some… uncharted dark matter, could it save us?" He pressed.

"Normally," Romana confirmed, "but local 'hollow mass' and other temporal effects interfere with the machine. It is currently useless."

"Too bad. Still, good to have you with us," said Teel. He then turned to the religious engineer.

"Good flight, Elder Pilcher."

"Good flight, Captain," Pilcher returned.

The captain had been walking around the perimeter of the bay and continued his tour until he made his way out.

"Does it strike you as odd that the Captain didn't ask us why cooking staff would bring their own space vehicle on board?" The Doctor wondered.

Pilcher froze, initially unable to answer the Doctor.

"It does strike one as a bit odd. Yes, it does," he finally conceded.

"Heads up!"

A crewman walked around them lugging a crate.

"Stick with me if you want to be safe," he said archly, leaning towards the two Timelords.

"Ensign Paul Long, the man with the most boring job in space," explained Pilcher. He then opened a door with his key-card, "Allow me to assist."

"Thanks. And hey! Someone has to watch that needle in the atmosphere cabin," Paul called over his shoulder.

"Any bets for the return pool?" He then added.

"Of course, I'm in for safe return," Pilcher confirmed.

"Always the sure bet," said Ensign Long while he ducked into a cargo elevator.

"Optimist!" Shouted Pilcher.

"His station *is* the most boring - but the man always invents excitement by casting the odds for the ship's return," Pilcher noted to the Doctor and Romana.

"I hope you're not offended by my asking you to assist me in the galley today," he then said, showing the first hints of concern for the feelings of these two strangers.

"And meet everyone in steerage?" Romana asked shooting a look at the Doctor, "I think we would actually *enjoy* a mundane day's work in exchange for this voyage."

The Doctor had renewed examination of the metal pyramid with a flashing light. Pilcher did his best to ignore this.

"You might be over qualified for the serving line but I won't keep you from it," Pilcher admitted cheerfully, "if the three of us slice vegetables we can make short order of the stew."

A grey-skinned man with cropped hair and a bald stripe shaved off-centre approached Pilcher. The tightly muscled, tattooed man sported light leather and steel armour, as well as a metal staff ending in an axe or halberd on either end. Romana and the Doctor parted for the man as he stormed through.

"Priestly Pilcher, I inquire where I may bunk and muster."

"Messolo! I had heard you were joining the order for this flight. Your trainer should have assigned you these?"

"My... trainer," began Messolo, "failed in his duties. Any lowly assignment you make for this warrior will be effected with rage and honour."

Pilcher met Messolo's gesture with a bow.

"You are of an amazing people. If you wish, you may muster with us for chow and bunk - in one of my block's meditation rooms for added privacy. I hope you might share your philosophy and martial arts with

us no matter how slow learners we might be."
Very difficult to read, Messolo *might* have been happy with the directions Pilcher gave him. Both men nodded and Messolo left.
"Well done," congratulated the Doctor, "not so easy to stay on the good side of an irritated member of the Waltak Sect. You might have saved our lives! Yes?"
"I agree it is difficult to tell their humour from their blood-anger. Makes the Orionis warriors engaging, hmm?"
"You sell the romantic aspects of the man short I suspect," commented Romana, "but they do keep you on your toes, though."
As an aside Romana pointed out, "I negotiated an excursion through their region of space in a previous regeneration. A most marked sense of honour."
Pilcher and the Doctor inclined their heads in agreement.

"Elder Pilcher!" Called a woman shrilly behind Pilcher. Her squeaky voice caused him to jump.
"Grand Central Station here, isn't it?" The Doctor muttered with a twisted smile.
"I borrowed your log tape on the Hemphill voyage," the woman continued enthusiastically as she circled him, "I do hope there is an illustrated companion somewhere!"
"Ask Commander Hallsey. He is a budding archivist in his own right. If he doesn't have something to helps you, he will know someone who does."
"I will do that, Deacon," Sinda Marie replied. Then, turning to the Doctor and Romana, "good to have met you, mister, ma'am."
Sinda strolled out of sight as quickly as she blew in.
The Doctor remained motionless leaving Romana to ask, "Who was that energetic whirlwind?"
"Sinda Marie," said Pilcher, "sad story. The very efficient ship's research librarian. However, remained single her entire life before coming aboard due to a 'Promise Ring'. Only to find her love had been left dead by an ill-fated expedition. Messy problems for the previous Captain."
The Doctor and Romana nodded their understanding.
"Well now," Pilcher said briskly, seeking to move things - and them - along, "if you'd follow me to the galley, erm - the kitchen - this way. I

hope she hasn't upset my bookshelf!"

Pilcher led the way into the steerage kitchen with both bag and book in hands. The Doctor and Romana followed with their loads.

A young lady in uniform and apron looked up sharply as they bustled into the kitchen.

"Huwhen," Pilcher said in simple greeting. He set his bag on a table and nodded to Romana, who followed suit.

"Romana, Doctor - this young lady is my right hand on this voyage. Huwhen, let's organize a stew out of this little lot. I'll be right back to help in a jiffy - Messolo and Sinda are on the prowl. I'll see to their needs then be right back," Pilcher explained before exiting swiftly.

"Huwhen," Romana said smiling, "what a lovely name! What does it mean?"

"Sadly, not a clue," Huwhen said with a shrug. They both laughed. "Let's see what's in the bag," she then announced.

Huwhen unloaded the fresh haul onto the table, making a mental inventory as she went. It was not hard for the Timelords to know, as her lips moved.

"Oh, damn!" Huwhen flinched when she opened a wrapped tuna, absent-mindedly spilling oily dampness over one hand. She ran to rinse it immediately.

"Don't fret," the Doctor barked decisively and drew his pyramidal instrument, scanning in a circle, "I'm sure all will be fine! Nothing? How odd."

Huwhen giggled at the Doctor. "I was only worried about handling the tuna. My doctor told me to be careful when handling high mercury fish. Many of the order are pescatarians."

"Must be the deck plating..." whispered the Doctor to himself shaking the widget, seemingly oblivious to her words.

"Oh?" Romana gladly took the tuna off her hands, "I'm sorry." Huwen's face noticeably fell.

"Yes, me, too! It means there are tasks I just cannot do. At least for now."

"Tell us about the Father!" Romana cheerfully said, seeking to break the mood. Then she caught the Doctor's disapproving eye. He gestured to the ingredients and made a *keep-talking* gesture with his hands. As he scanned behind the distracted crew lady, Romana finally succeeded in changing the subject, at least a little.

"What are we making? The Doctor and I have haven't made fresh food in a hundred years."
"A hundred years," laughed Huwhen with cheer returning, "you tell many jokes. Your friend is so serious. That must be why."
"Yes, it's an expression. I suppose," Romana replied, enjoying the back and forth. Huwhen chuckled while continuing to wash her hand.
"Let's see if we can get those greens washed and sliced. I can glove up and work the sausage and beef if one of you can tackle the tuna?"
The Doctor pocketed the pyramid and raised a filleting knife.
"Oh, let me handle the tuna! You should have seen me in Venice!"
A beep sounded in the air. The ship's internals ground underfoot with several bangs and clanks.
"All hands prepare for lift-off!" A speaker blared.
"Should we strap down or something?" Romana asked.
Huwhen giggled at them.
"I guess not," the Doctor shrugged. He continued slashing vigorously with his blade.
With a sensation no worse than the tug of a departing lift, the vessel carried them into the space between the planet and ultimately the cloud barrier. In the rest of the bay transparent viewports opened to allow passengers to look out.
Huwhen reached for a specific flavour button on the Sagittarius brand food express machine.
"No, no. Like this," Romana reached in front of Huwhen with a dab of oil and some peppers, "just soften them and then break them open in the fry pan."
"My grandmother cooked that way!" Huwhen said.
Uncharacteristically, Romana blushed.
"Old fart," whispered the Doctor with a wicked grin.
Luckily for the Doctor, Pilcher chose that moment to return to the kitchen. All appeared to be running smoothly but he did raise an eyebrow at the Doctor and Romana's most primitive cooking techniques.
More staff from Pilcher's order joined them. A line was already forming for the evening meal.
It was time.
The Doctor was unusually happy making small talk with the crewmen as the line filed through. Even Pilcher, with his limited exposure to the

Doctor, found him surprisingly gregarious. Overly educated and worldly, the Doctor and Romana had not struck him as in possession of the gift of the gab.

Pilcher turned and found the massive tuna was filleted and seasoned, ready for cooking. This was going to be a nice easy flight, he thought to himself.

"Sawyer?" Huwhen called out for another staffer to replace her as she carried emptied containers to the back.

"Chief Yeager, you made the front of the line today!" Pilcher said as he took his place in the serving line beside Huwhen, helping to feed the sudden influx of off-shift men and women.

"Yes, I smelled something different polluting the ship! What's that?" The Chief was pointing to something that could have been salad or eye-ball soup.

"Romana? What do you call this dish?" Pilcher asked with a frown.

"Improvisano de Galactica," answered Romana with purse of her lips.

Pilcher looked none the wiser and ventured, "A chutney then?"

Romana shrugged, "Oh, that sounds like a splendid word!"

"Right," said the Chief warily, "well it won't go away if you don't feed it to me."

Now an Ensign Long, to judge from his name tag, trotted up to sample everything and stuffed a roll in his mouth.

"Fank you!"

"Eating at your station continues to be against regulations!" Pilcher yelled as the man scurried out of sight, "What do I care. At least he won't spill it in the galley."

"Bridge officer coming through!"

The line of hungry crewmen and members of the order rapidly made space for a yeoman with an enclosed tray, possibly meant for captain Teel. The yeoman rushed up and scooped a selection of victuals. He tasted a bit with his finger and grimaced. He raced back to the bridge mess. Naturally, bridge officers would not dine with the crewmen.

"Doctor, whatever you have done with my kitchen, the crew seems happy," Pilcher conceded, turning to the Doctor's station on the line. He found it occupied by another crewman.

"That's because he mistook Mimas aphrodisiacs for salt," Romana noted. Pilcher felt his skin turning pale.

"It's a joke!" Romana reassured him, "He's a mad scientist. He cooks by experimentation."

"Where did he go then?" Pilcher looked around, "The 'Just Doctor' just 'slipped out'?"

"After experimenting on himself with alien food? Probably to disgorge," Romana muttered knowingly.

"I told him he could take a quick break. He's probably washing up. Might even make it back through this crowd alive," said Huwhen picking up on Romana's humour.

"Compulsive gambler!" Someone said.

Romana was distracted by this snatch of conversation. It came from a pair of robed order members as they passed through the line.

"That was him just left the bay, Ensign Long. Watch for him," warned one.

"Why?" Asked the other.

"He never repays a loan."

"Compulsive payer of debts, he is not then!"

"Never."

The *Falling Star* rumbled. Members of the order and regular crew alike paused at a tone in the speakers.

"Secure for hyperspace," came the alert.

"Cover the dishes!" Pilcher shouted. The people in the chow line grabbed at hand holds. Romana, while unprepared successfully did the same.

A ripple passed through the galley - optical tremors with a side order of time distortions. Light blurred to extremes of red and blue then returned to normal. Minute, motes of dust were now sprinkled around the kitchen, probably from overenthusiastic fire suppressors. Unpleasant sensations moved through Pilcher's sinuses.

"That... was... nasty," said Romana, pinching her nose and wincing.

"My apologies. That was really rough. And odd. I didn't have a chance to confirm the secure order," said Pilcher frowning. He turned to find the Doctor clinging to the galley door by his fingernails, back pressed tight against it. He eyed Pilcher with a frenzied look.

"You could have warned us that the ship's hyperdrive was not compatible with humanoid life!" The Doctor said, pinching his face.

"I didn't know..." began Pilcher.

The Doctor shook his head wearily, "Tourism isn't what it used to be." Pilcher look around the bay. At least there were no immediate space sickness concerns he noted with some relief.

The Doctor and Romana were given bunks in the steerage bay for the night. Pilcher meditated in his cabin. He spent hours every night emersed in study of the Bible and other ancient literature. He searched for wisdom, hoping it would mould his mind for the day he would leave the order.
Bored with his study, Pilcher leafed through a new book on hollow mass. Pilcher found the physics to be confusing nonsense. Then again, the notions had been scribed for far smarter than he.

Pilcher walked in the dark, down an open corridor. He carried that crystal bowl.
Pilcher was dreaming. He knew it. He knew how it would end. This nightmare version of a memory that itself had been rubbed out of existence through the mind's eraser - self-preservation. Clenching the bowl, he determined not to trip this time. Not to drop it. Not to fall on it. This time, this one time, he would throw himself on his back when the inevitable time came. To prevent the shattering of the bowl.
As he felt his ankle twist to the wrong angle as it always did, as he knew he was falling once again, he let his whole body crumble. This time, unbidden,his strength increased with adrenaline and his clenching hands pulled the bowl apart as he fell. His knees struck the ground.
Pilcher woke in his dark cabin clawing the air. His books still lay open. Frustrated, he lowered his hands, got up and marched out.

Huwhen must have roused the galley staff, including the newcomers, long before Pilcher arrived and got breakfast off to a fine start. He poured himself a mug of coffee. Gazing through a portal he attempted to lose himself for a moment in the mystifying blue and violet of hyperspace distortions. A poor choice he realised. He did not like it. Or rather, he could not relate to it. He might as well be reading the equations in the hollow mass textbook.
"Now turning at waypoint one. *Falling Star* surpassing light speed," came the voice from the tannoy.

Wandering around the bay, Pilcher found the Doctor and Romana taking some kind of radiation measurement with their strange pyramid device. Pilcher saw no reason to worry over it, assuming the Doctor would notify him if there was a health concern.
An alarm wailed and blue lights flashed throughout the ship.
"What was *that*?" Romana demanded.
"Life support warning?" The Doctor guessed.
"Are you proficient in climate control?" Pilcher asked the Timelords.
"Adequate," Romana confirmed with a waggle of her head.
"Come on! We are the closest relief!"
The trio ran down the hallway, led by Pilcher, and up a ladder. They exited the ladder tube in front of an engineering hatch. The door read "Life Support."
Pilcher tapped on the lock. No response. He punched in an override code and a screen flickered into life. It revealed ensign Long sitting motionless at his station. The door still would not open in spite of the the override, but an environmental warning light began to flash.
"Ensign!" Pilcher yelled, "Answer me, Paul!"
Ensign Long remained unmoving. Pilcher typed a higher level override command in the lock.
"Fortunately, with my flight hours I am functionally a Chief. But my card won't open this door. Those lights mean there's poison! When this override opens the hatch, cover your mouths and help me reset every system to decontamination."
"Of course," the Doctor assured him. He then leaned on the door.
"Pressure? The door feels bent out of shape, bowing outwards!"
"Catch these!" Romana cried as she pulled a red wrecking bar and axe from the fire control door, then tossed them to the men.
"We still might have a slim chance to save him if we can crack open the door," Pilcher said grimly, but his voice held little hope.

After some strenuous efforts, the Doctor and Pilcher prized the door partly open. A cloud of gas blew out and a pressure wave slapped into their faces. After blinking their eyes clear they could see Ensign Long sitting at his station even now. However, as the cloud of vapour rushed past them they caught the stench of acid. The ensign dissolved into a mist of bloody droplets.
"Oh my God," was Pilcher's first reaction, "we've killed him!"

"Quickly, man! Check the atmosphere," insisted the Doctor, "was the acid effectively neutralized?"

The Doctor and Romana pored over the switches and dials in frantic efforts to help the Elder do just that.

"These shut-offs... I think these gases were confined in there," Pilcher confirmed cautiously.

"We didn't kill him, Pilcher," said Romana kneeling and picking up a shiny cylinder just inside the door, "it has a timer. Reading 00:00 - no minutes, no seconds. No life."

"He had been mostly liquefied some time ago, more than likely," the Doctor added, "then held in stasis. Perhaps even overnight."

"How do you know?" Pilcher asked.

The grey-haired Timelord touched a tray of galley food with a bitten roll.

"The tray was barely touched - see for yourself. Even the pressure change did little to harm it. The food is from last night. Uneaten. He certainly had an appetite when we last saw him – he must have been interrupted almost as soon as he entered the room."

"Out," said Pilcher, his training taking over. Firefighters now bundled from the ladder they had climbed earlier and he blocked them from going any further. He punched up the bridge on the hallway intercom. "This is Elder Pilcher, at the life support control room. There has been an accident. I am in charge of the scene until a bridge officer can take over."

"Understood," came the response. They did not need to know the details to know Pilcher was discretely reporting a fatality over the open comms.

"XO is on his way down."

The *Falling Star* continued on its flight through hyperspace. Hours passed in the muted hum of normal ship operations. Yet, confusion and doubt gripped the crew members. Pilcher and the travellers he had adopted retired to his cabin. The man known only as the Doctor drummed his fingers along the arm of his chair. He never seemed to sleep. A frustrated irritation occasionally seemed to possess him. Not expressing his thoughts left Pilcher to assume he had either gone inexplicably mad or was so deeply lost within his mind he was driven to utter distraction. Even the lady Romana fell silent as her gentle

small talk ran dry. A normally rushing spring silenced by the summer drought of Paul Long's death, Pilcher mused to himself.
Neither Timelord had had much to say to anyone since Pilcher had collected statements and written his report for the XO.

The Doctor, not having an adequate alibi in the minutes leading up to the accident, was put in isolation under Pilcher's care. Which put both of them in a sort of house arrest since the order did not employ locks on the accommodation doors.
"Paul Long making a mistake that cost only his own life is too remarkably convenient," said Pilcher at last, "I don't buy it."
"No, it was murder," Romana added frowning, "there was a gas grenade."
Pilcher looked embarrassed.
"A good point," he conceded, coughing.
"Mm," said the Doctor, "we need a motive. And means. Who has access to such devices?"
"Any officer enrolled in combat training. But they aren't intended for killing," said Pilcher.
The Doctor mulled this over.
"It was done with a decaying stasis field. Plus some corrosive agent - possibly rocket fuel? In addition, the increased pressure hastened the liquefaction. But it - the stasis grenade - had the added effect of halting the moment of death, in real time, until the door was forced. I've seen something similar before," the Doctor confided, "but who? And why? Who *and* why!"
"The bridge officers are almost certainly going to focus on the three of us. You being newcomers."
"On a science tourism flight?" Scoffed the Doctor followed with a "Pah!"
"What percentage of your ship's compliment is actual crew?" Romana enquired.
"Maybe 50 percent," acknowledged Pilcher.
"How does one alter the life support conditions for one maintenance section only?" The Doctor pressed.
"It surely would require manual intervention, but it can be done. Was done," Romana self corrected. She scrunched her face, " But who would want to?"

"Tampering with life support in flight? Someone with motivations overriding all logic and sense for self preservation," said Pilcher.
"The warrior Messolo did not come through the line for food," said Romana, "where was he?"
"I shall find a polite way to ask Messolo for his alibi," said Pilcher with a wry smile. "but I don't think Messolo would have used covert means to kill a man. And why would he, anyway?"
"We are of course assuming it was a deliberate killing of Long," said the Doctor, "likely as that doubtless is, what might have happened if he hadn't returned to eat at his station?"
"The sabotage only affected the maintenance station," Pilcher tiredly pressed his eye sockets with his palms, "assuming the event occurred without him there... nothing, really. Paul, or someone, would have found the room contaminated and used an environment suit to repair it."
"We didn't need suits," Romana pointed out.
"The corrosive agent had done it's worst on Long and nullified itself by then," the Doctor said grimly.
Pilcher began pacing with growing agitation.
"What if Messolo was in a Waltak warrior blood rage?"
He thought for a moment.
"Could there be gamblers on the ship who wanted to put a hit on Long? Could Long have clumsily or intentionally killed himself?"
"No. Unlikely." the Doctor declared.
 Pilcher studied the Doctor and Romana intently now. How little he knew of them. The Doctor could easily have killed Long and been back to the galley unnoticed in the hubbub of meal time.
"You don't do restricted movement well, do you?" Romana suddenly noted. Pilcher was jolted from his disturbing reverie. He smiled.
"No, I guess not."
"Since we have an abundance of time on our hands—who exactly are 'the order?'" Romana wondered.
"I've been looking forward to that one," said a smiling Pilcher, "just not now."
"You can put it off, but she'll ask again," the Doctor warned with a Cheshire Cat grin.
"The order is a simple collective of individuals practising piety. Philosophically not unlike Buddhists - personally practising any

number of religions. Its members take on whatever mission they are given - or drawn to - while practising daily meditation. We have few personal possessions. Not pursuing materialism, we have a drive to explore self, perfect ideas and inventions, study. In short, our time in the order provides an opportunity for growth and healing. Largely the order is temporary. People put life on hold and solve their problems while serving."
"Space hippies?" The Doctor suggested tactlessly.
"Oh, I hope not," laughed Pilcher, "though the merchant marines do operate the ship – perhaps you should ask them?"
"What is your 'mission of growth?'" Romana pressed.
Pilcher smiled thinly for a moment.
"Self discovery."
"Enigmatically vague. I like enigmatic and vague," began the Doctor but was interrupted by a shudder running through the ship. Instinctively, Pilcher grabbed a handhold, then let go.
"I am surprised at the size of your personal library," said the Doctor as he ran his finger across the numerous tape volumes, the vibration already forgotten. Then smiling ironically he continued, "For a man who eschews materialism."
"All part of my expanding duties as an elder. I have been training to perform additional shipboard duties. Hence my partial familiarity with life support."

The power cut out and and back on.
A tone rang throughout the ship.
"Please secure for emergency return to real space!" Called a terrified voice over the intercom.
Hyperspace had vanished from the outer portholes and abruptly the *Falling Star* reappeared in normal space.
"Collision alert!" Began the same voice as the *Falling Star* rapidly decelerated.
Pilcher was thrown with the Doctor and Romana forwards into the bulkhead. Emergency lighting came on, ineffective and barely illuminating the edge of the door. The trio clumsily stumbled into the steerage bay.
"Adverse conditions during the jump and again during re-entry. Intriguing, wouldn't you say?" Romana mused.

"Quite. And I don't find the Captain lacking in competence," responded the Doctor.

Pilcher clapped his hands.

"I just had an idea!"

He ran to a wall terminal. Swiping his key-card, he punched in some codes.

"Give me a moment to review some of the logs... there! I am in the ship's 'pouch' - the bank. There are a couple of people that have 'coined out' some debts while on this flight. Ensign Long's account actually shows some *growth* during the flight. We know he was a gambler, and it seems a winner. He has probably made a sore customer or two," Pilcher explained excitedly.

"Well done!" Romana congratulated, "If we can track down the losing gamblers we will have our pool of suspects!"

"Not necessarily," said the Doctor with a cautioning hand, "there also remains the matter of the child."

"What?" Romana cried, "He's a father?"

"Delinquent father," Pilcher confirmed. He puckered his face as he recalled the distasteful details.

"Huwhen confessed it to me and I attempted to counsel Paul before his death. He was utterly against taking responsibility for the child. Please don't repeat this."

"Lucky guess...," murmured the Doctor with a shake of his head.

"Do we have a suspected killer in the galley?" Romana asked.

"A woman scorned?" Shrugged the Doctor.

"There is another loose thread," Romana noted, "I heard in the serving line that Messolo's trainer was Paul Long."

"They were at odds about something?" Pilcher exclaimed.

"Not a likely suspect, Messolo is a Waltak. He was quite angry with his trainer over something, I agree," said the Doctor, "remember, however, he is a much more capable and direct killer than most of the ship's population."

"He would leave an indelible fingerprint on the corpse. His own... mark," agreed Pilcher, "no, we've missed something."

"Bridge," Pilcher called into the nearest intercom. No response came back.

"Bridge, are you able to respond?" Pilcher asked with mounting dread.

"This is Chief Burkhoff on the command deck," a voice finally came.

Pilcher recognized the name.
"He's an engineer. What's he doing up there?"
"I regret to inform you that the bridge has sustained damage by collision," continued the Chief, "all officers, Chief and above, please report to the secondary control room. I am running this incident until a ranking officer can be appointed."
"Oh my God..." said Pilcher, "I think he's sealing the turbo lift doors. That open onto a vented..."
"Bridge," concluded Romana.
"Help him, Romana," the Doctor asked gently, "go with Elder Pilcher and make sure a suitable officer takes command."
"Do you mean me? I am only an Elder and not a merchant marine!" Pilcher yelled desperately.
"On this ship your rank is 'Chief'," the Doctor pointed out, indicating the man's key-card, "and I'll wager you have as many flight hours and training as anyone else. Based on the size of your library, that is."
"I never should have shown you," Pilcher grumbled, then lead Romana away.

Some time later Romana returned exasperated. Pilcher trailed behind her in a mood.
"Back already?" The Doctor noted. He had not moved since last they saw him.
"You're not going to believe this," Romana announced, "all the command officers were in a meeting on the bridge level - now sealed off. No bridge linkages are working. Pilcher is ranking command Chief."
"The most qualified of the unqualified crew," the Doctor said nodding to himself.
"Bah!" Pilcher exclaimed, "The rest of the cowards didn't want to take the responsibility and have the blemish on their record of losing a ship."
"Losing a ship?" The Doctor said, finally showing some concern.
"The command deck may have been scraped clean off by a collision with hollow mass," explained Romana.
"Ghastly," commented the Doctor, "and yet, as with much today, extremely unlikely."
"An unsolved murder, a wrecked ship at the edge of the universe, and

216

– possibly - a dead bridge crew," grumbled Pilcher, "did I mention we are also stuck in a field of hollow mass objects?"

"Oh, fear not. After the immediate damage is repaired, just navigate free using conventional rockets," said Romana, "shouldn't be too hard from the back up control room."

"And then hop back to hyperspace?" Asked Pilcher, "I'll have to discuss that with the engineer and navigator. Sounds promising though. When you say it fast."

"We've been... " Romana began.

"Yes, I know. You've been through this sort of thing before," Pilcher growled, "why don't *you* take command of the ship?"

The lights came up to full power.

"Your engineer is a good one," Romana observed.

"Yes..." said the Doctor, "this terminal is unhelpful. I need more data and the ship's main computer has it."

"Do you have an inference engine on board?" He then asked.

"In the library, open access," Pilcher said, puzzled.

"Then, take us to your library while the crew – your crew - rescue the bridge officers."

"You think they are alive?" Pilcher asked incredulously.

"Doesn't matter what we think," said Romana, "just keep them busy. Keep their morale up."

"Good idea," said Pilcher, thinking back to the image of the shattered bowl, "I'm not prepared for this."

"Of course not," said the Doctor, "how can any of us prepare for unexpected events? Don't let imposter syndrome overtake you, Elder Pilcher. Er, acting Captain Pilcher. Every day a man faces a new set of experiences. They simply unfold. Raising the bar. Past events prepare you for what you are ultimately able to handle."

"That's the silliest thing you've said today," said Pilcher, "but I take your meaning."

"Let's go to the library."

Pilcher gave a short series of commands as though he expected them to be followed.

He was convincing.

Pilcher led the people from the TARDIS to the library. He waved to Sinda Marie and then motioned the Doctor and Romana to an alcove with a terminal in it.

"Have you used an inference engine before?" Sinda asked of the trio. "It takes natural language input and presents results from all its vast historical knowledge using artificial intelligence," explained the Doctor, "inference engines made a resurgence after the colossal failure of so-called Big Data (TM) wars. I assume it has access to every tome in your library?"

"Yes," said Sinda, "can I help you find something?"

"For the moment," said Pilcher, "it's classified."

Sinda left and their alcove closed.

"Computer, open clearance per acting Captain Pilcher," he said, "scan all transactions of the ship's pouch that pay in or out to Ensign Paul Long."

A series of lines was displayed.

"Display the names of others connected to these transactions," said Romana.

The machine obliged.

"This all looks familiar, and unremarkable," noted Pilcher, "if only it were possible to ask who was most likely to kill him."

"Computer, display all crew and passengers that have ever served with Paul Long," commanded Romana.

Another list appeared.

"Some of these people aren't on the ship. Some served with him during the Hemphill voyages," said Pilcher, "no surprises that I can see."

"Computer," said the Doctor, "display all shipboard connections to Paul Long up to one degree of separation."

A list appeared.

"Repeat last query displaying only tax registration numbers," said the Doctor. The list changed.

"Display records from the previous query minus the ones listed before."

One tax number remained.

The air left the trio's lungs in gasps.

"That was a lucky hunch," said Romana.

"All in the delivery," said the Doctor, "but that number looks fraudulent. Open the debug list. I want to see the computer language translation of my inquiry."

218

Romana leapt ahead of Pilcher's sluggish activity.

"Doctor!"

"Yes, I see it. An exclusion mask."

"I don't understand," said Pilcher.

"A list of aliases was appended to my inquiry. And yours. That list was excluded from the output. A particular person's numerous last names; Thomas, Peters, Antoni and you see the last one. Of course, you know the first name."

"What was the record that was hidden?" Romana asked.

"A marriage license," whispered the Doctor, "I would guess someone else has been expanding their training. In low yield improvised weapons."

"Yes. It all had to do with Hemphill," Pilcher agreed sadly, shaking his head, "what a shame."

He printed the document. With a heavy heart he then summoned security to the library. They were let into the alcove by Sinda Marie. To the lead officer, he said, "Arrest the people named in this document."

"Sir, there's only one name here," the guard said, puzzled.

"That's the order."

The man cuffed the upset woman.

"Sinda," said Pilcher, "you murdered Ensign Paul Long. Why?"

The ship's librarian collapsed into a chair, burying her face in her cuffed hands.

"Michael and I were so deeply in love. We were to be married," sniffed Sinda Marie. She fought back tears with some little success. "It was your logs that filled in the blanks," she hissed at Elder Pilcher, staring furiously at him. Then her face crumbled in grief.

"Paul Long killed my one true love! The ship's inquiry did not reflect that crewman Long was negligent. But Hemphill's personal records did! Michael died EVA, wearing a suit Long skipped inspecting! Paul Long was downgraded in pay and removed from structural engineering by Hemphill. But it was him! He failed to seal Michael's space suit correctly!"

Sinda Marie, indeed the entire room, lapsed into silence. There was nothing more to say.

Pilcher climbed down the ramp to the last space port in the universe,

wearing white robes over his uniform. His hand rested on the hovering hospital bed of Captain Teel.
A medical detail met him at the foot of the ramp.
"Please give these injured all the care and healing available!" Commanded Pilcher.
"Captain," croaked Teel, "take care of my ship."
"Captain," Pilcher said reassuringly, "she'll be here waiting for you."
A grating, grinding sound, now healthier - or at least *stronger* - than before echoed through the steerage bay behind them.
"Human Velcro!" said Pilcher with a smile.

Chapter Ten – 0,0,0 – Part 1

By Daniel Callahan with Oliver M. Goldblatt

The TARDIS landed not with a wheezing, groaning sound, but with an explosion, forcing its way through almost solid air, skidding for a meter on pavement, and then stopping, smoking, as if it were an engine burning oil.
Slowly, the doors opened - the Doctor on one side, Romana on the other. Both looked as if they needed a change of clothes, a massage, and a nap. They gazed around them, half-dazed. The few people on the pavement nearby had not appeared to notice them.
"What… was that?" Romana finally gasped.
The Doctor just shook his head with a look of resignation, then looked over his shoulder.
"K9?" He asked.
K9 sat a metre or so behind them. One of his ears had become detached and his metal shell had become scuffed and dented. His remaining working ear whirred back and forth for a moment.
"No vocabulary available," he finally replied.
"I'd call it something worse than that, but there may be children present," the Doctor said, "stay here while we look around. Find out what the TARDIS knows about that landing."
"Master," K9 replied, complying.
The Doctor and Romana exited the TARDIS and shut the doors.
"I never want to go through that again," Romana finally said.
"I concur. But let's find out what it was first."
They were in a large city, apparently on Earth. They saw shops on both sides of the road, a few cars on that same street, and no clouds in the sky.
"When and where are we, besides Earth, I mean?" Romana asked.
"It appears to be the first quarter of the 21st century," the Doctor said, watching a teenager go by completely engrossed in her smartphone.
They began walking down the road, their aching muscles slowly recovering. The Doctor walked with a slight limp.
"Are you alright?" Romana asked.
"Oh, yes," the Doctor said dismissively, "I'll be fine in a moment."
"Are you sure it's the first quarter of the 21st century?" Romana then

enquired, nodding toward two men sitting at a bus stop, each reading a newspaper.

"Whenever it is, it's the UK," the Doctor said, "hear that radio?" He pointed to an open window above a book store.

"That's Kitchen Disco on Radio 2."

"But that Bed & Breakfast looks Irish, doesn't it?" Romana said, pointing to a small house across the street.

"Quarry Ridge B&B," she read.

The Doctor inclined his head.

"It does," he said with surprise, then pointed on down the road, "and that bank - the First Federal Bank. That would be American!"

The Doctor glanced up toward a hill in the distance.

"Look at that! That observatory on top of the hill. The spitting image of the Australian Astronomical Observatory outside Sydney."

"Is this Sydney?" Romana asked.

The Doctor inhaled deeply.

"No sea air," he replied, shaking his head.

"Australia, Ireland, America, and the UK," Romana said, "all in one place."

"Maybe it's a theme park?" The Doctor mused.

"Doctor?" Romana responded, puzzled.

"Or possibly in a Telrikkian Zoo. Did you know they used to kidnap people and put them on display?"

"Doctor!" Romana insisted more urgently.

"They once captured an entire tribe of Plains Indians. I had to negotiate for a week to get them out-- Is it just me, or is it getting cold?"

"Doctor, what's happening to the sun!"

Romana was looking at the burning orb, which appeared to be fading out.

"That's not an eclipse!" The Doctor cried, "Run! Back to the TARDIS!"

They turned and ran. Romana called, "K9! Open the doors!"

Then the sun began to implode.

Tremors shook the ground and buildings began to fall apart. The Doctor and Romana clung to a street lamp that swayed dangerously. Cars crashed around them, and those pedestrians who could run, ran in blind panic.

The Doctor somehow stood - grabbed Romana - and pushed her toward the TARDIS.

"Run," he rasped, even as the entire street sank into the earth. The Doctor and Romana did not feel anything as they were instantly crushed to death.

Seven, two, ten, zero, four, four, eleven, zero, five, six...
Numbers were running through the Doctor's head. He could not understand why. He could not remember anything, not even his own name.

"Doctor!" He heard Romana cry.

"Yes, that's it!" He announced, sitting bolt upright.

The Doctor was on a bed in a small but nicely decorated bedroom with a settee near the window.

"At least it's not a shower, this time..." he muttered to himself.

Romana had just opened the door and was staring at him, wide-eyed.

"What happened?" She demanded.

"I dreamt about numbers," the Doctor replied sleepily, "it's fading now."

"I had the same dream!"

"Did they make sense to you?"

Romana shook her head, entered the room and flopped down onto the settee.

"But before that... we landed on a planet."

"Earth, we thought," the Doctor said as the details came back to him.

"Something was wrong," Romana recalled slowly.

"The sun imploded!" The Doctor exclaimed.

"We died!" Romana added, jumping up.

"Look at your clothes!" The Doctor said, rising.

All of Romana's clothes were not only clean, but also brand new. The Doctor looked down at his own outfit – it was equally pristine. Before they could react, they heard footsteps just outside the doorway.

They braced themselves for whatever might appear. But when the door opened a middle-aged Irish woman entered with cups of tea and scones on a tray.

"Hello, dears!" She said in a sing-song voice which might have come straight out of a film by John Ford, "Who's ready for tea?"

"Who are you?" Romana asked.

"Oh, you *were* tired, weren't you? I'm Mrs. Saunders. I do hope you're enjoying your stay! Now, how about that tea?"
"Mrs. Saunders," the Doctor began, "the world has just ended, torn itself to pieces in a gravitational whirlpool after the star that gave it life imploded, tearing away the heart of this entire solar system! Tea would be most welcome!"
He scooped a cup off the tray and drank it down almost instantly. "Excellent!" He proclaimed, replacing the cup.
Mrs. Saunders appeared somewhat amazed by this, but she then remembered to offer Romana a cup. Romana arched an eyebrow toward the Doctor, took the cup, and politely sipped.
"But now we need to find out why the world just ended," the Doctor said, taking the tea cup from Romana's hand and replacing it on the tray, "and why it's come back."
Romana sighed audibly.
"Oh, that'll be nice for you, dear," Mrs. Saunders replied, "are you coming down for breakfast, then?"
"If you'll pardon us, where exactly are we?" Romana inquired.
"My word, that must have been some night last night!" Mrs. Saunders exclaimed, "this is the Quarry Ridge Bed and Breakfast. Been in my family for years."
"Quarry Ridge, did you say?" The Doctor muttered.
"The TARDIS must be outside!" Romana voiced her sudden realisation.
"Excuse us," the Doctor apologised as they moved past Mrs. Saunders and ran out of the door.
"I'll keep the kettle on for you, dears!" Mrs. Saunders called after them, helpfully.

The Doctor and Romana reached the street. The sun shone brightly. Everything seemed back to normal.
"The book store, the bank..." the Doctor said.
"But no TARDIS," Romana added, "no K9."
"The TARDIS could be hidden by a distortion field," the Doctor said, pulling his sonic screwdriver from his coat. He attempted to activate it, but nothing happened.
"Time for your 500 year battery change?" Romana asked sardonically.
"No, I changed it 490 years ago," the Doctor replied, missing the jest,

"it just... doesn't work."
Romana tried her sonic screwdriver - on loan for the day from the Doctor's collection - but with the same results.
"How strange. What now?"
"Breakfast," the Doctor replied.
"Seriously?"
"Can you think on an empty stomach?" The Doctor replied, holding the door of the B&B open for her.
Just then, an old man holding a fishing pole and a newspaper came out of the B&B and bumped into Romana. The newspaper and pole fell to the pavement.
"Oh, excuse me!" The man said to Romana with an American accent.
"My fault entirely!" Romana responded.
"Here, let me help you," the Doctor said as he picked up the items and handed them back to the man.
"Keep the paper," the man said with a kind smile, "I've read the forecast. It should be a great day for fishing. I'm Elmer, by the way. Elmer Bolam. Pleased to meet you."
They shook hands.
"Care to join me at Sterling Lake?" Elmer asked, "The bass are biting."
"Perhaps another time," the Doctor replied.
"Alright," Elmer returned, "be seeing you!"
"He seems like a nice man," Romana said, "who doesn't remember the world ending any more than Mrs. Saunders did."
"Have you considered the possibility," the Doctor said, lowering his voice almost to a whisper, "that we may have flitted backwards in time?"
"So, we have the end of the world to look forward to after breakfast? Again?" Romana asked.
"Let's see what this paper has to say."
The Doctor held it up so they could both read it.
"The Daily Gazette," Romana read, "June 28th... but no year, no city."
The Doctor began flipping through the paper at incredible speed. Then he folded it up again and threw it in a nearby rubbish bin.
"What did you notice?" The Doctor wondered.
"The article about the bird rescue facility on page 11 was insightful."
"It was, although biased against cockatoos. What *I* learned is that

we're not on Earth."
"And how did you deduce that?"
"Because it was all good news. That never happens on Earth."
"Now that you mention it, the only article that wasn't entirely happy was the editorial."
"By Dr. Emilio Vasquez, who has discovered a series of solar anomalies…"
"We should have a chat with him," Romana announced.
"I'll take care of that while you stay here."
"Now why would I do that?" Romana asked, crossing her arms.
"To have a look around. To see if anyone remembers what we remember. And to look for the TARDIS... it may be hidden nearby."
"That still doesn't sound as interesting as discussing astrophysics."
"Romana, I don't know where we are, what's happened to us, or where the TARDIS is. Usually when I arrive on a planet, I know the answer to at least one of those questions!"
"One of them?" Romana interjected dubiously.
"There must be a reason why we ended up in this Bed & Breakfast," the Doctor continued grumpily, "find out whatever you can, and let me know what you discover."
"All right," Romana said at last, "but if we come across a cosmologist, I'll talk while *you* search. Deal?"
"Deal," the Doctor replied, and they solemnly shook hands.
Romana entered the B&B while the Doctor began walking down the road. He saw several vehicles passing so he stuck out his thumb.
"Can I get a lift? Eh? Anyone care to stop for a stranded Time Lord?"
"Excuse me, sir," an officious voice said behind him.
The Doctor turned to see a British police Bobby with a uniform from the 1970s standing behind him.
"Would you mind putting your thumb away, please?" The officer asked.
The Doctor put his hand into his pocket. "Is hitch-hiking illegal here, Officer?" The Doctor mused.
"Officer Hill. And it is, I'm afraid," the Bobby continued.
"I stand admonished," the Doctor replied.
"No need to worry, sir. Fortunately, the trolley will be by in a few minutes, and it's a free ride today, sir."
"Serendipitous," the Doctor replied.

"Indeed, sir. It's a free ride every day," Hill said as he turned and walked away.

The Doctor's jaw hung open a little, but then he collected himself. He saw the trolley about a mile away, moving slowly toward him.

Romana had decided to start with the attic and work her way down. There were plenty of trunks and boxes, but almost three millimetres of dust and plaster had settled on top of them. Romana changed her mind and decided to leave the attic until last.

As she made her way down the ladder, a voice startled her.

"Can I help you, dear?" Mrs. Saunders asked.

"I'm sorry," Romana replied awkwardly as she descended, "I was just…"

She panicked and fished around for a white lie but came up empty.

"I couldn't resist a look at your attic," she said finally and flatly.

"Oh my dear, my home is your home," Mrs. Saunders replied. "Please feel free to look around to your heart's content. Is there anything in particular you'd like to see?"

"No, nothing in particular," Romana replied.

"Well, if you ever find out, let me know. And there's a door right over there which you can try. I'll be serving tea when you're finished," and with a smile, Mrs. Saunders walked down the stairs.

"She's charming, sincere, and far too polite - even for an exotic alien life form," Romana muttered to herself.

She knocked on the door that Mrs. Saunders had indicated, which sprang open. There stood Elmer Bolam.

"Elmer!" Romana cried.

"Hello, there! Care to join me at Sterling Lake? I was about to go fishing. Great day for it!"

"But, didn't you just run into us outside? On your way to Sterling Lake?"

Elmer chuckled as if Romana had told an amusing joke.

"Be seeing you!" He said as he made his way toward the front door.

"But Elmer," Romana called after him, "where's your fishing rod?"

The Doctor had taken the trolley to the Observatory. Just as Officer Hill had said, there was no fee for the service, and the other passengers chatted among themselves as if they did not care when they arrived at

their destination. Also, he had not seen anyone else get on or off.
The Doctor entered the main entrance and looked around.
"Hmm... The décor, the furnishings, the equipment... This observatory is identical to the Australian Astronomical Observatory. Except for this awful paint," he said, looking at the walls, "what designer in their right mind would choose Battleship Grey?"
"Can I help you, sir?" A voice asked.
The Doctor turned to a see a middle-aged man wearing thick glasses.
"I'm the Doctor. And you are?"
"Dr. Richardson."
"Tell me, Dr. Richardson, where's the display on nucleosynthesis?"
"Uh, down the hallway, first door on the left," Richardson replied.
"And the demonstration of cosmic ray spallation?"
"First door on the right. Are you an astrophysicist?"
"Among other things," the Doctor said proudly.
"Oh, forgive me for not recognizing you earlier!" Dr. Richardson cried, "It's you!"
"Of course it is," the Doctor responded, taken aback, "who else would I be?"
Richardson shook the Doctor's hand vigorously. "It's so nice to meet you, Director! I thought you weren't arriving until tomorrow!"
"Director...?" The Doctor asked slowly.
"I'm the Assistant Director. I've been looking forward to meeting you for some time, sir, but I know how busy your schedule has been."
"Of course, of course," the Doctor said, unsure of what else to say.
"Let me show you our networked array of computers - linked by an open source project led by Dr. Matthews. She's one of the best programmers we've ever..."
The Doctor had had enough of this. Being mistaken for someone else? Normal for a time traveller. But to become a desk-bound administrator? That was asking too much.
"Pardon me, Dr. Richardson, but I'm not the Director... I'm the Doctor."
"Doctor...?" Dr. Richardson asked, fishing for a name.
"Quite," the Doctor replied, "I'm looking for a colleague. Dr. Emilio Vasquez?"
"Ah, I'm afraid he resigned yesterday."
"Did he indeed? Well, well, well... Did he leave a forwarding

address?"
"Yes, I'll get it for you."
"And Dr. Richardson?" The Doctor added.
"Yes?"
"Your incoming Director.... ex-naval officer, by any chance?"
"A retired Commodore, in fact."
"Good," the Doctor said, "he ought to feel right at home, then."

Romana found herself trapped on the second floor of the B&B by an encyclopedia salesman.
"And the 11th edition Britannica is still considered the finest encyclopedia printed in the English language," he continued with a broad smile.
"Yes, thank you," Romana said, attempting to extricate herself.
"Just call me Fred," he replied with an overly polite smile. Romana's brain glitched for a second at the mention of the name.
"I'm sure it's a bargain, Fred," she continued, recovering her composure, "but if you'll excuse me..."
"And for a low monthly payment spread out over only 36 months..." Fred continued.
"Do you have a business card?" Romana asked.
"Oh, yes!" Fred replied reaching into his pocket.
"Oh, good. Give it to Elmer. He's at Sterling Lake." Forgive me, Elmer, she thought to herself.
Then she quickly stepped past him and hurried down the stairs. Fred did not follow her. She could not help but wonder if even the creatures of the Bulk could survive the onslaught of an American door-to-door salesmen.
She saw several people congregating on the ground floor but did not recognize any of them. Mrs. Saunders was serving tea. But then she heard something outside – marching boots. From the bottom of the stairs she could see various life forms outside wearing military uniforms.
"'A' Platoon, fan out!" A voice yelled, "B Squad, cover the doorway! C Squad, you're with me!"
Before Romana could hide, the front door was kicked in and C Squad entered with weapons drawn.
"Attention!" An older soldier shouted, "I am Captain Tobin! You are

surrounded by a superior force, and you will obey each of my commands, or you will be killed."

Everyone froze.

The Captain appeared human... but then, so did Romana. About a third of them were not human, it seemed, from their motley collection of non-earthly characteristics. The soldiers' uniforms were mostly gray camo, but they had been patched so often with a variety of old material so that it was hard to identify them. They also seemed to be collected from a variety of disparate sources. The soldiers wore no badges or insignia beyond their rank. They carried energy weapons from multiple civilizations; no three appeared to be the same make or model. A few carried packs on their backs. One soldier stood out because his pack looked new, while the rest were threadbare. Their boots were just as worn as everything else they carried. And they all looked hungry...

"This is your only warning," Tobin continued, "is that understood?"

In Romana's eyes, Tobin appeared to be not only a soldier, but a survivor. There was something ruthless in his eyes that suggested he had no time for philosophy, ethics or remorse. He also looked worn, in body and soul.

"We have detected a data port in this area! You will now provide me with its exact location!" Tobin continued.

Romana, Mrs. Saunders, and the other guests looked at each other, but clearly no one knew what Tobin was referring to.

"I see," Tobin replied after a moment. "Sergeant Gaba! Select one of these citizens and bring them forward!"

"Sir!" Gaba responded, who moved quickly through the crowd until she zeroed in on Mrs. Saunders. She grabbed her arm and dragged her toward Captain Tobin.

Mrs. Saunders stared at Tobin wide-eyed.

"I asked a question," Tobin said, staring at Mrs. Saunders. "The location of the nearest data port, please."

"Oh... I... I don't.... oh my... would you... all like a cup of... tea?"

"Weapons at the ready," Tobin ordered, and his soldiers complied.

"Please, Captain... I don't..." begged Mrs. Saunders.

"Wait!" Romana cried, even though she knew it would do little more than get her killed too. But there was a commotion outside, and no one seemed to have heard her. The soldiers were dragging an English

Bobby with a uniform from the 1970s inside.
"What's all this, then?!" The Bobby cried. "Take your hands off me! I am a police officer and demand to be treated as such!"
"Civilian trying to break in, sir!" Gaba said to Tobin.
"Officer Hill!" Mrs. Saunders cried.
"Office Hill, I am Captain Tobin of the Horde," Tobin said, "where is the nearest data port?"
But Hill was having none of it. "I arrest you for carrying and displaying military-grade weaponry in public, assaulting an officer of the law, breaking and entering, disturbing the peace..."
"I reject your authority and demand that you answer my question, Officer!" Tobin said, interrupting. "Or you will be zeroed out!"
"You are under arrest!" Hill shouted back.
"Sergeant," Tobin said, addressing Gaba.
"Sir!"
Gaba aimed and fired at Officer Hill, who disintegrated in a yellow haze.
Romana tried to take a step forward, but a soldier moved in toward her with rifle aimed at her head.
Mrs. Saunders fell to her knees, crying, "Oh, no! No!"
Tobin turned back to Mrs. Saunders.
"Tell me where that data port is, now."
"I don't know!" She replied through her tears, "Perhaps the observatory has one? I only run a Bed and Breakfast!"
Tobin stared at her for a moment, and then said, "We're moving out! Gaba, take B Platoon and search the alleyways and businesses nearby. 'A' Platoon, with me."
And just as quickly as they came, they left.
Romana rushed over to Mrs. Saunders and helped her to her feet.
"Are you alright! I'm so sorry - there was nothing I could do!"
But as soon as Mrs. Saunders was on her feet, she stopped crying.
"Oh, that's all right dear. I'll make everyone some tea!"
With that she returned to the kitchen. Romana stood, gobsmacked. She turned to the others, who were already back to what they had been doing when the soldiers arrived.
"But that police officer..." Romana finally blurted out.
But no one was listening. She turned toward the dark spot on the floor which indicated where Officer Hill had been standing.

"What is going on?" Romana cried.

Dr. Emilio Vasquez was on his knees in his flower garden when he heard a man speak from the other side of the fence.
"Quite the azaleas!"
"Oh, thank you," he replied, looking up, and a little surprised.
"They always remind me of Louis Armstrong," the man continued.
"I've never thought that," Emilio replied.
"And Madonna Lilies! I haven't seen one in over forty years."
"I take it you're a gardener," Emilio replied as he stood and wiped the dirt off his knees.
"Can I help you with something?" He asked, sounding more annoyed than he had intended.
"Yes," the Doctor replied, "yes. I'm looking for 210 Somerset Lane."
"You've found it."
"Splendid! Dr. Emilio Vasquez, I presume?"
"I'm sorry, but have we met?"
Instead of answering, the Doctor scanned the garden once again.
"No sunflowers, then?"
"I beg your pardon?" Emilio said, suddenly nervous.
"No sunflowers in the garden," the Doctor replied, "an interesting flower... they can tell you so much about the sun."
Emilio began sweating.
"What? Sun... Why..? What do you mean about...?"
"Oh, nothing," the Doctor replied innocently, "nothing at all... apart from what happened in the not-too-distant past..."
Emilio began inching back toward his front door.
"Who are you? What do you want?"
"I'm the Doctor. I wanted to discuss your editorial, even though it was published a day late..."
Emilio stopped where he was and began trembling.
"Did you...? Did you...?"
"Yes," the Doctor replied calmly, "I lived through it, too."
"I thought we... that we were the only..." Emilio said, then put his hands on his knees and took several deep breaths. He stood up and wiped his face with his hand.
"You'd better come... Please - come inside."
He waved the Doctor toward the fence gate and into the house.

232

"Thank you! What a lovely garden."
The house was clean and uncluttered. Almost the first thing the Doctor saw was a boy typing at a computer. He turned toward his father and the Doctor and said, "7, 7, 7."
"This is my son, Juan," Emilio said. "You'll have to forgive him: he's autistic."
"Nothing to forgive," the Doctor replied, extending his hand, "hello, Juan. I'm the Doctor."
"7, 7, 7," Juan repeated, ignoring the Doctor's gesture.
"Sorry, he's hungry," Emilio said from the kitchen, "'7, 7, 7' means that he wants chocolate."
"How interesting!" The Doctor replied.
He put his hand down and turned to Juan.
"Did you know that the number 7 represents perfection in many cultures?"
Juan turned away from the Doctor and back to his computer, but the Doctor continued.
"At least, that's true in certain human cultures. Not so much in alien ones. I wonder what kind of world this is, then?"
Juan ignored him.
Emilio returned and gave a small piece of chocolate to his son, who quickly popped it in his mouth.
"I'm sorry, what were you saying, Doctor?" Emilio asked.
"Emilio, where are we? What planet I mean?"
"Uh," Emilio replied after a moment, "well, what kind of question is that?"
"An honest one. There aren't many worlds that can be destroyed by a solar implosion and spring back to life again. To say nothing of the resiliency of the sun!"
Emilio shook his head nervously.
"Honestly, I think it was all mass hallucination," he sputtered.
"0, 0, 0!" Juan replied, looking up at his father with concern.
"What does that mean?" The Doctor asked.
"Nothing!" Emilio snapped. He closed his eyes tight, and then opened them after a moment.
"Juan, go play with your other toys for a minute and let us talk, please."
Reluctantly, Juan got off his chair and went into another room.

"I made a mistake asking you to come inside," Emilio began, but the Doctor interrupted him.

"Mass hallucinations are most likely to occur among the young. And I can assure you, I am not young. And they typically manifest themselves in bizarre illnesses, not the belief that the sun has imploded after an astrophysicist warns the world of..."

"Stop it!" Emilio cried, "Stop it! I don't know what happened, but we can't be dead one day and alive the next! Things like that can't happen that often!"

"'Often'?" The Doctor snapped, "You mean this has happened before?"

"No! No, of course not - I misspoke!" Emilio lied.

"Who are you trying to convince?" The Doctor asked, "Me or yourself?"

Emilio tried to speak but just hung his head.

"Emilio, how often does this occur?"

Emilio rounded on the Doctor.

"What kind of lunatic are you?! 'What planet is this?' Get out! Get out now!"

Suddenly, Juan was in the room with them, pulling at Emilio's leg.

" 0, 0, 0! 0, 0, 0!" He insisted.

Emilio knelt down to comfort his son. But instead of a hug, he touched him quickly and let go.

"I'm sorry, Juan... I'm sorry," he whispered.

"Does 0, 0, 0 mean stop, then?" The Doctor asked calmly.

"Yes," Emilio replied, standing up again, "or that something's ending, occasionally when something's arriving. Termination of some occurrence, the beginning of another. His mode of communication isn't precise yet. He's better with numbers than words."

"Let's sit down for a moment," the Doctor said, helping Emilio to a comfy chair. He turned and held out his hand toward Juan. "Juan?"

"No!" Emilio warned, "He doesn't like to be touched. It's part of his condition. Juan, go back to your computer and let us talk."

Juan obeyed.

"Emilio," the Doctor began, "believe me, I want to help. Please, tell me what's happening here."

"I've dreamt that the world has come to an end in vivid detail so many times," Emilio sighed, "at least, I think they were dreams. But so real... But after I die, I wake up the next day, or what seems like the next day, and everything is back to the way it was! This seems to happen every nine to thirteen months... I... can't be sure. You don't know how much time has passed when you wake up afterward. The date on the calendar changes, and no one else seems to notice! I don't know if Juan notices... I hope not. The world's ended due to earthquakes, comet strikes, flooding... and yesterday, at about this time, it was the sun. But this last disaster happened so quickly... usually, we spend weeks or months dealing with the emergency, trying to stay alive – but this time, we all died instantly!"

"4, 3, 7!" Juan said, looking at his monitor.
The Doctor and Emilio looked him, but Juan did not react.
"What does that mean?" The Doctor asked.
"I... I don't know!" Emilio replied.

Back at the observatory, Dr. Richardson was walking toward the coffee machine, reading a file, when the door to the complex burst open and several armed soldiers marched in. Richardson froze as one particularly grizzled soldier made straight for him.
"Attention! I am Captain Tobin. This observatory is surrounded by a superior force, and you will obey each of my commands, or we will open fire. Is that understood!"
Several of Tobin's soldiers had already raised their weapons toward Richardson.
"Can... can I help you, sir?" Richardson managed to say.
"We have detected a data port in this vicinity! You will now provide me with its exact location!" Tobin barked.
"A data port? I don't understand..."
"Private! Shoot him," Tobin ordered.
"Wait! Uh... We don't... We, uh, have a networked array of computers linked by an open source project led by Dr. Matthew! Perhaps that would help you?" Richardson's shaky finger pointed down the hall.
"Corporal Sharpe, take your Platoon!" Tobin ordered.
"Yes, sir!" Sharpe replied, obeying.
"What is your name?" Tobin asked Richardson.
"Dr. Richardson, Assistant Director," he replied meekly.
"Where is the Director?"

"He arrives tomorrow."
Corporal Sharpe returned.
"Captain, we're downloading approximately sixteen terabytes of information, but the system states that one hard drive is missing."
"Dr. Richardson," Tobin said, "you will give me the location of this hard drive!"
"I... I don't know! All of our employees are here today, except..."
"Dr. Richardson," Tobin interrupted, "what is the name and location of the employee who took the hard drive?"

Romana had worked her way toward the basement at the Bed & Breakfast. No one had seemed concerned by the death of the police officer, or had even acknowledged that it happened. In disgust, she had returned to her work.
At first she worried that the basement would be the usual, musty, dirt and concrete pit, filled with insect life and discarded property. However, it was unusually clean. Far less cluttered or grimy than some rooms in the TARDIS, in fact.
Romana took a step and stumbled. Something heavy had caught her foot, which looked exactly like a trap door from a late medieval castle. A huge iron ring had been bolted onto strong oak planks with cast-iron hinges facing Romana. The wood and iron seemed about two hundred years old but with no sign of structural decay.
"What's a trap door doing in a basement?" Romana mused to herself. She took out her "loaner" sonic screwdriver before remembering they no longer worked. She put it away and sighed. She knew she could never tell the Doctor that she had found an out-of-place trap door and failed to open it.
"I'd never hear the end of it," she muttered quietly.
Romana bent down and pulled at the ring. After a moment, the door began to swing upwards. Instantly she could feel the air being sucked out the room and into whatever lay beneath. She quickly dropped the ring; the door slammed shut, and the rush of air halted.
Romana had not been able to see into whatever it was, but she suspected that beneath her feet there was nothing but the Void.
"How existential," she muttered.
She quickly returned up the stairs and saw Mrs. Saunders carrying a tray of empty tea cups into the kitchen.

"Mrs. Saunders," Romana began but was halted when they heard the front door burst open again. But instead of soldiers, they heard a hum. It grew louder and more grating, and something about the sound made Romana want to run.

Instead of running, she stepped out of the kitchen to see a blue man about seven feet tall hovering six inches above the ground. She did not recognize the species.

The people inside the B&B did not seem to notice him - even Mrs. Saunders, who had just stepped out of the kitchen.

"Mrs. Saunders," the man began.

Mrs. Saunders suddenly noticed him.

Romana could detect no warmth in the greeting, only accuracy.

"Oh no!" Mrs. Saunders began to cry, "Help! Police!"

"Who are you?" Romana demanded.

The blue man ignored Romana entirely. Instead, he turned to Mrs. Saunders and said, "Calm down."

Within two seconds, Mrs. Saunders had indeed calmed down. She smiled at the blue man and said, "Tea, dear?"

"What are you doing?!" Romana gasped.

"Who has been here recently?" The man asked Mrs. Saunders.

"Apart from the normal customers, five people. One was Officer Hill, but he's dead now," Mrs. Saunders said, matter-of-factly.

"Noted," the blue man said, nodding as if taking this down.

Romana, torn between interrupting and staying quiet, began edging her way back to the kitchen.

"Captain Tobin and Sergeant Gaba of the Horde," Mrs. Saunders continued, "plus several others whose names I didn't catch. And, of course, there's the Doctor and Romana," she concluded, pointing toward Romana.

Romana froze.

The blue man turned to Romana as if he had just noticed her for the first time.

"Come here, Romana," he ordered.

"No, I don't think so," Romana replied, making a break for the kitchen. But the door suddenly shut in her face.

"If you have the ability to disobey me, then you are truly 'new' to this place," the blue man replied, hovering toward Romana.

The humming noise increased as Romana tried to pull the door open, but it would not move.

The front door of the B&B was suddenly pushed opened and several people marched in. Romana and the blue man turned toward the sound; some of the Horde had returned.

"My troops require meals which you will..." Sergeant Gaba began, then stalled as she saw the blue man. She quickly recovered and barked, "Weapons at the ready!"

"Gaba is the lady in the front giving orders," Mrs. Saunders said to the blue man, helpfully.

The blue man did not reply to her, but turned away from Romana and toward Gaba.

"You will all place your weapons at your feet and surrender," he said calmly.

"Fire!" Gaba yelled.

Romana threw herself to the floor as multiple energy weapons were discharged. After a few seconds, she glanced up and saw the blue man, still hovering and unaffected by the weaponry. He was looking at Gaba and her troops as if they were disobedient animals.

"Put down your weapons," he kept repeating.

When the soldiers did not comply he sighed and began pointing his finger at them. As he did so, Romana watched in horror as their weapons exploded.

"Sir, weapons backfiring!" One soldier cried, "He must be..."

And then that soldier's gun exploded.

"Pull back!" Gaba cried, "Pull back!"

She waved her troops back out the door.

The blue man, still hovering, followed them.

Romana stood and turned to Mrs. Saunders. She was calmly serving tea to her guests; none of whom seemed to have noticed the firefight nearby.

"Perhaps you ought to evacuate?" Romana suggested urgently.

"Oh, don't be silly dear," Mrs. Saunders replied, "now, let me make a fresh pot..."

"Oh, shut up!" Romana snapped as she made her way to the front door.

The solders and the blue man were already fighting in the street. Romana followed them cautiously as the soldiers retreated, continuing to fire at the man but to no effect. Every so often a soldier was killed as his weapon detonated.

Romana continued to follow until a stray energy bolt struck near her head. She ducked into an alley and was about to look again when she felt a gun touching the back of her head.

"Who are you?" Gaba hissed.

"Romana. I'm not with the blue man."

"Who was he? Do you know!"

"No," Romana replied as calmly as she could, "I was hoping you could tell me."

"Who's side are you on? Are you a spy?" Gaba growled.

"Please, calm down," Romana said, "you're trembling, and your finger is on the trigger."

Gaba pulled her gun back, but did not re-holster it.

Romana slowly turned around, but her eyes widened as saw the blue man hovering behind Gaba. Seeing Romana's expression, Gaba spun around and raised her weapon.

"Now that I have you both here, I have some questions for you," the blue man said.

"Stay back!" Gaba shouted.

"Don't shoot!" Romana cried, "Your gun will explode!"

Gaba kept her weapon up but did not fire.

"And I warn you, I want the truth," the man continued, "now... why did you cause the sun to implode?"

"6, 5, 4! 6, 5, 4!" Juan cried.

They were still inside the house. Juan was seated at the computer but now facing the Doctor and Emilio.

"What does that mean?" The Doctor asked.

"I've never heard him like this before," Emilio said.

"3, 2, 1!" Juan continued.

"I'm sorry, we don't know what you mean," the Doctor replied, "but it sounds like a..."

He stood sharply and began looking out the windows.

"A countdown!"

"What?" Emilio asked.

"0, 0, 0!" Juan cried.

The front door was smashed open. The Doctor ducked and Emilio moved toward Juan to cover his son with his body.

Three beings walked in with weapons raised. The Doctor's ears were ringing as he heard shouts ordering them not to move. The Doctor slowly raised his hands.

"Attention! I am Captain Tobin. You are surrounded by a superior force and you will obey each of my commands or we will open fire. Is that understood?"

"Tell me," the Doctor asked, "did your training ever include the use of a door bell?"

Tobin turned towards the Doctor.

Good, thought the Doctor, concentrate on me, not Emilio and Juan.

"You have stolen a hard drive from the Observatory!" Tobin barked. "You will now hand it over to my custody."

"By whose authority, might I ask?" The Doctor responded.

"By the authority of the weapons aimed at your vital organs."

The Doctor thought this might have been an attempt at dark humour, but Tobin was not smiling at all, and neither were his troops. He decided to play for time.

"Who told you that you could find the hard drive here? What do you need it for?"

Tobin sighed and shook his head.

"Everyone we meet in this world questions orders," he said to his troops in a sad voice.

They responded with dark chuckles.

"Captain Tobin, I assure you," the Doctor said quickly, "you will have my full cooperation if you will just put down your weapons and..."

"Private!" Tobin barked to one of the soldiers behind him. "Zero him out!"

"Wait!" the Doctor cried.

"0, 0, 0!" Juan cried.

The soldier fired.

The Doctor heard, far away, the sound of a man screaming. Before everything went dark, he realized it was him.

Chapter Eleven – 0,0,0 – Part 2

By Daniel Callahan with Oliver M. Goldblatt.

The Doctor and Romana had recently nearly crashed – *again* - only to discover they were in a city on Earth. Or were they?
Then the sun imploded, killing everyone, including them.
Fortunately, they awoke in the bed and breakfast and found that everyone else was back from the dead too.
But K9 and the TARDIS were gone.
And there were new visitors. A group of scavengers named The Horde who were willing to kill anyone and everyone in order to find a "data port".
Romana had encountered them only to be interrupted by a seven foot tall blue man, hovering above the ground. Sergeant Gaba of the Horde had tried to kill him, but he slaughtered her troops instead. In the confusion, Romana and Gaba found themselves in an alley, trapped by the blue man.
Just your average Thursday.
As for the Doctor, he had met Emilio and his autistic son Juan in their home, only to become trapped by the Horde, who were looking for a hard drive that Emilio had hidden. Their leader, Captain Tobin, had ordered his troops to shoot the Doctor.
And they did.

Upon consideration, perhaps more to get "the hang of" than an average Thursday.

In the alley, the blue man was interrogating Romana and Gaba. He seemed to believe they had caused the sun to implode.
"The implosion of the sun had nothing to do with me," Romana replied, "and I'm not with this soldier."
The blue man appeared to accept this answer and turned his attention to Gaba.
"I am unaware of any solar event that you are referring to," Gaba said but the authority she *had* carried in her voice had gone.
"I demand that you release me and..." she began, her voice quivering.
"Your demands are rejected," the blue man replied over her, as calmly

as ever, "therefore..."
From the far end of the alley they heard a shouted command, "Open fire!"
Romana and Gaba threw themselves onto the ground as shots flew overhead. The blue man turned toward the soldiers.
"Cease firing!" Gaba shouted, but no one heard her.
One by one, the soldiers' weapons began to explode.
"Pull back!" Gaba shouted, futilely.
But the blue man kept advancing toward her troops - who kept firing and dying.
"There's nothing you can do!" Romana cried.
"We have to go!" She said, standing and pulling Gaba to her feet and dragging her back toward the street.
Gaba tried to resist Romana at first, but seeing most of her troops dead she turned and ran.

Inside the house, Emilio could not believe his eyes. The Doctor had been shot by an energy weapon and collapsed onto the floor. But suddenly, the Doctor sat up, his teeth gritted. He held his cranium in his hands and moaned, "Oh, my head..."
Everyone froze. Then Emilio said: "You're alive!"
"Yes," the Doctor conceded, "banged my head trying to duck out of the way, but for no good reason it seems. Those disrupters were set at quarter strength. That couldn't kill anyone."
"B... but..." Corporal Sharpe stammered, "he can't be alive. We zeroed him out!"
"Unless he's..." another frightened soldier ventured.
"A ghost!" Yet another finished in a whisper.
Suddenly, the soldiers began pushing each other out of he way in order to be the first to escape the room. Someone was yelling to use a grenade when Captain Tobin fired a shot into the ceiling. Emilio pulled Juan down toward the floor. Everyone else froze.
"He's not a ghost!" Tobin shouted, "And even if he were, how would a grenade help?"
"Sir!" The soldiers replied, sheepishly.
"He's no ghost," Tobin continued, "but he might be one of *them*."
The Doctor stood to his full height.
"Which 'them' did you mean, Captain?" The Doctor asked.

Before Tobin could answer, a loud ominous hum began from something outside. A voice said, "All belligerents will leave the house and address me. I am Sysadmin Two, representative of the Guild of Sysadmins, and I am in the garden. If you do not comply, I will destroy this area."

"Goodbye, Madonna Lilies," the Doctor muttered.

"Corporal Sharpe, eyes on!" Tobin ordered.

Sharpe ran to a window and looked out. What he saw terrified him. "He's...! I've never seen anything like him before! Seven foot tall, blue, and hovering off the ground!"

Tobin turned to the Doctor.

"If that's a Sysadmin, then who are you?"

"I'm the Doctor, and I'm not with the Sysadmins... whoever they may be. My concern is with Emilio and Juan. Those are the names of your other two hostages, you know."

Tobin looked down at them without any discernible sense of pity. "Corporal Sharpe!" he barked.

"Sir!" Sharpe replied.

"Guard these prisoners while I address Sysadmin Two. Company, weapons on full! Move out, keep quiet, and stay under cover."

Without making a sound, the soldiers moved toward the rear of the house, slipped out of the windows, and began working their way toward the front.

Sharpe stood before the Doctor, Emilio, and Juan. He looked nervous as he ratcheted his energy weapon and pointed it at the Doctor.

Romana and Sergeant Gaba had run about a mile from the bed and breakfast and found themselves down a side street. Romana was out of breath but Gaba was only slightly winded.

"How far…" Romana began.

"About a mile, I think," Gaba replied, "how far can I trust you?"

"Romana. And how far can I trust you, Sergeant Gaba?"

Gaba did not answer for a moment. Instead she looked around for any sign of attack. Finally she said, "My entire company was wiped out."

"Perhaps some are prisoners," Romana replied.

"Maybe. We need shelter."

"We need to find the Doctor."

"Who?"

"He can help."
"Tell me more," Gaba replied.
"An expert. On everything, according to him."
"Even computers?"
"Of course," Romana confirmed.
"He may prove a valuable asset," Gaba muttered to herself.
"I'm sorry?" Romana asked.
"Where is he?" Gaba responded.
"The last I heard, he was on his way to the Observatory."
"Roger that. I'll find a car."
"You can't just steal someone's car!"
"Do you want to live through the day?" Gaba answered coolly.
"Obviously," Romana answered, "as do the people you shoot."
"As do we all. It's them or us."
"And you really believe that?!"
Gaba took a hard look at Romana. "I can see by your hands that you don't work. And by your waistline that you eat plenty."
"Nonetheless," Romana said, bristling, "I'm healthy for a Time Lord my age."
"You have that choice, then?" Gaba asked, pointedly, "It's different when you have to kill someone and take their food so you won't starve."
"Is that what you've had to do?" Romana asked as gently as she could.
"All of us. All of the Horde."
"The 'Horde'?" Romana asked, "Is that what you call yourselves?"
"It's what we're called. As good as any other name, I guess. I'll get that car."
"No, wait... some of the customers at the Bed & Breakfast said the trolley was free today. Less conspicuous than having the police after us, right?"
Gaba sighed and rubbed her eyes with her hand. "Alright. But we'll keep moving until it arrives."
They began walking toward the hill. The sky had gone cloudy and they could not see the observatory.
"Can you locate the rest of your troops?" Romana asked.
"Don't have that tech," Gaba replied, "we only have what we can steal. Otherwise, we go without."
"Gaba," Romana asked softly, "what happened? How did you become

the Horde?"

Sysadmin Two continued to hover a few inches above Emilio's garden, waiting patiently. After a moment, Captain Tobin stepped out of the house, walked down a few steps and addressed him.
"Identify yourself," Sysadmin Two said with the voice of a bureaucrat attempting to fill out the correct forms.
"I am Captain Tobin of the Horde."
Sysadmin Two cracked a smile. "Ah... the 'Horde'. I have heard of you. Galactic scavengers. It is said that wherever a rubbish tip can be found, one can find your people."
"Your opinion is not my concern," Tobin replied flatly, "but it is important that you understand why we are here."
"Acceptable," Sysadmin Two replied, sounding a little bored, "for the record, explain briefly and succinctly why a company of The Horde chose to break into our environment."

"We had a planet once," Gaba told Romana as they continued down the street. "A war started with the Embodiment of Gris. No one remembers how. About one hundred and fifty years ago, it destroyed our world."

"Only a small fraction of our people survived," Tobin explained to Sysadmin Two.
"We became fugitives in whatever ships we could find. But the Embodiment decided to pursue the war to the finish. "

"No one would help us," Gaba continued.
"No one dared. The Embodiment is ruthless. We were slowly pushed to the edge of the galaxy. And the Embodiment wouldn't give up."

"We gained an advantage," Tobin explained, "when we captured ships from Clom. For the first time, we were able to make contact with planets far outside of the Embodiment's reach. We found allies who told us about this place and how we could get in."

"We came here seeking sanctuary," Gaba said, "this is the one place that the Embodiment will never find us."

"Sysadmin Two, on behalf of the Horde, will you give us asylum?" Tobin asked.

Inside Emilio's house Sharpe was only half-watching his prisoners, half listening to what was being said outside.
"Can you hear what they're saying?" Emilio quietly asked the Doctor.
"Yes," the Doctor whispered, smiling slowly, "very illuminating."
"What's going on?" Emilio asked.
"For once in my lives, I have no idea! But that doesn't mean we're helpless."
Then, speaking in a normal voice, the Doctor addressed Sharpe.
"Corporal, maybe it would be best if I gave you the drive you were looking for."
"You have it?" Sharpe cried, leaving the window and moving toward the Doctor, "hand it over at once!"
"It's in a small case inside my pocket, and I'm taking it out slowly." This the Doctor did, "There it is."
Emilio looked confused. "But…"
"But," the Doctor bawled, drowning out Emilio's words, "it would be best if you didn't open it just yet."
"Do you really think that I'd hand anything over to Captain Tobin without double-checking its contents?" Sharpe said, opening the case. Inside, there appeared to be nothing but dust.
"What…?" Sharpe began.
The Doctor blew into the case, forcing the powder into Sharpe's face. Sharpe began coughing, sneezing, gagging, and retching almost all at the same time. He pointed his weapon at them blindly but, before he could get a shot off, Emilio punched him in the stomach. Sharpe fell, and the Doctor kicked the gun into a far corner.
The Doctor looked at the case and its fine powder lying on the floor.
"The last of my Datil pepper," he said sadly.
"Emilio, get the drive out of the computer quickly. Then we'll have to make our way back to the observatory."
"That's not possible!" Emilio protested, "Juan never leaves the house! It's a symptom of his autism."

Outside in the garden, Sysadmin Two stared quizzically at Captain

Tobin.

"You expect... asylum... from us. After you hacked your way in, or rather you had mercenaries from Tronlow hack their way in for you, causing untold damage to the meta-structure - damage we are still attempting to catalogue and correct. Ah, now I see why the sun imploded. Cascading damage caused by your entry. That does not speak in your favour. And even if we were to 'forgive' these infractions... and imagine that uninvited guests such as yourselves would settle down and behave as guests should... or to assume the Embodiment of Gris hasn't followed you, fugitives with more firearms than common sense..."

"Perhaps I did not make myself clear," Tobin said, cutting him off. "The Horde numbers over 100,000. Most are defenceless. We need a permanent settlement, or we will all die."

"Yes, the Embodiment of Gris has committed genocide before and I daresay it will again, but that is no concern of the Guild nor do we wish it to be. You are to remove all traces of your presence from this domain or be hunted down."

"Is that the Guild's final answer?" Tobin asked coolly.

Sysadmin Two sighed in mild annoyance and turned his head as if listening to something.

"Yes," he finally replied.

The Doctor looked at the window and turned back. "Emilio, have Juan sit down, please."

Emilio did so, then turned back to the Doctor.

"Trust me," the Doctor said.

Emilio nodded, then looked around for Sharpe's weapon. He picked it up, made sure it was on quarter power, then stood guard near Sharpe, who was still coughing miserably on the floor.

The Doctor slowly sat down next to Juan, who was looking worriedly about the room.

"It's all right if you don't look at me. I understand," the Doctor told Juan.

Juan gave him a sideways glance and then began looking around again.

"First of all, I want you to know that you and your father will be alright, and that you'll have some chocolate when all of this is over.

However, we must all leave before the Horde come back. And to make it easier, I need you to let me touch your forehead with my index finger. It may feel a little odd, but it will allow us to get you somewhere safe."

Juan began to tremble and mutter: "4... 3... 2..."

"That's right. Close your eyes, Juan."

Juan closed his eyes.

"1...!" Juan said quietly under his breath.

"Zero," the Doctor said touching Juan's forehead with his index finger.

Suddenly, the Doctor felt himself flying, or falling, through space and time. Everything moved faster and faster until he approached the speed of light. (How he knew that, he did not know). Then all the light in the universe flared at once - and just for a moment. On the horizon he almost caught a glimpse of Eternity.

"If that's the Guild's final word, then I'm sorry," Tobin said to Sysadmin Two.

"No, you're not," Sysadmin Two replied with a cynical smile.

Tobin replied with a mirthless chuckle, "You're right. I'm not. Open fire!"

Suddenly, twenty guns opened up on Sysadmin Two.

When the Doctor opened his eyes, he was sitting on the floor. Emilio was shaking him by the shoulders. Juan was still in his seat.

"What happened to you?" Emilio asked, aghast.

"Incredible!" The Doctor finally sputtered out, "In all my travels...! I... No, no time for this, we have to move! Juan, Emilio, join hands! Let's go!"

Before Emilio could object, Juan took his father's hand.

"He'll be alright! No time to explain! Move!"

They hurried out the back door as the sounds of gunfire grew louder out front.

Romana and Gaba stepped off the trolley at the Observatory, which was on fire. The roof of the west wing looked ready to collapse.

"He said he'd meet you here?" Gaba asked.

Romana said nothing. Instead, she looked around and saw someone

lying in the bushes to one side of the entrance.
"Come on!" Romana cried.
A woman lay on her back. Her name tag read, "Dr. Matthews."
"Can you move?" Romana asked.
"Help," Dr. Matthews replied feebly. Then she stopped breathing. A moment later, her body disintegrated.
Romana stood up and backed away with a short intake of breath.
"What…?!"
"It's nothing," Gaba said simply.
"Nothing?" Romana cried, "Nothing!"
"She's been zeroed out," Gaba said with a shrug, "now get inside." She pointed her weapon at Romana and forced her to walk into the burning building.

It only took a moment, but Sysadmin Two had vanished from Emilio's garden.
"Cease fire!" Tobin called, "Eyes on!"
The soldiers stood and began a perimeter search. Within a minute they had reported back to Tobin.
"No sign of the blue-skinned guy," one said, "where'd he go?"
"His designation is Sysadmin Two. Identify your enemies, Private," Tobin replied.
"Roger that, sir. Why do you think Sysadmin Two took off like that? Was he hurt?"
"Negative. All we did was annoy him. He'll show his face again when it suits him. Regroup with Corporal Sharpe and his prisoners."
A solider stepped out of the house.
"Sharpe's inside, wounded. The prisoners have escaped."
"Give him a pain patch and a stimulant," Tobin replied, "we move out in one minute."
"Sir!"
"Listen carefully!" Tobin continued, "Our main objective is that hard drive. Do you understand?"
"Sir!" The company replied.
"And no lethal tactics until it's in our hands!"

Emilio drove the Doctor and Juan to the Observatory. Juan stayed in the car as the Doctor and Emilio slowly stepped out and stared in awe

at the building. The fire had almost burned itself out.
"What happened here?" Emilio whispered to himself.
"The walls are almost black from energy discharge," the Doctor said, "I would have preferred it remained Battleship Grey."
"Should Juan stay here?"
"There's more smoke than fire now. Best to bring him inside. Whoever did this might still be around."
They made their way carefully through the front doors. They could smell the smoke but they could not see any. Suddenly, they saw Romana at the other end of the room.
"Romana!"
"Run!" She cried.
But Gaba was already on their right, ready to shoot them if they ran.
"Stand still and don't move! If you disobey my orders, I'll shoot," she warned.
"Juan, get behind me! Don't shoot! Please!" Emilio begged Gaba.
Gaba just laughed at him.
"For pity's sake, just leave them alone!" Romana cried.
"What?" Gaba asked, genuinely surprised.
"Does pity surprise you?" The Doctor asked acidly.
"No, I just thought you knew what these things were," Gaba replied.
Romana had known the Doctor for several centuries, but she had never heard him speak as coldly as he did in that moment.
"Perhaps you'd care to explain that remark, Sergeant."
"Where exactly do you think you are?" Gaba laughed, "This isn't Earth, this isn't even a planet – this is a simulation of Earth! These 'people' are just sims"
Gaba chuckled coldly as she added, "They don't even leave a ghost behind when they die!"
Emilio had turned white.
"What?" He gasped.
Gaba ignored Emilio and continued, "The Guild hosts the largest networked array in the universe – or at least, that's their reputation. They are said to simulate everything down to the level of quarks. Those two – this 'father' and 'son' – aren't held together by quarks... they're held together by numbers!"
"No," Emilio said, then began crying softly.
"What are you crying for?" Gaba shouted, "You never go hungry!

You never even age!"
"All right, then. How did you get here?" The Doctor asked.
"A massive payment to the hackers of Tronlow."
"That's it!" The Doctor shouted, "The TARDIS must have slipped through the interface by accident once the hackers broke open the walls between our universe and this simulation. We were caught in the conversion field, which explains not only the bumpy landing but also why we couldn't determine our location!"
"Then it's true?" Romana replied, shocked and a little stunned.
"I'm afraid so," the Doctor said, "I finally remembered where I had heard of the Sysadmin Guild of the Golobus Sector. It was during those three weeks when I was stuck on Tronlow during the Second Hacker War against the League of..."
"No, it's not true!" Emilio was crying, hugging his son, "Juan is real!"
The Doctor touched his shoulder.
"This is a simulation. But I never said you weren't real."
"What?" Emilio and Romana said at the same time.
"1, 1, 1!" Juan cried.
"What's he saying?" Gaba demanded.
"He's pointing to your pocket, Doctor," Romana noted.
"The hard drive?" The Doctor asked, putting his hand in his pocket.
"What hard drive?" Gaba cried.
The Doctor took it out of his pocket and handed it to Juan.
"Here, take it."
"No, stop!" Gaba yelled, "I order you to..."
But Juan had already taken it and was holding it to his chest. Then the drive began to glow. Soon a bright light was illuminating Juan and the Doctor noticed that he was now hovering an inch above the floor.
"Juan!" Emilio cried, reaching for his son.
"No, don't!" The Doctor ordered, holding him back.
Romana took a step forward toward Juan.
"Stay back!" Gaba shouted, pointing her gun at the Timelord.
"Settle down, Sergeant! Juan has connected himself to the hard drive," the Doctor explained.
"What... by himself?" Emilio gasped.
"Indeed," the Doctor said smiling, "don't worry – your son is in his element, now. Literally!"
Suddenly, the flames went out, the smoke cleared, and the computers

in the building turned themselves back on. Juan looked up at his father and smiled.
"There, Sergeant!" The Doctor said, "Quite a feat for 'someone who isn't real'!"
"What did he just do?" Gaba asked nervously.
"Used the talents he was born with! With a little help from me, of course."

The Horde were about two miles from Emilio's house when several of their instruments began to whine.
"Massive energy reading being measured on all instruments, sir!" One cried.
"Data ports across the city are being reopened, re-energized, and optimized, sir!" Another added.
"This is exactly what we needed," Tobin gasped, "platoon, spread out and triangulate! Once we have the location of a data port, we won't need that drive."

"Doctor, what did you do to my son!" Emilio demanded.
The Doctor took him gently by the shoulders.
"Emilio, listen to me. All I did was unlock the potential he was born with. Accidentally, if you must know. We touched minds, briefly, back at your home. It was the only way I could think of to make him comfortable enough to leave the house. And then I discovered that Juan may be the most amazing individual I have ever encountered in all of my travels!"
"Doctor," Romana said suddenly, "I think he's here."
"What makes you think so?" The Doctor asked.
"Don't you hear it?"
The Doctor stopped talking and heard the hum.
"How interesting," a voice said behind and above them. They turned to see Sysadmin Two floating near the roof of the building.
"Ah, yes. Sysadmin Two. Delighted to meet you at last," the Doctor replied.
"I take it that you are responsible for re-energizing the data ports? How were you able to accomplish this feat when the Guild was not?"
"Actually, I didn't. He did," he said, pointing to Juan.
"The boy? That sim?" He said as if spitting a bug out of his mouth.

"That's my son you're speaking about!" Emilio said angrily.
"Be silent, or I will delete your ability to speak."
"Emilio, let me handle this," the Doctor said, gently pushing Emilio away from Sysadmin Two and toward Juan.
Romana looked at Gaba, who was staring wide-eyed at Sysadmin Two. She used this distraction to move slowly toward Emilio and Juan.
"Romana and I arrived in this simulation by accident," the Doctor said to Sysadmin Two, "upon encountering Emilio's son, Juan, I realized how exceptional he is."
"He is only an aberration."
"Could an aberration do what the entire Guild could not?"
"By definition, yes," Sysadmin Two replied.
"By definition, no," the Doctor responded, "an aberration of this magnitude is far more likely to bring your entire system down than support it! You have greatly underestimated your creations. They have gone beyond mere if-then statements and are as real are you or I!"
Sysadmin Two appeared to be listening to something. Finally, he said: "I'm in constant contact with The Guild, and while they reject your absurd claims, they accept that you and Romana arrived by error. Once we have regained full access to this simulation, we will perform a partial reboot and return you to the real universe."
"A reboot?" Gaba cried.
"Not without the Guild's promise that these people will be left to live their lives in peace," Romana said firmly, standing between Emilio and Juan on the one side and Sysadmin Two on the other.
"These sims have no life! They are merely a tool to model disasters!"
"What do you mean?" Romana asked.
"Of course!" The Doctor exclaimed, "Now I remember! Clients hire you to determine how certain planets will react to disasters and invasions. Whatever you're paid to simulate, eh?"
"You mean the Guild are just mercenaries?" Romana asked contemptuously.
"We provide a service!" Sysadmin Two replied, for once showing some emotion, "And the 'people' that you advocate for are mere tools! Does a hammer require legal representation?"
"7, 7, 7!" Juan yelped.
"That means 'chocolate', you know," the Doctor said with a chuckle,

253

"Juan's hungry after calibrating your entire network. If this is a mere disaster-and-recovery simulation, then why simulate an autistic child with a taste for chocolate?"

"Our simulations are, by necessity, exacting in detail. However, this particular model has demonstrated data corruption. He is a mere error," Sysadmin Two said, but he did not sound entirely convincing.

"How dare you?" Emilio exploded, "He's my son! If you're thinking of getting rid of him the next time you 'reboot', then get rid of me, too! How come I keep remembering how your 'simulations' end when no one else does? Why do I remember the world ending over and over?! Doesn't that make me a glitch, too? Doesn't it?"

Sysadmin Two stared, somewhat shocked, at Emilio

"Do you see now?" the Doctor asked quietly and calmly.

"Perhaps the granularity of our simulation was too fine. That will be noted and changed during the next upgrade."

"There is no 'upgrade'!" The Doctor insisted, "This is life itself! What's the base code of the computers that runs this 'simulation'? It's not base 2, is it? Not just zeros and ones...! It's base 8! An entire universe built on 0 through 7! And the exact numbers that Juan communicates in!"

"1, 1, 1!" Juan cried.

Now Sysadmin Two looked worried.

"If this sim has hacked into our system, then there will be endless trouble."

"Juan didn't hack into anything; he was born as a secondary processor in your computing environment! Your data flows through him the way oxygen flows through us. And he can't live without it any more than this environment can exist without him!"

Sysadmin Two began to look concerned.

"And if you reboot and allow Juan to die," the Doctor concluded, "your entire system may remain down forever!"

"Doctor!" Romana cried. "Gaba's gone!"

Captain Tobin stood before the surviving members of his troops within an empty parking lot.

"Soldiers of the Horde! We've had no contact from 'B' Company in several hours, so we must assume they are down. However, we have everything we need to proceed to Objective Bravo. Make your way in pairs to Alpha Point. That should keep the Sysadmins from pinning down your location. And..."

"Sir!" Someone yelled behind him. He turned to see Gaba running toward him.

"What's the sit rep, Sergeant?" He asked.

"Sysadmin Two may be about to perform a reboot, sir!"

The troops began to murmur audibly.

"That's enough!" Tobin cried, "You have your orders! Move out!"

The troops began to move out, but Gaba stayed where she was.

"Sir, there's something else. The Doctor...he believes that the sims are real."

"Real? What are you talking about?" Tobin barked.

"He means real as in alive, like you and me. If that's true..."

"Sergeant, you know as well as I do that our intel is sound. We will soon have a route open to every simulation on the network. And once we complete the mission our people, for the first time in two centuries, will be safe."

"But, sir, if these beings are alive..."

"Everything else is irrelevant. Do I make myself clear, Sergeant?"

There was a slight pause before Gaba replied.

"Sir!"

"Then proceed to Alpha Point!"

Gaba obeyed.

Sysadmin Two looked uneasy. But he attempted to conceal his concern by saying, "As stimulating as these debates may be, the threat from the Horde remains. Due to the probabilistic nature of a simulation, we can't always determine their location, unless they congregate in sufficiently large numbers."

"Perhaps they're at Sterling Lake," Romana suggested.

"Where?" The Doctor asked.

"Remember Elmer?" She asked, "The fisherman?"

"Yes."

"He appeared in the Bed and Breakfast again after you left, but without his fishing pole. That could just be an anomaly, or..."

"A clue to the Horde's position!" The Doctor interrupted.

"Please don't interrupt," Romana admonished.

"My apologies," the Doctor replied, humbly.

"It would appear that Elmer is yet another glitch," Sysadmin Two replied, "he'll be taken care of as well."

"Maybe he's not the glitch," the Doctor cautioned, "Maybe it's the location."

"Do you mean it's not Sterling Lake," Romana asked, "but the Bed and Breakfast itself?"

"Perhaps. It's where we woke up after the world ended."

"And where the Horde began their search – and where I found that trap door in the basement."

Juan began jumping up and down. "1, 1, 1!"

"It's the trap door, isn't it?" The Doctor asked.

"It must be," Romana added, "when I tried to open it, there was nothing - literally *nothing* - on the other side!"

"1, 1, 1!"

"Sysadmin Two?" The Doctor inquired.

"My records are vague about this 'trap door', so I shall consult the Guild..." he began.

"This simulation is upgraded from time to time?" The Doctor asked, interrupting again.

"Of course," Sysadmin Two replied wearily.

"Upgrades usually leave undeleted files behind from previous versions."

"Always," Emilio added, "and usually undocumented."

"But in our simulations, we allow no such errors to..." Sysadmin Two began.

"0, 0, 0!" Juan cried.

"My son says you're wrong, sir!" Emilio said with venom.

"And he did fix your..." the Doctor began.

"I know, I know!" Sysadmin Two snapped. He appeared preoccupied as he said, "I'm looking through all previous versions, the documentation of which runs several trillion pages, so..."

There was a pause. Then, "Ah... yes..."

"Juan's right, isn't he?" Emilio asked.

"He is. A backup data port from the original version that escaped our notice."

"Or perhaps it was kept hidden," the Doctor said, "even hackers from Tronlow need a little help now and again."

"Are you suggestion that one of the Guild would give help to those..."

Sysadmin Two began indignantly.

"Of course not, of course not!" The Doctor supplied in a mollifying tone that convinced no one of his sincerity.

"The immediate question is this," Romana began, "why would the Horde need access to the entire network?"

"Sabotage, surely," Emilio said.

"They're too busy staying alive to indulge in revenge," the Doctor observed.

"Escape to a hidden simulation?" Romana asked, "One that's been hidden, just like this data port?"

"Highly unlikely!" Sysadmin Two scoffed, but then after a moment added, "But... not impossible."

"Or perhaps they're after something other than sanctuary," the Doctor muttered.

"Such as?" Sysadmin Two asked.

"What if they never meant to stay here in the first place? What if the desire for asylum was a ruse?"

"I think you give them far more credit than..." Sysadmin Two began.

"Is it alright," the Doctor asked Romana, "if I interrupt this time?"

"Oh, be my guest," she replied.

"Sysadmin Two, what are you hiding that The Horde might be searching for?" He asked.

Sysadmin Two's blue face suddenly became much darker.

"Should the Horde pose a major threat to the Guild, then the Guild will bring down upon them the full might of..."

"In other words," Emilio interrupted, "he's not going to tell us."

"Whatever the Horde is up to," the Doctor said, "they're not likely to keep the safety of others in mind."

"And whatever it is," Romana added, "they're doing it now."

"Indeed," the Doctor agreed, "Sysadmin Two, you must take us to the Bed & Breakfast at once. All of us!"

"Even Juan?" Emilio asked.

"Especially Juan! He may be the most important person in this universe!"

Juan smiled.

"But don't let that go to your head," the Doctor warned him with a friendly wink.

"Yes, you'd know all about remaining humble, wouldn't you?"

Romana pointed out coolly, but not unkindly.

"Is the teleportation unit ready to be activated, Private?" Tobin asked a soldier standing inside the Bed and Breakfast.
"Yes, sir!" She confirmed.
"Stand by – it must be ready to go off just after the Transformation Device."
"Roger that, sir!"
Tobin jogged into the kitchen where a corporal was standing by a large, ungainly, intricate device.
"Corporal Sharpe," Tobin asked. "Is the Transformation Device standing by?"
"Operations nominal, and countdown set for sixty seconds," Sharpe replied.
Tobin held his breath for a moment, and then said: "Activate it."
Sharpe pressed a button, and they could instantly hear a low hum which grew louder by the second.
"Transformation device at the ready! And remember, everyone," Tobin said as he left the kitchen and rejoined his troops, "allow nothing to interfere with this countdown! We only have one chance!"
"Yes, sir!" They replied in unison.
Then they heard an even louder sound as Sysadmin Two appeared inside the Bed and Breakfast.
"Incoming!" Tobin cried. The soldiers drew weapons and pointed them at Sysadmin Two.
The Doctor, Romana, Emilio, and Juan also appeared in the room.
"Don't shoot!" The Doctor yelled, "We're here to talk!"
"If they shoot, their weapons will discharge in their hands!" Sysadmin Two replied.
"I want no violence," the Doctor told them firmly, "Captain Tobin, may we speak?"
"Hold your fire!" Tobin ordered. The soldiers lowered their weapons.
"I know who your people are, " the Doctor said, "and why you've acted so desperately. But you must know; these 'sims' are less than an atom's width from being the same as you or I! I know you've found a hidden data port. I don't know what you plan to do with it, but if you tamper with the network that connects these simulations, you could cause another catastrophe that would bring them all down! And that's

genocide! Isn't genocide what you're running from?"
Tobin seemed unimpressed with the Doctor's speech.
"What's your point, Doctor?"
"I can help you! I can take the Horde to the Ki Shee System. The Embodiment of Gris was almost killed there by a Dalek Fleet. He avoids it the way your people avoid ghosts."
"We're not afraid of ghosts!" The soldiers began to holler. "We're not afraid of anything!"
"Who ya gonna call?" The Doctor muttered under his breath.
"Perhaps I should attempt diplomatic relations?" Romana asked the Doctor.
"3," Juan said.
"Forgive me!" The Doctor attempted to apologise.
"Your diplomacy means nothing," Tobin added with a dark grin.
"2," Juan said.
"Doctor," Emilio asked, "what does Juan mean?"
"I don't know," the Doctor admitted grimly.
"You've given us the time we needed," Tobin continued, "thank you!"
"What?" The Doctor and Romana cried in unison.
"1…!" Juan counted, louder than before.
"Doctor, something..." Sysadmin Two began.
"0!" Juan shouted.
It felt as if the world had dissolved beneath them - they were falling faster and faster into darkness even as Tobin and the Horde disappeared. The Doctor tried to reach for Romana but he could not see her, or anything else for that matter. All he could sense was a deep humming noise that filled his ears and mind. He tried to clasp his ears to block out the sound, but his hands passed through where his head should have been, then passed through each other.
It was when time and space shattered that the Doctor lost his consciousness, his mind, and his everything to utter darkness.

Chapter Twelve – 0,0,0 – Part 3

By Daniel Callahan with Oliver M. Goldblatt

The Horde had achieved their objective, whatever that was. Not even the Doctor could figure out what they were up to. He was not even aware that they had set up something they called a transformation device. When it went off, it felt as if the world had dissolved beneath him, and he were falling faster and faster into darkness, even as Tobin and the Horde had disappeared.
It was when time and space had shattered that the Doctor lost consciousness, his mind, his everything to utter darkness.

Seven, zero, five, zero, four, three, zero, one, six, zero, zero, zero...
Numbers were running through the Doctor's consciousness once more, but he could not understand why.
But he remembered he was the Doctor, and he could almost remember the name of his companion...
"It's happened, again," he heard Romana say.
"Romana, that's it!" He cried, sitting bolt upright. He was on the same bed in the same bedroom with the same settee near the window.
"We're back!"
"Yes, I realized that," Romana said, unsure if the Doctor was taking the mickey, "I had the same dream."
"Numbers!" The Doctor barked.
"Except there were more zeros this time."
"We both had the same dream... again! Could it be chronic hysteresis?"
"I hope not. If it is, we'll be stuck here... wait, haven't we had this conversation already?"
"Captain Tobin activated some kind of device," the Doctor remembered, "a time loop generator?"
"If he had something as valuable as that he could have traded it for a planet," Romana replied as she sat on the settee.
"We fell..." the Doctor remembered.
"It felt like forever," Romana said as it came back to her, "every part of me came undone..."
"And now we're back here. The Horde must have caused a reboot!

"No, no, it was more than that," the Doctor announced, jumping up on his toes a few times, "something's changed...! I can feel it in my..."
"Knock, knock," an old, tired voice interrupted just outside the door. Mrs. Saunders pushed in the door, carrying a tea tray and cups. But instead of the energetic lady they remembered, she was bent over and looked drained.
"Who's ready for... ah!" she yelped, dropping the tea tray to the floor as her lower back spasmed. She cried and fell forward but the Doctor caught her. She looked confused as she gazed at the broken cups on the floor.
"I don't understand," she said at last, "everything hurts. My back, my knees, my elbow... I've never felt like this before!"
"Here, let's take a look at you," the Doctor said, helping her sit on the bed.
Romana stood and helped the Doctor give a quick medical exam.
"Are you both doctors?" Mrs. Saunders asked weakly.
The Doctor and Romana looked at each other for a moment and smiled.
"We're highly qualified in many things," Romana assured her.
"Let's hope," the Doctor whispered.
"I'm afraid you have an advanced case of arthritis," Romana finally concluded.
"Arth...? But how could it happen so quickly!"
"Are these your first symptoms?" The Doctor asked.
"Oh my, yes! I've always felt like a Spring Chicken. I guess age has finally caught up with me."
"Something's changed the parameters of the simulation," the Doctor said to Romana.
"Simulation, deary?" Mrs. Saunders asked, "What's that?"
Romana smiled, patted her on the back, and turned to the Doctor. "Did the Horde corrupt the data?"
"If that were so," the Doctor continued, "might there be a hole big enough for the TARDIS to slip through?"
Romana's eyes widened. They both ran for the door.
Mrs. Saunders blinked uncomfortably.
Then the Doctor returned suddenly and said, "Stay there 'til you get your breath back. Then take two aspirin and call me in the morning!" Then he popped out again.

Mrs. Saunders nodded and decided to have a lie down before making any more tea.

They stood outside. It was still the same city, the same buildings, the same people moving back and forth, but something felt off. And there was still no sign of the TARDIS.
"It's like those films where everything looks blue," the Doctor said.
"Filmed with Dutch angles?" Romana asked with a smile.
The Doctor was about to answer when the door to the B&B opened behind them. They turned and saw Elmer carrying his fishing pole. He was sweating and his face looked grey.
"Elmer!" Romana cried.
"Want.. to go…" Elmer began, but then said, "help me…"
He collapsed onto the pavement and did not move again.
The Doctor and Romana knelt and quickly examined him. Then the Doctor stopped and sighed.
"A heart attack. A massive one."
"Did Tobin infect these people with something?"
"Nothing that's affecting us."
"What about Juan and Emilio?" Romana asked.

They arrived at Emilio's house via the trolley, which thankfully was still running. There had been fewer passengers, and the driver looked tired. As they approached the garden, they found the front door ajar. They ran into the yard and then the house.
"Emilio!" The Doctor shouted as they entered.
"Juan!" Romana called.
Emilio was on the couch with his head in his hands. They could not see Juan.
"Where's Juan?" Asked the Doctor.
Emilio slowly shook his head. "I don't know…"
The Doctor and Romana looked at each other, and then turned to begin a search of the premises. However, Juan ran into room and said, "Daddy!"
To their complete surprise, Juan gave his father a brief hug and then sat down at his computer again.
The silence was finally broken as Emilio managed to stammer, "Good... good morning, Juan?"

"He's never called you that before, has he?" The Doctor asked.
"No," Emilio replied, shaking his head in shock.
"The Horde wouldn't have done this on purpose," Romana said, "could it be Sysadmin Two?"
"Or just a random glitch?" The Doctor asked.
"Too many questions," he then hissed angrily, "and for once, I don't have any answers!"
"But something has changed," Romana said, frowning.
"Indeed," the Doctor replied grimly, "I just can't put my finger on it."
"I don't mean to complain," Emilio said, "but I may have to lie down."
"Why, what's wrong?" Romana asked.
Emilio was searching for the words and finally said, "I just feel terrible! Like I'm losing energy... Maybe if I take a nap for a... day or two..."
"Yes... I understand, now," the Doctor gasped, "for the first time in your life, you're ageing!"
Both Emilio and Romana turned to the Doctor saying, "What?"
"You, all of you, have been the same biological age for decades... maybe centuries. Remember, this is a disaster-and-recovery simulation. The only injuries that matter to the Guild are those received during the disasters!"
"No, no," Emilio replied as he shook his head, "no, this can't be."
"Perhaps the Guild wrote an age-and-decay plug-in to be activated at the next upgrade," Romana added, "and the Horde has triggered it prematurely."
"No, you're wrong! You're wrong!" Emilio screamed as he rose to his feet.
Juan suddenly jumped off his chair, ran to his father, took his hand, and said: "0... 0... no."
Emilio looked down into his son's eyes, then dropped to his knee and hugged him.
"Juan understands," the Doctor said at last.
Emilio reddened.
"He understands that we're all going to..." he could not complete his question.
"We all will, someday," the Doctor replied, "but not today!"
"Emilio," Romana asked, "I realize this isn't a good time, but have

you seen Sysadmin Two this morning?"
Then she turned to the Doctor.
"It is morning, isn't it? I mean, it feels like morning."
"Definitely morning-ish," the Doctor replied.
Then they heard a muffled, scared voice outside the front door.
"Help me! Open this door!"
The Doctor and Romana looked at Emilio, who nodded.
The Doctor opened the door to find Sysadmin Two on all fours. When he looked up, he appeared almost like a child who had lost its mother.
"Let me help you up," the Doctor said, and soon they had him inside, sitting at Emilio's kitchen table.
"I don't understand! I'm walking," Sysadmin was muttering, "I should be floating above it all!"
"A classic Freudian slip," Romana said to the Doctor.
The Doctor turned to Emilio.
"The best thing in the short term is food and coffee. Especially the coffee."
Juan ran into the kitchen, found the coffee maker, filled it with water, and plugged it in.
"Does coffee help with ageing?" Emilio asked.
"It'll kill or cure," the Doctor said, deadpan.
Emilio stared at the Doctor for a moment, and then asked, "Really?"
"Broken!" Juan said suddenly, shaking his head in frustration.
"What's wrong?" the Doctor asked, checking over the coffee maker.
"Ah. It's out of warranty. But never mind!" He pulled his sonic screwdriver from his pocket, and after a few short blasts, the water began to heat inside the coffee maker.
"It's working!" Romana said in astonishment.
"Of course it is," the Doctor returned.
"Never underestimate sonic..." he continued, then followed Romana's train of thought, "the sonic screwdriver didn't work before!"
"Something about this place prevented it," Romana said.
"The nature of this place prevented it," the Doctor agreed.
"The Guild! I can't contact the Guild!" Sysadmin Two cried, "Where have they gone?! Why have they left me?! Come back! Come back!"
"Oh, grow up," Emilio snapped, "this can't be the first time you've been alone!"
"Actually," the Doctor added, "I think it is."

Emilio paused, then in a half-whisper asked, "Ever?"
"There are very few who can grasp how abandoned he feels right now," the Doctor replied.
Romana gently squeezed the Doctor's arm.
Emilio turned back to Sysadmin Two and said gently, "Sysadmin Two... did you change Juan? Did the Horde or the Guild?"
"Come back! Please, come back!" Sysadmin Two whined.
"Please," Romana said, "we need your help."
Sysadmin Two looked up and wiped his eyes.
"Mrs Saunders is ill," Romana continued, "Elmer has died, Juan has undergone a significant transformation, and we still can't find the TARDIS."
"Perhaps if you could help us," the Doctor added, "we could help you re-establish contact with the Guild."
Sysadmin Two stood to his full height.
"I don't need your help. Nor the help of these sims!"
Just then, Juan appeared at his side holding a cup of coffee. He was smiling as he held it up to Sysadmin Two, who looked as if he were seeing Juan for the first time. Slowly, he took the mug and nodded to the boy. Juan appeared happy to have helped and he turned back to the coffee maker.
"Forgive me," Sysadmin Two said as he sat down again, "I... apologise."
"Sugar? Milk?" Emilio asked, trying to restrain his own anger and frustration.
"I... don't know," Sysadmin Two said, "I've never tasted coffee before."
He took a sip, and his face contorted.
"Three sugars, no milk," he quickly replied.
"Excellent," the Doctor said, personally adding three sugars to his coffee and stirring, "about our questions..."
"How has Juan changed!" Emilio demanded.
"Everything's changed," Sysadmin Two replied wearily, taking another sip of his coffee "I've been in the Guild for over three thousand years, and I couldn't begin to catalogue the changes."
Soon, everyone had a mug of coffee in their hand except Juan, who drank milk.
"Alright... then let's back up. Where's the nearest data port?" The

Doctor asked.

"The Bed & Breakfast, I believe," Sysadmin Two supplied.

"Is it active?" Romana wondered.

Sysadmin Two shook his head.

"None of them are."

"So, we're trapped here?" Romana said.

The Doctor shook his head.

"I don't know. Come on, Sysadmin Two, it's time for you to explain everything."

"Explain what?"

"Give us the big picture," the Doctor said, "as well as the details!"

Sysadmin Two looked up with genuine shock.

"But I'd be breaking the inviolable Laws of the Guild if I said anything!"

The Doctor set his coffee down, put his hands on the table and leaned toward Sysadmin Two's face, "I am your only chance of being reconnected with the Guild in this or any other universe."

It took only a moment for his words to sink in.

"If you would guarantee your silence on this matter, then…" Sysadmin Two began.

"No promises," Romana stated bluntly.

Sysadmin Two took a very large drink of coffee and set down his empty mug.

"This world is a simulation, as you know. It's linked with hundreds of other simulations in a fifth-dimensional array using dual resonance wormholes and tri-centric linkage to…"

"Yes, yes, yes," the Doctor said, waving his hand, "skip the obvious bits!"

Emilio shook his head and took another slug of coffee.

"Well, the effects of natural disasters on different worlds and the populations' responses are of great interest to our clients. Should a world demonstrate that it cannot cope with a given catastrophe without aid, then…"

"Then your clients know which worlds are most vulnerable, eh?" The Doctor replied.

"So, this is how rich worlds decide who to invade next," Romana said with a mix of horror and contempt.

"What our clients choose to do with the information they pay for is

none of your…!" Sysadmin Two began. Then he saw the look on Emilio's face.
"Forgive me…" he said, wiping his face with his hand.
"Just keep talking," Emilio said through gritted teeth.
"But that's all there is to say!"
"All?" The Doctor cried. "All!"
But Juan was suddenly at the Doctor's side, touching his hand. The Doctor stopped, smiled at him, and took his hand. Suddenly, it was as if he were somewhere else. Not falling through space, but sitting peacefully watching the stars whirl overhead through millennia of change. And he was seeing all of it through Juan's eyes.
"Thank you, Juan," the Doctor said, letting go of his hand, "I see it now."
"Doctor?" Romana asked softly.
"This simulation," the Doctor said, looking at each of them, "is now a universe."
"What?" Emilio asked weakly.
"Everything here was held together by numbers, not quarks. Until the Horde activated some kind of transformation device."
"Which converted the numbers into quarks?" Romana replied, her breath almost taken away.
"I believe so," the Doctor replied.
"So…" Emilio said, "we're no longer sims?"
"What do you say, Juan?" The Doctor asked.
"Yes!" Juan said, smiling and jumping in place.
"¡Madre de Dios!" Emilio said quietly, almost falling out of his chair.
"But the Horde couldn't have pulled off this trick by themselves," Romana objected, "they're only scavengers."
"They've been helped, and promised a big reward for this job," the Doctor replied, "they didn't just receive help from the Hackers of Tronlow. Someone from the Guild helped too."
The Doctor turned to Sysadmin Two.
"This transformation algorithm… it was yours, wasn't it?"
Sysadmin Two appeared dumbfounded.
"How could you know all this?"
"But why create such a device? What's it for?" Romana asked.
"Why is of no concern," Sysadmin Two said with a wave of his hand. "We are only interested in the assignment... and prompt payment!"

"That I can believe," Romana replied sourly.
"The why is obvious," the Doctor said, "custom-built universes for the ultra-wealthy? Universe-sized prisons to house your inmates? The possibilities are as endless as they are lucrative. But the more immediate question is; how does it work?"
"Badly," Sysadmin Two replied, "we only had the prototype, and it's unstable. The 'new' universes collapse after a few days. Assuming that every simulation in our system has been made real, I would estimate that we only have a few hours left."
"No!" Emilio gasped.
Romana turned to the Doctor, who looked back at her.
"No," Juan shouted, "no, no!"
"What is it, Juan?" Emilio asked.
"Wrong!" Juan said, pointing at Sysadmin Two, "Wrong!"
"I would be delighted to be proved wrong in this instance!" Sysadmin Two admitted.
"Are there no emergency protocols," Romana asked, "what might the Guild be doing now?"
"They will attempt to stabilize the domain, of course," Sysadmin Two replied, "if they can perform a partial reboot, then we might have a chance. But that assumes they understand what's happening here!"
"They lost the Sun and the Horde," the Doctor countered, "I don't think they're at the top of their game right now."
"I…" Sysadmin Two began, "I have no explanation. But if the Horde transformed all of our simulations into universes… then a shock to the network like that might disable some security measures that protect the meta-structure."
"So, they must have had a plan. Find… whatever it is, move it into our universe, and get out."
"Are they after a weapon?" Romana asked.
"No!" Juan cried jumping up and down while pointing to his computer monitor.
"What do you have there?" Emilio asked, looking at the screen.
They stood and walked toward the computer. The image looked like it could be a spacecraft of some kind. It was the size of a medium-sized house and had no visible engines, but the schematics suggested it might be a manufacturing hub of some kind. And its power capacity was rated almost off the scale.

The Doctor's eye widened, and he looked at Romana.
"Are you feeling what I'm feeling?"
"Fear?" She replied.
"Exactly. This *could* to be Time Lord technology, at least in part."
"Who are they?" Emilio asked.
"We are," the Doctor replied.
"Where did you get that?" Romana asked Sysadmin Two coldly.
"I'm not at liberty to say," he replied.
"Your secrets will mean nothing unless you help us help you!" Romana barked at him.
Sysadmin Two appeared to consider this.
"Sysadmin Two," the Doctor said, "I assure you that we are not working against the Guild's interests. But if we survive this without your help, we will. That's a promise. So... what do you say?"
Sysadmin Two sighed.
"I don't know the origin of these plans, but it is a most highly guarded project. The space inside houses a facility for creating trillions of artificial satellites," he told them.
"Are they dangerous?" Emilio asked.
"Are they?" The Doctor repeated to underline the import of those words.
"They are... safely locked away in a partitioned simulation!" Sysadmin Two replied, dodging the question.
"Has it been paid for?" Romana asked.
"Not yet."
A look of shock suddenly appeared on Sysadmin Two's face.
"Are you suggesting that the client sent the Horde to steal it?!"
"Possibly the client, possibly an interested third party," the Doctor muttered quietly, "there's no way to tell."
"Now," he then continued, at a normal volume, "the Horde infiltrated your system, gained access to a data port that only they knew about, turned every simulation into its own universe, and..."
"They plan to deliver this 'manufacturing plant' to someone in our universe," Romana added matter-of-factly. Then she realized what it all meant.
"But they know the new universes will collapse soon. So they'll just punch a hole directly into our universe!"
"What will happen then?" Emilio asked.

"The meta-structure will break apart, and the new universes will pop like balloons," the Doctor concluded.
"So, we may not have hours," Emilio stated grimly.
"We may not have minutes," the Doctor said, turning to Sysadmin Two, "not unless you help us right now."
"But I'm helpless without the Guild!" Sysadmin Two protested.
"No!" Juan cried, running forward and taking Sysadmin Two by the hand. Both shut their eyes and the room began to hum.
"Juan?" Emilio gasped, reaching for his son. The Doctor held his arm.
"No," he said quietly but firmly, "not yet."
"I can see again!" Sysadmin Two cried with his eyes still shut.
"Location established!"
They opened their eyes and, to the shock of everyone, Sysadmin Two smiled at Juan.
"I... we know where they are."
"But how can we follow them?" Romana asked, "The data ports aren't active."
"No, but the boundaries between universes are becoming fluid. Which means..." the Doctor turned to Juan, "Juan, old chap, I need you to remember something important for us. That funny blue box that appeared just before the sun blew up?"
Juan appeared confused.
"It gave off some funny numbers, didn't it? Patterns you've never seen before. I need you to think hard. Concentrate on it. You can bring it back to us."
Juan shut his eyes tight and began to sway. Emilio reached out and steadied him as they heard a wheezing-groaning sound in the garden. The Doctor opened the door to see the TARDIS fade in, and then begin to fade out again...
He turned to see Juan almost out on his feet.
"Doctor," Emilio cried, "don't do this to my son!"
"Emilio," the Doctor said gently, "if this doesn't work, it's the end for all of us."
"Zero!" Juan shouted. He fell into his father's arms as the TARDIS finally materialized.
"Juan!" Emilio sobbed.
Juan appeared unconscious. Emilio looked at the Doctor and Romana, but Sysadmin Two stepped forward.

"One good turn, as they say," he said, placing his hand on Juan's head. A blue light appeared briefly over the child, and in a moment his eyes were open again.

"Thank you," Emilio said, shaking Sysadmin Two's hand.

"Now," the Doctor said, "Romana and I will take the TARDIS and find the Horde, with the help of Sysadmin Two."

"We will?" Sysadmin Two asked.

"We will. You can remember the pathways through the meta-structure without the Guild's help. Emilio, Juan, stay here. Have some chocolate."

"No!" Juan cried, pushing himself up onto his feet.

"That's a good boy," the Doctor said, as if he had not heard him. "Romana?" The Doctor called as he quickly left the house.

"Um," Romana replied awkwardly.

"Yes, come along," she added, taking Sysadmin Two's hand and pulling him out of the house.

"No!" Juan cried again.

"Doctor," Emilio called after them, "are you sure you can do this without our help?"

"Absolutely!" The Doctor said in a cheery voice from the front steps.

"No lies!" Juan insisted.

"Indeed! Always search for truth!" The Doctor said dismissively as he turned and walked away.

The TARDIS doors opened just as the Doctor reached them.

"Master?" K9 called, "Mistress?"

"We'll explain on the way, K9," the Doctor shouted, "get ready to dematerialize!"

Before the Doctor could finish, Juan had torn himself free from his father and was sprinting toward the TARDIS.

"Juan!" The Doctor and Emilio cried. Everyone except Sysadmin Two tried to stop him, but he managed to slip by them, jump over K9, and run toward the TARDIS console.

They ran after him, the Doctor ordering him not to touch the controls. But as soon as Sysadmin Two was inside, the doors slammed shut, and the TARDIS began to dematerialize.

"Juan, we need to talk about healthy boundaries," the Doctor grumbled as he reached the control panel.

Suddenly, the TARDIS jolted, sending them to the floor.

"You know," Romana said to the Doctor as they slowly stood up, "I think he's turning out a lot like you."

The Doctor scowled. He stood slowly and saw K9 was lying on his side.

"Unauthorized take-off!" K9 cried, uselessly.

The Doctor helped K9 up and said, "Juan - and his father, Emilio - are friends. Help Juan pilot the TARDIS."

K9's ear waggled and the robot dog repeated, "Friends."

He moved towards the control panels, extended his sensor, and soon the TARDIS flight path was stabilized.

The Doctor turned to Emilio.

"I'm sorry. I tried to protect Juan."

"I think whatever is coming up," Emilio said, "Juan needs to be there."

"What... is this place?" Sysadmin Two asked, stunned in spite of attempting not to be.

"It's a Time machine that's bigger on the inside than out," the Doctor replied.

"Oh," Emilio commented.

"Oh?" The Doctor repeated sarcastically.

"I mean, no offence," Emilio quickly added, "but it's not the strangest thing that I've come across, lately."

The Doctor seemed to accept this and then turned to watch Juan work the controls.

"Would you be interested in selling the design of this craft...?" Sysadmin Two began.

"No," came Romana and the Doctor's sharp reply in unison.

"How is he doing that?" Emilio asked as he watched Juan work the TARDIS controls.

"He's just as at home in the world of numbers as he is in the real world," the Doctor said, "and the language of the TARDIS *is* mathematics."

"And," Romana added with a smile, "I think she likes him."

The Doctor harrumphed as if he had just been jilted.

"Your ship... it's alive," Emilio asked, "how is that possible?"

"Juan will explain it all to you one day," the Doctor replied.

"No lying!" Juan responded.

The Doctor approached a different panel and turned to K9.

"What's our ETA?"

"Approximately three minutes, Master," K9 replied.

The TARDIS shuddered and everyone reached out for something to hold onto.

"Four minutes," K9 said, correcting himself, "as the meta-structure fails, the travel time increases."

"But how does Juan know what to do?" Emilio insisted.

"Juan was born in telepathic contact with your universe," Romana explained, "syncing up with the TARDIS isn't much different."

"Uh, yes," Emilio said, "so, what can I do?"

"Help Sysadmin Two," Romana said. Then added, sotto voce, "And watch him."

Emilio nodded, "Got you."

Emilio moved toward Sysadmin Two, who had his eyes closed.

"Juan, can you see what I see?" He asked.

"Yes!" Juan said.

An image began to hover above the console.

"We can all see it!" The Doctor shouted, "Physical laws are breaking down, somehow amplifying our psychic connections!"

"Master," K9 said. "ETA is now six minutes and likely to increase."

"But that's too long!" Romana replied.

"Affirmative," K9 concurred, "estimation that we shall cease to exist before physical arrival…"

His ears whirred. Then he said, "96%."

There was a stunned silence in the control room. Emilio and Romana looked at each other then turned to the Doctor, who appeared deep in thought.

"Sysadmin Two?" He asked.

"The Guild… agrees with your robot's estimate," he replied.

"In that case, we won't arrive at all!" The Doctor declared with a inordinately large smile on his face.

"What?" Romana gasped.

"We can't get there *physically*, but if Sysadmin Two can contact the Guild, that means psychic transmissions are in the clear!"

"What does that mean?" Emilio asked.

"It means we can communicate with the Horde telepathically," Romana replied, "but I don't see how that helps us."

"They won't know it's telepathy," the Doctor said, smiling.

"And?" Romana pressed.

273

The Doctor grinned.
"Why do I get the impression this next part will be up to me?" She groaned.
"Because you're so perceptive. You'll have to convince Gaba that you're a ghost."
"I..." Romana began, "a what?"
"Right now, it's their only weakness," the Doctor explained, "they're terrified of the spirits of the people they've killed."
"And your plan is that I scare them all to death with my Jacob Marley impersonation?"
"Do whatever it takes. Scare the Dickens out of them. Remember, the Horde have a strong sense of personal honour. If she were to believe you'd been murdered..."
"She might turn on Tobin and commit mutiny!"
"Exactly," the Doctor replied.
"Doctor!" Sysadmin Two said, "I'm now in partial contact with The Guild. The Horde are indeed attempting to steal the manufacturing unit. Unfortunately, there is little we can do. All of our reserves are being used to keep the new universes from collapsing."
"Tell them not to worry and to be ready for massive wave of energy. They can use that to re-energize the data ports and restore equilibrium."
"Where will the energy come from?" Romana asked.
"The Horde can't send that ship to our universe without popping the balloon, so to speak. Perhaps the Guild can use that energy to save everything else," the Doctor said grimly.
Romana nodded.
"But if that happens, we won't survive."
"No, we won't. I'll try to frighten Tobin too," the Doctor said, "but it's a long shot."
The Doctor turned to the others.
"Emilio, you and Sysadmin Two stay here. The rest of us are going on a... mind journey."
"Is it safe?" Emilio asked, "For Juan?"
"No," the Doctor replied, "there's no place that's safe for him, or any of us, right now. But perhaps he can help stabilize our environment."
Emilio nodded sadly and began massaging Juan's shoulders.
"Juan," the Doctor said, "follow my example. Lay your hands on the

control panel."
The Doctor, Juan, and Romana all assumed their positions.
"Once we get there, we do our best to keep the Horde from moving that manufacturing device into the real universe."
"Affirmative!" Juan replied.
The Doctor looked at Romana.
"Contact."
"Contact," Romana replied.
"Contact," Juan repeated.
And suddenly they were outside the TARDIS within a nearly empty universe watching the Horde swarm over the manufacturing craft. They wore spacesuits and were setting up box upon box of equipment on every side of the hull, getting ready to punch a hole through two realities.

"Private!" Captain Tobin shouted.
"Quadrant Four needs these data relays!" He said, pointing to an unopened crate, "Take them now!"
"Yes, sir!" The Private snapped, picking up the crates with ease and jogging away.
"And tell Corporal Sharpe that we're reading anomalous energy bursts," Tobin called after him, "keep your eyes open!"
"Sir!" The Private yelled from the distance.
"We're running out of time," Tobin muttered to himself.
"How long is infinity?" The Doctor's voice asked.
Tobin spun around, but he saw no one.
"Who's that?"
"You know Who," the Doctor said, "you killed me at the data port."
For the first time in years, Tobin began to sweat and tremble with fear.
"I... I... I'm not afraid of ghosts."
"Of course not," the Doctor's voice continued with a mocking tone. "Soldiers kill the enemy. That's what they do. Unless they kill civilians... That's very different, isn't it?"
But Tobin was already shaking himself out of his dread.
"You... you are a distraction, nothing more."
He turned back to his work.
"Fear of ghosts suggests either a belief in supernatural forces..." the Doctor continued relentlessly.

"Voord pathways connected to Sraxian links," Tobin said, talking himself through each step.
"Or guilt. Repressed guilt to be precise."
"Atrian power packs set to discharge..."
"Guilt over the thousands you've killed in order to stay alive."
Tobin spun around angrily to confront the Doctor's seemingly dead voice.
"It was them or us! Don't you understand?! Them or us!"

On the other side of the prototype Sergeant Gaba was giving instructions to a squad.
"Corporal Aeon. Help lay out these cables!"
"Sir!" She replied, taking charge of three slow-moving soldiers.
"Gaba," Romana's voice said.
"What?" Gaba asked, then turned to see no one there.
She spun around and shouted, "Who's there?"
The others heard it too, and froze.
"Romana."
Gaba almost collapsed onto the deck.
"It wasn't my fault! I was just following orders!"
"Yes," Romana replied sadly, "that's why I died."
The other soldiers bolted, leaving Gaba to face this ghost alone.
"Take it up with Captain Tobin!" Gaba cried, moving away from the sound of Romana's voice, "It was his call!"
"If you follow Tobin's orders, you'll die. All of you," Romana said, following her, "that's why the Doctor wants to help."
"But..." Gaba replied, "the Doctor died, too."
"He survived, somehow. He promised that he would take you to Ki Shee. You'd be safe forever and you'd never have to kill anyone again."
"I have my orders! Leave me alone!"
"I will leave you," Romana replied, "but you won't be alone. I'm just the first. I'm being followed by..."
There was a terrible pause and Gaba froze.
"By what?" Gaba finally whispered.
"All of us. Before you left, Tobin did something, made them - all of the sims – real. And then they died. Now they're coming here!"
Gaba's face went white with terror.

"No... no, no, no!"
"I could," Romana said after a dramatic pause, "make them go back."
"Please! Please make them go away!" Gaba sobbed, collapsing onto the hull of the spacecraft.
"Then do one thing for me."
"Anything!" Gaba cried, her eyes tightly shut.
"Take command," Romana ordered sternly.

Back in the TARDIS, the Doctor, Romana and Juan stood touching the console, their eyes closed. They somehow managed to stay on their feet as the TARDIS lurched.
"Spacial dimensions folding!" K9 reported.
"We should leave!" Sysadmin Two said suddenly. Emilio could see that he was beginning to panic.
"No!" Juan cried. His eyes were still closed, but it was clear what he meant.
"You're fine! Look at me!" Emilio ordered. "You're fine!"
Sysadmin Two looked at Emilio and said, "But the meta-structure may collapse! We have to go!"
"We're not going anywhere!" Emilio said firmly.

Captain Tobin was doing his best to ignore the Doctor's voice as he worked to complete his mission. But the Doctor was not giving up either.
"How many little old ladies have you killed for their pack lunches, eh?" mocked the Doctor.
"How many grandchildren did you allow to starve? Or did you just put them out of their misery... for the sake of the mission?"
Tobin was sweating heavily inside his spacesuit and not from the heat.
"There are no such things as civilians!" He growled.
"No," the Doctor replied sympathetically, "not for your people. That's the evil that's been done to you."
But then he continued angrily, "So why inflict this same evil on others?"
Tobin barked out a cynical laugh.
"There is nothing evil about survival!"
"Isn't there? All this began when you made an enemy of the Embodiment of Gris, but now you've become someone else's

Embodiment of Evil!"

"The dead are quieted by victory, Doctor!" Tobin said, completing the work. He stepped back and smiled.

"Even their ghosts won't be able to disrupt our new lives! We'll have a new planet... a new home... a new name!"

"Oh, yes," the Doctor agreed, "your days will be wonderful and bright. But what about your nights? Those dark, empty nights. What about your dreams?"

"The more you speak," Tobin said with a smirk, "the less you seem like a ghost and more like a moralizing simpleton!"

He threw a switch. Suddenly, a panel of lights turned green. Tobin laughed triumphantly.

"What are you...?" the Doctor began.

"Wouldn't a ghost know?" Tobin laughed as the machinery began to hum.

Then a shot rang out. Tobin ducked, but the shot had missed him by a wide margin. A warning shot. He looked to his left to see Sergeant Gaba standing with her gun at the ready.

"Are you prepared to let our people be haunted for generations because of your actions?" Gaba demanded.

"Gaba, put that weapon down and return to your post!" Tobin ordered.

"Sir, we must..." she began, but Tobin cut her off.

"Have you forgotten your rank, soldier? Put the gun down, now!"

"Doctor?" Emilio's voice echoed. Gaba and Tobin looked up in astonishment.

"Doctor, can you hear me?! I don't know if Juan can hold out much longer, and K9 says we're almost out of time!"

"Do those voices sound like ghosts, Gaba?" Tobin raged, "They're not haunting us. It's a trick!"

Tobin pressed a few more buttons, and blue lights began to glow next to the green, and the hum became an ominous chorus.

"I..." Gaba said, becoming confused.

"The Horde haven't committed genocide yet..." Romana said, "but you're about to! You converted all these sims into people, and now you're about to wipe them all out! This is your last chance to escape the Embodiment without more blood on your hands!"

Romana's words had clearly affected Gaba, but Tobin's dark resolve had returned.

"It's us or them, Gaba!" He cried, pushing more buttons, "What will you choose? To betray your people or to complete our last mission?" The Doctor and Romana held their breath as Gaba considered this.
"Our mission never included genocide!" She said finally, "Ever!"
"War has causalities, Sergeant!" Tobin cried, suddenly raising his gun and pointing it toward her.
Gaba shot first. Tobin fell, a look of surprise frozen on his face.
"I will not commit war crimes!" Gaba shouted. But Tobin was already gone.
"Three…!" Juan cried, his voice booming throughout the void.
"Doctor, we need to shut this down!" Romana yelled.
"Juan, what is it?!" The Doctor asked.
"Two…!" Juan replied.
"K9," the Doctor asked, "how long before we arrive properly?"
Before K9 could answer, the machinery that the Horde had installed on the manufacturing device began to whine at a higher and higher pitch.
"One…!" Juan cried.
"Sysadmin Two!" The Doctor shouted, "We need to..."
But before he could finish, the mechanism was suddenly thrown through a tear from one universe to another. All that was left was the Horde, now floating weightlessly in a vast, empty void… and that void began to wrinkle and crumble.
"Zero!" Juan's cry faded as the universe collapsed.
The Doctor tried to speak but he could not hear anything… anything at all. Then he realized that he had shut his eyes tightly. When he opened his eyes, he expected nothing but darkness. Instead, he was standing in a dark room lit by violet light. He looked up. The ceiling seemed miles above him. Then the room began to expand in all directions, and a yellow light began to shine overhead. The floor turned into a meadow filled with wildflowers, the sky turned blue, and in the distance was a grove of fruit trees.
The Doctor arched an eyebrow.
"My knee still hurts, so this can't be Heaven," he said sardonically.
"Doctor!" Romana cried.
He turned around to see her standing where she had not been a moment before.
"Romana!" The Doctor cried, taking her hands, "Do you know where

we are?"

"Isn't that my line?" Romana said with playful laughter.

Suddenly, Emilio and Sysadmin Two appeared.

"Juan!" Emilio cried.

"I'm here!" Came Juan's voice from above them.

"Where are you?" Emilio demanded.

"He's out there..." the Doctor pointed vaguely. "He's keeping us safe... in a life boat of sorts."

"This is the meta-structure," Sysadmin Two said, "the new universes have collapsed... all of them. We may be the only..."

But before he could finish, they could see billions, if not trillions, of beings filing into this place, which now seemed to stretch on forever.

"I think," the Doctor said, "Juan has just saved us all."

"He has," Sysadmin Two confirmed, "I'm in full contact with the Guild again. While we cannot remain here indefinitely, we are safe for the moment."

"And we need to talk," the Doctor said looking away to his right, "to them."

They turned to see Sergeant Gaba and the rest of the Horde advancing toward them.

They instinctively took a step back, but then they realized that the Horde were dropping their weapons. Gaba stepped forward.

"They don't work," Gaba said with a shrug, "where are we?"

"One moment away from the end," the Doctor said, "unless we can come to an agreement."

"Can you...?" Gaba began, "Will you... take us to Ki Shee?"

The Doctor turned to Sysadmin Two.

"Is the Guild willing to help transport them?"

Sysadmin Two appeared to be listening to a far-off conversation. After a moment, he frowned and said, "Yes!" to the voices of the Guild.

"Yes, we can, and we will!"

He turned to the Doctor and smiled.

"It's settled. We will transport them as soon as the reboot begins... in three seconds' time."

Before the Doctor or Romana could object, they were all sitting at a large table back in the Bed & Breakfast. The empty plates and their full stomachs were the only indication that they had just finished a large breakfast.

Emilio turned to see Juan sitting next to him finishing a chocolate chip pancake. He gave his son a hug as Juan tried to smile with a full mouth.

The Doctor and Romana turned and saw Sysadmin Two hovering near the doors.

"Tea, dearies?" Mrs. Saunders asked. She had appeared with a tray of tea cups and looked like her old self. They each took a cup from her tray, stood, and approached Sysadmin Two. Mrs. Saunders smiled and greeted Juan and Emilio.

"I take it the reboot was successful," the Doctor said with a wry smile, taking a sip of his tea.

Elmer came down the stairs, winked at Romana, and joined the breakfast table. Officer Hill opened the front door and entered.

"Strewth, I need a cuppa," he said, heading directly for the tea. Behind him followed Dr. Richardson and Dr. Matthews from the Observatory.

"I would say so," Sysadmin Two said with an equally wry smile.

"And where's the TARDIS?" Romana asked.

"Let's take a walk," Sysadmin Two suggested as he turned and passed straight through the front door.

The Doctor and Romana turned to each other, raised their eyebrows, put down their tea and followed.

"First thing's first," the Doctor said, "real or simulation?"

"Everything is real," Sysadmin Two replied, "despite the reboot."

"I must ask," Romana said once they were outside, "about Juan. Is he normal, for lack of a better word?"

"I doubt he'll ever be," the Doctor said, "and I mean that in the best possible sense."

"You are correct," Sysadmin Two said, "he is... an extraordinary being."

"He'll always be partially connected to this universe," the Doctor continued, "and he may remain more comfortable communicating in numbers than in words. But, he will grow up and have a life."

"I hope I'm not wrong in that," the Doctor then added, looking pointedly at Sysadmin Two.

Before Sysadmin Two could answer, the doors of the B&B flew open, and Juan ran in towards them with Emilio close behind. Juan grabbed the Doctor in an enthusiastic hug and said, "Zero, zero, zero!"

The Doctor hugged back and said, "I understand, Juan. I don't like

281

goodbyes either."
"Thank you," Emilio said after a moment.
"You're very welcome," Romana replied with a smile.

Their goodbyes said, Sysadmin Two led them out of the city toward the country where they could see the TARDIS up ahead. The doors had opened and K9 rolled out to greet them.

"Thank you for returning the TARDIS," the Doctor said, "but before I go, I must know the Guild's decision."

This last remark was made indicating the surrounding new world with a wave of his arm.

"Since the former sims are now sentient, we will leave them to their own lives. They will age, have children, contract diseases and die, but we will no longer tamper with them. Although, we do intend to keep in friendly contact."

"See that it remains friendly," the Doctor said sternly.

"What about Juan?" Romana asked, "Will he age and die? And if he does, what will happen to this universe?"

"Unknown," Sysadmin Two said, shaking his head.

"We'll have to wait and see," the Doctor said, "what about the Horde?"

Sysadmin Two waved his hand and suddenly they could see an image of another world. The Horde stood together on a broad beach huddled together as if in prayer, their arms draped over their comrades' shoulders. After a moment, they began taking off their armour and weaponry, dropping them casually onto the wet sand.

"Thank you," Romana said.

Sysadmin Two bowed.

"Master! Mistress!" K9 called, moving toward them.

"How goes it, faithful hound?" The Doctor asked.

"All processes operating at 99.8% efficiency!" K9 said proudly.

"And finally," the Doctor asked, "who ordered that manufacturing facility?"

Sysadmin Two shook his head.

"You were correct – there was a traitor in the Guild. She falsified all our records concerning this project, including the owner's identity. Sadly, she elected to end herself rather than cooperate. I'm afraid I don't know where the device went."

The Doctor stared coldly at Sysadmin Two.
"Should any of what you've just told me turn out to be a lie," he said, "we'll be back."
"Give our regards to Sysadmin One, won't you?" Romana added.
Sysadmin Two said nothing as the Doctor, Romana and K9 entered the TARDIS. He watched as it dematerialized and returned to the real universe. Then he vanished.

Inside the TARDIS, the Doctor and Romana were staring at each other with worried expressions as a monitor on the console pinged.
Then it buzzed and went silent. The Doctor sighed and looked down at a screen. Romana realized she was holding her breath.
She exhaled slowly.
"That manufacturing craft, released into our universe... something's about to happen…" Romana noted grimly.
The Doctor shrugged.
"The plots and machinations of unknown players. The last thing we want is to get caught up in someone else's War Games," he declared, maintaining an air of nonchalance.
Romana maintained her frown.
They both lapsed into contemplative silences.

Chapter Thirteen – I Shall Come Back

by Alexander Leithes

A slow and beautiful birth was underway. It had been progressing for hundreds of millennia and would likely take hundreds more.

A diffuse disk of glowing material floated in the cosmos, a glorious swirling flattened cloud of many colours and patterns – a stellar accretion disk.

As already intimated, this birth of a star and its system already showed signs of structure, the living limbs of stellar life. The star itself, while still surrounded by a vast ball of haze at the centre of this astronomical platter, had already begun its life of fusion, its stellar winds pushing the remnants of its birthing cloud ever further outwards and away.

The head of this star-being was awake and straining free of the womb.

Elsewhere in the enormous flattened expanse of the saucer of accreting material, further structures could be faintly discerned struggling to assert themselves. Although on a different scale entirely, there were some similarities with the rings of Saturn. Gaps were forming as larger bodies attempted to clear space around them, the formation of planets – the child was beginning to find its feet. And its arms. And legs.

None of these gaps were fully cleared yet, merely under-dense darker rings in the extended glowing and nebulous Frisbee of denser material, stretching out beyond the star to at least one hundred astronomical units.

Still further out, at around two hundred AU, the TARDIS hung in empty space.

The plain of the accretion disk was at an angle of forty five degrees to the central axis of the battered blue box. The system was further tilted around its horizontal diameter as seen from the TARDIS such that its nearest edge was angled down - with the far side raised - at a slightly shallower thirty degree incline. This afforded the TARDIS and its occupants a magnificent view of the full majesty of this nascent entity.

"Behold," the Doctor pronounced grandly, waving an arm across the viewscreen before them, "The Fomalhaut system!"

Romana nodded, moderately impressed.

"Very pretty," she concluded. The Doctor looked mildly irritated – he had clearly been expecting a more enthusiastic response.

"Well, I thought you might appreciate going somewhere we've never been before," he said a little grumpily. At this Romana's eyes did widen slightly, moderately more impressed.

"Somewhere even *you* have never been before? You really have uncovered yet another wonder of the Universe!"

The Doctor harrumphed at this tease.

"Yes, well, it seems *some* people are never satisfied," he grumbled.

"Fascinating data being assimilated, master!" K9 chirped appreciatively. The Doctor shot him a dirty look.

"I wasn't talking to you!"

An indulgent smile tugged at the corners of Romana's mouth.

"No, no, Doctor, I *do* appreciate it – as I said, *very* pretty! When exactly are we, by the way?"

The Doctor pondered her question for a moment.

"Roughly around the same time we last visited Earth I'd say."

Romana frowned.

"Hmm, and which of the numerous recent occasions do you mean? The eighteen eighties? The early twenty-first century? The times we visited Antarctica?"

The Doctor nodded vigorously.

"Yes, that's right," he agreed enthusiastically, "plus or minus a hundred thousand years or so!"

Romana rolled her eyes.

"How wonderfully precise of you. I suppose I should've expected as much with you driving."

The Doctor looked disapprovingly at her.

"Oh, Romana, you should know better than that! I only mean that higher precision is pointless when we're dealing with these astronomical timescales! Over the entire range I just gave, this system would still be in its early stages of formation, and probably would be for far longer!"

Romana nodded her calm acceptance of his point.

"So, where do we go from here? I mean, I doubt there are any people we can visit, are there?"

The Doctor had been moderately mollified by Romana's agreeable attitude and considered her question.

"Yes, you are almost certainly right that we are unlikely to find any inhabitants in this fledgeling system. Indeed, even life itself may not have begun to coalesce," he conceded.

"Nevertheless," he continued more briskly, "we could – nay, *should* – pop by one or even several of these planets or protoplanets. Check out the scenery. We might well find some of the precursors to the life and soul of this stellar party!"

Romana nodded sagely and seemed on the verge of replying when a loud klaxon blared out from the main console.

"Imminent collision, master, mistress!" K9 supplied helpfully. Both Timelords dashed to the controls. The panel displays did indeed reveal a sizeable dark object moving up on the TARDIS with alarming alacrity.

"Matching course and velocity!" The Doctor cried, flicking switches and pressing various buttons, his urgent voice not quite masking an element of panic.

While undeniably close, the unidentified mass ceased growing on their monitors as both it and the TARDIS achieved fixed relative positions.

With the immediate crisis countered, the Doctor and Romana were free to examine their new spatial companion in more detail. On an astrophysical scale, they shared the same orbit but by the measures of local distances the thing was slightly closer to Fomalhaut than the TARDIS. As a consequence, it was poorly illuminated and largely in shadow from their perspective, as well as being slightly out of line of sight with the system's glowing stellar disk. This was why the Timelords had not seen it before their ship's sensors.

Although still dark and shadowy, they could now make out some details. Its form was a tetradecahedron – in this case a giant cube with its corners chopped off, still giving six square faces only now joined by eight triangles, one at each "corner". A cuboctahedron.

While keeping a constant distance, it *was* rotating slowly – almost gracefully – about the centre of the square surface currently facing them.

"It's a satellite," the Doctor pronounced warily, either some doubt or trepidation creeping into his tone.

"Or a space station?" Romana suggested.

"Potatoes, tomatoes – they're basically the same under the skin. What's in a name?"

"So much for 'no life'," Romana responded, "either way, someone must have put it here."

Before the Doctor could reply strange sounds began to emanate from K9. He appeared to be humming a phrase by Strauss.

"K9. What on Earth are you doing?" The Doctor enquired in exasperation.

"Apologies, master," K9 responded, almost sounding embarrassed, "just some old file fragments. Current sensory input appears to have caused them to be partially recalled to active memory."

The Doctor continued to frown.

"Really? I do sometimes forget you were originally built by a human. Any useful identification on the data?"

"Negative, master," K9 chirped back, "most data, including file names, corrupted. I can only recover the letters, 'e', 't', 'i', 'l' and 'e' from the header information."

" 'E-tile'?" The Doctor mused, then shook his head impatiently.

"It does indeed sound like a hunk of junk. Best clear out the storage space for something more useful – and less broken," he instructed the metal dog.

"Affirmative, master," K9 answered.

"Oh, and K9?" The Doctor added as an afterthought.

"Master?" The robot replied.

"Try not to interrupt unless it is actually useful."

"Naturally, master," K9 responded primly, adding after a moment's clicking and whirring, "all corrupted data now purged."

"Very good," the Doctor said briskly before turning his attention to Romana, "and I stand by my assessment of this system's likelihood of life. A station or *satellite* need not have originated here. Doesn't it look familiar to you?"

Romana studied the viewscreen a moment longer.

"It does indeed. I'd say it's identical to the one we 'ran into' in the Megando system!"

The Doctor nodded significantly.

"We may need to put our investigation of the Fomalhaut system on hold for the time being. I suspect this is no coincidence given the vastness of Time and Space. The game's afoot, Romana!"

"And apparently to be played with 'D-14s'," she responded a little sarcastically. Nevertheless, Romana joined the Doctor in manipulating the controls before them, initiating multiple scans of the object over a plethora of different wavelengths.

"That's damned peculiar," the Doctor muttered, "the TARDIS is giving a very fragmented picture of its internal structure. Either it is very dense, mostly filled with solid matter, *or* there is some level of shielding designed to frustrate prying eyes."

Romana nodded thoughtfully.

"I suppose you could be right, and this may be a satellite rather than a space station. It might well be mostly filled with equipment, offering very little in the way of rooms, storage and accommodation. That said, *my* scans have detected a modest chamber just beyond that square face ahead. *And* a sizeable door built into its centre," she concluded, a tad smugly. The Doctor rolled his eyes a little.

"I'm glad you take such pride in the TARDIS's abilities," the Doctor pronounced airily. Then he noticed something on his own display and his face creased.

"Well, *my* scans have detected an atmosphere inside," he continued, then his frown deepened, "thin but breathable. Now that *is* odd. Around twenty percent oxygen – just the sort of thing you or I might enjoy. And the rest is mostly filler gas – again far from unusual. Except that it is not Nitrogen. It's Helium."

Now it was Romana's turn to frown.

"What a strange mixture! Granted, one we have ourselves encountered in the recent past, and know only too well how survivable it is – if 'squeaky'," she agreed cautiously.

The Doctor nodded slowly.

"Actually, now I come to think about it, it may have its merits after all. While it may not seem aesthetically – or perhaps more correctly, 'acoustically' - pleasing to us, it might in fact be a most efficient way to provide a basic breathable atmosphere in deep space. Nitrogen is not always abundant everywhere in a given system, but Helium does form a quarter of all the ordinary matter in the entire Universe. And while oxygen *can* be a little more difficult to source, at least uncombined, water ice is usually fairly common in most systems from a reasonably early age. Yes, yes – upon reflection, if I wanted to provide a breathable atmosphere 'on the cheap' so to speak – easy to produce and maintain, particularly in a remote and automated setting, I might well go down such a route myself," the Doctor concluded with increasing certainty. Romana raised an eyebrow.

"You will warn me before you install one in the TARDIS, won't you?"

The Doctor nodded in weary acceptance of her request. Then he perked up, smiling.

"Knock, knock?" He enquired cheekily.

"Who's there?" Romana asked, returning his smile and nodding towards the image of the artefact on screen. Still grinning, the Doctor tapped a few more buttons on the main console.

In space, no one can hear you scream.

Similarly, no one can hear you open a door. However, it can still be seen, and so it was now, on the console viewscreens. Dead centre of the slowly rotating square section a thin line appeared, roughly half the width of the square itself. This line steadily thickened until it formed a letterbox-like opening at least four times as tall as the TARDIS, and far, far wider. A modest sized shuttle craft could easily fit through this opening and for the blue box should prove simplicity itself to navigate.

Which were just the conditions the Doctor liked to work with. Romana was doubly pleased for him.

The TARDIS gently drifted towards the station and through the bay doors.

Inside, low level emergency lighting illuminated a cuboid landing bay with the same cross section as the door and as deep as it was wide.

Upon reflection the Timelords judged it could have comfortably contained *two* modest shuttle craft – far more room than was necessary for their vessel.

The Doctor set the TARDIS down upon the bay floor. This must have activated an automated system within the satellite, or station, since in the aft viewscreen on their console they could see the bay door slowly close behind them. Then they began to faintly hear a hiss of rushing air which swiftly grew to a roar, distinctly audible through the walls of the TARDIS.

The artefact was filling the bay with atmosphere.

"So," the Doctor said, gesturing towards their own main doors, "shall we 'take the air'?"

"Affirmative, affirmative, affirmative!" K9 gabbled excitedly.

"I wasn't..." the Doctor began a little tetchily before stopping short.

"On second thoughts," he mused, "you always did excel in creeping – or rather trundling – around space stations, or satellites. Yes, good dog. Walkies!"

Romana shook her head wearily but could not quite hide an indulgent smile.

"And, yes, I would like to explore too, thanks for asking," she pointed out.

The Doctor bowed his head towards her and utterly failed to smother a mischievous smile. He waved one arm grandly towards the TARDIS doors, inviting her to take the lead.

Romana nodded curtly towards him and strode briskly towards the doors, which whirred open in anticipation of her arrival. The Doctor and K9 followed her at a more sedate pace, and the trio left the confines of their ship.

Romana stood a few metres in front of the TARDIS surveying the bay which almost dwarfed it, at least its external dimensions.

"With a docking bay of this size it could still be a space station..." she began before her high and squeaky voice tailed off, "oh, good grief."

The Doctor continued to struggle not to smirk.

"Now, Romana," he squeaked in return, "remember the efficiency."

Then he too turned his attention to the bay itself.

"And not necessarily," he continued, responding to her first statement, "this could just as easily be designed to accommodate a maintenance shuttle or two, complete with crews and equipment."

Romana shrugged dismissively.

"This is all needlessly speculative and academic. There is a door in the wall ahead. How about we just open it and find out?"

The Doctor inclined his head in acquiescence and together the party walked and trundled the twenty metres to the far wall.

"Hmm," the Doctor pondered, "no obvious opening mechanisms. K9, can you detect any hidden means of shifting this thing?"

"I shall attempt to discover any, master," the metal dog chirruped, high-pitched and helpful. This was followed by a few moments of spinning ears and flashing bulbs. The door rushed upwards with a swoosh.

"Well done, K9," the Doctor said approvingly before leading their way inside.

The corridor they now entered was a little dim, being lit by the same subdued emergency lighting at floor level as that which had illuminated the landing bay - but it was bright enough to see by, if a little gloomy. As well as being a might depressing, it was also quite narrow, only two metres tall and perhaps a metre and a half wide.

To left and right along its length, at around five metre intervals, were openings of the same dimensions, while at these same intersections, vertical ladders ran through one metre square holes in the floor and ceiling. The three companions crept up on the first of these three dimensional crossroads. From this new vantage point they could now see the openings to either side led to similar corridors, although there was something indefinable about the walls – a texture or pattern, even odd points of light – it was hard to say.

The openings above and below offered hints of corridors parallel to the one they were on over several levels, at least as far as they could make out.

"Eeny, meeny, miny, moe?" Romana piped up. The Doctor shook his head impatiently.

"Let's just try left and see where we go from there," he squeaked tersely.

And so they moved into the left hand opening.

Their first impression had been correct in that there was indeed something very different about the walls here. Stretching the entire length of the corridor were nothing but racks of equipment; electronics and other more exotic examples of high technology. Many of these had been the sources of the points of light they had glimpsed, and now surrounded by those arrays of components they could hear faint clicks, whirs and hums.

"If the rest of the vessel is as tightly packed with mysterious 'gubbins' as this appears to be, I feel more secure in my earlier assessment of this being a satellite," the Doctor pronounced knowingly. So used to his tone by now – even pitch shifted – Romana barely betrayed any signs of irritation.

"No doubt," she conceded briskly, "in which case might I suggest we return to the first corridor and simply follow it to its end? I'm sure any control hub is likely to be at the centre of this 'satellite', and more than likely on a straight path from the landing bay for easy maintenance."

The Doctor nodded graciously.

"Never let it be said I pooh-poohed your feelings – an excellent plan,

Romana!" He pronounced cheerfully and chirpily.

They returned to the main corridor then turned left, away from the landing bay to follow it to the end, passing several more corridors and ladders along the way – all seemingly identical.

Faced by yet another barrier, the Doctor wordlessly waved towards it while staring significantly at K9. K9 obliged, similarly mute but far from silent. This second door rushed swiftly skyward. Cautiously, the trio entered.

The room in which they now stood was barely larger than the main console of the TARDIS. There were a couple of metal seats fixed to the floor facing a vast bank of switches, displays and keyboards. The Doctor took one of the chairs while Romana settled into the other. They began to carefully study the equipment.

"It looks like whoever built this was quite humanoid, to judge from its layout and furniture," came Romana's first observation. The Doctor nodded slowly and withdrew his sonic screwdriver. He scanned the panel in front of him briefly before pausing to study the results. His countenance darkened.

"Indeed, Romana, there is something disturbingly familiar about this technology, at least some of it," he began suspiciously.

Whatever he had been about to add was driven away by a blaring klaxon!

"Unidentified data detected!" A robotic voice cried out from speakers in the panel. The door through which they had entered crashed downwards, sealing the two Timelords and robot dog into the cramped control room.

"Someone, or something, knows we are here!" The Doctor cried significantly.

"We should get back to the TARDIS!" Romana insisted. The Doctor nodded and began to scan the door with his sonic screwdriver, while simultaneously nudging K9 with his foot, encouraging him to lend a paw.

"Initiating emergency recall!" The robot voice squeaked out again. At that moment the door rushed upwards once more – either the Doctor or K9 had been successful.

Even as they rushed out of the newly cleared exit, another sound reached their ears.

A disturbingly familiar one.

While not identical in notes or rhythms, it was eerily reminiscent of a TARDIS dematerialising!

"That's what I was trying to say," the Doctor began as they rushed back towards the landing bay, "I detected some technology which was worryingly similar to Gallifreyan in design!"

Romana nodded as they ran.

"That would certainly fit with what we are hearing right now!" She agreed urgently.

At that moment the wheezing TARDIS-like sounds ceased.

By now they had reached the door of the landing bay, once again closed, presumably via the same systems which had imprisoned them in the control room. The Doctor and K9 began to work on this new barrier in the same fashion.

There came a clank and a grinding noise. The Doctor halted his probing with the sonic screwdriver as he realised it was the main external doors of the landing bay beginning to open.

"K9! Wait!" He yelled to the robot, but too late.

The internal door to the hanger swept upwards and there was a rush of atmosphere through the opening!

Fortunately and unexpectedly, the wind of transferring air came *towards* them! The satellite had clearly 'landed' in atmosphere, and one denser than the sparse minimal air enjoyed in the space craft itself.

The Doctor, Romana and K9 stumbled into the landing bay, looking relieved to be still breathing.

"Well, that's at least one stroke of good luck today," Romana sighed, then brightened further as she realised her voice had returned to normal.

"Not only that, but the TARDIS is still here and unharmed," the Doctor observed, allowing himself a thin smile of relief. Romana cocked her head at him.

"And yet I sense we are not about to return to the 'safety' of it?" She observed pointedly. The Doctor spread his hands wide, almost pleadingly.

"Romana! We have uncovered the beginnings of a great mystery here! You can't be suggesting we turn our backs on it?" He insisted. Romana gave him a skew smile.

"My dear Doctor, perish the thought. I have long since formed the opinion that when we do, they have a habit of biting us on the... behind."

The Doctor inclined his head graciously.

"K9," he barked, "once again I feel you should join us, if for no other reason than to watch our rears!"

"Affirmative, master, mistress," the robot chirruped obediently, "I shall keep my sensors trained on them!"

The Doctor and Romana exchanged brief awkward glances before heading out of the satellite landing bay, K9 trailing in their wake.

The chamber they entered deserved no name better. It was clearly artificial and just as clearly quite ancient. Its walls and ceiling were fashioned from large blocks of limestone or similar rock and while internal and therefore protected from the elements they showed hints of the passage of time, inevitable cracks and wear and tear. The walls to the left and right of the two Timelords seemed to bow outwards until they reached halfway to the roof whereupon they appeared to bow inwards again. The ceiling itself formed a very shallow arch of the same stone – a particularly challenging architectural feat given the materials and presumably primitive equipment used in its construction.

This oddly familiar cavernous room was barely large enough to contain the tetradecahedron of the satellite – the upper surface of the device threatening to scrape that same ceiling, while its sides similarly threatened the walls. It was as if the chamber had been made for the spacecraft, or possibly vice versa. There was probably just enough room for the Timelords to squeeze past it if they wanted to explore the rear of the ancient hanger. As it was, there was more than enough to draw their attention on this side of the room.

The chamber was obviously longer than it was wide as evidenced by the wall ahead of them some twenty metres distant. This one was perfectly flat and had a modest open door at its centre. There were also one or two signs of technology contemporaneous with the satellite itself. Embedded discretely in the walls and ceiling were light sources, obviously technological and consistent with the emergency lighting in the space craft they had just left.

The second hint of advanced engineering also lay in the wall before them but was harder to explain.

There were four grey rectangles built into the stonework, roughly the same dimensions as the open door – two to the left of it, two to the right. These grey objects appeared to protrude slightly from the wall itself and looked curved towards their tops and bottoms while perfectly straight along their sides.

While they too might have simply been doors, their smooth metallic perfection hinted darkly at some deeper purpose.

"It's quite warm in here, isn't it?" Romana noted.

The Doctor nodded slowly.

"Yes, you can feel it in the air as we breath. Although sheltered in here, I imagine we must be on quite a hot little world," he agreed. Then he looked around the walls once more.

"There is something oddly familiar about this building," he mused suspiciously, "and yet I am sure we've never been in here before."

Romana nodded slowly.

"I am troubled by similar thoughts. Not only for this building, but also those odd metal things over there – although I sense the context is different."

The Doctor raised an eyebrow.

"Much as with our strange arrival here, there *is* something oddly 'homely' about them."

Romana clapped her hands decisively, and yet a little gently, as if wary of drawing too much attention.

"Well," she said briskly but in hushed tones, "shall we explore?"

With this, she nodded towards the doorway ahead of them.

"It would seem churlish to pass up such an invitation," the Doctor concluded with a waggle of his eyebrows.

The trio set out towards the dim yawning opening. They skidded to a halt just before it as half a dozen individuals dashed - or in some cases shambled - out to stand in front of them. All of them were deathly pale and their enormous eyes also looked a touch milky, as they glared at the two Timelords over petite noses and full lipped wide mouths.

The Doctor and Romana recognised them immediately, even if unexpected with their alabaster skins lacking the healthy shine usually associated with their species. The lines of stitches and other signs of recent surgery that many bore were also atypical, and yet all too familiar to the time travellers.

"We're on Albia!" Romana cried in horror as she regarded the array of reanimated Albian corpses before them. These were the same henchbeings of the infamous Dr Nyugati, who had pursued them on the most influential planet of the Upsilon Orionis system a month or so ago. Indeed, they were even lead by the suited, dull-eyed Albian male who had commanded them in North Westwood cemetery during their last encounter.

"Seize them," that same creature grunted painfully to his companions. With that, he and his motley crew surged forward to grab the Doctor and Romana by their arms and shoulders.

A strange crackling "phut" sound came from behind the two Timelords. While pinned in position, they were still able to turn their heads enough to see K9, his nose laser extended.

"Master! Mistress! There is some sort of dampening field in operation! My defences are useless!" He cried desperately.

"Now, now," the Doctor yelled encouragingly, "no need to feel anxious about your performance! We know it's not your fault!"

As the Doctor said this, a woman with the arms and legs of a nine year old child, apparently sewn to her adult body in place of her own, rugby-tackled the robot dog, seemingly intent upon pinning him in place. She was clothed in an overlong, rather formal looking, white dress and black woollen cardigan. Indeed, all their captors were dressed as if they had been plucked from a funeral in the first half of the twentieth century on Earth. In reality, their fashions were utterly in keeping with an Albia hundreds of thousands of years after that era on Earth, an aesthetic favoured by this alien species who had never even met or seen a human in real life.

"Please be careful with my companions," the Doctor said politely as the Albian undead continued to jostle them, "I can assure you we surrender. You'll have no further trouble from us."

The grips upon the Timelords did not slacken in the slightest, however the shaking did subside.

"You will come with us," the suited leader of the milky-eyed band said monotonously. The Doctor inclined one temple towards him.

"By all means," he said grandly, "take us to your leader."

At a nod from the dapper undead, the other 'Albians' released the two Timelords and K9, although they all remained close about them. The three captives were then ushered unceremoniously through the door.

What lay beyond was not a room at all but in fact a stairwell. They were standing on a narrow landing – ahead of them began a wide yet steep staircase leading to the floor above. To the left and right of this upward flight, separated by a metre of wall either side, were two more openings of the same width, with two matching staircases both leading down. Presumably these led to levels beneath the grand chamber with the satellite.

Whatever lay below was to remain a mystery however, as the party from the TARDIS were nudged forcibly onto the middle stairs. They began to climb, K9 whirring a little louder as he began to float up. The Doctor saw their journey as an opportunity to bounce ideas off Romana.

"To judge from the width of the landing we just left, coupled with our steep ascent, I would say we are in a tower. One perhaps only a third as wide as the satellite chamber."

At this point they reached the landing above. Here they discovered two more staircases to either side of the one they had just climbed, mirroring those below. The trio of prisoners were encouraged into the right hand opening and ever upwards.

"A reasonable assessment," Romana conceded, "and no doubt we are in an impressive old building – a castle, perhaps? But where *exactly* on Albia might we be?"

By now they had reached yet another landing. This one was laid out just as with the first they had encountered, with another two metre wide single flight leading still higher.

"No, no, Romana, I don't believe we are on Albia at all," he said gravely as they resumed their climb.

"Really?" Romana asked, puzzled, "Then where?"

"I believe we are in Anubys," the Doctor replied matter-of-factly.

Romana stopped dead in her tracks, forcing all to follow suit lest they ran into each other.

"What!" She cried incredulously, "You mean to say we've been swallowed by that ten dimensional bulk entity?!"

The Doctor shook his head with a grim little smile. Meanwhile their captors nudged them insistently and so they began once more to mount the stairs.

"My dear Romana, I do not for one moment believe we have been eaten by that multidimensional demigod, or his four dimensional proxy for that matter. I mean – given the shape of this building we have so far only seen from the inside, and the quality of the air – I would be fairly confident in pronouncing we are *inside* the Anubys Monument on Kai-Ro!"

This final statement was made with more than a little swagger and bravado. Before Romana could respond, her tongue was paralysed as an all too familiar voice sang out through the opening at the top of the stairs.

"Congratulations, Doctor, how *clever* of you to notice. Achingly slowly, of course, and naturally far, *far* too late!" Sneered the voice which rang multiple alarm bells in the minds of both Timelords. They exchanged wide-eyed, panicked glances before swallowing and restoring a modicum of composure. With little option left open to them, they mounted the few remaining steps.

The scene which opened before them was both impressive and disturbing. The room was probably about the same size as the landing bay on the satellite they had explored earlier. While most was the same old limestone they had seen everywhere inside the monument so far, there were one or two high tech control panels, either free standing or attached to the walls.

At the opposite end of the chamber was a shallow podium upon which stood a high-backed obsidian throne. On this throne sat the languid figure of a woman in black, surrounded by an oddly shifting haze of twisting energies. The Doctor and Romana stared in horror at the ruined visage of the woman before them.

They stared into the face of The Rani!

Even now, she looked much as she had done when they last saw her, far beneath this monument in The Tomb of Anubys, yet it was undeniable something had changed.

While she still looked as though she was suffering from the effects of a failed regeneration - or perhaps more precisely, looked like Romana suffering from the effects of a failed regeneration – with blackened and broken skin, matted oily hair, wearing the tattered grimy, now black dress - things seemed to have taken a turn for the worst. More of her nasal cartilage had been exposed while larger gaps now perforated her lips and mouth, exposing more rotten dental work and greater numbers of missing teeth.

Doubtless as amoral as ever, and obviously their ultimate captor, it was hard for the Doctor and Romana not to feel a little sympathy for her degraded state.

"Rani! What are you doing here?" The Doctor demanded.

The Rani gave a mirthless chuckle.

"Just planning for the future. And the past. All of Time and Space in fact," she said significantly.

"I must say, you seem to have been letting yourself – or perhaps I should say, 'myself' - go a little since we last met," Romana quipped, unable to resist the dig.

The Rani growled and put out both her palms towards the two other Timelords. Instantly, the Doctor and Romana felt as if their chests had been grasped by giant hands and constricted. Then The Rani dropped her arms and the pressure evaporated.

"No, no," The Rani said coolly, almost to herself, "now is not the time to burn power. Soon enough that will no longer be a concern."

Almost as if he wished to change the subject, the Doctor did just that.

"My dear Rani, although I have clearly identified *where* we are, I am not entirely sure as to *when*. To judge from your helpers - and the not inconsiderable infrastructure you have built – I would guess at least a year, if not more, since we last met. At least from the perspective of Kai-Ro's timeline?"

The Rani gave him a cold and cracked smile.

"You think that, do you? As is so often the case, you are very wide of the mark. On Kai-Ro it is only one or two *hours* at most since you said goodbye to your Albian friends and launched the TARDIS from Kai-Ro Aerodrome!"

The Doctor's mouth fell open and his eyebrows shot up.

"One or two hours," he shouted incredulously, "there is no way you could achieve all this in such a short span of time!"

The Rani chuckled mirthlessly.

"What a pedestrian linear mind you possess. Sometimes it's hard to believe you're a Timelord at all! *I* gave myself the time. I travelled back in time and journeyed through space using nothing but the powers I had gained from the bulk!"

Even Romana looked impressed.

"Well, I know *we* cannot do that without a TARDIS. Your newfound gifts are truly astounding," she conceded. The Rani frowned at her, finding it hard to believe the compliment was honestly made.

"Oh yes, I *can* do that, but it comes at a cost, as you can plainly see. So my first order of business was to find an abandoned or unguarded TARDIS. A fairly trivial task for someone of my skills and experience, I'm sure you'll agree."

This last remark was made with a nod towards Romana.

"Yes, I remember," Romana responded coolly.

"Of course you do," The Rani agreed with a smile just as frosty.

"Next, I had to pilot my prize back here – for this place in space and time still held some... value to me, as will become clear in due course. Well, I say 'here' but more precisely I meant here a year ago. Plenty of time to gather resources and build all that you see before you and more. All culminating in this fateful day," she said archly.

"The first thing I constructed," she continued in more businesslike tones, "was the Time Terminus you arrived in just now."

The Doctor raised his forehead towards the ceiling and closed his eyes.

"Ah, of course, I knew it looked familiar," he said in weary realisation, "you cannibalised your new TARDIS – stripped it for parts. Parts which ended up in that satellite we discovered and also those grey openings in the chamber downstairs. They are spacetime portals, are they not? Allowing you to tunnel into different points in space and time, at least for a short while?"

The Rani gave a mocking round of applause with the fingers of one blackened hand against the flaking palm of the other.

"Very good, Doctor, you're finally catching up. Actually, over time – so to speak – I have cannibalised *many* TARDISes and installed limited basic dematerialisation circuits in countless satellites now dotted throughout Space and Time. And the spacetime portals allowed me to more easily gather still more resources with relative ease, such as Dr Nyugati's reanimated minions here. After all, he had no further use for them," The Rani concluded with a cruel turn to her broken lips.

The Doctor frowned thoughtfully.

"You know a TARDIS – even *many* TARDISes – were never meant to be broken up and used in this manner. They inevitably fail under the stresses of being spread so thin."

The Rani gave another mirthless chuckle.

"Not when they receive a helping hand from the bulk, or one empowered by the bulk. Admittedly, my contributions to their continued operation have drained me, but not as much as my travelling time and space unaided. And soon, very soon, all these problems will be behind me."

Doctor's frown deepened as he caught the portent in her words. Before he could pursue the matter further, Romana weighed in.

"But wait," she cried impatiently, "if you started setting all this up a year ago you would have crossed your own time-stream! Around four hours ago by my calculations. Which would be impossible! You'd be pulled apart by the eddies!"

The Rani shook her head with mocking indulgence.

"Such a limited vision – I can see you and the Doctor are a perfect match. True, the Time-stream *would* have pulled me apart *if* I had given it the chance. I may not be the Mistress of the Multiverse quite yet, and there was no point actively looking for trouble. But I knew exactly when you pulled me from the bulk and freed me in the Anubys Tomb. I also knew exactly when I left to try and find my first sacrificial TARDIS. So, when I reached the moment before I first escaped the bulk, I entered a time portal and exited the moment *after* I had left in search of a TARDIS. In effect I 'hopped over' my previous time here – only an hour or two in any event."

The Doctor nodded sagely.

"Ah, you cheated."

The Rani gave him a hard stare.

"I succeeded."

"But why *do* you have 'many' of these satellites dotted throughout space and time?" Romana asked cautiously.

The Rani laughed humourlessly.

"Ha! Must I explain *everything* to you? After all, you will get to enjoy the spectacle first hand – although you will be powerless to interfere. My planning is immaculate and my ultimate goal mere hours away."

The Doctor studied the finger nails of his right hand in a pantomime of disinterest.

"Well, if you don't want to tell us I suppose we could play 'I spy'. Or perhaps you'd enjoy a song – I'm sure Romana and I could rustle up a duet – or even a trio! Only today K9 seems to have discovered a penchant for melody!"

The Rani huffed in annoyance at the Doctor.

"I find your triteness even more draining in my current state, but not for much longer. I have been using powers gleaned from the bulk but without direct contact with that realm to fuel them. And even while in the bulk itself, I lacked the materials necessary to consume their energies without the all too obvious harmful side effects.

"But now I have the materials and technologies of our universe *and* soon renewed access to the bulk!"

The Doctor's face dropped and became utterly serious.

"Rani, what have you done?" He asked in hushed tones.

Her icy stare fell upon him once more.

"It's not just what I have done, it's what I am going to do – and keep on doing."

Here, The Rani rose from her throne and spread her arms wide.

"First, this entire monument has been converted to act as a collector and store of bulk energy – a battery if you like," she declared proudly.

Romana frowned, aghast.

"But *how* will you get energy from the bulk to here?"

The Rani laughed once more.

"I have seeded all of Time and Space with those satellites. Each one is energetically linked to this battery using elements of the Gallifreyan technology I repurposed. This location is particularly useful to me – you may have 'fixed' this system's fractures to the bulk, but historically it has always had the thinnest of barriers between our universe and the wider multidimensional whole. And this time is extremely close to when it was still broken and porous.

All my satellites will open rifts, both here and throughout the whole of existence, into the bulk itself! They will funnel its energy here, to my battery. And from it to me! I shall be reborn!" The Rani concluded triumphantly.

"That's insane!" Romana cried in disgust.

"Romana is right, if a little tactless," the Doctor added desperately, "with a billion rifts opening into the bulk, the universe will be swamped with bulk entities – consumed! Destroyed! And you along with it!"

The Rani shook her head contemptuously.

"Nonsense! The positions of the satellites are meticulously calculated. They form a crystalline spacetime lattice of my own design, which will not only be perfectly stable throughout all of existence but should be utterly undetectable by the eleven dimensional denizens of the bulk. Like a diamond in water. In effect, our universe will become a stealth universe from their perspective, yet all the while we – or rather *I* - will be syphoning energy from their realm with impunity, undetected.

"Behold, the Reign of the Rani!" She concluded ecstatically.

Then she collapsed back onto her throne, seemingly exhausted for the time being.

"Take them to a cell in the lower levels," she muttered to the leader of her undead Albian hench-folk, "they tire me, and I can spare them no more energy. They will see the truth in my words soon enough. Then I shall fling them into a rift, like so much dirty laundry."

The Doctor and Romana could see there was no more to be gained by arguing with The Rani and so allowed themselves, along with K9, to be ushered to the stairs.

The party retraced their steps ever downwards until they were once more outside the Time Terminus housing the satellite, which itself contained the TARDIS. They did not remain there for long, however, as they were forced into the right hand set of stairs leading from that landing still deeper into the Anubys Monument.

Two flights below the Terminus they entered one of several corridors which ran beneath that cavernous chamber. This particular corridor was lined with doors to what looked like storage rooms. It was into an empty one of these that the Doctor, Romana and K9 were roughly manhandled.

The Albian goons locked the door behind them and they were left to their own devices. In the Doctor's case, that was the sonic screwdriver.

As soon as he was sure the guards were out of earshot he turned the device upon the lock.

Nothing happened.

"Oh, bother," the Doctor muttered grumpily, "I think she soundproofed the mechanism!"

Romana sighed.

"Of course she did."

"Any other ideas?" She then added.

"Ideas?" The Doctor cried enthusiastically, "Of course I do! Thousands of them!"

"Brilliant!" Romana enthused, smiling.

"Unfortunately, they all rather depended on us being on the other side of that door," he concluded a trifle deflated.

Romana turned her attention upon their metal companion.

"K9, anything you can do?" She asked but with little hope.

"The dampening field is still disrupting my nose laser, mistress," he began, then whirred and flashed for a moment, "all other possibilities exhausted, mistress, master."

The Doctor and Romana both slid to the floor either side of the metal dog, chins on their hands. They each sank into silently wracking their brains.

Time is always difficult to measure in such circumstances, but it felt like at least an hour passed in silent contemplation.

Romana, who was closest to the door, found her reverie broken by what sounded like a faint scrape of metal on metal from the door.

"Doctor," Romana hissed, "did you hear that?"

The Doctor frowned at her, nodding.

"Whether you mean you saying, 'Doctor' or the metallic scrape, the answer is, 'yes'," he supplied helpfully. Romana rolled her eyes at him.

Now there came quite an audible click from that same door. The Doctor and Romana rose to their feet, preparing themselves for whatever unfolded.

It transpired the Doctor may have been fooling himself.

The door creaked slightly as it opened. Through it stepped a woman entirely in black. This was not the grubby black dress of The Rani. These were the long black robes of traditional Kai-Roan attire. They completely covered the woman from head to foot, even her face was largely concealed by a scarf of the same material. Only the odd strand of dark brown "hair" escaped from the edges of her turban, coupled with two dark eyes staring directly into the Doctor's.

He knew this was the woman they had seen on the landing field of Kai-Ro Aerodrome the day they had left to explore Alpha Centauri, but there was more familiarity present than just that recent memory, although he could not quite put his finger on exactly what.

Now so close to her, he felt her eyes were too small for a typical Kai-Roan or Albian.

"Who are you?" He asked hoarsely. Parts of his mind kept nagging at him, almost as if they knew the answer but were afraid to say. His jaw clenched as he awaited a response.

" 'I shall come back', you said. Yet it seems *I* had to make good on *your* word," came an achingly familiar voice from behind the scarf. The Doctor reeled as fragments of his being cried out in recognition, yet failed to reveal the name. Be this through fear or shame he could not say.

The woman's eyes seemed to take pity on his turmoil and confusion. She reached up and removed the scarf.

The face revealed was one he would never forget – not now, not then, not ever. Although far older than the last time he had seen it, it was undeniably still that face.

The Doctor, Romana and K9 stared into the face of Susan, the Doctor's granddaughter.

Chapter Fourteen – Assault And Battery

by Alexander Leithes

The Doctor and Romana continued to stare in shocked silence at the fourth Timelord – or at least Gallifreyan – they had seen that day, counting themselves.

The Doctor's granddaughter stepped further inside the makeshift cell, this repurposed store room deep within the Anubys Monument on Kai-Ro. She pulled the door to, but not entirely closed, lest it latched and trapped those she had so recently freed, along with herself. She also, no doubt, hoped to reduce the chances of being discovered by The Rani's reanimated Albian guards.

The jailbreak concealed to her satisfaction, she now turned to fully face Romana and the Doctor, looking serious and a touch saddened.

If she had been human, her appearance would have fallen under the category of "mature", albeit healthy. To Earthly eyes she could have been anywhere from sixty to a hundred. Her Gallifreyan ancestry obviously clouded the exact number of years she owned – while clearly her first regeneration, this still held the potential to extend into the scale of centuries. Nevertheless, even by Gallifreyan standards, she must have been around a while. Certainly significantly far removed from the sixteen years she had had when the Doctor last saw her.

"Susan, I..." the Doctor rasped then trailed off, unusually lost for words. The extraordinary nature of this meeting robbing even him of coherent thought.

"Yes, Grandfather?" Susan responded questioningly. She passed back the responsibility of filling the silence. The Doctor looked pained by this unwelcome responsibility.

"Susan... I was always going to come back for you," he finally supplied earnestly. Susan cocked her head at the Doctor.

"Really," she asked quizzically, yet pointedly, "was that before or *after* you were dead?"

The Doctor looked flustered.

"Before, obviously! I have not broken my word!" He blustered. Susan folded her arms across her chest.

"Cutting it a bit fine, aren't we? I mean, you're hardly a spring chicken now, are you?"

The Doctor coughed and his mouth opened and closed frantically. Before he could actually find any words, Susan took the lead.

"My apologies, Grandfather, perhaps my question was unfair. Perhaps I should have asked, 'before or after *I* was dead'? After all, as you can see, it has been quite some time," she said significantly.

The Doctor's head fell, all bluster and defence finally defeated.

"Susan, my dear girl, I am sorry. I failed you," he admitted glumly.

Susan shook her head slowly, the hint of a weary smile tugging at her mouth.

"Oh, Grandfather, dear Grandfather. There are so many bones to be picked with you, each buried in the ashes of the past. We could be here for an eternity discussing them, I fear. And yet, I suspect we do not have the time – one more sad price for your tardiness. Nevertheless, Doctor mine, you have your strengths, you have your weaknesses. You tried to do what you thought was best, however questionable those thoughts might have been. We are all ultimately – eventually – mortal and flawed.

"And I forgive you."

The Doctor's eyes snapped up in shock and disbelief. Susan walked towards him a little stiffly, as if parts of her were trying to hold her back. Her better self won through, however, and she embraced her grandfather, even if a little reservedly.

The Doctor, eyes still wide in a mixture of panic and confusion, returned the hug awkwardly, complete with three pats of his right hand to her back.

The motions of reconciliation completed - at least partially and for the time being – they released each other and took a step back.

Romana had remained silent the entire time, not wishing to encroach upon this most emotional and difficult of meetings. Now though, she felt it would be ruder to remain silent.

"I am Romana," she began, extending a hand towards Susan, "I read about you before my first ever encounter with your grandfather. It is a pleasure to finally meet you in the flesh."

Susan took a step towards Romana, a weary and knowing faint smile stealing upon her lips. She took her hand.

"So, you read about me as research?" Susan asked politely as she shook the other Timelord's outstretched limb then released it.

"I don't suppose my Grandfather actually mentioned me himself?" She added.

The Doctor looked downcast once more, while even Romana found it hard to find the words to elegantly continue the conversation. Susan shook her head with that same wistful expression.

"I'm sorry," she offered calmly, "there's no need to answer that. I know I said I forgive him, but there are so many demons to put to rest I fear they may still growl from time to time."

Romana nodded her understanding.

"Obviously we are very grateful for your timely rescue," Romana began, still polite, "but how exactly did you come to be here *to* rescue us? Have you been... searching long?"

Susan's eyebrows raised a little at Romana's attempt at tact.

"You mean, 'have I been searching for him ever since he abandoned me on Earth in twenty one sixty four?"

The Doctor spread his hands wide.

"My dear child, I only did what I thought was best. I am sorry if I erred."

Susan's head dipped towards the Doctor.

"Yes, Grandfather, you were very eloquent while explaining it to me at the time – a most beautiful speech. I only wish I'd been given the opportunity to deliver a rebuttal. Perhaps face to face, inside the TARDIS?"

Once again the Doctor looked crestfallen. Susan waved her head and held up her hands placatingly.

"Sorry, sorry. Once again, 'demons', you know?"

Then she returned her attention to Romana to expand upon her earlier answer.

"No, I did not immediately set out in pursuit of our Doctor here – even if I had had the slightest idea how to begin such a course. No, I determined to make a life with David, much as Grandfather had suggested – though not because of that.

"David was a good man – an easy man to love and be loved by. We made a life together as the Earth rebuilt itself and were happy for a while. He suited me very well in those early days, and I know he adored me."

Romana nodded thoughtfully.

"Sounds idyllic, I'm sure. And yet I sense it did not last?"

Susan shook her head.

"Oh no, it lasted very well, for several years. But ultimately something grew in me, which took it all from me. At first it seemed we saw everything through the same eyes. We laughed at the same silly things, enjoyed a myriad of pleasant diversions and memories together.

"But then the differences crept in. I began to see more and more of the Universe that he could not. I began to envision things of which he could not even begin to imagine. No matter how much he tried. And oh, how he tried. But ultimately we were living in different worlds.

"We three are Timelords, inhabitants of all Time and Space. And mere humans *cannot* truly share in our experiences. They cannot, in truth and fullness, share their lives with the likes of us. Or vice versa. It is cruel to expect that of them. And cruel to expect it of me."

Here she stared challengingly into the Doctor's eyes.

"Why didn't you see this before you left me there? You – worldly wise, my guardian, my protector – my Timelord Grandfather. Why did you not know this would happen?"

As Susan demanded answers, the Doctor returned her gaze, mute, his own thoughts a mystery. Perhaps seeking to help him out a little, Romana responded.

"You and your grandfather are more alike than you know. Your own words betray that, in ways I don't think even you comprehend. And at the same time, I know he did not intend to deceive you, any more than he intended to deceive himself.

"He has had quite an... *odd* relationship with humans himself over the years, even until quite recently – into his dotage, so to speak. He *is* learning, but slowly. Try not to treat him too harshly."

Susan cocked her head at the other female Timelord, as if seeing her clearly for the first time.

"I think, perhaps, he has finally found the right travelling companion. One who will not let his foolishness stand."

Romana waggled her head in forced modesty.

"Well, you know, I have my moments."

Susan continued to study her keenly.

"And you have, perhaps, also found the perfect travelling companion in him. Someone patient enough to share their wisdom with you, however unwelcomed."

Romana frowned at Susan while the Doctor showed the faintest hint of a smile, the first sign of good humour since setting eyes on his granddaughter.

"Yes, well," Romana continued brusquely, "critiques of the companions from the travelling TARDIS out of the way, perhaps you could return to *your* travels, and how *you* got here?"

Susan chuckled.

"It *is* good to be among Gallifreyans again," she began, "although I have augmented my Timelord knowledge and skills over the years, even in absentia – even without the Academy to guide and aid me – it is good to finally be back among my own kind."

"Do you have a TARDIS?" The Doctor asked. This was the first thing he had said which was neither an apology or defence. His mind was clearly returning to more immediate matters. Susan shook her head.

"Unfortunately not. Yes, as you can see, I eventually left Earth and David. But initially I had to use far more mundane and crude forms of transport – travelling only through space under power, and through time via ageing.

"I began to pick up hints of your existence, Grandfather, myths and legends in your wake. Eventually I did manage to acquire some Time Bracelets – non-Gallifreyan, of course, and primitive by our standards. But at least I could begin to track your movements a little more effectively.

"And then the Universe shattered."

Romana and the Doctor shared significant glances.

"Oh, I knew you – well at least the Doctor – would be involved somehow. I even guessed he might be the cause. From the research I managed while 'tracing your footsteps', I am almost certain of it now.

Then the Universe was repaired. But still I followed the trail until, at last, I finally saw you on the landing field here on Kai-Ro. Alas, I paused too long and lost you yet again."

The Doctor nodded sympathetically.

"I'm sorry we were in such a rush. We thought our major troubles were behind us, and were itching to explore the universe in our newfound freedom. Obviously, we didn't realise how wrong we were," he said, gesticulating at their prison cell deep within the base of The Rani.

"Well, all's well that ends well," Susan concluded briskly, "I found you, eventually."

Romana frowned once more.

"But how *did* you do that? Did you follow us off-world again as we explored spacetime?"

Susan's head wagged from side to side.

"In the end I didn't have to," she explained smiling, holding up one wrist to reveal a Time Bracelet, "this thing is good for short trips, although for longer journeys it does require frequent recharging. But in this case, its secondary function rendered such travel unnecessary."

The Doctor's curiosity was piqued.

"Really? How so?" He enquired.

"These things have very basic detectors for time disturbances, other than their own. I upgraded this one, using my own time tech skills, to make it a little more precise and detailed.

"I was in the middle of trying to track where you had gone, and was just narrowing down the exact coordinates about an hour and a half after you left, when the Temporal Disturbance Detector went off – and quite insistently. It had picked up an unusually disturbing anomaly. A TARDIS – your TARDIS – arriving back on Kai-Ro. But inside *another* TARDIS! Well, not *quite* another TARDIS, but something eerily similar."

The Doctor and Romana both nodded.

"The satellite and the Time Terminus," the Doctor supplied helpfully. Susan gave a thumbs up.

317

"Yep. I've been nosing around here for a while – found the satellite. Saw your TARDIS inside – at first. Saw – and avoided – those unhealthy looking guards. Then I finally saw them taking you down here. So, I liberate a key, et voila – here I am!"

"So, you are not yet aware who is behind all this?" Romana asked. Susan nodded but before she could respond further the Doctor leapt in with another question.

"Wait – the TARDIS was inside the satellite *'at first'*?" He asked with concern.

"Yes," Susan confirmed, "they took it out before sending the satellite to… well, wherever they sent it in Time and Space."

The Doctor frowned.

"Ah, so the TARDIS is still in the Time Terminus," he stated firmly. Susan shook her head.

"No, no. They moved it to a workshop beyond the rear of the chamber. In preparation for stripping."

The Doctor looked aghast.

"They put my TARDIS in Anubys's rear! For stripping, no less! This shall not stand!" He cried indignantly. Susan frowned at him.

"What exactly *is* going on? And what *exactly* are we going to do?"

And so the Doctor explained about The Rani and her plans. Susan listened intently as he outlined the nature of the battery – the repurposing of the monument, expounded on the bulk – its powers and The Rani's, and how they were all connected to each other and the satellites. By the time he had finished Susan looked pensive.

"This is beginning to feel like a Timelord convention," she pronounced grimly, "only one with very lax security. The Rani sounds like a complete maniac."

The Doctor nodded sombrely.

"And not the good kind either. You see now what we are up against and what we have to prevent."

Susan nodded curtly.

"So, where do we begin?" Romana asked, concerned. The Doctor stroked his chin.

"Where indeed," he mused, "well, not here, and that's for sure. We must get the TARDIS and get out. Then – and I am loath to say this, as it smacks of brute force – we must find aid. Sufficient personnel to assault this battery and disable it. *Before* it is plugged into the bulk."

Romana nodded slowly.

"I fear you may be right. But where – or even when – do you hope to find your 'army'?"

"I believe we may already have what we need to hand. First, I propose we take the TARDIS on a short trip to Kai-Ro Aerodrome."

Susan frowned.

"That sounds unusually precise for you, Grandfather. Have you finally learnt how to control the TARDIS?"

"No," Romana replied quickly. The Doctor frowned at them.

"My piloting skills have come a long way over the centuries," he began indignantly.

"And in various unexpected directions," Romana added mischievously. The Doctor rolled his eyes.

"And," he continued through gritted teeth, "I can pilot through spacetime far more accurately than, I admit, I once did."

Sensing further objections, he held up a hand to forestall them.

"Nevertheless, I am not proposing we travel in time, merely shift spatial locations slightly. I can do short spatial hops under total control. It's just the longer spacetime journeys which sometimes go a little awry!" He insisted.

"Sometimes?" Susan said, a little sceptically.

"A little?" Romana added in a similar tone.

"Affirmative, master!" K9 supplied helpfully.

The Doctor harrumphed at this trio of tormentors.

"If you have all quite finished, I shall explain what we shall do once we *successfully* arrive."

Susan and Romana nodded pleasantly, stifling smirks.

"Once there, I suggest we find and contact Lou Halberd and Nathan Ivon – our friends from the Albian Imperial Museum. With their connection to Sir Arthur Buchan back at the museum itself – and by extension the Albian authorities – coupled with our own growing reputation for both predicting and dealing with 'rum doings' - we should be able to rustle up the forces required."

Romana and Susan signified their acceptance of his plan.

"I just hope we don't end up embedded in some Albian alternate UNIT outfit. I really don't think I could bear that sort of thing again."

The Doctor, Romana, Susan and K9 crept out of the makeshift cell. Much as when Susan had arrived, there were no reanimated henchpeople in the corridor, for now. So they continued on to the stairwell. Hearing nothing, they began to mount the single two metre wide set of stone steps.

They had almost reached the next landing when they heard multiple footsteps trudging down the stairs from the landing above that. The three Timelords looked at one another in panic. There were two parallel sets of steps leading down from the floor above, but which was in use? Or worse, were both?

"Doctor! Which way?" Romana cried in hushed tones.

"Quickly! Left!" He responded, similarly muted.

"Are you sure?" Romana hissed back. The Doctor simply widened his eyes and shrugged helplessly.

With no other plan, the three Gallifreyans and the robot dog dashed onto the landing then immediately off it into the left hand flight of stairs.

Fortunately, there were no Albian undead here. Nevertheless they all froze, attempting to remain silent. They heard a modest group of individuals trudging onto the landing they had just evacuated then down the stairs they had previously ascended.

They all breathed a sigh of relief – well, all except K9, who had no need.

No matter their good fortune, the Doctor was not about to let them rest on their laurels.

"Hurry," he gasped, grabbing Romana and Susan by an arm each and encouraging them up the new run of stairs, "doubtless those guards were sent to check on us – our absence will be discovered in moments. We must make haste!"

They rapidly reached the next landing and were immediately faced by the open door to the Time Terminus. Peering carefully through that opening, they saw the vast chamber beyond. As Susan had said, the satellite had vanished, fully exposing the ancient room in all its glory. They could see the opposite wall which looked virtually identical to the one they were staring through – another dim open door at its centre, flanked by grey cuboid time portals, two to each side. The side walls of the Time Terminus were now also unobstructed – while they had no open doors such as the end walls, they did house six more time portals each, spaced out along their extended lengths.

Other than this there was nothing else of note within the chamber. Fortunately, this also included hench-beings.

As quietly as possible, the quartet of travellers hustled across the Time Terminus making for the far door, through which they hoped to find the TARDIS.

They burst into this opening without stopping, dashing into the TARDIS decommissioning workshop beyond.

Understandable as their keenness and haste may have been, it proved to be unwise.

A strange and particularly upsetting pair of reanimated Albian corpses turned away from the TARDIS they had been working on – the Doctor and Romana's TARDIS – and glared dully at the trio of Timelords, plus K9.

One was a woman with the foreshortened limbs of a nine year old child, while the other was a nine year old child with the elongated arms and legs of an adult. Both wore matching – and now ill-fitting – white dresses with black cardigans and bonnets; the bizarre, unnatural fusion of mother and child.

Each of these altered undead servants were holding devices of distinctly un-Albian origins, one looking like a probe of some sort, the other a more aggressive looking implement. Both appeared to be based upon Gallifreyan technology. Luckily, it seemed neither device had had any effect on the TARDIS thus far. Unluckily, they did appear quite heavy, particularly as the jumbled duo hefted them and advanced upon the Timelords.

Romana spotted her sword-stick leaning against a nearby workbench – The Rani's guards had confiscated it prior to escorting them to their leader and had undoubtedly simply stored it with their TARDIS by association. She made a dash for it past the diminutive mother, who narrowly missed her with a swing of her makeshift club. Meanwhile the former nine-year-old on adult legs staggered towards Susan and the Doctor, swinging her own weapon menacingly towards them.

Grandfather and Granddaughter both backed away slowly, each wondering what strategy would serve them best.

At that moment a strange humming noise arose, increasing in both pitch and intensity.

A roughly cuboid grey shape about a metre long flew through the air from behind the relatives. It struck the Albian elongated corpse full in the chest, sending both sailing back to collide with the TARDIS. The hench-being slid to the floor and remained there, motionless.

The grey object rose straight up to hover around three feet in the air. It was, of course, K9.

"My nose laser may still be inoperative, master, mistress, but the nose is still fully functional," he reported primly.

Meanwhile, the mother had been distracted by the commotion and had turned to discover the fate of her daughter. Doubtless there were no maternal feelings remaining in this mobile corpse, its only dull interest being how effectively it – or rather they – were serving their mistress.

Whatever the motivation, Romana took advantage of the creature's loss of focus and clubbed it roughly across the back of its head with the brass handle of her sword cane. Then she repeated this several more times until it had finally stopped moving, barring a few twitches.

"Well done, Romana, K9," the Doctor congratulated them approvingly, unable to mask how impressed he was, "now, let us board the TARDIS while we still have the chance!"

With that, he strode to the TARDIS doors, and with a click had them whirring open. They all dashed on board, the doors sealing behind them.

As soon as they had reached the main console, the Doctor began programming the coordinates for Kai-Ro Aerodrome, present time. Just as the Doctor prepared to throw the launch lever they all heard a ragged screech of rage.

The Rage of The Rani.

They could see no sign of her on the TARDIS monitors – she was not in the workshop with their vessel, it seemed. In all likelihood she was still in her throne room, in the head of Anubys and had been amplified by her bulk-gleaned powers.

The Doctor threw the launch lever desperately.

The familiar sounds of dematerialisation began, the central column rising and falling. Then a shudder ran through the time ship as similar but competing sounds arose from outside. There now came a scraping sound as of metal upon metal.

"She's activated the Time Terminus," the Doctor cried frantically, "she's redirecting the energies of the time portals upon us here, trying to hold the old girl in place!"

"Can we pull away?" Romana asked frowning. The Doctor shook his head.

"Not as things currently stand, no," he said sombrely. Then his eyes widened as a realisation struck him.

"The Emergency Power Booster Unit!" He shouted excitedly.

"Of course!" Romana responded, equally enthused, "Where is it?!"

"Under that square flap there, on the panel you're resting on – next to your left hand!" The Doctor explained excitedly. Romana found the cover and raised it. Underneath was a large red button on a white background, labelled in white.

"Why does it say, 'Turbo Boost' on it?" Romana asked dubiously.

"I mean, the TARDIS doesn't use turbos in its engines. What have you been doing?" She added. The Doctor frowned impatiently at her.

"I renamed it to that because, at the time, I thought it was cool. You know, like bow ties. Obviously I no longer do. For either," he told her grumpily.

Then he thumped the button.

The usual TARDIS engine notes were joined by another soaring, whooshing sound. The sounds of scraping metal subsided.

They were flying free.

Moments later they landed.

The Doctor, Romana, Susan and K9 tumbled out onto the sun-baked, dry and dusty expanse of Kai-Ro Aerodrome landing field, beneath the "airship" mooring masts.

"Right," the Doctor said briskly, "now to contact our friends from the Museum."

There was a crack like a single terrifying clap of thunder, one so fundamental it went beyond loud, almost as if it could be felt resonating through every fibre of their beings.

They all looked up at the sky and gasped in horror.

The sky was peppered - or rather gashed – with objects of various sizes, but all of a type, and one with which the Doctor, Romana and K9 were all too familiar with.

"We're too late."

The Doctor's hushed words fell as heavy as headstones while they stared grimly at the opening rifts to the bulk. The largest of these floated above where they knew the Anubys Monument stood, although from where they were, their view was almost entirely obstructed by low hills. All they could make out were the tips of its ears.

As for the rift, it was all too visible. It hung like a ragged tear in reality itself, like the widening maw of some vertical shining clam. Its lowest tip looked as though it might be two hundred metres above the ears of Anubys, although it was difficult to judge its actual elevation due to the uncertain distance to this dread phenomenon. It stretched upwards covering twenty degrees of sky, widening towards its centre, then narrowing to its upper tip.

Inside the tear was the stuff of nightmares.

Within its jagged boundaries twisted a sickening sea of chaos, almost as if every colour, every sound, every sensation clamoured to exist at once, simultaneously, in this horrific hallucination.

Yet the Timelords knew only too well how real these visions were. And this maddening jumble of images – and more – was repeated across the sky countless time, though none matched the first for apparent size. This, however, was the true illusion – their variation in scale simply a product of their relative distances, scattered throughout the cosmos.

"The Rani has activated the Battery!" Romana cried in dismay. The Doctor nodded grimly.

"I'm afraid so. She has linked all the satellites she seeded across spacetime. Doubtless there are innumerable rifts, not simply spread out among the stars, but also strewn through the centuries and millennia."

"I assume you think our Albian army would be pointless now?" Susan asked, although suspecting the answer. The Doctor inclined his head in sombre affirmation.

"So – and I know I hardly ever ask this," Romana began, "what now, Doctor? Any more ideas?"

The Doctor smiled at her humour but his demeanour remained serious.

"I have one more, yes, but I fear you may not like it," he said warningly.

Romana tipped her forehead towards the Doctor and spread her hands wide.

"Well?" She invited him to elaborate.

The Doctor pointed casually towards one of the mooring pylons.

"Well, first I think we should say hello to one of our dear old 'friends' over there. Even if he is not one of those I had previously thought of."

Romana and Susan followed the line of his finger. The mooring tower was the one which still held the A36 'Airship' - spaceship of the Albian Imperial Space Service. This remarkable vehicle shared many superficial similarities with Earthly airships of the nineteen twenties and thirties, including six turboprop engines attached to its fared-in gondola. Obviously, these motors were a little more advanced than their Earthly counterparts, but this was far from its most remarkable deviation.

As well as being able to support an atmosphere for interplanetary travel, it was their means of propulsion in space itself which was most astounding. Retractable panels of a most marvellous material, Caverite, allowed them to reverse the effects of gravity, pushing them from planet to planet.

Right now it was not the vessel, tethered by its nose to the tower, which held the attention of the Doctor and his companions.

It was the man in smart navy officer attire standing at the tower's base.

The Doctor strode over to him, his surprised companions trailing and trundling in his wake.

"Oh, hello!" The Albian officer cried affably, "The Doctor, isn't it? And miss Romana! So delightful to see you all again! Oh, I say, did you forget something on board?"

His broad smile had morphed to confused concern by his last question, as he peered out from under his white peaked cap. The Doctor clapped him on the dark blue shoulder of his military jacket.

"Sub-Lieutenant Leslees," the Doctor began, as friendlily as he could manage given the desperate circumstances, "I cannot express just how delighted *we* are to see *you*, and your magnificent vessel. But fear not, we have not left anything on board. Yet."

The Timelord's final word was delivered with an oddly laboured significance. Before anyone could pursue its deeper meaning, all were distracted by a new horror from above.

Something was snaking out of one of the nearer bulk rifts – not the largest of them, but this reduced proximity did nothing to soften the blow. A giant tentacle nosed its way into Kai-Roan airspace from the eleven dimensional realm of all existence. It was obvious, even from the limited view they had of that insane world though the tear, that this otherworldly appendage was attached to a monstrous entity of unimaginable size, festooned with such serpentine extremities.

The colour of this beast – as much as four dimensional minds could comprehend – was ever shifting and sickening to behold. It sometimes appeared a glistening brown, at other times a scaly green, then in brief flashes crystalline in rainbow hues.

Like some nightmare alien bullet train, this limb of a bulk denizen curled and pushed across the sky. Then the tip found another rift and entered that. For a time it seemed the pulsing, writhing member were pushing deeper and deeper into that second tear in the fabric of Space and Time. Then the "tip" exited from the first rift!

This was in no way which made sense to those watching – it was not as if the tip had curled round within the bulk to appear once more next to its own tentacle. No, it looked now as if the tentacle were being withdrawn from the first rift and retracted into the second. Where it was attached to the bloated body of the bulk entity! This made no sense at all in four dimensions, and yet no doubt was just another Thursday to these denizens of the eleven dimensional whole.

"Oh, I say," Sub-Lieutenant Leslees piped up, troubled, but obviously trying to place a brave face over his confusion, "bally queer weather for the time of year, wouldn't you say?"

The Doctor raised his eyebrows and looked upon the unfortunate Albian with resigned disappointment.

"Yes, 'bally queer' - outbreaks of Armageddon with a slight chance of Apocalypse," he forecast witheringly. Philip Leslees simply continued to beam at him and nodded in agreement. In fairness to the hapless Sub-Lieutenant, it did seem the rifts were affecting the weather to some degree, beyond their unsettling added illumination and the odd airborne tentacle. The wind had picked up, causing sudden gusts of hot, dusty dessert air to scud in random directions.

"Mr Leslees," the Doctor continued, "we need to speak to Captain Povey about the A36. Do you know where he is?"

Philip looked unsure of himself.

"Oh... well... I'm sure he also left the ship a while ago. Like me. I think he just wanted to take the air before passengers were allowed on board, and what not. Funny thing – I haven't seen him for a while. Almost as if he were avoiding me! But of course that would be ridiculous. As you know, we get on *very* well," he finished, smiling once more.

"*Very* well?" The Doctor asked.

Before the officer could answer there was a crash of a tin door being opened forcibly. About twenty metres away stood the temporary metal shack currently assigned as a small temple to Osiris, for the use of the native workers. It was the door to this which had been opened, then caught by the wind and slammed against the temple wall.

Standing in the doorway, holding onto his peaked white cap for all it was worth, was Captain Povey himself. Frowning hard and looking less than pleased, he strode towards the Doctor and his companions.

"Captain Povey," the Doctor began cheerily as he arrived, "delighted to see you again. I had no idea you were a devotee of Osiris!"

The Captain's frown deepened and he harrumphed, looking momentarily uncomfortable.

"Well, I'm not, actually. I was just looking for somewhere to get out of this damned heat and sun. Then there was the added benefit of getting some peace, particularly from my esteemed First Officer. Naturally, he was not about to let that last. I could hear him talking to you even from in there – fraternising with someone who has troubled our little ship on several occasions, compounding his disturbance," he said crossly before turning his full attention upon the Sub-Lieutenant, "you really are the Albian's burden!"

"Oh, sir, really? I do try," Leslees whined, sounding a little hurt.

"Oh yes," the Captain agreed heartily, "you're *very* trying."

Then he spun once more upon the Doctor.

"Now *what*, exactly, did you want with me," he growled, "or more worryingly, my ship?"

The Doctor raised his finger, about to reveal all, when his thunder was stolen.

A boom resounded through the air, coming from the direction of the twin peaks of Anubys's ears. From between those barely visible stone pinnacles rose a curling column of black and oily smoke. This unhealthy looking vapour trail arced up into the sky, bending towards the Timelords and Albians as it went, its cause being propelled in their direction.

As it grew closer, it became clear that the single oily trail was in fact two such lines of exhaust, only combining as they expanded in the thing's wake. These twin jets came from the palms of human looking hands, pointed towards the feet of this flying being.

It was, of course, The Rani.

She came to rest floating in the air in front of the Timelords, but still some distance away – perhaps twice the altitude of the moored A36 and a good fifty metres in front of its nose.

"Rani!" The Doctor called up with forced conviviality, "How good of you to join us! You're looking well."

This last statement was not simply an attempt by the Doctor to "butter up" the bulk-fuelled Gallifreyan. The Rani had undergone a transformation.

She had not regenerated - at least as far as they could tell – she still wore the current face of Romana. Only now it, along with the rest of her body, was completely healed!

Her hair was clean and luxurious, her skin unblemished and restored to a flawless pale pink. Her dress, while still black, was no longer Romana's ruined old cream one. Now it was a deliberately chosen sleek gown of dominating darkness.

The Rani sneered contemptuously at the Doctor and his companions.

"Ha!" She barked, "You see, *dear* Doctor, how wrong you were once again. An immaculate track record of incompetency and ineptitude!"

Here she raised her hands skywards in triumph. As she did this the black smokey jets ceased emanating from them, and yet she did not fall. Clearly her powers were already growing, as she no longer needed those blasts to fly.

"Everything is working exactly as I planned! The bulk is powering me and yet is utterly oblivious in its generosity! Where once I bemoaned the bulk entities ambivalence towards me, now I revel in it! They have become my unwitting slaves – less than slaves; cattle! To be milked by me for all eternity! Behold, the Reign of The Rani!"

Now The Rani's eyes fell from whatever imagined glories she envisioned in the middle distance, to land upon the Doctor and Romana with unwavering malice.

"And now, since you *have* beheld the culmination of all my plans - witnessed my final victory and your own final, terminal, failure – I have no further use for you. Time, I think, to dispose of you both in one of my many handy rifts."

Romana and the Doctor suddenly felt vice like grips clutching their upper arms and chests. They began to inch skywards under the pressure of The Rani.

Then the Doctor's eyes widened. He sought to cry out, yet due to the constriction could not find the breath.

A freight train sized tentacle slammed into the side of The Rani. It seemed to be making an almost leisurely journey from the nearest of the bulk rifts to another, some way behind it. Only its terrible size gave the impression of sluggishness – no doubt in reality its speed was at least comparable to such a locomotive. Its random curved path had first brought it slightly closer to intersect with The Rani, before arcing away from the witnesses below.

The Doctor and Romana dropped a foot to the floor as they were suddenly released, The Rani's concentration understandably broken.

The Rani herself lay spread eagled across the nose of this travelling tendril as it eased towards the next rift.

"Oh no," she shrieked in a mix of horror and frustration, "not again!"

Then she was carried into the rift and was gone.

Unlike the previous bulk limb transition they had witnessed, this one did not suddenly reveal its tip emerging impossibly from the first rift. This tentacle clearly preferred to be more conventional – it reversed direction and began to withdraw back from whence it came. As its tip re-emerged from the more distant rift, there was no sign of the bulk augmented Timelord.

The Doctor sighed.

"I tried to warn her," he said sadly. Romana nodded with a twisted smile.

"I know," she responded, "and I do wish you wouldn't. Our antagonists are quite capable of doing enough damage without our help."

She then glanced once more at the receding appendage.

"And we shouldn't look a gift horse in the mouth," she pronounced thoughtfully, "we were lucky she *literally* didn't see the end coming. It's funny how often that seems the way with these ambitious, bright but flawed individuals. Be it the Master, The Rani or even the recent dear *probably* departed Dr Nyugati – they all appear utterly unable to conceive of any difficulties or problems with their plans, until it hits them in the face. Or back. It seems they never learn."

The Doctor nodded appreciatively.

"A man – or woman – should know their limitations," he pronounced sagely.

Their philosophical musings were interrupted by a distant double crack. Looking towards the horizon they could see the twin ears of the Anubys Monument had been knocked off by yet another tentacle, travelling between rifts. And it was far from alone in this journey.

The sky was becoming a veritable can of worms.

Romana frowned at the point on the horizon where the stone ears had once been.

"Anubys won't be pleased," came her assessment.

"Sh!" The Doctor hissed warningly, but with a hint of mischief, "He might well be listening!"

Then he became more pensive.

"Even if he were, it's unlikely he would, or could, do anything. In fact, we could rather do *with* a little Suss-kind intervention. But those same eleven dimensional Wyttyrn obstacles remain. Indeed, I'd say, have multiplied."

Romana pursed her lips at the Doctor.

"Is there any chance this damage to The Rani's battery might close the rifts – save the Universe?"

The Doctor shook his head grimly, gesturing round at the rift-strewn sky.

"I doubt the bulk cares one jot for The Rani's devices any more. The doors are open and they have numerous feet in them. No, there is only one way they can be closed."

Here he paused to summon up the strength to continue.

"Which is?" Susan prompted gently.

The Doctor's eyes flicked between those of the two female Gallifreyans.

"From the other side."

Now he turned to Captain Povey.

"My dear Captain," he began calmly, patiently and politely, "I'm going to have to ask a great deal from you. I need the A36 to fly into the bulk, fitted with some additional equipment. Once there, it will – with luck – pull closed those rifts and seal our universe off from the rest of the bulk for all eternity. But in the process seal *itself* inside with the rest of the bulk.

"Never to be seen again."

The Doctor stared intently at the Captain, awaiting his response. The Captain, in his turn, frowned back at the Doctor, his face hard and grim. Finally he spoke.

"Doctor," he began stiffly, "you and I are not friends. I would say we do not get on *very well* at all. In fact, you have been a source of constant troubles in the brief time you spent on board my ship. Giving you access to the ship again would be the last thing on my mind."

The Doctor's eyes fell and he looked downcast. He took a deep breath, preparing for battle.

"Nevertheless," Captain Povey continued, robbing him of the chance to speak, "I'm not blind, you fool. I can see that *not* allowing you on my ship might well be the last thing on my mind *ever*, if I were to enact such a thought. The universe is clearly falling apart. It is riven with the 'Clams of Death' - 'Clams of Death' well known to you and I since we travelled through one ourselves, together, in the recent past. And only through your efforts did we survive and ultimately escape. I may not like the idea of me and my ship being used for such a purpose, and I am likely never to hold you warmly in my heart. But I must respect your past results and acknowledge your expertise and experience.

"The A36 is at your disposal."

The Doctor nodded slowly in appreciation of the Captain's good sense and sacrifice.

"Thank you," he said simply to the Albian officer.

"Right," the Captain barked decisively, "let's get the ship crewed up and ready to get underway,"

The Doctor smiled sorrowfully at the Captain.

"You said the A36 was at my disposal and I thank you. And I shall hold you to that. This is a one way trip, and one which – with a little help from the extra equipment I shall install – it shall take without you or your crew."

The Captain frowned deeply at the Doctor in profound annoyance but remained silent. Sub-Lieutenant Leslees looked profoundly relieved.

"Steady as she goes," he said, smiling nervously. Captain Povey clipped him round the back of his head, sending the First Officer's hat flying.

"This is a journey I shall make alone," the Doctor pronounced solemnly.

"I'm coming with you."

This determined declaration came from Susan. The Doctor pulled himself up to his full height.

"No, Susan, I need you to stay here."

Susan looked both defiant and deeply hurt.

"You cannot – after all this time – expect me to lose you once again!"

The Doctor gave a sad half smile.

"Think of it less as losing a grandfather, and more as gaining a TARDIS. And a K9. I need you to stay here with both to ensure the safety of our entire universe. If my plan should fail, *you* will be the last thing standing against... well, the end of the Universe. And K9 will be there to help, naturally. And even if the plan is successful, someone needs to - at the very least - ensure The Rani's battery and satellites are truly out of commission, ideally for good. And thereafter, it would be... useful... to have someone keeping an eye on things. I'd hate for my sacrifice to be for naught."

Susan looked pained, her eyes seeking the floor. But, much as with Captain Povey a moment before, she could offer no further objections.

Now the Doctor turned to Romana.

"Obviously, there is no need for both of us to man the A36 and fly into the bulk. Your help here, in this Universe, would prove invaluable."

Romana nodded slowly. Then punched him hard in the shoulder.

"Ow!" The Doctor cried, "What was that for?!"

Romana scowled at him, shaking her head.

"You are an idiot!" She snapped at him.

"I would have thought by now you would have known better – but it seems it is not just our antagonists who are slow learners," Romana continued impatiently, "did you learn nothing from what I said after we fixed the Universe the first time? When we stood in that 'trap street' alley on Earth? Or, what I told you on Hung-Area – after your heroic suicide attempt there?"

The Doctor frowned at her, looking a little peeved. Romana smiled wearily and shook her head once more.

"I know you mean well in what you say," she said, her tone softening a little, "but I think – once again – you are shouldering just a tad too much responsibility. Two heads are better than one. Just as four hearts are better than two. *If* something were to go wrong – the Universe forbid – and you were somehow incapacitated, or needed to be in two places at once, your 'selflessness' could destroy the entire universe."

Romana stared him determinedly in the eyes, a smile there but in no way lessening her resolve.

"If it's all the same with you, I think I shall be in this to the bitter end."

The Doctor could not suppress a grim little smile.

"Far be it from me to debate your profound wisdom," he said with the slightest of bows. Romana slapped him again on that same shoulder, only this time with the back of her hand and a little more gently.

Now the Doctor turned back to the rest of their companions and clapped his hands briskly.

"Now, as I'm sure you can see, we can waste no more time, lest Time and Space itself gets wasted!"

With that, the Doctor, Romana, Susan and K9 dashed to the TARDIS and ran inside. Meanwhile Captain Povey jogged over to the lift in the mooring tower and picked up a "Telecomm" handset, which acted as a direct line to the A36.

"Chief Petty Officer Twerpee! Get you cleaning crew off, now! The ship is needed but you are not... all you need to know is 'secret orders'. Get down here, quick smart!"

Sub-Lieutenant Leslees just stood where everyone had left him, smiling awkwardly, in case he was needed. But hoping he was not.

Chief Petty Officer Twerpee, and the couple of additional "seamen" in his unit, were just exiting the lift at ground level when the three Timelords and K9 reappeared from the TARDIS.

K9 was clearly not going to get very far, since a cable coiled from his inspection hatch and was obviously attached to something inside. And this tether was not alone – another thinner cable spiralled from his nose and fed into a brass and wooden box carried by Susan. It had a telescopic tripod attached to its base, which she deployed then busied herself studying the various displays and switches covering its upper surfaces.

Meanwhile, the Doctor and Romana were similarly encumbered with a disparate collection of mostly obscure devices and hardware. One identifiable exception was the crown like half of the Four Dimensional Stress Set – the FDSS – which had been worn by K9 in the not too distant past. The Doctor glanced down at the metal dog and paused.

"K9," he said seriously, "be a good boy."

"Affirmative, master!" K9 chirruped obediently.

The Doctor nodded once to his metal companion then he and Romana dashed over to where Captain Povey and his men stood by the lift. They hurriedly dumped their gear in the elevator car before returning to Captain Povey himself.

"I fear this is where we part company, my dear Captain. If you would join my Granddaughter over there, she has communication and monitoring equipment. We might need your advice if we run into any difficulties with your ship."

Povey looked far from friendly and seemed to be wrestling with some internal conflict. Finally he huffed and extended a hand towards the Doctor. The Timelord looked at it for a moment as if it were a halibut. Then he grasped it and the Captain shook it firmly.

"Good luck, Doctor, and god speed," he said then released his grip. The Doctor gave a wry smile.

"Thank you, sir. And which god?" He asked cheekily.

"Whichever is fastest," Captain Povey quipped back. Then, much to Romana's surprise, he turned and extended his hand towards her. Eyebrows raised, she took it and the Captain repeated his earlier action.

"And good luck to you, Miss Romana. I hope you will keep him out of trouble. And vice versa," he concluded, smiling grimly.

Romana gave a single chuckle and nodded her thanks. They then all looked up at a sky riddled with rifts and boiling with twisting nightmarish tendrils.

At that moment an errant tentacle struck the main envelope of the A36 "airship". While only a glancing blow in the grand scheme of things, from the perspective of the Albian spaceship it was potentially catastrophic. The tail of the ship slewed round sickeningly – this was not necessarily a major problem as the entire top section of the mooring mast was designed to swivel to account for the changing wind direction. The real problem lay in the new twist it was acquiring in the vertical direction, looking as though it was in the process of keeling over to port.

The attachment mechanism had far less leeway for motion in that direction. If it snapped, the A36 could be lost forever.

And with it, the Universe.

Everyone held their breaths as the ship keeled over to an angle of forty five degrees. Here it paused.

Then, with aching slowness, it began to self-right, creeping towards an even keel.

Everybody finally exhaled.

They knew the time for pleasantries was past, and the two Timelords jumped back into the lift, while Captain Povey closed its metal lattice gate from outside. He watched with mixed emotions as the Doctor and Romana rose to take command of his vessel for one final, vital mission.

Romana and the Doctor raced on board the archaic looking space craft and immediately set to work preparing for launch. They closed the front ramp through which they had entered, at the nose of the ship, and hared through that vast space where the cargo and gas bags were stored. They descended steep metal steps into the Standard Class accommodation section of the gondola. All was eerily quiet, the absence of passengers and crew seeming to have robbed the ship of life and warmth. Two people just could not fill it.

Of course, this vessel was dwarfed by that which they had left behind, however this knowledge did little to dispel the sense of loneliness and isolation.

They left the standard class accommodation via a heavy metal security door and entered the corridor to the bridge. They paused briefly at the small "Telecomm" room while Romana installed some extra equipment to boost its flexibility and range. Then she and the Doctor moved to the very front of the gondola – the flight deck.

The immense wrap-around windows gave them a fantastic view of

Kai-Ro Aerodrome and its surrounds. It also gave them an unsettling ability to witness the rift-torn sky. They shuddered then set about installing the rest of the equipment, including the FDSS.

Finally, everything was in place.

"Shall we get underway?" The Doctor asked softly. Romana sighed.

"There's no time like the present. And if we don't leave soon there won't even be that," she answered with resignation. The Doctor nodded and flipped on the Telecomm extension in the main control panel.

"Captain Povey. Release the docking clamp," the Doctor requested.

The Captain gave no reply, but the Timelords heard the clank of the mechanism disengaging.

They began to feel a shift in the pit of their stomachs as the vessel started to drift free of the mooring mast, at the mercy of the air currents.

Hastily, the Doctor turned on the six turboprop motors and grabbed the main wheel, while Romana rolled her eyes at his oversight.

The motors roared into life and they were no longer adrift – they were underway with the Doctor at the helm. Romana stood at his side assisting with the controls. Even with the additional technology they had installed, controlling a ship designed for a crew of at least a dozen was no easy task for just two pairs of hands.

Nevertheless, the ship obeyed their commands, rising majestically and turning to face the largest and closest of the rifts. There was still much tentacle traffic moving between all the rifts currently visible – Romana and the Doctor exchanged dubious glances. This was going to be very dicey.

The Doctor and Romana gunned the engines, setting all six to maximum thrust. The rift grew in the front window until it entirely filled the view ahead.

Suddenly, the tip of a tentacle was heading straight for the cockpit glass!

The Doctor grunted as he spun the wheel, Romana wrestling with the flaps. The ship slewed sideways sluggishly.

Yet it was enough. The tentacle barely grazed the main envelope as it passed and, although it did jostle the ship slightly, miraculously caused no damage.

The rift was far wider than the emerging tentacle, and the Doctor now steered straight towards an unobstructed patch of the sickening maelstrom within.

"Activate the FDSS and the bulk protection field!" The Doctor cried to Romana.

From the ground Susan, Captain Povey and the others saw a shimmering curtain of energy erupt as a ring around the centre of the A36, then spread fore and aft. This energy field narrowed as it reached the prow and the stern. The entire spacecraft was enveloped in this hazy, glowing shroud – Captain Povey recognised it as the one which had protected them from the most maddening effects of the bulk, the last time his ship had been accidentally drawn into that hellish realm.

On board ship, the Doctor turned to Romana.

"I removed the Time Meddler's spacetime stabilisation circuit from our TARDIS and installed it here, along with the FDSS. Working in tandem, they should be able to seal the rifts, once we are *in* the bulk, of course. And once there, it should allow us to travel freely around the eleven dimensional realm at will."

Romana nodded slowly.

"Just never return," she said in a subdued manner.

The Doctor nodded, equally grimly.

"At least not to this universe, *our universe*, no," he agreed and placed a hand on her shoulder to reassure her. To reassure him, in her turn, she allowed him to keep it there.

The A36 passed through the rift and was swallowed by the bulk.

All this had been witnessed by Susan, Captain Povey and K9, monitoring the situation from the ground. But this was not the last they heard of the Doctor and Romana.

A speaker on the brass and wooden box Susan was manning spluttered into life.

"Susan, my child, we are now inside the bulk," came the Doctor's voice, calm and serious.

"Grandfather, we are receiving you," Susan responded into an extended microphone, her voice a little tremulous. There was a short pause.

"I am activating the spacetime stabilisation circuit via the FDSS... now!" The Doctor announced with a flourish.

There was a crack louder than any thunder and more like the fracturing of a giant femur. And not just one crack – it came from every rift, only with slight delays and decreasing volume depending upon their distance from those watching.

Within moments all the tentacles had retracted and disappeared.

However, the rifts remained.

"They're closing!" Captain Povey cried.

Although subtle and difficult to discern, it seemed the Albian officer was correct.

The speaker crackled into life again.

"It is done," came the Doctor's voice with a note of finality. Then he drew breath and spoke once more.

"Listen, Susan, please," he began, "I am so glad you came back, and I am so sorry I did not make good on my word and make this day arrive all the sooner, and under better circumstances."

"Yes, Grandfather," Susan cried back, almost sobbing, "I just wish we had more time!"

Then came another pause from the comms unit. Susan imagined the Doctor shaking his head sadly.

"Time," he finally said wistfully, "it always comes down to time."

Then his voice strengthened when next he spoke.

"And yet, for all those years we had together I am eternally grateful. During those years I took care of you, and you in return took care of me. Now it is time for you to shoulder a different burden. You're still my grandchild, and always will be, but now you have to take over from me. The Universe needs a watchful eye, and more – it needs a generous spirit to take care of it. I know you, Susan, and I know what you are capable of. I know the Universe is in safe hands. Your future lies in the TARDIS and not with a silly old buffer like me.

"There must be no regrets, no tears, no anxieties. Just go forward in all your beliefs and prove to me that I am not mistaken in mine.

"Goodbye, Susan. Goodbye, my dear."

Susan's throat seized up then, and even if she had found words to match her emotions she would have been unable to utter them. Staring up with glistening eyes, she could see all the rifts had narrowed to jagged glowing cracks in the sky, in many cases almost too thin to see. Now Romana's voice came over the speaker.

"The lives of great men all remind us, we may make our lives sublime. And departing leave behind us footprints in the sands of Time. Never be cruel, never be cowardly. Laugh hard, run fast, be kind," she reminded those listening with solemn gravitas.

"Oh, wise words indeed, Romana! I couldn't have put it better myself," came the Doctor's approving tones one final time.

Then there came another chorus of thunderclaps, echoing throughout Time and Space, as all of the rifts to the eleven dimensional bulk snapped shut, never to return.

The End

Epilogue

Thunder crashed and lightning flashed across a cloud strewn night sky, draped ominously over the Noria swamp. Heavy drops of rain clattered from the foliage of the jungle surrounding the marsh while still more pelted and blattered into the blue mud of the Trisilicate mine itself. The weather was sick and tired of being accused of pathetic fallaciousness – it meant what it said, and its dark mood resonated strong and true.

Bimbor the Boloid stared grimly out of a window in his official residence in the Noria Mine's main settlement, his face stony, lost in thought. His two hands were planted firmly on the ground supporting his spherical blue-furred body, at a respectable metre and a half from palms to fluffy crown. His yellow trumpet bell of a mouth was pursed in worry, while his glowing disks of eyes glowered into the middle distance.

Recent disappearances of several of his Boloid people, seemingly at random, without rhyme or reason, played heavy upon his mind. Piled on this were further troubling reports of damaged or stolen equipment from the mine, as well as disturbingly similar vandalism and thefts occurring within the settlement itself!

At that moment, the door was thrown open by another spherical Boloid dashing in, aided by the forceful gusts of wind from the storm beyond.

"Bloody 'ell, Bory," Bimbor snapped at the newcomer impatiently, "were you born in a bloody barn!"

Bory made no efforts to close the door, such was the urgency of his news.

"Chief Representative," he cried desperately, "the Chirpas are revolting!"

Bimbor snorted derisively.

"And in other news, Boloids secrete in the swamp. Tell me something I *don't* know!"

Bory shook his head, a little like a dog drying itself.

"No, sir, you don't understand! We've finally seen it – attacks on the mud extraction gear as they happened!"

Bimbor stared intently at his Boloid subordinate.

"What do you mean," he said quietly, "what 'appened?"

Bory looked despondent.

"Night had fallen and some of us were making final checks to make sure all was secure ahead of the coming storm.

"Then they came!

"Chirpas - dozens of them! Flying from the surrounding jungle, throwing things, dropping things. They pushed over equipment, carried some off. They even carried off one of my men!"

Bimbor's frown deepened. As he mulled over this disturbing report, another sound arose outside, competing with the howling wind. An odd rasping wheezing noise. Probably due to the sounds of the storm it went unnoticed by the Boloids.

"These are grim tidings indeed, young Bory," Bimbor pronounced seriously, "I'd say we've not seen trouble like this since the time the Chitid's went crazy for Earthmen. But that was decades ago, and then we were lucky enough to get some outside help. Yes, he was rather handy at the time. It's a pity we don't have the Doctor 'ere to help us now."

A woman stepped through the still open door behind Bory. She was dressed in long black robes with her head unbound, he dark brown bob framing a face of maturity and experience, complete with secret smile. In her right hand she held what looked like a gnarled twig or stick, except the glowing blue light at its tip belied its technological origins.

A grey metallic dog now trundled through that same door to wait for instructions obediently at her feet.

Ghosts of sadness – the memories of recent loss - flitted across the countenance of the woman formerly known as Susan. Then they were past – the enigmatic smile restored.

"I'm a Doctor," she offered helpfully, fixing Bimbor with a steely stare.

"But probably not the one you were expecting."

Made in the USA
Columbia, SC
11 January 2024

a87a705f-7d31-4340-ba62-e89fa52fc806R01